find himself in this tender treasure of a book. *Never Been Kissed* has my whole heart!"

—**Alison Cochrun**, author of *The Charm Offensive*

"A cinematic daydream guaranteed to steal your heart, *Never Been Kissed* is a delightful debut. The perfect balance of charm, swoons, and unforgettable laughs. Readers will be deeply in love with this second-chance romance!"

—**Julian Winters**, award-winning author of *Running with Lions*

"*Never Been Kissed* is a wonderfully upbeat and sweet blend of self-discovery and second-chance romance. This book warmed my heart—I can't wait for readers to fall in love with Wren and Derick!"

—**Suzanne Park**, author of *Loathe at First Sight*

"*Never Been Kissed* is an absolute delight! Wren is the hopelessly romantic film nerd I was missing from my life. I ached for him as he sussed out his dreams for his future, navigated his own sexuality, and blossomed into his first love. I caught myself cheering out loud for Wren and for Derick, gobbling up every word as fast as I could to get to their HEA. This story will thaw even the coldest heart and leave it with the warm fuzzies. A stellar debut from a fresh, new voice."

—**Xio Axelrod**, author of *The Girl with Stars in Her Eyes*

"A tribute to movies, drive-ins, and figuring out who you truly are, *Never Been Kissed* is a pitch-perfect second-chance summer romance. Watching Wren and Derick navigate their past and their present while fighting for their community and what they believe in will make you want to cheer. This book made my queer heart so very full and deeply happy: everything a rom-com should be."

—**Anita Kelly**, author of *Love & Other Disasters*
and the Moonlighters series

"In this sparkling debut Janovsky offers a queer romance NA readers are going to gobble up. Its uplifting message of identity and belonging will resonate with readers of all ages, and the quirky nostalgia-filled setting is the perfect backdrop for all the first time falling in love feels, which lead to a stand-out swoon-worthy romance readers will want for their keeper shelves!"

—**Annabeth Albert**, author of *Conventionally Yours*

"Grab the popcorn and curl up with *Never Been Kissed*. Timothy Janovsky is an incredibly gifted storyteller—his unputdownable debut novel brims with sparkling wit, high-stakes drama, and a swoony, slow-burn romance worthy of the classic movies that Wren, the book's flawed but lovable cinephile, holds dear. I can't wait to read what he writes next!"

—**Erin Carlson**, author of *I'll Have What She's Having: How Nora Ephron's Three Iconic Films Saved the Romantic Comedy*

Also by Timothy Janovsky

Never Been Kissed

YOU'RE A MEAN ONE, MATTHEW PRINCE

TIMOTHY JANOVSKY

sourcebooks
casablanca

Published by Sourcebooks Casablanca, an imprint of Sourcebooks
P.O. Box 4410, Naperville, Illinois 60567-4410
(630) 961-3900
sourcebooks.com

Cataloging-in-Publication Data is on file with the Library of Congress.

Printed and bound in Canada.
MBP 10 9 8 7 6 5 4 3 2 1

For Tarah,
the Ed to my Taylor

Author's Note

The holiday season can be a time of immense joy and celebration, but for those struggling with mental illness, it can also be a time of pressing anxiety. This book contains frank depictions and discussions of generalized anxiety disorders and anxiety attacks. I hope I have treated the experience, my characters, and you, dear reader, with care and grace. If you need resources or support regarding these topics, please flip to the back matter of this book or visit timothyjanovsky.com/youre-a-mean-one-matthew-prince. Sending you love and well wishes.

CHAPTER 1

I bought an island. So what?

It's not even a big island. It's only, like, twenty-five acres.

The guy who sold it to me said it's an international boating/sport-fishing destination with several private beaches and that it possessed *strong development potential*. My parents are always telling me to *reach my full potential*, so I spent a measly couple million dollars on an early Christmas gift to do just that.

Apparently, that was *taking it too literally* and *a gross waste of hard-earned income*.

I guess they would know.

Dad's an investment banker from old money. Mom's the author of a beloved sweeping fantasy series called A Game of Dark Dissension that spawned four books, two spin-off novellas, a hit TV series, and an upcoming musical adaptation thanks to two prodigious teens on TikTok. She's new money all the way.

Right now, I'm no money. Cut off. My black and gold cards were ceremoniously snipped with the sharpest scissors Mom could find. I almost dropped to my knees and wept, but my usual theatrics would do me no good in front of those two.

I stopped being sympathetic and started being a liability to them ages ago.

At least this time I've given them a good reason to believe it.

So, here I sit in the back of a Town Car as my driver winds an uphill, forest road toward Grandma's house in picturesque but downright stifling middle-of-nowhere western Massachusetts. My rose-gold tablet stares menacingly at me from its charger. Pulled up on its screen is an email from our family publicist, Sarah Pearson. The damning body of the email is like the cut of Sarah's tragic bangs: blunt.

> We need to contain this story ASAP. No way to spin this.
> Suggested action: Social media blackout + complete image rehabilitation

My parents do just about anything Sarah says to avoid being canceled, so this single email is largely to blame for my current predicament. Why *parent* your twenty-one-year-old when you have a PR titan to do it for you? What a joke.

Sitting alone with this frustration will only cause me to spin out like a truck in a snowstorm, so I whip out my phone for a surefire distraction.

The service is bad, but before it disappears altogether, I call Bentley Eng, my best friend. Or the closest I have to a best friend, anyway.

She answers on the third ring, even though she's already tucked away in her Aspen ski-in estate for the better part of the holidays. Snowcapped mountains provide her with the perfect scenic backdrop for our fuzzy, cutting-in-and-out video call.

"What's up, Matty Baby?" she asks, followed by the sound of her famously long, pointed fingernails tapping on a nearby countertop. As this call continues, the tapping will speed up, and once it reaches a fever pitch, I'll know her friendly patience has run out for the day. I've got to make this quick.

"What am I going to do?" I whine. "I'm not going to last four seconds, let alone four weeks here. No clubs. No boys. Already barely any phone reception. I'm not a monk!" My driver, with his thick, dark hair tucked under a rigid hat, catches my gaze in the rearview mirror. "Driver Man, keep your eyes on the road and your ears to yourself. Thank you." I can't remember if his name is Mikhail or Maxim or Marcus or someone else entirely. Not that it matters.

The only thing that matters is that I've been banished to the Berkshires for the holidays. The rules of my sentencing are as follows: I will stay with my grandparents in their homely cabin for the entire holiday season—help with "chores" (*seriously?*) as needed, partake in Christmas traditions (*yuck!*), and reflect upon the actions that led to Island Gate. I will not use social media, get into trouble, or *make a further mockery of the family name*.

It's a vast overreaction, if you ask me.

I mean, yeah, sure, maybe a bunch of Dad's big clients would threaten to pull investments from major accounts if they saw how Matthew Prince Sr. *lets his son handle the family finances*. And it's possible Mom's musical producers might back out because bad press from the creative team is certain death for advance ticket sales. But this would hardly be the first time I've sent the media into a tizzy over a price tag.

My entire closet probably costs more than that stupid island.

I have a sneaky feeling something else is up. I just can't put my finger on it.

"I want to say I feel for you, Matty Baby, but my Xanie just kicked in, so I'm not feeling much of anything." Bentley's eyes are spaced-out orbs only half staring back at me. "Which is exactly where I need to be before my cousins arrive. Those little shits don't deserve the droves of expensive athleisure my parents bought them. If they still believed in Santa, you best believe I'd be shoving coal down those spandex stockings."

"Bee," I intone. "Focus. Please. I'm in crisis mode here!"

"Hard to catch the urgency when you won't even tell me what you're being punished for," she says with an unsympathetic groan.

"It's nothing, Bee. I swear." I'm sweating as I rack my brain for something convincing to say. I might think the island is no big deal, but everyone else seems to think it's the end of the world. So, I've been instructed to keep it under lock and key. Even from the people closest to me.

"I maxed out my cards again and they freaked. It's, like, the eighth time now," I lie.

I know Bentley's my best friend, but she's the reason the phrase "loose lips sink ships" exists. Literally. She caused a famous DJ's yacht to sink off the coast of Ibiza once because she was gossiping with the captain. He was so engrossed in her chitchat that we ended up hitting a submerged coral reef. No one was injured, thankfully. But it was still scary as hell.

She adjusts her Ivy Park bucket hat like it's doubling as her thinking cap. "Just call, pretend to be your dad, and get your limits upped like I did. Problem solved."

"Not the problem I need solving right now, remember?"

"Right, right." She puzzles. "Wait. Doesn't your grandma own that Hamptons house and that Paris apartment? Why don't you just steal a key and sneak off to one of those?" The nail tapping increases in speed.

If Mom and Dad were hearing this, they'd say, as they've said before, that Bentley's a bad influence. However, I'm in the camp that believes *bad* is a highly subjective term. I wouldn't be New York City's reigning Party Prince (yes, it's a play on my last name, deal with it) without a proper bad—excuse me—bad*ass* Party Princess.

"You're thinking of my dad's mom. This is my mom's mom who lives in a log cabin overlooking a river. She runs a used bookstore in the center of town."

"If there is anything worse than books," Bentley says, "it's books people have already sneezed in."

"Gross."

"Epically gross." She pastes on a clownish frown. "Ugh! Matty Baby, what about our New Year's Eve bash? You already secured the Greenpoint warehouse and the Russian aerial silk artists. That vodka ice fountain carved in our likenesses is probably already being…made, chipped at? I don't know the details, but it's getting done." She pouts. "I *need* that party after all this family holiday bullshit. What are you going to do? You *can't*, and I repeat, *can't* cancel."

It's like she doesn't think I know that. It's like she doesn't realize that's the whole reason I called. The only time I'd cancel a party is if I died, and even then, I'd probably strike some deal with the devil to come back as a ghost to throw an epic funeral for myself.

I must sit in silent, stony contemplation of this for too long because—

"Hello? Are you frozen? Did the wintry weather already turn you into an ice pop?" Bentley taps her screen like a kid on a tank at the aquarium. "All I've gotta say is you better not be planning any wicked parties while you're away. Do you hear me? I'll murder you. I'll murder you, and I'll get away with it too. I have people who know how to make it look like an accident."

Maybe that funeral won't be so far away after all.

Bentley is *very* serious about her parties. She took me to my first EDM rave, forced me to go on an ayahuasca retreat, and talked me into dropping Molly at a former president's daughter's birthday celebration. We may or may not have destroyed a bouncy castle. I'm adventurous, but Bentley is downright wild.

"No murder necessary," I assure her with feigned confidence. I use what little I have left to declare: "I'll be back by then. My parents will be checking in with my grandparents for updates. All I need to do is convince them that I've learned my lesson, and I'll be home free. I have to be." The last remaining shards of my reputation depend on it.

Since high school, every New Year's Eve, Bentley and I throw a massive, balls-to-the-wall party and invite everyone who's anyone in young New York City society. Over the years, it's morphed from a chaste evening of chatting and dancing to a Bentley-approved rager fueled by top-shelf alcohol, amphetamines, and shirtless, tatted DJs spinning sick, frenzied sets.

But now, the one night it gets to be about me, and *not* about my imposing parents, has been taken away in the name of punishment to *conceal a story* or some shit.

"Matty Baby, you better make sure your ass is back by then. I can't do all this myself. You need a plan and you need—"

A crackling starts, then a full-blown cutting out. My phone screen blinks *disconnected*. I mutter expletives under my breath. That didn't make me feel any better.

The Welcome to Wind River sign flies by out the window. Population: Who fucking cares? This is the kind of town you drive through on your way to your summer home or make a pit stop en route to a ski slope. This is not the destination for most, but tragically, it is for me.

As we pass through the center of town, a holly-jolly bubble of nauseating joy, I do what I always do when the panic of a situation starts setting in:

I begin planning a fake event in my head to distract myself. This one is an I Should Be Home for the Holidays Hoedown. I'm envisioning a dress code of leather chaps (pants optional) and designer cowboy boots. For drinks, there would be a Blue Christmas bourbon concoction. Aside from authentic square dancing, in the center of it all there would be a pellet-shooting game where you could ping metal cups stacked in the shape of a Christmas tree pressed with pictures of people on your own personal naughty list. I'd have Mom and Dad set up as the prize-winning bull's-eye.

It's petty and kitsch but calming somehow. A coping mechanism designed by my highly sought-after therapist.

Our car clips the last few miles uphill until we come to a stop at the end of a long, bumpy driveway. We've pulled into Isolation Station, and I don't have a return ticket.

In a clearing sits a house smaller than even the most modest vacation homes I've stayed in. Patches of dirt sit dormant where greenery thrives in sprouts of color in the spring months. The plentiful tree branches hang down low like ominous, barren arms reaching out to grab hold of me.

I slip out of the car, careful to avoid the huge, slushy puddle we've parked in. It takes me a moment to adjust to air that isn't tinged with the stale scent of single-bagged bodega garbage cluttering the street. It would almost be nice if this was just a quick visit and not a staycation.

The cabin has an A-framed roof and a rustic porch where a bench swing sways. Twinkle lights chase each other down every slanted edge, making it look like an oversize sparkling gingerbread house even in the dwindling daylight.

Driver Man—whose name I now remember is Maxim, thanks to a helpful name tag tacked onto his lapel—drops the last of my bags at my feet, trying hard not to get any water on my Gucci black-leather ankle boots.

"Do you think their housekeeper will come grab these?" I ask.

He looks at me with sympathy before shaking his head. "No, Mr. Prince. I've been told they refused the housekeeper your mother hired for them. I'd help you myself like usual, but unfortunately, the drive took longer than expected. I'm due back to meet your father at the office to ferry him to an important business dinner. You understand."

I do understand. I understand that in the family hierarchy I'm the least important Prince. The Prince that gets punished for no decent reason.

"No chance you'll take me back with you, I presume?" I flick on the false charm.

"None. I was given very specific instructions."

"How about now?" I fish into my wallet and produce a fifty.

"I can't take a bribe."

"Consider it a tip."

He gives me a pained smile. "No, but thank you all the same, Mr. Prince. Enjoy your stay."

Maxim's refusal, compounded with Sarah's email and Bentley's bad advice, ticks my fuck-off-o-meter to full blow. If I were half the bitch the tabloids make me out to be, I'd text Dad and have Maxim on the next bus to Unemployment Town just for the hell of it, just to *feel something*, but I let it go due to the sheer fact that my hands are already too frostbitten to take out my phone. Not that it's of any use to me without service.

I stand there in the middle of the muddy driveway, alone and optionless. I curse whatever higher power is orchestrating this hopeless practical joke.

As if in response, that higher power sends slush flying up from Maxim's back tires. An icy waterfall cascades down my side. I'm soaked and shivering in seconds flat.

Why me? I ask the universe as I lug my two overweight suitcases up the steps of the front porch. The cold wind and the wetness seep through my layers, kiss my skin, and cause my anxiety to rush right back to the surface.

I Should Be Home for the Holidays Hoedown, I remind myself.

Chaps. Square dancing. Bourbon. Breathe. *Breathe, dammit.* Gingham tablecloths. Sliding barn doors. Horse-drawn carriage rides. *Exhale, exhale, exhale…*

When the campy scene colors itself all the way to the edges, I reopen my eyes, but don't find relief. *Fuck.*

Summoning my last nerve, I ring the high-pitched bell and prepare myself for what lies beyond the threshold.

CHAPTER 2

There's an old-school camcorder in my face the moment the door swings open. Grandma hangs behind it like she's Steven Spielberg.

"Matthew!" she shouts. "Wave to the camera!"

Old habits die hard with her. Each Thanksgiving she insists on filming every single relative's entrance into the house. She says one day she'll super-cut them all together, so everyone can see how they've changed over the years. That is if she ever figures out how to work iMovie.

"Did you go for a swim before you got here?" She tugs on my damp sleeve. I suppress a groan. No dry cleaner in this town is going to know how to properly care for an off-the-runway overcoat.

Her face lights up brighter than her ornate wreaths as she sets down the camera on a nearby end table. I had hoped we'd outgrown the cheek-pinching phase, but that's obviously not the case. She grabs fingerfuls of face flesh. I *ouch, ouch, ouch,* yet she doesn't take the hint.

"Let me get a good look at you." Her long, thin gray hair is spooled into a bun atop her head. She's got the same high cheekbones Mom does, but rounder cheeks, a dimpled chin, and a paler, whiter complexion from less sun and no bronzer. "You're so tall. What's it been? Two years?"

It has, in fact, been two years. I skipped last Thanksgiving to jet around Morocco with the heir to a breakfast-sandwich fortune and his musician husband in an ill-advised polyamorous throuple. If you ever want to feel like a third wheel, date a happily married couple and try planning a couple's massage. They don't even put out a third bed; they just make you rotate every fifteen minutes.

Grandma thinks hard on when she saw me last in the flesh and not on a screen. "Yes, it must've been two years ago because you were in London that one Thanksgiving visiting the British boy with the butterfly tattoo." She pauses. "Wait, no. I think that's a book title."

"No, you're thinking of *The Girl with the Dragon Tattoo*," I say. For someone who runs a used bookstore, she has a terrible time remembering book titles, yet she can recall every single guy I've ever been photographed with.

The Thanksgiving she's referencing was one where I ditched with my girlfriends to see a certain former boy-band front man perform a concert. What he and I did or did not do after his show is, quite frankly, none of anyone's business. Even though certain gossip sites seemed to think it was. And my own grandma, for that matter.

Recently, the closest I'd come to Grandma and Gramps was one spotty video call a week or so ago. I sent them my well wishes and then snuck off with Bentley to take tequila shots out of the navel of a consenting and well-paid underwear model, which, if you can believe it, wasn't even the highlight of our night. It was the perfect way to ignore my blown-out-of-proportion financial faux pas.

As I stand here, I take stock of what's changed since last time. The house smells of cinnamon, clove, and something cooking in the oven. Christmas has thrown up all over every windowsill and doorknob—from stuffed snowmen figurines with false smiles to a reindeer wall clock whose nose lights up on the hour. It's overkill, and it's killing me already.

Ever since tradition ceased to exist with my parents, the holidays are nothing more than an inconvenient hurdle on the sprint to New Year's Eve.

The foyer leads into the kitchen, which is still retro and not in a fashionable way. There are pea greens and muted yellows sprawled across the backsplash as if my grandparents had watched *The Exorcist* once and then asked the designer to color match Regan's projectile puke. Not appetizing to say the least.

The oval light-wood table where many Thanksgiving meals have been shared sits up against the far wall. The windows beside it look upon the perilous slope with its path down to the river, which is entirely iced over this time of year, a perfect slate for Joni Mitchell to skate away on.

I never could picture Mom growing up here. All my images of her are superimposed against sleek stainless-steel appliances and balconies backed by impressive skylines. She has a Midas touch, and this just doesn't compare to some of the gilded places we've been over the years.

Gramps comes charging around the corner of the far hall. He's not much taller than Grandma, though his gut is rounder than I remember, testing the seams of his argyle sweater vest. He's got me in an embrace before I can even say hello. This is far more physical affection than I'm used to or, frankly, comfortable with.

"Picture time!" Grandma's fiddling with her camcorder again like Mom didn't send her the newest iPhone when it came out earlier this year. "Oh darn. I never figured out how to work the timer on this thing. Hector! Oh, he's outside chopping wood. Be right back!" She dashes off, leaving me in the dust of confusion.

I ask Gramps a question I'm not sure I want to know the answer to: "Who's Hector?"

"A former student of mine. His family hit a patch of financial hardship sometime last year. He doesn't talk about it a lot, but before the start of the fall semester, he sent me an email letting me know that he may not be able to return to classes due to the cost of room and board. You should know, he's immensely bright, so his tuition is largely covered by scholarships," Gramps explains, as if I asked for a full biography with sources cited. "If a bed and some food were all he needed to continue his college education, then Grandma and I decided we'd scrape together a bed and some food for the boy. That's all there is to it." He beams at me. "It's the Wind River way."

The Wind River way sounds worlds apart from what I left back in Manhattan: high-exposure fundraising events and large-sum donations tactfully boasted about by publicists. Those are expected. Housing the displaced and downtrodden for the holidays is unheard of. And for good reason.

What if this Hector is an ax-wielding murderer? I want to ask how well they know him, but recalling how many years it's been since my last visit, I suppose I could ask them the same question about me.

"You look different," Gramps says after a bit of studied silence. "You eating?"

"I'm eating." I tug my coat self-consciously away from my center. It wouldn't be a visit with family without them poking at your sore spots. The very same spots you obsess over in every single candid photo taken of you and scrutinized on numerous gossip sites.

"Traffic bad?"

"I was asleep most of the ride." Alas, I was up late last night, trying to argue my way out of this. When Mom realized I had packed next to nothing, she and Oksana, our au-pair-turned-housekeeper, erratically stuffed my belongings into the closest luggage they could find. They rolled me out of bed and into the car this morning with barely a wave.

A slap on the wrist is usually what I get for overstepping my spending limit. Something's different about this time, and I just want to know what it is.

My thought is interrupted when the mysterious Hector arrives wearing a corduroy jacket over a red-checked flannel that complements the sweaty, appealing flush on the crests of his cheeks. He's got tan skin and long, black hair that unfurls from beneath his modest knit beanie.

"Hector, this is our grandson, Matthew," Grandma says, overly chipper.

"I know who he is," Hector says, clipped, expression unmovable.

Classic stranger, thinking they know me just because they've seen my pictures online and read about my family too many times. Nothing irks me more than preconceived notions about who I am.

Grandma and Gramps are preoccupied again, bumbling with a jammed button on the camcorder. Hector extends a hand anyway as he looks me over with striking emerald-and-gold eyes. "Nice pants."

His voice—decadent and gliding with a low timbre that's in sharp contrast with his untrimmed facial scruff and rustic wardrobe choices—rings like a compliment, but his smirk and slight chuckle make the statement land with a sting.

Instantly, an insulted heat races down my neck. "Thank you, but my eyes are up here," I shoot back, calling his attention away from the front of my waterlogged, pink-painted crackle jeans with the zippers on the thighs. I was being rushed this morning and grabbed the pair nearest the front of my walk-in closet.

Do they not match my sweater? Should I have paired them with different boots?

Wait, no. What does that matter? I shouldn't be receiving passive-aggressive fashion critiques from a guy wearing shabby, holey denim that could've been retired two years ago. Or better yet, never purchased from some tragic bargain bin to begin with.

I meet his hand, grip so strong he knows I'm not here to play games. "They were a gift from a prominent global designer. Pieces like this are entirely en vogue." I narrow my eyes. "In case you missed the memo. Looks like I arrived just in time. You could use the inspiration."

I watch his thick throat as he swallows a balk. My gaze lands upon three distinct brown birthmarks orbiting his Adam's apple. A tiny, unique constellation. Mesmerizing in an obnoxious way. "I'm good. Not really my style," he says. "I prefer clothes that are more...*practical*." By practical, I'm certain he means less flashy, less flamboyant, and more *traditionally masculine*. Every sentiment I've had hurled at me in countless comment sections since the dawn of time. Screw this guy and his scratchy-looking flannel.

"I didn't realize 'practical' meant drab." I'm all smiles, while harshly shaking his hand.

"And I didn't realize 'fashionable' meant blinding." He matches my smile, giving me one last hearty shake. At full volume—in an amiable show for my grandparents who are listening once again—he says, "It's good to meet you, dude." Though it doesn't sound *good* at all.

"Good to meet you too, *dude*." His lip twitches, but not with pleasure, at the way I echo him. His firm glare grows more unreadable. It's infuriating. Agitating.

I pull my hand away first, which I never, ever do, as a rule. But I can't help it. The way he hasn't so much as rolled out the welcome wagon for me is disarming. The relentless prickling on my scalp confirms it.

"Shall we take the picture?" Gramps asks.

Grandma and Gramps usher me in front of the doorway, which is strung up with strands of golden tinsel. I attempt to look as happy as possible for the picture, which I'm sure will be on Facebook within the hour. I'm not looking forward to having to discreetly untag myself.

"Say 'Best Christmas Ever!'" Hector announces with a dash of irony as the camcorder fires off and my annoyed curiosity about him fires up.

When the photo shoot finishes, a timer rings from somewhere in the kitchen. Grandma asks Gramps for help with her chicken, leaving Hector and me alone in the foyer. He clicks through the seventeen different pictures he took, not even acknowledging my presence.

"Gimme." I hold out an upturned hand for the camcorder.

"Excuse me?" he asks, quirking a bushy eyebrow at me.

"The lighting in here sucks, they positioned me on my bad side, and I'm certain you're not familiar with flattering camera angles. You're no Annie Leibovitz."

"And you're no hotshot celebrity, so I guess we're both disappointed."

I gawk at him. "Just give me the damn thing. I need to delete any evidence of this encounter before it ends up online and in the wrong hands." I leave my palm there but, even with my airtight explanation, he makes no move to meet it.

"It's a family photo for Facebook, not the cover of a fashion magazine. I think you'll survive if a single hair was out of place," he says, iciness evident. I rock back, physically stunned. Nobody ever takes such a cold tone with me. Yet there I go, like a fool, patting my head for flyaways that may or may not be there. He smirks at that.

I squint back at him, off-balance. "Do you have a problem with me?" I ask outright. Needing to hear it for certain. People usually course correct their attitude when I call them out on it.

"No," he says, unperturbed by my defensiveness. "It's just…for someone whose last name is Prince, you're not very charming."

The cutting remark causes my mouth to fly open and a surprising tingle to race down my spine. I struggle for a comeback, which is so unlike me. "Well…well, for someone who's a guest here, you're not very polite."

He laughs. "If I'm a guest, what does that make you?" He motions down toward my bursting-at-the-zippers baggage.

"A *prisoner*," I retort.

Annoyed beyond belief and needing to remove myself from this conversation before I get myself into trouble, I struggle with my bags toward the guest bedroom. Hector doesn't offer to help. Not that I expected him to after needling me like that. My cheeks are still burning from the exchange.

When I kick open the door, I'm faced with multiple full bookshelves and Gramps's ring-stained desk. The room has been transformed by antique lamps with gold-balled chains and fine art pieces, gifted by my parents, that have been cramped into craft-store frames. A crime of the eye, truly.

I see they've done some reorganizing. This all used to be in the basement study. What once was Mom's childhood bedroom, as hinted at by the faded pale-pink border paper still lining the tops of the walls, became the guest room where I stayed every Thanksgiving while my parents luxuriated at the fanciest (read: *only*) inn in town.

This room was the one bit of normalcy I was counting on. Change and my anxiety are not compatible.

"Oh dear. Didn't you read the text I sent you?" Grandma asks, appearing down the hall.

I did not read her text. It was at least two paragraphs too long. I deleted it because I felt if I could ignore the situation, maybe it would go away.

"With Gramps's bad back, he can't do the stairs so well anymore. We moved everything up here so he'd have easier access." I'm aware this is information I probably should've had already, but I'm not in the mood to shame myself for more of my shortcomings right now.

"Okay then." Exasperation rolls right off my tongue. "Where am I supposed to stay?"

She gestures for me to follow her. I don't even dare attempt sliding both my suitcases down the steep steps into the basement. I hoist up only one, regretting it with a throaty groan, and leave the other on the landing.

Their house sits on a hill, so the basement is a walkout. There's a sliding glass door at the base of the staircase that leads to the icy-looking patio.

Around the corner, there's still a threadbare rocking chair and a brown rug, an end table and floor lamps, but now there are also *bunk beds* where the bookshelves used to be. The top bunk has disheveled flannel sheets and dog-eared paperbacks sprawled across it. The bottom bunk is made up for, gulp, *me*.

"What is that monstrosity?" Dread envelops me. When I look over, Grandma's biting her nubby nails.

"I know it's not ideal," she chirps around her cuticles, "but you'll have to share the room with Hector while you're here."

I'm going to be sleeping underneath a *stranger*? It wouldn't be the first time I found myself lying beneath someone whose last name I didn't know, but these circumstances are much less enticing. Especially since his dismissive attitude rubs me in all the wrong ways.

"What happened to the twin bed from the guest room?" I ask. *Is it too late to hitchhike back?*

"We got rid of it when we moved the office. You stopped visiting, so we had no use for it." There's a bit of accusation folded into her voice. I refuse to feel guilty for having a life. "Nevertheless, when we decided Hector was to move in with us, the best we could find in our price range on Facebook Marketplace was this beaut." She slaps the side of the bunks, and I swear the wood wavers and creaks like it's about to comically crumble.

I can't sleep in that death trap. This couldn't possibly get worse.

"You'll have to share the bathroom too."

Just kidding. It's worse. So, so, so much worse.

She gestures to a small bathroom hidden in the corner that I'd almost forgotten about.

My expectations for this month, if I ever even had any, plummet out my ass.

Share is such a foreign concept to me. As an only child, I've never once needed to share anything, except the occasional Town Car to school with some of the kids who live in my building. I'm not looking forward to finding unidentifiable hairs on the tile or listening to some stranger toss and turn above me all night as the bedsprings squeak.

The ghost of that sound brings me back to Hector's full lips, his stern gaze, and his gruff, provoking comments. My mind tips to the other ways springs could groan and give and moan...

I stop myself before I overheat. That is not appropriate.

Mom and Dad sent me here to keep a low profile while the island gets sold and the story gets squashed before it gets out. Not to fuck one of Gramps's students.

Even if it has been ages since I've allowed myself the privilege of touch. Nursing wounds after a majorly public breakup is difficult business. The last thing I need is people commenting on my choice of rebound. The rumor mill cares too much about where my lips have been, which is why I'm practically starved at this point.

I push aside that inconvenient hunger to give Grandma a proper response.

Mom and Dad expect me to be gracious, humble, and repentant, so I mask my upset (and stupidly horny) feelings. "Fine. This is all fine. In fact, it's great. Thank you." The nerve signals telling my brain to move my mouth into a smile are responding with: *Are you sure?* Which I'm certain makes my face look like a melting wax figure's.

"You're welcome." Grandma seems pleased. "I've put fresh towels out for you. If you've forgotten any toiletries, there's a closet with some odds and ends in the hallway upstairs, but if you need anything specific, the drugstore in town should be able to sort you out," she says. "I'll leave you to get settled. Holler if you need anything."

As soon as she's gone, I want to holler my head off.

I miss my king bed with its four-poster canopy done up in golds and blues. I miss my freestanding whirlpool tub in my *private* bathroom. I even miss the cacophonous sounds of the city spilling inside, keeping the silence and the thoughts that come with it at bay.

I've never had a roommate before. I've never wanted a sibling. I like being alone.

I've been alone most of my life and that's what I'm used to. That's what I know.

Unable to stand still any longer, I trudge into the bathroom with a silk pajama set pulled from the top of my luggage. Not appropriate for the weather, but I'll deal. I want to get out of these still-damp clothes. Hopefully, I can sleep off this sick feeling.

The sink is practically on top of the toilet, so I can't swing open the medicine chest without pressing my entire body up against the far wall. The shower looks like something out of *Elf*. I'm going to be crouching the whole time to keep my head under the water.

Once I put away my plethora of peels, moisturizers, and serums, I catch my flinty reflection in the mirror. I take stock of my dirty-blond hair, my baby-blue eyes, and my smooth, boyish complexion, which is seconds away from a stress breakout. My pores are screaming.

On an exhale—a cleansing, arduous exhale—I remind myself that if I make nice and make good for the time being, there's a chance I'll be back in New York in time for the big party. I just need to prove to my grandparents that I've changed. Enough for them to convince my parents of the same.

Upending your entire attitude and worldview can't be that hard, right? I've seen Scrooge do it a million times in all those *A Christmas Carol* adaptations I watched with my parents back when we still cherished Christmas like other families do. I'm sure there are plenty of meddling ghosts in this house to help me.

But that thought paired with the situation makes the back of my neck start to sweat. My heart rate spikes like it did in the car, a relentless hammering against my rib cage. I'm staring down the barrel of a second spiral within a single hour. A record, no doubt. Except this time, the hoedown doesn't do it for me. Flashes of down-home cookin' and sweat-stained flannels churn my stomach over and over, until I feel like my body is rebelling against me.

Quickly, I flip to something flashier, glitzier. Closing my eyes, I imagine a sweeping ballroom.

A Make This All Go Away Masquerade. Black-tie attire mandatory. Guests in evening gowns and tailored tuxedos glide across an opulent room where bulbous bottles of champagne get poured into crystal flutes. A string quartet plays as people caress their lovers in slow-dance embraces, hands on waists, arms draped over shoulders. Everyone's identity is a secret, which is perfect for me, someone who needs that feathered mask to conceal at least some of the hurt my visage carries.

And as my breath settles into a more natural rhythm, I imagine myself waltzing with a broad-shouldered man. His eyes are two dazzling torches underneath his beaded mask; I'm liquid gold beneath his touch.

The classical cover of a pop song ends, and the man asks to see my face—*all* of my face—but my gaze dips bashfully to the brilliant marks making a geometric pattern on the soft underside of his throat, and I know in an instant I've made a horrible mistake.

Eyes snapping open, I force myself to swallow down the rest of the anxiety along with that unwelcome fantasy about *Hector*.

I look myself dead in the eyes and jab a stern finger at my reflection. "Don't you dare get any ideas," I warn before shutting out the lights and forcing myself to sleep.

CHAPTER 3

Thwack.

I'm awakened from my depression nap by the sound of a possible murder taking place. I shoot up, hair flattened to my forehead, drool dangling from my lower lip.

Smack.

My head is throbbing the moment it makes contact with the hard wood of the bunk above me. These beds were made for prepubescent tweens, not college-aged men. My vision goes starry for a second, and the unfamiliar room is spinning.

With my forehead radiating pain, it takes me a second to realign my world. When I remember where I am, I need all my strength not to dive headfirst back into the non-memory-foam pillow.

Thwack.

I'm up now, more careful this time, and my heart is racing. I inch toward the glass sliding door, stepping over what I assume are Hector's stray, smelly sneakers, to see what hillside horrors await me.

Just beyond the patio, the sneaker owner himself is chopping wood for the family room fireplace. He moves with the certain, calculated grace of a man who does this by trade. His lean, limber arms are misleading. He wields the tool with semi-impressive strength.

Not impressive enough to distract from the pounding ache he indirectly caused. If we're going to be roommates, he needs to be more considerate when I'm napping. GADs—generalized anxiety disorders—are difficult enough to manage without my much-needed rest being interrupted. Not that I'd share that personal information with him.

Aggravated, I fling open the door and call into the yard, "Do you mind? Some of us are trying to get some beauty rest."

"Judging from that huge red mark on your head, it must not have worked." Hector inspects the glaring spot right below my deflated bangs but keeps his distance. I resist the urge to touch it. He doesn't deserve the satisfaction of knowing he's jostled me. "Jeez, dude, that looks bad. Who's that guy from that children's song again? 'It's Raining, It's Pouring' or something?"

"Yeah, yeah, yeah, he went to bed and bumped his head and couldn't get up in the morning. Very funny." If only I could slip into endless slumber and hibernate through this hellish experience. "Is that what an English degree here gets you? A spotty grasp of basic nursery rhymes?"

"Careful now," Hector cautions. "Don't go treading on your grandfather's livelihood or he just might go throwing you out too."

That comment burrows under my skin until I feel his words crawling around in there between the layers, laying eggs and multiplying tenfold. I shiver.

"Say, couldn't hurt to try and earn your keep while you're here. If you aren't holding too many silver spoons, that is."

"It's silver spoons in your *mouth*, actually," I correct.

"Well, how was I to know, when you haven't stopped running yours?"

I freeze. Never in my life has someone come for me so directly like this. Everyone hides behind their computers, writing articles and mean tweets they think I'll never see, but here's this stranger unabashedly going toe-to-toe with me.

Fuck. Do I find that…*refreshing*?

Up against the house is a pile of already split logs. It's almost like he made those last two whacks extra loud just to startle me. Since we'll be sharing a room and a bed frame for the foreseeable future, I slip on a coat and boots and switch to playing faux nice.

"Fine, I'll help. Hand me the ax," I demand, stepping into the frigid late-afternoon air. Gramps showed me how to do this once as a kid. Albeit with a toy ax, and the wood was obviously already split, but the principles are the same.

"This is a wood-splitting *maul*. An ax would stick."

"Right. And I should care because?"

"Because around here, you can't chop wood if you can't properly identify the tool."

"Oh, I think I've properly identified the tool, all right." My eyes prod him with a pointed once-over.

He tuts. "You should just carry the ones I've already split upstairs, so nobody gets hurt." He puts on his safety glasses and tan gloves again, giving me the brush-off.

Slowly seething, I watch him prop the dry, semi-frozen chunk on a stout stump, square off his pelvis, and swing from his waist with force until the log parts. I'd almost be awed if I wasn't so annoyed.

"Are you waiting for something?" he asks, already preparing the next piece.

I hold out my hands. "Princes don't back down from challenges. Mom and I once beat the editor-in-chief of a prestigious fashion magazine and her daughter at an impromptu game of doubles tennis. And we hadn't even warmed up. So, hand it over."

He laughs, louder this time. "You're joking, right?"

"What, like it's hard?"

I step closer, daring him to deter me again. This guy thinks because I'm well-groomed that I'm inept. Well, I'll show him.

He shakes his head, gives in, and hands me his gloves and the maul. I shoot him my most sneering smile. He backs away quickly, sussing out the safest distance like I'm planning on taking his head off.

This will be perfect for letting out my frustrations about being here, stranded and abandoned for the holidays.

Hector's scrutinizing gaze cuts through to my uncertain core though, reminding me of my dream. All too aware of his eyes on me—and the dream memory of his arms around me—I overcorrect, loosen my grip, and overshoot my swing. With a surge of almost slow-motion force, the tool misses the round, hits the chopping block, and bounces out of my hands. It clunks to the ground at the foot of a nearby tree, followed by an echoing sound of defeat.

A gaggle of birds fly away, squawking in fear. What I wouldn't give to have weightless bones and the ability to soar and escape this.

"I meant to do that," I say, covering up that catastrophe. I don't dare cast a look in Hector's direction. Just hearing his amused chuckle is enough to make my mortification skyrocket.

"Sure, dude." He picks up my sad attempt. "I've got an extra pair, so you can keep the gloves. I wouldn't want you getting even a tiny splinter in your manicured hands."

I hate that he thinks he has me figured out, but that doesn't stop me from sliding off the gloves and checking my nail beds, which are two weeks overdue for some TLC. My manicurist is probably worried sick about me.

I chop Hector with my words instead. "Is your masculinity really so fragile that you have to belittle my beauty regimen?"

"Is your ego really so big that you have to look perfect every single second?"

"Oh, so you think I look perfect?" I puff out my chest.

His newfound flush tells me he flubbed. Big time. "Don't flatter yourself, dude. Perfect is overrated."

Happy my grandparents aren't around to witness this, I give in to my basest heated impulses.

"Listen, Lumber-*jerk*, I don't like your attitude," I say finally, crossing my arms over my chest so he knows I mean business. I've watched Mom do this with more than a dozen assistants, and it never fails to ignite the fear of God in their eyes.

"Yours isn't exactly a winner either, Capitalist Crony."

"Ah, I get it now. I'm the enemy because I'm rich."

"Your *parents* are rich," he corrects with far too much gleefulness. "What is it you contribute to the Prince family fortune again?"

At that vicious attack on my worth, my mind goes blank. No thoughts. Just miserable, *miserable* vibes. Never before has someone been able to banter me into submission.

Hector pulls back suddenly, voice becoming gruff instead of acidic. "If you care to contribute now, you can pick up those logs I already split. As I said before, they need to go inside." He gestures toward the stack he's created that sits a few inches off the ground.

I narrow my eyes at him before picking up an armful of logs, angry they're snagging threads on a brand-new Fendi. Marching around to the front of the house, I stew the whole way.

When I get back inside, Grandma's in the kitchen hovering over a pot of soup simmering on the stove. A couple of chopped carrots sit on the cutting board beside her. She barely hears me sneak up on her over the Nat King Cole Christmas record spinning across the room.

"I thought you didn't use this anymore," I say of the fireplace. I set the wood down in a decorative holder next to the already roaring fire. The warmth feels nice. It makes me miss my family room back in our sprawling Fifth Avenue apartment with its plentiful windows, Aubusson rugs, and views of Central Park.

"We didn't for a long time. Gramps can't spend his summers felling and chopping anymore, and he's too proud to buy the split stuff." She grumbles something unintelligible and then dumps the contents of her cutting board into the pot. Steam rises in wispy swirls. "Hector has been so helpful since coming to live with us. When he first arrived, I'll admit, I didn't think it was going to work out. He's a bit of a workaholic. Coming and going all hours of the day. Up all hours of the night studying. But a month or so in, I realized Gramps and I were managing so much better with him around. He cleaned out our gutters without being asked and helped string up the lights outside. He knows the bookstore stock like the back of his hand. He even taught me how to make this delicious Puerto Rican bread pudding called budin a few months ago from his family recipe." She wipes her wet hands on a mistletoe-patterned apron before taking a seat at the island.

"What a saint," I mutter to myself, but Grandma catches it.

"As Hector likes to say, 'Hard work feeds the soul.'" She winks at me as if hoping that will make the sentiment sink in better. I grimace. "Anyway, I made mention of how much we used to love spending the holidays around an open fire, so Hector found some cheap seasoned rounds in town. He brought them back as a little gift for letting him stay with us, and he's been chopping away ever since. I think he likes it to help clear his mind." She shrugs. "We're using the wood for special occasions."

"What's the occasion?" I ask, staring straight into the flames.

"Your arrival, dear."

Some of my anger whooshes out of me.

Grandma's words should make me feel good, but for some reason they don't. They make me feel remorseful for how I'm acting. Despite how comforting it can be to reunite with family, the circumstances and living arrangements—especially the snippy roommate, no matter how *helpful*— are less than ideal.

I fumble for a distraction.

"What's the Wi-Fi password?" I'm fiddling with my phone again.

Grandma grabs a sticky note from the fridge. "Try this, but good luck. Ever since we switched carriers, it's a miracle if you can get anything to load around here. I told Gramps it wasn't worth saving the few extra bucks, but he insisted."

"My service here is terrible too."

"Oh," she utters, tapping some salt into her concoction. "The service is always spotty here. We're in the middle of the woods. Our landline works just fine though, if you need to make a call. There's an Ethernet hookup down in the basement if you want to use your laptop."

Landlines? Ethernet cables? What kind of twisted looking glass did I fall through to end up here? I forgot Dad used to set up the ultra-fast mobile hot spot whenever we visited to ensure no work email was ever missed. I slump into an easy chair near the coffee table. I sit there catatonically for a while, wondering what to do with myself, how to make this new reality less abysmal.

About twenty minutes later, Gramps comes in the door, newspaper under his arm, clumps of snow still clinging to his boots. I was almost certain that print media was dead, but this town seems set on proving me wrong in every way.

"Hey there. You should take a walk into town tomorrow once you're settled. It's changed a lot since you were a boy." He unravels himself from three layers of winter wear, an amusing Russian nesting doll of weatherproof garments.

I do remember loving the center of town during Thanksgiving visits. It reminded me of an old-timey movie set where people actually lived. We'd always drive in to the municipal center after dinner, past a myriad of mom-and-pop stores, to see the annual tree lighting.

This town is and always has been an anomaly to me. Like something plucked out of a fairy tale and plopped into the Berkshires.

There are two central hubs of activity: Havensmith Hollow and the Downtown District. Havensmith Hollow is where the Havensmith College campus is located. It's surrounded by student housing and a smattering of estate-like Victorian homes. It's haunting in its historical glory. The Downtown District is what Gramps means by "town." It's about five or so tree-lined streets of clay-colored buildings with striped awnings and decorative signs.

Main Street itself is backed by a breathtaking, if somewhat menacing, view of the Berkshire hills. Those hills are where most of Wind River's residents reside in remote cabins and hidden colonials with riverfront views and access to hiking trails. What is a woodsy paradise to some is my geographic prison for the next four weeks.

Don't get me wrong, this place was quaint for the two days a year we spent here, but by the time I was sixteen I was itching to get back to my friends and the hustle and bustle of a big city right after the turkey was carved. Cranberry sauce be damned.

That's probably how my parents felt as well, making up excuses for the last few years regarding Hong Kong trips, rewrites, and this year, thanks to me, Island Gate.

"Dinner will be ready soon. Go freshen up, dear," Grandma says, giving me a once-over.

You know it's bad when your grandmother comments on your appearance.

At the stairs to the basement, I find my second suitcase still waiting to be brought down. I'm sure there's a dinner-appropriate outfit tucked in there somewhere. Mom may be neglectful, but she has taste.

I pull up the rolling handle, unwilling to carry its full weight down the eight slender steps…which is a huge mistake. The wheels snag on a lip in the carpet, sending the brimming bag catapulting down before me with a tumble and a tuck. The whole thing bursts into a mess of cashmere sweaters and designer briefs. I stare at it like it's a crime scene.

"Everything okay?" Grandma calls, concerned, from the kitchen.

"Just my life exploding. No big deal," I mutter.

"What was that, dear?"

"Nothing!" I call cheerily. "I just dropped some things." I shut the door and start cleaning up, imbuing each item with all the metaphorical things I've dropped lately. A pair of Versace underwear. "My dignity." A Burberry scarf. "My sanity." A Gucci belt. "My will to go on…"

CHAPTER 4

"Why are all my flannels on the floor?" Hector asks angrily as soon as he steps back into our room.

Our room. Ew. I'm not going to be able to get over that.

"I think the real question is: Why do you own so many flannels?" I don't even look at him as I hang a pair of drop-crotch pants over one of his former hangers. "Ever heard the saying, 'Variety's the spice of life'?"

He clomps further into the room, gathering his discarded items up off the floor. "Dude, you just took all my stuff out of the closet and hung up yours?" When I opened the accordion door earlier, I was punched in the face by a wall of questionable flannel, all of it already wrinkled. I didn't think twice before flinging it all out. Not like he was giving me a very warm welcome.

"My wardrobe needs just that...a *wardrobe*," I explain. "I can't live out of a suitcase for four weeks. All my custom, curated pieces would get ruined beyond repair." Now that everything is neatly inside, I step back, ignoring Hector's foreboding presence, to consider how I'd like to organize it. Mood? Occasion? General vibes? "Besides, you leave your shoes all over the floor. I figured your shirts didn't need special treatment."

"You can't just take whatever you want whenever you feel like it," he growls.

I roll my eyes, produce my wallet, and flash him the crisp fifty-dollar bill Maxim refused earlier. "Here. Happy?" He goes stock-still, slack-jawed, so I slip the bribe into the unbuttoned front pocket of the shirt he's wearing with a wink.

I'm afraid he's about to riot due to how red he turns, but instead he plods into the bathroom. Good, he's accepted defeat. That's what I hoped would happen. Except the fan doesn't turn on, nor does the shower. All I hear behind me is something opening and then a rainstorm of objects hitting the carpeted floor.

When I turn back, my skin-care products have crash-landed in the center of the room. "What the hell!" I drop to my knees and begin scooping them up, but Hector is faster than I am. One by one, he's tossing my tan, white, and green tubs and bottles of La Mer off like they're nothing. Like they aren't *literally* all I have left!

"If you get the closet, dude, then I get the medicine chest," he says, chucking the last of my items. "And the underneath cabinet!"

"For what? Your surplus supply of three-in-one shampoo, body wash, and conditioner?"

"It's efficient and cost-effective!"

"It's full of harsh chemicals and probably smells bad!"

"Why do you care?" he asks sharply.

"What?"

"Why do you care what I smell like?" he asks, borderline smug.

I gulp back my masquerade fantasy, nearly choking on the heavenly imagined scent of him. It's unfair. I can't read him, but it's clear he thinks he's got me splayed open like a book.

"That's what I thought." He rolls his eyes before whipping open his newly claimed cabinet. I don't know if it's the abruptness with which he pulls or what he finds underneath, but either way he shrieks like he's seen a ghost. He hits the far wall with his back. "What the fuck is *that*?"

A laugh flies out of me when I remember what I stored under there. I race over and shove my way around him. "It's a SpectraLite mask, you fool." Feeling suddenly, unexpectedly playful, I slip on the pink-and-white mask and flip off the bathroom light. With the click of a button, the red LEDs underneath illuminate only my eyes and mouth. I ask in my eeriest voice, "Are you afraid of me, Hector?"

"Stop it! That's creepy, dude!" He bumps me with his hip, reaching for the switch. I wrestle him away slightly, not realizing that the brush of bodies could morph into a frenzied press. "Come on. Quit it," he says, and it almost sounds like he's holding back a laugh. A genuine one. He shoulders me friskily, and it takes my breath away, which is beyond weird.

When we're back under the harsh-white buzzing light, I realize how close we are, and swiftly the light isn't the only thing that's buzzing. My skin is vibrating, and my own heart rate ratchets up. I'm glad I'm wearing this mask because otherwise he'd see my blush. This is too much like my masquerade daydream to handle.

He must sense my clogged-up thoughts because he skirts away, embarrassed maybe. "Jeez, where did you learn that voice from?"

"You pick up a few things when you practically grow up on the set of a high-fantasy TV series," I say, sliding off the mask when the heat on my cheeks subsides.

He nods, the childish fighting coming to a cease-fire.

"What's going on? What's all the ruckus?" Concerned voices grow louder as Grandma and Gramps come racing (well, shuffling) around to where we are. "We heard screaming!"

Grandma's face is aghast. "What a mess! Did a tornado blow through that we didn't hear about?"

Hector and I step out of the bathroom sheepishly. Inspecting the scene, I realize it looks like two puppies had a tug-of-war over shared toys, and instead of playing nice, they ripped them all to shreds. The wreckage is everywhere. Hector and I don't look at each other, and we don't dare look at Grandma.

"I'm surprised at you two. I thought you were grown men. Not little boys." She folds her arms and *tsks*. "What's the meaning of all this?"

Neither of us has a decent explanation, so we remain silent, chastised, with our heads hung.

She shakes her head. "I was about to tell you dinner was ready, but never mind. Naughty boys don't get to eat dinner until they've cleaned up their messes." She pivots, but thinks again. "And apologize to one another for their nastiness." Another shake of the head. Another *tsk*. Gramps looks just as disappointed—if not more—as he goes.

Hector begins picking up his shirts, and I begin cataloging my beauty products, making sure none of them cracked or leaked. I need these for the duration of my stay or else I'll be a blotchy, pimply mess.

When I glance over at the closet, even though it's tiny, I realize I could stand to give up some of its real estate. Though it would severely ruin the flow and overall aesthetic of my garments, I have a mind to give him something close to half the closet for his homogenous attire. His reaction to the mask made him a little more human to me. Made me feel a little more reasonable. Generous, if you will.

I'm about to say something when—

"I don't know why I feel guilty here. You started it," he huffs.

My generosity vanishes in a cloud of smoke. "I start a lot of things: trends, passion projects, parties when I walk into the room, but that? What just happened? I give credit where credit is due, and that was all you, Hector."

"You're seriously something else." Hector finishes folding his shirts and slides them into a wonky drawer in the defunct entertainment console. A compromise on his part, perhaps.

"I'm choosing to take that as a compliment."

"I hope you know I'm keeping this for emotional damages," Hector says, pulling the cash from before out of his pocket.

"How lovely for you." I clap my hands together. "Now, I'm starving. I trust you can pretend we apologized to each other?"

"As well as I can pretend we're both going to make it to the new year alive."

"Fantastic." I smile wickedly at him. "Let's eat."

CHAPTER 5

"Coffee Girl, can you make me a cinnamon macchiato, two-and-a-half shots of espresso—no, wait, make that three-and-a-quarter shots—almond milk with a splash of oat milk and some stevia?" My order flies out of my mouth the moment I enter Moon Beans, the only coffee shop I could find on my weary amble down the main strip.

I had no idea how long a night it was going to be.

After the closet fight, a terse meal, and an argument over who got to use the bathroom first, I thought Hector and I had given each other permission to rest. That idea flew out the sliding glass door the moment the snoring started.

Hector sleeping sounds like a mother demon is having a baby inside his mouth, and then that baby is respawning while simultaneously killing the mother in a loud, violent battle to the death.

That's putting it mildly.

No matter how I covered my head with the pillows, I couldn't stop the grating sound from penetrating my earholes. Sleep was futile while listening to that, so I had plenty of time to lie awake and think about everything I'm missing back in the city—including my favorite coffee shops.

"We only do lattes, Americanos, and cappuccinos." A Black woman about my age with a natural Afro and dangly snowflake earrings looks up at me from the large paperback book she's reading. She's got bright-blue decorative nails with snowman decals that catch the light of the overhead fluorescents. "Also, my name is Noelle, not *Coffee Girl*. In case you were wondering."

"Okay, *Noelle*." I take a deep, cleansing breath to reset. "Please tell me there is a Starbucks around here somewhere that can make me what I want."

She laughs, deeper than expected. "Closest Starbucks is two towns over."

"Perfect, and that's how far?"

"Probably a two-hour walk." She shrugs, doing the mental math. "That's if you walk fast."

I grunt loud enough to make her jump. I'm gay; obviously I walk fast!

But that's beside the point right now as I attempt to shake away the trek over here: Snowflakes stick in my unwashed hair. The heat is on full blast, so I pull off my scarf before my body goes into temperature shock. I flop down on one of the barstools, fatigued. Without caffeine, getting here was a Herculean feat.

The road down the hill from Grandma and Gramps's house barely has a shoulder and is poorly salted. It takes about twenty minutes before civilization even appears on the horizon.

I'm so used to the ease and convenience of an elevator ride and a waiting Town Car. Now, I fear I'm going to need to invest in a pair of sensible walking boots, which goes against everything I stand for in the name of fashion.

"You're Matthew Prince, right? Lorna and Doug's grandson?" Noelle asks with a tone that suggests she already knows the answer.

"What gave me away?" I ask. My now-ruined Louboutin boots? My three-hundred-dollar haircut? My Alexander McQueen puffer jacket that probably cost more than her entire inventory? I stick out like a sore thumb in this town.

She just shrugs like she wants to say something more but decides not to. With finesse and ease, she brews me an almond-milk latte with one pump vanilla and some cinnamon sprinkled over the top. It's a solid compromise. I blow on it so I don't burn my tongue.

I sit there, the lone customer in this strange establishment with chalkboard menus done up in faded, space-themed jewel tones. The seating area is an assortment of shiny chairs in varying degrees of distress. The walls are covered in celestial tapestries that clash but still don't feel out of place. It's a bit of a tried-and-true bohemian dream in this endless nightmare.

God, what I wouldn't give for a good nightmare right now. Walking a red carpet in my underwear? Bring it on. Even fitful sleep would be better than no sleep. No sleep maximizes my anxious tendencies, and I'm already a ball of fritzing nerves.

"Okay. I'd regret it if I didn't, so I just have to say..." Noelle hesitates for a half second and then launches it all at me, clearly not catching my *I can't handle anything more this morning* aura. "I love your mom's books. I mean, like, I *love* them! The world building in A Game of Dark Dissension is some of the best I've ever seen. And the romance, ooooh. Don't even get me started on the inter-kingdom romance. Swoon city, baby. Beligley forever. I've read each of them three times." There's far too much excitement in her voice for this early in the day.

I flinch. I hate when someone brings up Mom's work. They always see me as a tether back to her. Actors itching for auditions for the musical adaptation they're making. Fellow writers looking for someone to give feedback on their manuscripts. It's exhausting. I can barely get Mom to do *me* a favor, let alone some nobody.

"Didn't love her novellas though. Seemed more like cash grabs than actual stories." I shoot her a skeptical yet amused glance. I didn't expect that hot take. "What? I'm just being honest. I didn't need a backstory for Malum, the bloodthirsty, head-collecting king who died by dragon in the third book."

Maybe I misjudged her. "Yeah, I skimmed the novellas when she sent me the drafts. She's clutching to that series for dear life, draining it for all it's worth, afraid if she strays her readers will leave her or something." My sleep deprivation causes a second lapse of discretion, which catches Noelle's rapt attention. Afraid I've said too much already, and not wanting to anger Mom any more than I already have, I change the subject. "Speaking of my mother, do you happen to have Wi-Fi here?"

She slides over a small, stand-alone sign on a metal stick with the log-in information. "Wi-Fi's for paying customers only." Her wholesome smile is as sparkly as her earrings. She nudges the tip jar forward with her elbow for added effect. Against my ingrained nature, I like her already.

I reach into my wallet, hand her a ten-dollar bill, and tell her to keep the change. I should be a bit more frugal with my spending now that I'm broke with a capital B, but my parents can't keep me off the leash forever. Once they see my grand transformation from rakish party boy to saintly small-town guy, they're going to call me right back.

At least that's what I tell myself so I don't curl up in a ball on the dirty floor of this establishment right now.

I slide into the booth over in the corner and lean my phone up against the napkin dispenser. Mom answers with a flourish. Her sharp angles are made more prominent by a full face of professionally done makeup.

"Can you make this quick? I'm en route to an important meeting with the musical production team. They have the opening number ready for me to listen to. It's titled 'Swinging Swords.'"

I almost choke on my coffee, trying to stifle a laugh. "Are you sure that's what they want to go with?"

"Yes, Matthew," she says, the portrait of seriousness. "The show begins with a battle sequence. It just makes sense. The lyrics are all about the different types of swords—short sword, long sword, aiming sword." She shakes her head at me. "Why are you laughing?"

"No reason," I say. I'll let the creative team sort out their own messes. "When can I come home?"

She doesn't miss a beat. "After New Year's. How many times do I need to repeat myself?" She doesn't even have the decency to sound like she's partially on my side in all this.

"Look, I walked thirty-three minutes into town this morning down what I'd consider to be a treacherous ice rink for half-decent coffee. Did you know I'd be sleeping in the basement?" Mom doesn't react. "In bunk beds?" Is she even listening? "Under a stranger?"

"There's no need to yell, Matthew. Yes, I knew about the basement and the bunk beds and the college boy. I'm your mother. I know everything." She loves to tout that fact, but rarely does she act like it. "If you had read Grandma's texts, you'd have known as well."

"I have no privacy! It's like I'm living in a castle's servants' quarters in one of your books." Mom always brightens at the mention of details from her books, but not today. "It's not just the beds. I have to share a bathroom! The drugstore didn't have my hydrolyzed vegetable protein shampoo. I've learned my lesson. I'm suffering."

"What do you know about *suffering*?" Mom lets loose a mocking scoff. "I grew up in that house for eighteen years, so you can handle four weeks. The same amount of time you survived NYU."

There she goes again, bringing up the lost deposit and wasted tuition money from nearly three years ago. Like she doesn't wipe her butt with the check we wrote that hack institution. I guess I would've been more serious about it had most of my prep school friends not forgone college for start-ups and modeling gigs, luring me into underground clubs and a party scene that was more interesting than my 8:00 a.m. gen-ed lecture.

"It's part punishment, part kick in the ass. Until you've seen the error of your ways and we ensure the story of your island misadventure doesn't get out, you're staying put. No use obsessing over something you can't change. It's tough love. Ever heard of it?" She raises a daring, penciled-in eyebrow. "And be aware, Grandma and Gramps will be sending us reports on your behavior. So, you best be on your best."

I shove my hands into the pockets of my coat. "But what about my New Year's Eve party?"

"What about it, Matthew? You don't get to buy an island and then pout over a silly little party. You lost pouting privileges when you could've scared Dad's investors shitless and lost me my musical!"

"Oh, please. There's no way this is all over one stupid island. Sarah is making sure nobody knows, and even Dad said it would've been a good investment under the right circumstances. What is going on that you don't want me home for?"

"Matthew, I love you, but you're too nosy for your own good. Leave grown-up things for the grownups." I don't bother to hide my eye roll. I *am* a grown-up. I have been for almost four years. When are they going to start treating me like one?

She's not even looking as she signals her driver to drop her off a block away. There's too much traffic for her to sit still any longer. She must think she decomposes or something if she's not on the move. "Think of this as a winter retreat to reevaluate your priorities. You're staying there. End of story." Classic her, treating me like one of her characters. "Keep me updated. Got to run. Kisses."

I don't even get to say goodbye.

Noelle tries hard to make it look like she wasn't listening, but I know better. I chug back my now lukewarm latte just to feel something inside me that isn't buzzing stagnancy.

"Can I grab another of these to go?"

"Oh, you want more *half-decent* coffee, do you?" I see from her knitted brow she's not going to let that offhanded comment go.

"I was just saying that to be dramatic. It was hyperbole." She's unmoved, lips pursed. "I didn't mean it." I bat my eyelashes for added effect. Her glare goes on for what feels like forever, but she ultimately nods and dips behind the shiny, silver coffee machine.

As I wait, I text Bentley:

SOS.
I have a roommate here.
We're sleeping in bunk beds.
Kill me.
It's like Summer Camp 2.0

She texts back within minutes, instead of her usual seconds:

Bentley: Stfu, you went to theater camp in the Catskills.
Me: And???
Bentley: Your "cabin" was a refurbished hotel room… 🙁
Me: You're one to talk. You spent summers at Princess Prep IN A
          LITERAL CASTLE.
Bentley: And I grew up to be a fuckin' queen. Get over it. 💅
Me: You're being VERY UNHELPFUL RIGHT NOW.

I say *right now* but I do mean over an indeterminate period of recent time. Bentley and I were joined at the hip in high school, existing on a wavelength above everyone else, but ever since my reputation started taking a rocky turn, she's begun putting distance between us, and it hurts.

Her next message is a link to the Wind River Inn. The image attached is the bright-white exterior, all stunning porches and a slideshow of its loudly wallpapered (probably haunted) rooms. Duh, how had I not thought of this myself.

Bentley's last text reads: Don't say I never did anything 4 u, matty bb

✳ ✳ ✳

"I'm sorry, Mr. Prince, but there's no room at the inn," says Rosalie, the elderly innkeeper wearing owlish glasses, from behind the reception desk. I gape at her, and she snorts to herself. "Sorry! I've always wanted to say that to someone."

My eyes narrow. "I'm not looking for a *room*. I'm here for a *suite*." She doesn't seem to be comprehending the difference. "I don't require anything fancy. Just a king bed, a claw-foot tub, a sitting area, and if you have one with a view, that wouldn't be the worst thing in the world, but if you don't, garden-facing is fine."

Rosalie blinks back at me as if I'm from another dimension and then steps aside, doing a Vanna White gesture to the wall behind her. There are at least a dozen empty hooks where brass keys usually hang and sway, tagged with room numbers. I've been here before when my parents checked in during Thanksgiving, and I've never seen that wall depleted in my life. "No rooms. No suites. No vacancy, sweetie."

"Are you serious?" I hope my incredulity conveys that something must be done about this. Though in fairness, this isn't the kind of place I can flash my parentage for favors. Mom went from hopeful town youth with shiny prospects to bestselling urbanite author and never looked back. The town has never quite forgiven her for that.

Except Rosalie, who took her business annually.

But whatever. I'll make like Mary and Joseph and sleep in a manger behind this former carriage house if I must. Anything to not be sharing a room with that human snowblower. Those close quarters will force me to crack.

"Unfortunately, I am serious," Rosalie says. "Joking aside, a local lawn architecture company is launching a walk-through Christmas light exhibition, and it's drumming up a lot of interest online. All part of the big town-revitalization plans or whatnot. We were booked solid by last weekend. Everyone wants to be there for opening night. Lots of out-of-towners are making a weekend out of it."

I bite the inside of my cheek until I taste blood. This was my only hope. I assumed since they knew my parents here they could bill the suite to the last card on file. Which, now that I consider it, may have expired at this point.

"What's your availability for Monday?" I ask, hoping for some certain reprieve to look forward to. She completely ignores my question, enraptured by another thought.

"You remind me of your mother when she was young," Rosalie observes, resting an elbow down in front of her. Like Grandma, people here refer to Mom as *your mother* more often than not. Anna Winston-Prince is practically forbidden. "One time, maybe when she was thirteen or fourteen, she burst in here saying she'd had a fight with Lorna and Doug and was looking for a place to hide out. She was a ball of teenage angst, almost adorable, entirely frightening. I had girls of my own, so I knew the drill." She tucks a wispy hair behind her ear.

"I said, 'Okay, if you can't pay, you'll have to work off the room. Do you understand?' She said, 'Sure. I'll do whatever.' I took her right back into our kitchen and showed her the sink piled high with the plates from the breakfast buffet and said, 'You said you'll do whatever, right?' She took one long, hard look at those dishes covered in hollandaise and said, 'You know what? I just forgot I have a book report due tomorrow,' and fled here like a bat out of hell."

Rosalie's laugh is so booming it makes her rosy cheeks jiggle. I'm unamused by her trip down memory lane. Her apologetic eyes make my stomach sink even lower. "I wish I could offer you a similar deal, but my hands are tied. Let your parents know that the next time they're in town, we'll prepare the singular suite for them well in advance. No dish washing necessary."

"Sure, yeah. Will do."

Rosalie dips into her office, leaving me alone.

Dejected and out of options, I don't let the door hit me or my bruised ego on the way out.

While lost in thought, considering how to get back to Grandma and Gramps's house—walking: not my favorite option, after seeing the havoc it's wreaked on my fresh-from-the-box boots—I don't notice a patch of pesky black ice right in front of me.

Suddenly, I'm graceless Adam Rippon, slipping and sliding down the front walk, arms flailing. My life—once fantastic, now a joke—flashes before my eyes. I grab for the rickety sign to keep myself upright, but the terrible tread on my boots has me speeding away before I can grasp it.

"Matthew?" comes a voice that makes my predicament even more unfortunate. I don't have time to look up before I'm bumping chests with a certified snoring extraordinaire. The force of my body knocks Hector backward and backward further, until we both tumble into a melting snowbank, landing with me on top of him in an ungainly sprawl. "Oof!"

The blow knocks the wind out of me. It's seconds before I'm opening my eyes to ensure I haven't killed a man. Thankfully (or not thankfully, depending on how you look at it), Hector is breathing, glaring up at me from beneath his wayward beanie.

"You cause chaos everywhere you go, don't you?" he snidely remarks. It's so like what one of my married exes said to me on that fateful day at the Fire Island beach when I was broken up with.

"You're chaotic, Matthew. And we don't need that energy in our life any longer..."

I cringe. That comment stings worse than the cold or any scrapes I may have sustained from that spectacular fall.

"Can you get off me now?" Hector's breath is a torrent of peppermint-scented gum.

Using my last remaining might, I roll over in the snow before picking myself up and dusting myself off. That coffee earlier did nothing to prepare me for another encounter with Hector. I'm running on empty.

"What are you even doing here?"

"Trying not to die," I half joke while racking my brain for an appropriate lie. My eyes land on the bright-orange HELP WANTED sign in the front window. "I was…applying for a job?"

Hector laughs right in my face, no holding back while still absent-mindedly holding my arm. If I'm cut off forever, perhaps I can make a living doing stand-up comedy. At least I know I have one fan, even if my jokes are entirely unintentional. "No, seriously. What are you doing?"

"I could ask you the same question."

"Not that it's any of your business," Hector starts, "but Rosalie's youngest daughter, Cherry, is in my Victorian literature class. We're writing a joint final paper on *A Christmas Carol*. She asked me to meet her here so we could work in the tearoom."

I remember the tearoom as the place where Mom, Grandma, and I would go when I was young. Though, back then, I hated the taste of bitter hot tea, so Rosalie would bring me warm milk and all the macarons my stomach could handle. This town isn't just small; it's crushingly small. Reminding me of everything I once had.

"Wait," Hector says, jolting me from the memory. "Hang on, were you trying to get a room here?"

"No." He doesn't budge, struck with skepticism, so I give in. "I was trying to get a *suite* here."

"Seriously?"

"There's a difference!"

He throws up his hands. "You're seriously something else!"

"Why do you keep saying that?"

"Because I don't know what else to say to you. You whirled in here like the churlish roommate from hell…"

"Says the boy who snores like he's possessed…" I mutter to myself, but not quietly enough apparently. I need to work on that.

"Shit, I snored?" He appears so disheartened—a sharp about-face. I'm almost afraid to nod, but I do it anyway. He has no interest in sparing my feelings. He's just like the internet vultures.

"Ugh, my ex used to hate that. I mean, *haaaaaaaate* that. It happens a lot when the weather gets cold."

"Your ex?" Curiosity kicks the question right out of my mouth. I shouldn't be intrigued by this, but of course I am.

"Yeah, she always begged me to try those sticky strips, but I don't know, dude. Do those even work? They make no sense to me."

I shrug and make a mental note of his ex. Not that I need to file that information away for safekeeping, but it should hopefully squelch some of my sudden-onset interest. That doesn't mean this dude is *not* into dudes; it just means he's got an open thing with a recent ex. At least an open-enough thing that he'd bring it up. Unless he's one of those weird people who gets emotional closure after relationships and then still talks about them fondly. Gross.

"Your point is?" I ask, reverting to our natural snarky state.

"My point is that I can't control that, so deal with it, dude."

"I was dealing with it by trying to get a room here!"

"A room? I thought it was a *suite*." His comment is a sandpapery caress of derision.

"I…" I stop short before saying something I might regret. "You're the worst."

"Yeah, well, the feeling is mutual, and for both of our sakes, I hope you were successful securing that suite." He shoulders his way past me to the porch.

"I wasn't. They're booked. We're stuck with each other." I groan.

We stand there in a gridlock. Him on the top step. Me down below. Heated eyes that linger too long, and for a second, it feels like there's a flicker of detestable lust lapping off his hard countenance. Like at any second we could rip into each other in a wild, animalistic way. Shed our layers to get to the root of our loathing.

But it evaporates just as quickly as it came. My imagination is going to get me into trouble.

Hiking his backpack farther onto his shoulder, he says with a smirk, "Can't wait until your grandparents hear about this." My heart *thunks*. Mom mentioned that she'll be taking reports from Grandma and Gramps. The first one can't be bad if I plan on showing them I'm turning over a new leaf.

"You wouldn't dare." I do the power pose again. The one Mom taught me. It's even less effective this time around.

"Wouldn't I? Hmm." He arches a caterpillar eyebrow. "I guess you'll just have to wait and see."

CHAPTER 6

I think about Hector's threat for the rest of the day.

I thought about it on the awful walk back. I thought about it as I tried to nap. I can't even stop thinking about it now, before dinner, as Grandma asks for my help setting the table. I aimlessly lay down bowls on place mats, trying to control the mounting dread. It seems my brain has mutated into a menacing Krampus—a shadowy half goat, half demon that instead of bringing gifts brings torturous mental imbalance.

I try to focus on a fake event. But the hoedown doesn't work, the masquerade was sullied by Hector's abrupt appearance in it, and I'm not feeling particularly creative at the moment, so I can't come up with anything new. Instead, I cling to the positive thoughts Krampus hasn't stuck his horns through and deflated yet, which in fairness are few and far between.

Hector is rude, sure, and surly and brusque, but he's *not* vindictive.

At least I don't think.

It was probably an empty threat. Grandma and Gramps scolded us, and he dutifully folded his flannels for storage in the entertainment unit. He can be agreeable to my whims when he wants to be.

"Do you know where everything goes?" Grandma asks me, while taking a call on the cordless landline phone. Distorted words come out of the receiver. "No, not you, Jack. Matthew." Beat. "My *grandson* Matthew." Another beat. "Yes, my *only* grandson. The *only* child of my *only* daughter."

An excruciating beat where Jack can be heard soapboxing on the other end of the line about the state of capitalism, the downfall of man, and how Mom has disowned this town for the umpteenth time. Grandma looks at me, covering the speaker. "He says hello and happy holidays."

My eyes roll so fast and so hard they may just roll right out of my head.

"Oh, and soup spoons go on the right side of the bowl, dear," Grandma says, watching my every move even though she's midconversation. "What? Were you raised in a barn?"

I want to say: *No, I was raised in a world where people do this menial stuff for me. Thank you very much.* But I know that's the kind of arrogance that got me sent here in the first place. I simply shake my head as if to say *silly me* and reset the spoons.

Hector arrives, fresh from the shower. His hair hangs in damp strands around his tanned face. Even tousled, he's a vision, and I hate that.

I work hard to perfect and maintain my image. I'm photographed enough to make the expense worth the investment. I use the best skin creams and conditioners and get the occasional tasteful tan, but I've never been a natural looker. I may have inherited wealth, but I didn't strike gold in the gene pool like he apparently did.

"Dear, Hector usually sits there," Grandma informs me. I didn't even notice I'd sat. Hector stands over me wearing a curt smile, like he's ready to spill any second. I don't even argue that it's where I sat last night because I don't want to upset him into tattling on me.

Gramps ladles us each a hearty serving of leftovers—more of Grandma's famous chicken noodle. This is what my life has come to: leftovers. A never-ending parade of recycled soup.

I must admit the steam alone, for a second time, sends me floating away on a memory cloud back to my childhood. Grandma and Gramps would babysit me while my parents attended book-launch parties and office gatherings. I'd slurp down this soup with world-record-setting speed and always ask for seconds.

But, I'm no longer a soup guy. I'm a bisque man now.

My spoon hovers over the bowl. The utensil is a bit rusted, water stains on the handle. This isn't the highly polished stuff set out for me at my favorite Upper East Side French bistro where the escargot is to die for.

My palate has changed. *I've changed.*

The phone clangs back into its holder. "I just heard the absolute *worst* news," Grandma cries as she takes her seat. "Jack, from the music shop down on Spruce, has the flu. He's dropping out of being the point person for the annual Holiday Charity Gala. It's a little over two weeks from now. We're never going to find someone to replace him."

"Wouldn't someone on the town council be able to fill in?" Gramps asks.

"No. They've got their hands full. I could never ask Pat or Jude. Maybe Alma, but with the grandkids on the way, it would be wrong. It's Christmas. Nobody wants to be running around like a chicken with their head cut off when they could be present shopping and spending time with family. But somebody must!" She scratches her head. "Unless we cancel…"

"You can't cancel. Especially since you worked so hard to have the Small Business Association as the beneficiary of this year's event. There are too many struggling Wind River businesses holding out hope for that grant money," Hector says between slurps.

I'm happy there's a distracting topic of conversation. Hector seems too engrossed in this to even remember he ran into me in town today. I'm the last thing on his mind, and that's the way I like it.

"What is this gala exactly?" I ask, anticipating a lull. I need to keep them talking.

"It's a huge community event," Grandma chirps, broth trickling down her chin. "The gala committee chooses a town-wide initiative each year to raise money for. One year it was the underfunded school music program. Another year it was the agricultural society. It's always a worthy, close-to-home cause. There are a theme, a red carpet, a silent auction, some kind of performance, and a sit-down dinner."

"So, like a low-budget version of the Met Gala?" My question is met with blank, unblinking stares. "Hello? The Met Gala? Do none of you know what I'm talking about?"

"Of course we know what you're talking about, Matthew," Grandma huffs.

"Yeah, it's the big party they throw after the opening game of a new season for the New York Mets, isn't it?" Gramps asks.

Oh dear Lord. I'm in hell. I have to be. There's no other explanation. Just the thought of the Met makes me miss Manhattan more than I already do. What I wouldn't give for an afternoon in the Temple of Dendur or the Greek and Roman Sculpture Court. I suppress the feeling as best I can, the anxiety spiraling out once more.

To ward off the panic, I explain it in simple terms to them, getting swept up in blissful memories of before. "The Met Gala is a high-profile fashion event that takes place at the Metropolitan Museum of Art. Designers and models and celebrities all attend to compete for media coverage and raise money for the Costume Institute, which is the only self-funded department in the museum." I smile longingly. "I've been a few times. It's divine…"

Grandma goes from downright depressed, sighing into her napkin, to excited, eyes ablaze. "Matthew, you know all about big, fancy parties. Couldn't you lend a hand?"

My whole body stiffens. I'm looking for a way out of this town, not to get embedded in its local politics. While towns surrounding Wind River host summer arts festivals with New York's biggest stars and house impressive skiing and tubing resorts, Wind River doesn't traffic in flashy upscale events. There's absolutely no way I'm stooping that low.

"While I'd love to, I just don't think I'm the right person for the job." I haven't even touched my soup, and now my stomach doesn't want me to.

Grandma's persistence grows stronger. "Oh, come on now, dear. What else do you have to do while you're here?"

"Uh, I don't know. Soul-searching? Journaling? Maybe I'll record bedtime stories for one of those calming sleep apps people seem so enamored with. I always come up with something." Any excuse in the book would usually work, but Grandma's not buying them this time.

"It would mean a lot to us if you'd consider the gala as that something," Gramps says. "Think about what good you could do for the small businesses."

I feel my chest start to tighten, cutting off my ability to protest. The sweating. The labored breathing. I'm a ticking WebMD checklist.

"Yeah," Hector starts. *Oh no.* "Like the small business you tried to frequent today…"

It's clear what's happening here. He's using blackmail to make me fall in line. Admirable. Inspired, almost. But wholly annoying.

Grandma looks surprised. "What small business did you try to frequent today, Matthew? I didn't even know you were in town. You should've stopped by the bookstore."

My eyes signal *Don't you dare*, but Hector's eyes signal back with equal gall, *Try me.*

"No, he was at the inn," Hector says. His tone conveys everything his words don't.

"Getting afternoon tea like we used to?" Grandma smiles, remembering simpler times.

"No, actually…" Hector starts, staring me down as if waiting for me to grow a heart and interrupt. He and I both know the truth will only hurt my grandparents. I wasn't just running away from him. I was running away from them. This. A holiday season stuck in their humble (*majorly* humble) abode.

I don't want to care. I *don't*.

"I wasn't feeling well," I cut in despite myself. "I needed a place to sit. I had a scone. It passed."

Hector relaxes back, satisfied. Anger bubbles right up to the surface when I realize how he's got me under his thumb. And I can't spend another hour—let alone another night—in his presence, no matter how it makes my grandparents feel. I can make it up to them later.

This is not my world. This is wrong. I shouldn't be here sharing and playing pretend and taking the heat for doing something so innocuous, so unworthy of punishment.

Island or not. Inn or not. I'm out of here.

"Actually, will you excuse me?" I ask as politely as possible, pushing my bowl away. "I think I'm gonna be sick again."

CHAPTER 7

Back downstairs, safely out of earshot, I start repacking everything. Hector can have his precious closet back. If I'm making a run for it, I'm doing it stealthily in the cover of night and leaving nothing behind.

Folding and managing space are not in my skill set, so everything gets rolled or bunched and shoved inside a suitcase. I'll buy new stuff when I get back to reward myself for surviving the past twenty-four hours. Look out, Bergdorf Goodman!

I put my entire body weight on top of one suitcase just to slide the zipper closed. I pray the Louis Vuitton gods forgive me for these sacrilegious acts.

After an hour or so, I hear footsteps at the top of the stairs. I assume it's Hector come to gawk at me some more, but I'm surprised to find Grandma. She knocks on the wall to signal her entrance.

I sit up—more like *crouch* up—in bed. I'd shoved all my packed bags under the bunk, so she doesn't suspect anything. I pull a random book from the dog-eared stack on the TV tray next to Hector's ladder and pretend to be reading.

"Feeling any better?" Grandma asks. She's holding two full mugs of tea.

"Not really," I lie. I'm good at playing sick. I once got out of an entire month of school using the hot-water-on-a-washcloth bit. Though I had no other fever symptoms, Oksana was happy to have me home with her where we'd play games of checkers, and then she'd put on the afternoon soaps while she dusted and I mindlessly texted Bentley.

Grandma hands me the brown mug with gingerbread men dancing around the perimeter. The sweet gesture pokes a hole in my resolve. I sip slowly, getting notes of pumpkin and cardamom. She sits down in the old rocking chair with an *oof* followed by an *ahh*. Comfort comes in the unassuming things for her.

"You know, we really are happy to have you here."

"Happy to be here." Though *happy* is another one of those relative terms like *bad*.

She sighs. "You know I've been around the block with your mother, so I know fake sick when I see it."

My stomach squeezes. I know she hasn't done anything wrong, this isn't her fault, and I shouldn't be deceiving her like this, but telling her the truth will only upset her more. Aren't I saving her the heartache? I should be sainted for this chivalrous display.

"No, really, I'm…"

She holds up a sun-spotted hand. "It's okay. I get it. You want your space. I'm sorry we can't give you more privacy, but Hector is a good person. He comes across a little stern at first. Just like someone else I know…" She's clearly talking about me. It's been a good bit since someone has called me a good person. A spoiled person? Constantly. A privileged person? Always. But a good person? Maybe the one time I volunteered for the Trevor Project right after I came out? Since then, my goodness has been buried under a barrage of bad press.

I guess that's one thing my parents did semi-right for me: tried to save me from the onslaught of internet trolls over the island, even if it mostly is for their benefit.

Grandma continues. "I know your parents can be a bit…" She looks around, trying to catch the right word.

"Much?" I ask.

"Sure." She laughs. "A bit much. But I think underneath it all they usually mean well, and I think they try to do right by you when they can, so if they believe you need to be here, then I trust that you need to be here. Does that make sense?"

Nothing makes sense. I'm almost twenty-two years old. I don't need two babysitters. A metaphorical flick on the ear is what I usually get for stepping out of line. There's more to this story, and I think Grandma knows something. "Did they say anything?"

"It's not for me to divulge."

I set my tea down and press the heels of my hands into my eyes. "Dad has been talking about buying resort property for years. It's not like I bought a yacht I'd never sail or an exotic pet tiger I wouldn't take care of. I had a whole plan…"

I shake my head, but even that feels like it's too much work.

Misery loves company, yet it's clear by Grandma's pursed, chapped lips that she's not going to play accomplice to my flights of woe-is-me.

"Sometimes space to reflect and reset with family is exactly what you need." Her hands are shaky, but her voice is a steady calm. "I've been telling your mother that for years, but those books and that business are her family now."

I would say I agree, but what would be the use? I've come to terms with my place in the family hierarchy. Flesh and blood does not outweigh cold, hard capital or heavy, tangible books.

I hold space for Grandma to say more on the topic, but she doesn't.

"I think you'll find Wind River to your liking and the gala to be a worthy project while you're here."

"Maybe," I huff.

"Maybe? All right. 'Maybe' is fine for now."

I tell her I'd like to sleep, and she says she should do the same. She comes over to hug me, but stumbles on a stray LV luggage tag poking out from beneath the bed. I clock her gaze as it lands upon the repacked suitcases, but if she thinks it odd, she doesn't say anything, much to my relief. After a quick kiss atop my head, she disappears up the stairs.

I burrow myself down into the blankets, hoping to strike that conversation from the record. I don't want to build up any more guilt. I start planning a fake event in my head—a Getaway Go-Go Party.

Each detail comes with difficulty and varying levels of clarity. Teased hair. *Inhale. Count to ten.* Caged dancers. *Exhale. Inhale. Count to ten.* A Belinda Carlisle performance. *Exhale. Inhale.*

Count to ten... Count to... Count...

My mind is racing too much to keep track of the numbers. I start at four and end up going to twelve, and then starting over without much more success. The thought of hearing "Heaven Is a Place on Earth" live doesn't even calm me down. That's how bad this must be.

To try to clear my head, I flip through the book I pulled from Hector's collection. I realize it's a copy of *A Christmas Carol*, but not just any copy. It's the copy I borrowed from Gramps at ten years old. Gramps allowed me the privilege of leaving pencil notes in the margins of his books when he lent them to me so he could track my thoughts. I doodled ghosts and lit candles, questions about differences from the movie versions, and exclamation marks where I was scared or surprised by the action.

Where did that little boy go? Running the pad of my thumb over a detailed depiction of Tiny Tim, I hope to absorb some of that lost whimsy. I contemplate the prospect of finding that forgotten self. If I stayed longer, would I revert to being wonder-struck and hopeful? Would I even want to?

I'd like to think I'm better now, stronger. A top-tier version of myself with good hair and nice clothes and friends in high places. That's what my parents raised me to be, prepared me for. I'm more equipped to take on the world and all the bullshit it throws at you. Right?

So much for clearing my head.

My face grows hot, and my back clams up again. Krampus—the name I've christened my anxious brain with—reaches an arm out of my earhole and uses its claw to put me in a choke hold. I rise quickly, rushing into the bathroom to splash some water on my face, which cools me down enough to think a little more in the moment. I realize I'm not in any danger. Not really.

Returning to my bunk, I let a thought of Hector's whereabouts pass. I'm happy to have a little breathing room as I set myself up for escape. I read passages in his book, lazily looking for answers, until I calm myself down enough to fall asleep.

CHAPTER 8

At midnight, my alarm goes off, vibrating the underside of my pillow.

It's time. Now or never.

I listen for signs of Hector having returned.

Not a peep, and all the lights are still on.

When I slip out from my bunk, everything is as he left it when I excused myself from the dinner table. Sneakers still tossed off in the center of the room. Towel still hanging from the top bedpost. I wonder where he could be at this late hour.

Without time to think about it, I rush up the steps and into the only corner of the family room that gives me enough bars to get my RideShare app open and working. I'm thankful Dad's business card is still linked to my account. It takes forever, but the server finally loads.

I plug in my destination as Bentley's apartment in Williamsburg. She gifted me a spare key for those nights out where she would invariably forget her own. She's away. She won't mind. Or maybe she will, and I just won't tell her. I tap the last button between me and sweet, blissful freedom.

The "searching..." message mocks me. In minutes, Gramps could be in here looking for a midnight snack, a weird nighttime habit of his I remember from childhood. I don't know how I'd talk my way out of this one.

I'm surprised when the app says there is a driver ready and waiting for a passenger within two minutes of here. Finally, a win for me. I'm borderline giddy as I race back downstairs, fling on my outerwear, and traverse the steps with care and quiet feet.

When I nearly crash into a table covered in Precious Moments figurines, I curse Mom for packing me so extravagantly. I'd make a bad criminal on the run from the law. My shoes need their own suitcase!

I roll my cumbersome baggage onto the front porch. The Christmas lights are out now, but the porch light is on, a weak yellowish glow illuminating the shoveled steps. A lone vehicle sits idling in front of me. If this were the city, I'd need to check if this was my car. Out here, I'm more than certain.

With some oomph, I stow my bags in the popped trunk and jump into the back seat. The cabin is warm and the music is soft, a Christmas carol played on the piano. I relax, allowing the adrenaline to subside.

"Making an escape?" the driver asks in an almost-familiar voice. I notice then that they wear a hat with fuzzy flaps pulled down over the ears. The rearview mirror is angled away, so I can't get a good look at their face.

"What's it to you?" I'm not looking to make a friend on this long ride. Chatty drivers are the bane of my existence.

The young driver laughs and shrugs, setting the car into motion. Only we're moving at a snail's pace. Inching down the driveway. Squeaking onto the main road. I know it's dark and the streets are icy, but damn, this is ridiculous.

"RideShare Person, can you step on the gas? I'd like to make it home before sunrise," I say, tipping forward in my seat to insure they hear my directive.

"You got it, Back-Seat Person," they say. Except they only tap the gas a tad. We're going one or two miles per hour more than before. It's late, so I decide not to fight it; however, this bizarre attitude is churning up my anxiety.

I take a breath, try to conjure an event. Maybe the driver's just chilly and cautious. Doesn't want to catch a cold or get a speeding ticket. Both are good. This car is carting precious cargo after all. No reason for Krampus to come out.

"You have left the planned route," drones the GPS. The car is turning down a tight-squeeze lane. Trees bracket us in. Branches are dangerously close to scratching the windows.

Okay, maybe Krampus *should* come out. Can my brain demon become real and save me from what might very well be a kidnapping-extortion plot?

"Where the hell are we going?" I ask through a thick throat.

"Do Lorna and Doug know where you are right now?" the driver asks, voice pitched lower.

I'm about to ask how they know my grandparents, but this is a small, community-driven town of only about a thousand citizens strong. It's spread out in physical distance, yet close in relationships. I let out a sigh, but it's neighboring on a yelp. "Yes. Yes, they do," I lie. "And *you*—you're going to be in big trouble if you don't tell me where we're going or let me out of the car this instant."

"Am I? Just hold tight. It's a shortcut," they say ominously, waving a hand like I'm panicking for nothing.

But I know it's not for nothing. The perceived threat alarm is wailing inside my head. This situation is slipping out of my control. "Okay, fine. What is it you want? Money? I have cash. I don't have my cards anymore because… Well, it's a long story. But there are luxury designer items in my suitcase. Help yourself to anything you want." I pause, midpanic. "Well, not *anything*. If you have a heart, leave the yellow Balenciaga padded mohair jacket," I plead. "Oh, and the Givenchy metallic leather pants, please! Those are just, like, only flattering on the right body type." The driver scoffs, and the panic surges again. "Not that you couldn't pull them off! You probably totally could! It's just they're custom fit and—"

I stop blabbering long enough to notice we've somehow ended up back in Grandma and Gramps's driveway. The porch light appears like a beacon in the near distance. Did we take a really long U-turn?

"Okay, seriously. What's going on?" I ask, getting my breath back. "You could've just canceled the ride if you didn't want to take me. I know it's far. I'll tip you big, okay?"

"Oh, like the fifty you flipped me last night?" The driver taps on the overhead light. Hector stares back at me with *Gotcha!* written all over his face. My heart drops like an elevator in a disaster movie.

Of course this callous jerk would intercept my only means of escape. I grow clammy. Frustrated. Embarrassed. A hodgepodge of horrific feelings gurgle in my stomach, and I'm struggling for words.

"What…what a great, funny prank you just played." I inhale sharply. "You're just full of fucking jokes." I should've known something was up. There's not even another house within two minutes of here. How stupid of me. Stupid, stupid, stupid.

I struggle to get the seat belt unclipped. It feels like it's crushing my sternum, but that might be the brand-new anxiety attack starting to spread like a rash across my torso.

"I thought it was pretty funny." Hector's pleasure is profuse and grating.

"What the fuck is wrong with this shitty seat belt?" I ask-shout, my chest rising and falling quicker than ever before.

"It sticks sometimes. You just have to pull."

I shout that I am pulling. I yank and press and pull some more. The belt digs deeper into my shoulder. *Please don't let this happen right now.*

Inhale. Count to ten. Exhale.

It's no fucking use.

"Chill, whoa. *Chill.*" Hector jumps out of the car and runs around to the back passenger's side. He nearly elbows me in the face while he frees me from my polyester prison. "Dude, you could've broken this," he says, inspecting where the belt began to fray.

"Well, maybe if you want to be a RideShare driver, you shouldn't have the world's faultiest seat belts." I'm suddenly hyperaware of his closeness. He smells of cedar, something smoky, and ocean-scented three-in-one cleanser. Not as a bad a scent as I'd suspected, but there's no space to think on that. The combination is causing my head to whirl more. I wiggle out from underneath him and hunch over in the gravel.

Fire burns underneath my skin. My brain bangs against my skull for relief.

Hector takes a beat before placing a hand on my lower back. "Are you okay?"

I jerk away from his touch, already too busy fanning my internal flames. "I'm fine," I lie. "I just need a minute."

As he kills the car engine, I try to right my breathing, but my mind won't let me.

It's been so long since I've had an anxiety attack like this. I've worked so hard to make sure that kind of tight-chested dread wouldn't control me any longer. With everything going on—all this abrupt change—I guess it was inevitable.

"Here," Hector says, handing me a chilled bottle of water. I accept it and gulp it down with fervor. My body registers normalcy once more. I'm mortified, both for being caught running off and freaking the fuck out in front of him. As if he didn't already think I was an abomination of mankind. "Come sit." He ushers me over to the bench swing on the porch. Its gentle glide lulls me into semi-rational thought.

So much for being back in the city by sunrise. Grandma's conversation comes ringing back to me with striking clarity.

God, I wish I could go back and unbuy that stupid island. Scrap the plans. Throw out the notebook I pored over with my exes. Never take a risk or a chance on myself again. Survive the rest of my life being the spoiled, looked-down-upon prop in my parents' ascent to American power-couple status.

Wouldn't that be easier? I should be grateful for my lot in life. Shame on me for wanting something more. My heart rate spikes again as my thoughts gain speed.

What was my plan, anyway? When Grandma and Gramps found out I was gone, they'd have told Mom and Dad right away. My parents would never be caught dead in Brooklyn, but that doesn't mean they wouldn't send someone after me. It doesn't matter that I'm an adult. I'll always be a loose-cannon kid in their eyes.

And maybe sometimes I do act on impulse or lash out or throw a tantrum like one, but maybe that's because that's the only way I can guarantee their attention.

I've been told time and time again that my biggest problem is not thinking things through. In hindsight, it's so easy to see when I've done it, but in the moment, when I'm hit with an overwhelming urge to act—my anxiety growing unbearable—I follow through without hesitation.

"Has this happened to you before?" Hector asks. There's newfound kindness intermingled with serious concern sparking in his eyes. The jutting elbows and sharp jabs we've been prodding each other with for the past two days fall away. For a flash, in the glow of the moonlight, we're looking at each other without the pretenses.

I nod, head full of pressurized, overinflated balloons, ready to burst.

"Okay. Is there anything that normally helps when you experience this?" He sits next to me, leaving a person's-width of space between us, allowing me to keep my security bubble. Inside that invisible bubble, I'm safe. It takes a lot of energy to remind myself of that.

"Sometimes, but it's stupid." He's seen enough unfiltered Matthew Prince for one night. I can't risk him learning more about me than even my closest friends know. Yet he doesn't drop it.

"I'm sure it's not stupid." His voice is gentle for once. "Tell me about it."

Nobody has ever sat with me like this before, spoken to me like I'm a person when my mental health springs out of control. At least not someone I don't pay for that express purpose.

Flashes of my first anxiety attack come upon me.

During a particularly important book conference Mom dragged me to, an inflammatory reporter asked me if I ever felt neglected by my parents like the young, dragon-obsessed prince character, Quigley, in Mom's books. I knew the honest answer was yes, but how could I say that? I was eleven or twelve. I was basically one giant, insecure pimple in the public eye. I didn't want to cause a problem or a scene, but I also didn't want to lie. So I froze up. *Bad.*

Mom didn't even flinch. She had Sarah Pearson bring me back up to the hotel room, put on a Pixar movie, and order me strawberry ice cream from room service. I thought, *Well, at least Sarah is here. I'm not totally alone.* As soon as she tipped the bellboy, she was back out on the conference floor.

It took an hour for my heart rate to settle again. I had no idea what was happening. I thought I was dying in some sad hotel in Tampa. When we returned to the city, Monday morning Mom marched me into the office of the nearest child psychologist without a word about what had happened. It was both the right thing to do and the wrong way to handle it.

We've never talked about it. It's the silent expense nobody brings up.

"You still with me?" Hector's question calls me back to the moment. When I readjust, I find my breathing is less labored, giving me the leeway to be vulnerable without overthinking.

"I plan a fake event in my head. Something silly to get my mind moving." Already I'm overcome with a color scheme: millennial pink and natural green. A soundtrack of new-age music, lots of lilting flutes and ambient sounds. "Whispers only, please" whittled into light wooden signs.

The right corner of Hector's lips threatens a smile. If I train my eyes right there, right on those twitching micro-muscles attempting to turn up, I can stay locked into the present. "What kind of event are you planning right now?" There's genuine, surprising curiosity in the question, which prompts a free flow of frilly ideas.

"A Self-Care Slumber Party with complimentary kimonos and cozy slippers." Just saying this out loud feels like dropping into a hot spring, worries floating away on the wisps of steam. "Maybe a screening room showing sweet, low-angst romantic comedies." His smile forms fully. "Complimentary spa treatments, of course."

"The kind with cucumbers over the eyes?" Hector asks, playfully but not teasingly. "I've never gotten one of those, but I've always wanted to. Though to be honest, dude, I think I'd be too tempted to eat them."

"Obviously there'd be cucumbers, both for eating and eyes." He seems pleased by this answer. "We'd offer 24-carat gold facials, milk baths, and sound therapy with Tibetan singing bowls for energy healing."

"Sounds…*luxurious.*" He says it with an almost British accent so it comes out like *lux-jour-e-us.* I pause to figure him out for a second. For once, I can tell he's not mocking me. And when I realize that, he succeeds at making me laugh by saying it again, only with a worse accent, which softens me.

I decide to meet him where I'm at because he's already doing ten times more than any friend of mine ever has.

Even if my vulnerability ends up being entirely misplaced, I need him to keep looking at me like that and listening to me this way because it's reassuring and nothing like what I'd expect from him.

"It would be very *lux-jour-e-us*, bringing the world's best treatments to one place for a serene evening." Imagining myself at said event does wonders for my internal temperature and my chaotic brain. Stasis comes, slowly but surely. "At the end of the night, everyone could retire to their own personal sleeping pod for heavenly rest after all that sweet rejuvenation." A yawn tickles my upper lip at the thought of sleep.

Hector laughs, but not at me this time. Not completely. It's almost as if he thought this exercise was cute, that my yawn was puppy-in-a-TikTok adorable. "It's not a special sleeping pod, but there is a bottom bunk downstairs waiting for you." With a twist of his wrist, he checks his watch and uses his phone to clock out on his RideShare app. "We should probably get to bed."

I agree, and when I go to grab my suitcases from the trunk, he stops me. "You go ahead. I'll get them." His smile falters. "Should probably work for that fifty from yesterday, right?"

My body seizes. "I, uh, yeah, about that..." Guilt gnaws at me. I'm not one for apologies. Forever, my parents have instilled in me that saying *I'm sorry* is a bad habit that loses you the upper hand in business negotiations. I remind myself that they're not here and that this *isn't* a business negotiation. This is just two people in a unique situation making amends for two days of bad, rash decisions. My mouth morphs around the unfamiliar syllables. "I'm sor...*sorry*. I shouldn't have acted so rudely when I arrived." I cast my face away so he can't see how hard I had to work just to say that.

"Thanks." He breaks for a beat. "Same. I said some shitty things." He flicks the zipper on the pocket of his coat. Its tinkle sounds like sleigh bells. "It's just you waltzed in here like you owned the place. Like you were better than me. You're not entitled to more than me just because you have money."

There's a long-lived pain lodged in that truth begging to be excavated.

It's for that reason that I don't make any more mention of his terse assessment of my outfit before that first handshake. I'm sure he has his reasons for remaining guarded around someone new. I didn't give him a chance to show me his true self. Instead, I filled in his Mad Libs blanks and, right now, I realize I may have chosen all the wrong adjectives.

Isn't that my biggest pet peeve—people judging me before they get to know me? I know it's not the same in any regard, but have I been doing the same to others all along without realizing it? And if so, does that make me a bad person?

Being here is all the answer I need to that question.

"But that's not an excuse. I took my anger too far just now." Hector juts his chin toward the car. "I'm not a dick, not usually... I promise."

It's hard to pinpoint exactly when I started playing into the tabloid poster-child persona. The one I cultivated over the last few years after stumbling out of the right spots and into the wrong arms. How long have I been breezing through life, offending people for sport? "Take it from someone who *is* a dick usually." I let out a self-deprecating laugh that sounds sadder than I mean it to. "I can tell you're not."

Judging by how Hector talked me down just now, helped me find my calm, I have to believe he's telling the truth. That the Hector I first met was a fluke born of my abrupt, blustery arrival. I do have a tendency to roll in like a hurricane, careless of my own destruction.

"I'm going to try to do better," I declare. "About my dickishness, I mean."

At least toward him. At least for now.

He nods, reasonably uncertain, then hops up, offering me a hand. Feeling balanced again, I insist I help with my bags. "Fine, you can take the heavier one." He throws the menagerie of shoes in my direction, and even as I struggle to lift it, I feel a teensy bit grateful to be stuck here with someone like him.

An hour later, when we're both tucked into our beds, lights out and snoring not yet started, Hector whispers into the static void of the room, "Are you awake?"

I'd been awake this whole time, listening to the house sounds. A creak here. A pipe bang there. A woodland creature scurrying across the back patio not far from the door. My anxiety makes it hard to adjust to new sleeping arrangements. Every noise is a possible threat.

"Yes," I whisper back, though I'm not entirely sure why we're whispering since we're not going to wake anyone up down here.

A rustle comes from overhead. The lump of his body, the impression of which I can see through the wooden slats, readjusts.

In the darkness, with my sight dulled, we could be anywhere and be anyone. While I wait for him to say something else, I imagine for a moment that we're in the undercarriage of a boat. Two guys belowdecks on a yacht charting a Mediterranean voyage. I imagine toasty sand, bothersome sunburn, cocktails in coconuts. It's soothing, and I'm nearly asleep when—

"I get why you did it, dude." His words hang heavily, like a mobile of rocks above my head.

"What?" I ask groggily, not understanding in the slightest.

"Why you tried to run off tonight," he explains. The toilet runs in the other room, the water sounds only making the Italian coastline fantasy more potent. Maybe I wasn't looking for a real escape, just a mental one. "I wish I were home too," he admits.

Home. What another highly subjective word. By the way he says it, I can tell Hector means where his family is. The place where he's welcomed with warm hugs and homemade dishes. For me, home is purely a place I can point to on a map. The Upper East Side is a neighborhood, a subway stop. The apartment—at Sixty-Seventh and Fifth—is a necessary smattering of impeccably designed rooms that I call my place of residence. It's where I go to rest my head.

They say home is where the heart is, but my heart always seems to be chartering a jet to its next destination, unable to settle down, running from the fear that if it stops for too long, it might get squished. People will learn too much, look too hard, dismiss me for real reasons and not the bullshit ones I can hide behind.

There was no hiding tonight out on that porch, but I'm too sleepy to let that worry me right now.

"I wish that for you too," I say finally. Softly. And I mean it. Sincerely, which... Ew. I don't *do* sincere. But just this once...I allow it.

He snorts, probably at the tone of my voice, but I think he's thrown for a loop. "Why, so you can have your own room?"

I have to hold back a "no." The impulse surprises me. *No* is the truth because that would mean I'd be alone down here, stewing in the sludgy feeling of being exiled. At least with him, I have something to focus on. Someone to commiserate with. Someone who, after tonight, maybe doesn't hate my guts.

If he's as good a person as Grandma says he is, then maybe he's someone worth getting to know.

"That would be a perk," I joke to cover up my other thoughts. "But, honestly? Because I feel like shit right now. Absolute shit. And I wouldn't wish this feeling on anyone."

"Not even me?" he asks, clearly still beating himself up over playing a prank that caused my anxiety attack.

"No," I'm quick to say this time. "Not even you."

I hear his smile. I don't know how. I just do.

Maybe I even see it, shining above me like a wavy, ombre sunset over an imagined ocean that helps me drift, like an unanchored yacht, to sleep.

CHAPTER 9

An alert buzzes my phone on my walk into town:

Snowstorm Warning in Effect This Evening

The weather has been blustery, wind whipping up, giving this town's name real context.

On every street I've walked down, people are stockpiling cases of water and canned goods in their trunks like the apocalypse is upon us. You'd think living in a place like this where storms are frequent people wouldn't freak out so much, but that's obviously not the case as a woman in a Patriots hat carries three gigantic bags of dog food out of a pet store, a precarious balancing act as a yellow Labrador Retriever on a leash pulls her forward.

Me? I don't have time for a weather-related meltdown. I'm on a mission.

I clear the notification and tap back into my Google Maps walking directions. I don't remember which street Grandma's shop is on. All small businesses seem to look the same to me. Cheerful window displays. Garland on the streetlamps. Sickeningly festive, but I have enough patience to ignore them today. Especially since I might be in the business of helping them soon.

The Havensmith College buildings loom large toward the south, peppering the skyline with tall dormitories and a classic bell tower. To the east, fog is rolling in from the hills I trekked down. I'm so mesmerized by it all that I hardly notice when I step into a crosswalk painted the colors of the Pride flag.

I stop in the middle of the road, perplexed by this lovely display of solidarity and celebration. Has this always been here?

Honk comes the sound of a car waiting to turn. It's not even an aggressive honk like the ones in the city. It's an *Are you okay?* honk. That's a very good question.

The welcome bells to Lorna's Used Books & Beyond signal my entrance. A lone man in earmuffs peruses a copy of *The Complete Works of Edgar Allan Poe*. Being stuffed inside a wall honestly doesn't sound so bad right about now.

Oh, the tales my heart could tell.

I welcome the blast of warmth in here, feeling almost content to be in a place that hasn't changed at all since I was last here. There's an antiquatedness that couldn't be copied. My chest is a roaring, open hearth.

That's until I'm confronted with a table full of Mom's books and the warm fire extinguishes. The display copies are TV show tie-in editions with the actors holding daring poses in front of a gated castle. Lukas Clifton and Bella Borden, the youngest cast members in the ensemble, embrace in the corner, colorful swirls looping around them to signal their star-crossed love.

A shiver races down my spine at the thought of Lukas's arms around me like that in his trailer at thirteen figuring things out the way questioning boys do until we were caught, chastised, and scolded into never seeing each other again. I'd go on to very publicly and very loudly come out, following the script written by Sarah Pearson, the very woman who imposed the wedge between me and the only boy I'd ever had feelings for. Lukas would go on playing straight for the sake of the series, his future movie career, and his mostly female fan base.

Yet another case of my feelings not mattering.

Anyway, so much for a hometown author spotlight. There are discarded signed copies galore. Not that I'm surprised. Mom has been vocal about her distaste for small-town life versus big-city living. Those early-career comments really cemented her legacy in this town. Rosalie's story only proved it.

Next to a pricy Game of Dark Dissension box set, a sign reads: STAFF PICKS…HECTOR.

In the center are copies of books by James Baldwin and F. Scott Fitzgerald, Toni Morrison and Jane Austen. There's every book Miguel de Cervantes ever wrote. Some even in their original Spanish. Hector couldn't be more of a literature nerd if he tried.

"Can I help you with something?" comes a voice from behind the counter. I expect to see Grandma, but Hector stands by the register. A navy-blue beanie is pulled taut around his head. He looks surprised but not altogether unhappy to see me. That's a first. "If you're looking for your grandma, she just stepped out to grab lunch." He presents a smile, no more hostile smirking or sneering.

"Actually, I'm here to see you." The animosity is gone, but it's clear we're still unsure how to navigate each other. Last night in our bedroom, in the bunks, we couldn't see each other. Expressions and circumstances could be imagined.

Here, face-to-face, it's clear we have some renegotiating to do.

Some real negotiating, period. At least, I hope so. If he'll hear me out.

Earmuff Man asks to be rang up, so while Hector is occupied, I wander. The store fans out with no rhyme or reason. Hand-painted signs touting genres from Fiction to Religion and Self-Help to Cooking hang crooked from nails half-falling off the walls. Some books are stuffed into overcrowded shelves, while others sit in towers on the floor like an entire city of paperback skyscrapers. Prices are denoted by colorful circle stickers on the spines. Most books cost from fifty cents to twenty dollars, based on cost guides taped onto end caps.

It's hard not to feel like one of these books. Rehomed. My parents cherished me when I was a brand-new hardback, displayed forward-facing on the shelf, but the novelty faded so they pawned me off. Sent me here.

No amount of revision can change my past, I suppose.

"How are you feeling?" Hector asks after the man leaves with his purchases. "Um, since last night."

"Okay. Yeah, I'm feeling okay. Thanks for asking." Though I struggled to get to sleep again, I did manage a few good hours before Hector's alarm—some wintry Billie Eilish song—woke me up. There was something comforting, if still irritating, about his snores last night. Not that I think I'll get used to them, but they were a nice reminder that I wasn't alone.

Funny, I'm so used to being alone. I *know* alone. It wasn't until I was dropped off on Grandma and Gramps's front doorstep that I realized just how *lonely* I was. Never had I been well-acquainted with that feeling before.

"Good, good." Hector picks up a box that reads "New Buybacks" and carries it into a nearby aisle. "What did you want to see me for?"

Before my nerve falters, I blurt out, "I have a proposition for you."

He stops what he's doing to give me his full attention.

"Hear me out." I clear my throat, suddenly worried he might say no. A word I'm not used to hearing. "We got off on the wrong foot. We're very different, clearly. We're from two different worlds. Planets. Universes, maybe. But I realized there's one thing we have in common."

"We're both queer?" he asks. It's so casually cool that I choke on my own spit. This conversation has taken a hard right turn.

"What? No, I didn't... You are?" I hate being caught off guard like that, but I love this new information.

The right corner of his lips folds up into an apostrophe. "Based on your reaction, I guess I misjudged where this was going, dude." He scratches awkwardly behind his neck, his bicep bulging under the sleeve of a cream-colored sweater with rainbow speckles in the knit. It's no doubt the department-store version of a designer piece I have hanging in my walk-in back home. Except somehow this one looks better on him than mine ever did on me.

Suddenly, I'm flushed with the thought of him without the sweater. I can't stop studying him the way I would a figure model in one of the drawing classes I took as an elective in high school. He's made up of lines that extend out into infinity, some pointed, some more loopy, all adding up to a pleasing portrait.

"To be fair, you did use the word 'proposition'..." he teases in almost a purr.

"Not that kind of proposition, you perv!" I yell, trying to cover up the entirely uncelibate thoughts I was just having about him.

"Sorry, jeez." He goes back to re-alphabetizing, his mouth all screwed up. "I assumed your grandma told you I was bi, and you… Well, never mind."

"No, no *never mind*. I, what?" I ask, interested.

"You're very open and out in public. You've been spotted on dates with a lot of guys. That's all, dude."

"Excuse me, *dude*," I shoot back. "I've been spotted out with a completely reasonable number of guys. Thank you very much." I don't love what he's insinuating.

He dips his head, holding his hands up in truce. "I'm not judging you. I swear. I just got the wrong idea. It seemed like you were…" If he says checking him out, how could I deny it? "My bad."

"Your bad is right," I scold, fixing the collar on my coat so he can't see me sweat. So I don't have to come clean.

"So, what's the other thing we have in common then?"

I pivot this conversation back to a comfortable place. "We both want to go home." He rocks back on his heels, losing some of the rigid, frisky fight I saw tightening his muscles earlier. "Listen, after what you said last night, I realized we were fighting because we both want the same thing and neither of us knows how to get it."

He seems taken aback, as if the exchange in our bunks last night existed only inside a lucid dream we were bound never to speak of, but I can't stop thinking about it. The quiet intimacy of that conversation. The fantasy that sparked in my mind. It's all too vivid and real.

"I'm listening," he says.

"You want to go home to be with your family for part of the holiday. I want to go home so I can reclaim my rightful place as Party Prince for the new year."

"Do you get a crown for a title like that or something?"

"Shut up, I'm not finished." I roll my eyes. "But, yes, if you must know, I do own a crown. It's unrelated though." His jaw drops. "Only a small one. My last name's Prince, for God's sake. It would be ridiculous if I *didn't* have one. It was a gift from Cartier. Anyway, focus. We need each other."

"How so?" His eyes go wide, sexier somehow.

Leveling is not an easy task when you're fighting off attraction. "If you agree to team up with me to throw the charity gala, I will make sure you have a round-trip plane ticket to wherever your heart desires."

Hector grips the orange book in his hand with frightening tightness. His knuckles turn a strange shade of red as something resembling hope spreads across his cheeks. "What exactly do you mean?"

"I *mean*"—I inch closer to him—"that right now I'm cut off because of a bad investment."

"What kind of investment?"

"That's none of your business," I counter.

"You want me to help you, and you aren't even going to tell me what you did to get sent here, dude?" he says. "Seems sus. I'm not interested in hearing any more about this *proposition* until you tell me."

"If I tell you, I'd have to kill you." I raise my eyebrows, hoping that will be enough to placate him.

Undeterred, he raises his eyebrows back. "I'm not buying that." He's too good at challenging me.

"Fine. If I tell you, and you tell anyone else, there will be reproach from my very powerful, very litigious family lawyer. Do you understand?"

"I understand."

"I bought a stupid island," I murmur, backed into a conversational corner.

"You what?" He leans in closer.

"I said, I bought a stupid island!"

"You what?" he repeats, incredulity maximizing his reaction. "In my family, buying a used car is a big fuckin' deal. I can't imagine owning an entire body of land. What were you going to do with it?"

"That is on a need-to-know basis, and *you* do not need to be in the know," I say, trying to shake off the project that was meant to pull me out from my parents' monstrous shadow and into the limelight for the right reasons. Too bad I went about it the worst way and it all backfired.

It's bad enough he knows about the island now. I can't risk him learning any more information that he could leak to the media.

"What I'm willing to tell you," I say taxingly, "is how much it cost."

"Do I even want to know?" It's a fair question, but one he needs the answer to so he can fully evaluate the leverage I hold here.

I lean in and whisper the figure in his ear, just for the fun of making the hairs on the back of his neck stand up.

He shouts, "No way, dude! I knew you were rich, but I didn't know you were that rich." He's abandoned the buyback box now, and he's pacing the aisle—the number alone sending him into a frenzy. It's funny to watch.

"Yeah, well, now you know." As much as I love my flashy shows of material wealth—like the pants he read for filth when I arrived—I do get hit with pangs of self-reproach for occupying that space. For having so much when so many have so little. A swipe of plastic is all it would take for me to be flying first class to just about anywhere in the world right now. Hector is stuck here because he goes without that privilege. I promised to be less dickish. This is the first step in fulfilling that promise. "Do you see how easy it would be for me to get you home in time for New Year's?"

"Wait, but you just said you don't have that money."

"I don't have that money *now*," I correct. "The whole reason I'm here is to hide away so I can't do anything else stupid while they keep the story under wraps. For image rehabilitation or whatever, but do you know what my parents will love even more than no story?" His expression is empty, and I'm annoyed that I must spell this out for someone as smart as him. Even if his face looks a whole new shade of adorable like that. "A new story! A story of redemption and changed behavior. A son who throws a charity gala out of the goodness of his heart to help a small town's struggling small businesses."

The fabulous headlines in *Variety* and *Vanity Fair* and other outlets that begin with V practically write themselves.

Sarah Pearson could finally hop off my ass. Dad's investors would be thrilled. Mom would feel justified for sending me here. And I could go back to who I was; the status quo would be restored.

I'm already imagining a Welcome Back BBQ at my favorite Korean restaurant when Hector throws a wrench in my plan.

"In theory, I see where you're coming from, but what if it all flops? What if your parents don't care?" He stops his pacing. "How do I know I can trust you to hold up your end of the bargain?"

I fiddle with the tie on the front of my wool trench coat, willing my brain to come up with the exact right thing to respond with, and when it does, I decide I have to show him my hand. The real one. Not the cards stashed up my sleeve for downright trickery. Those won't impress him. Above that, he doesn't deserve them. Not after last night.

"You can't." My reputation precedes me. He made that clear with that comment about the men I've been seen out with. While I used to not give a damn about any of it, now I guess I don't have a choice in the matter.

There's not enough time to jump through hoops and make him see that I'm trustworthy. That I may be frivolous, but I'm not maniacal. I have a heart. A small, mostly broken one currently, but it still beats just fine. I feel empathy. On most days.

Hector laughs to himself. "Someone needs to teach you what *not* to say when striking a deal with someone."

Funny, considering my dad wrote a pivotal book on striking deals. Hector's way out of his depth here. I know exactly what I'm doing. The only true thing I can do: attempt to forge a connection. "I'm being honest. Isn't honesty worth more in the end?" I slip between him and the shelf so we're eye to eye. "You can't know if you can trust me. I can get what I want from you, turn around, and then stab you in the back, couldn't I? My promises could be worthless for all you know."

"Seriously, dude, you're not making a good case for yourself."

I hold my pointer finger up to his full lips—a plush place for my own lips to land, surely. If that were an option.

"But I could be offering you a mutually beneficial opportunity. Don't you want to see what could happen? Aren't you a little curious?"

His eyes dart down to my finger. Those flecks of gold are practically dancing with the dizzying idea of being home. Not that here is hell or anything, but it's not ideal for him either. "Why do you even need me?"

"I don't ever plan alone. That's not how I work." I look him over. "I'm an ideas man. You're an *action* guy." What an awkward way to say he's more capable than I am. "I come up with the concept, and then you help me execute it. I can't throw a Prince-level gala in two weeks with only one pair of hands. Not one my parents would be proud of."

The reality of that hits me hard. Something crinkly in my chest cavity crumples a little bit more. I didn't mean to get *that* real with him, but now it's out there, and I think he can tell how packed that statement was.

"Plus I need an outsider to tip off the media of my goodwill, which is also where you come in," I tell him.

He strokes the five-o'clock shadow outlining his strong jaw. "I'll think about it."

"What?"

"I said, I'll think about it, dude. You may run on impulse, but I come from a family that thinks things through before they agree to them." Two parentheses crease between his eyebrows. "Well, I thought I did."

I would question what that means, but I'm too busy watching him chart the disbelief all over my face, and his classic smirk coming back. "You're used to getting what you want just because you're handsome and influential, huh?"

My brain nearly combusts. "You think I'm handsome?"

"That's what you took from that?" He reddens. "Objectively speaking." Clearly, I'm not the only one having a hard time keeping certain sentiments under wraps today. Maybe he *wanted* it to be that kind of proposition.

I grunt in defiance but it does nothing to sway him. He's stalwart and smug, chuckling at me. And because I have no ground to stand on or any ammunition to force *his* hand with, I withdraw for the time being.

Later that night, after helping Gramps salt the driveway and bringing all the firewood inside before the impending storm, I find myself in bed, wrestling myself to sleep again. All the unknown noises of a creaky old cabin on the side of a hill in the middle of the woods create a pulse-quickening orchestra that's going to take a million years to get used to.

I know Hector's not asleep either, since his snoring hasn't added an instrument yet.

Suddenly, he whispers into the darkness. Just like last night. Just as slight. "Are you awake?"

"Yes," I groan back. "Can't sleep when you're snoring. Can't sleep when you're not either, apparently." It's frustrating, my anxiety keeping me up like this, but I sink further into the blankets, letting my heavy head roll to the side. It doesn't feel so stuffed. Now that I shared a little piece of the island ordeal with Hector, there's significantly less pressure up there.

"I don't need to sleep on it," he says faintly. "I'm in."

I don't react at first. For a hazy half second, I convince myself I dreamed it. Maybe I reconfigured the sounds of the windy snowstorm outside into a pleasant gravelly baritone, but then—

"Did you hear me? I'm serious. I'm in."

I suppress a squeal. A literal *squeal*. Never before in my life have I had to dryly swallow an ecstatic sound. It's unnerving—the fact that I could be excited over planning a gala for tragic townies, especially one for Christmas, a holiday I've considered cursed since I was thirteen. But I am. There's no denying it because it means I'm one step closer to getting what I want.

Bring out the mistletoe because I'm ready to kiss this town goodbye.

CHAPTER 10

We're snowed in.

When I get out of bed the next morning and walk to the back door, the fuzzy light bounces inside off a shifted landscape. There's at least a foot of snow blocking the exit, covering the patio, draped over the trees. The blanket of white sparkles. There's still a flurry coming down, light but steady.

The scene is nothing like snow over New York City, turning sludgy and gray the moment it hits the pavement. This is pristine. Calming in a way I couldn't have expected.

Upstairs, Grandma, Gramps, and Hector are taking a snow day too. All are wearing chunky sweatshirts and enjoying bowls of oatmeal at the kitchen table. Grandma reads the newspaper, while Gramps grades papers. Hector's nose is nestled in *A Christmas Carol*.

"Good morning, bedhead," Grandma says. No sudden urge to slick down my flyaways comes over me. While grabbing a mug from the cupboard, I relish the fact that I don't need to look my absolute best while I'm out here. Away from the bright lights of the city and even brighter lights of camera flashes, I can simply exist. I can breathe. It might be nice.

"The roads are completely iced over. We're all going to be stuck here for the next twenty-four hours at least," Gramps says.

I did say *might*.

"Let's enjoy the peace of our first full snowfall together before we have to shovel ourselves out."

Shovel? I thought I met my quota of *chores* for the week when I lugged that salt bag up and down the front walk yesterday. My back is already killing me from that lumpy mattress and all the hiking into town.

I scoop some oatmeal into a bowl and sprinkle assorted nuts and seeds over the top, while I consider how to play this conversation. With Hector's approval, it's time to advance my pawn in the gotta-get-home game. My sudden about-face around the gala might sound suspicious to Grandma and Gramps. I need to be delicate about how I bring it up.

"Hector and I are going to plan your gala," I blurt out sans a dash of delicacy. My mouth moves faster than my mind sometimes.

All three heads at the table snap in my direction, thanks to the verbal avalanche I unleashed. Hector furrows his brow at me beneath his disheveled hair. I expect Grandma to shriek with happiness, but her expression is sheathed in founded skepticism.

She sets the newspaper down with little grace. "You know we won't pay you, right?"

"Of course."

"And you're aware it's for local businesses, not some flashy charity like celebrity pet adoption or coral reefs or whatever it is your mother is always posting about?"

"Naturally."

"And you can't just give up on it if the going gets hard, tiring, time-consuming, or it's not what you expect?"

I drop my spoon like I've been wounded. That one got me.

"Dear, be serious. I'm not trying to be a nag. I'm only saying you have a habit of…well…" There she goes again, looking around as if the right word is written on a cue card somewhere off-screen.

Gramps grabs the conversational baton. "Quitting in the middle of things."

Protesting is futile. I know I have a history of running in the face of a challenge. In childhood, I went through phases. There was my acting phase—did one commercial and got mad they cut my lines. Never auditioned again. There was my diving phase—got an Olympic-level coach, climbed the ladder to the board for the first time, and chickened out. Never went back. Kept the Speedo though.

In adulthood, I'm sure they're referencing my brief stint at NYU after Mom pulled all the strings to get me accepted. My grades were less than stellar and my application was written by someone I paid, so there's that.

"This is different. I don't quit at things I'm good at, and I'm *very* good at parties."

Grandma sighs. "That might be well and true, but the two of you don't seem like a match made in event-planning heaven. No offense to either of you."

Offense taken.

Yes, I shirked their offer before, but it's still torture to know that even my grandparents think I can't be serious. My successful parents have always begrudged my lack of drive, but to be fair, who needs drive when you have a driver? Who needs perseverance when you can just give up on ice-skating and pick up rhythmic gymnastics? Hard work may feed the soul, but my soul was fed with constant change based on my moody whims.

I was never in town long enough to get good at competitive double Dutch, too busy being whisked off to a television studio or a promotional tour to play prop at. My ballet teacher thought Mom's books were a tawdry plague on society—too much fantastical sex and bloody violence—and belittled me before every class, making my stomach hurt at the thought of showing up to the next one. That's not even to touch upon the recreational soccer league I joined in middle school that used my picture—wearing horrendous neon orange shin guards, I might add—on all the advertising materials, but never rotated me in to play.

Excuse me for falling into traps that were laid and set for me long ago.

But, again, I guess that's partially why I'm here. To undo the undoable. So, I hoist myself up and say straightforwardly, "What do I need to do to prove to you that I—*we*—can do this?"

Grandma and Gramps look at each other, bemused, before Grandma's gaze drifts outside. A delightful pucker appears on her face. "Since you two don't seem like a pair we can hang our hats on, especially after all the ruckus we saw and heard the other night"—the closet fight seems like an eternity ago now—"I have a task for you."

With oatmeal on the edges of his lips, Hector says, "I have finals to study for."

"Oh, it'll only take an hour or so." She dances into the kitchen where she already has ingredients laid out on the island. "Noelle loves to send me cookie recipes from Pinterest. I planned on trying one today since I can't open the shop, but I have another idea." She pulls a box of chai tea bags from the pantry and a carton of eggnog from the fridge. Slapping both down on the island, she smiles. "My arthritis is acting up, so I think you boys should do the honors."

I already don't like this. Nothing about baking has ever appealed to me. The measuring, the precision, the waiting to eat carbs. It's all crap. Even the gentle, comfort viewing of *The Great British Baking Show* displeases me. This is not how I hoped to be spending my day. I want to vision board or go to town in my planning notebook. Not get my hands down and dirty in raw cookie dough.

But Grandma's practically jumping up and down, or whatever the old lady version of that is, so *no* doesn't seem like an acceptable answer. I glance over at Hector, who appears intrigued by the challenge.

"What kind of cookies are we talking about?" Hector asks, licking his lips, like that bowl of oatmeal didn't even register in his stomach. He's ready for dessert.

"Chai sugar cookies with eggnog icing," she says. Hector moans. "You have all the ingredients you need. Just have to follow the instructions and work together." Grandma claps her hands. "Oh, this is going to be great! It's like having a mini baking competition right here in our home!"

"Does that make us the judges?" Gramps asks, rubbing his belly.

Grandma snaps her fingers. "Doug, that's genius! Not only do you have to bake the cookies but we'll score you too. If you two can work together to make a tasty Christmas cookie, then I think I can trust you both to plan our gala."

My aversion to Christmas is a cumbersome Yule log in my stomach right now.

"Need I remind you, you don't have many other options and very little time? This seems like a waste when I could be researching chefs and designing centerpieces." Anything but this.

"Suck it up, dude. It's just a cookie. It can't be that hard." Hector pats my shoulder, the first moment of intentional contact we've ever had. His warm hand lingers longer than it should; the heat of his palm burns right through my shirt.

"We'll be in our room watching TV if you need us," Grandma says. "Holler when you're ready to be evaluated."

Gramps adds as he goes, "Just don't destroy anything, please."

Well, I guess the only thing I'm planning to destroy now is their expectations.

"Fire extinguisher is under the sink!" Grandma yells, then shuts their door.

Before I know it, I'm donning an apparently feminist apron that reads Mrs. Claus Deserves All the Credit and reading through a printout of a recipe. A total waste of paper, but whatever. Hector collects the bowls and spoons and measuring cups we'll need, since I wouldn't know where anything is nor am I particularly versed in baking instruments.

As he reaches to grab the mixer, his long-sleeved T-shirt rides up his torso, revealing a treasure trail of black hairs. I busy myself by preheating the oven to 350, so I don't get caught staring. Our proposition conversation is still weighing heavily on my mind.

I pause over the instructions. That can't be right. *Beat the butter in a large bowl for about a minute.* Beat?

I shrug. After unwrapping the stick of unsalted butter, I wash my hands, set a timer on my watch, and go to town, punching that yellow sucker into submission. Yet another way I can pummel out my frustrations about being stuck—

"Dude, what the hell are you doing?" Hector catches the bowl before it flies off the counter from the force of my inexperienced fist.

I hold up the paper with my clean hand. "Beating the butter like it says to do."

Okay, now he's laughing *at me*. Full-fledged belly-laughing with tears forming at the edges of his gemstone eyes.

"What is so funny?"

"With a mixer," he chokes out, trying to catch his breath. I'm glad I'm a fucking clown to him.

"It doesn't say *mix*." I point to the paper with so much force I nearly tear it. "Mixers are supposed to mix. It's in the name."

Calmer now, he snaps one of the extensions off the mixer.

"Great, now you've broken it," I say. "We're never going to get this right."

"I didn't break it. It's an attachment, and it's called a beater. You beat with a beater. Didn't you read the part where it says 'on medium'?"

"I thought that meant the pressure. Like when you knead dough. I don't know. I'm new at this!" He's swapped his smirk for a tickled grin. "Wipe that look off your face. I'm trying here!"

"Whatever you say, Rocky Balboa." He taps me out and starts in on the proper *beating* technique. It's like the damn maul all over again. I hate how useless I seem to him.

As he adds the vegetable oil, he asks, "Not much of a baker, huh?"

"Nope," I huff. "Not even at *this time of year*." I hate all those Hallmark movies that show this as some sort of yearly ritual that all families *should* do. As if my parents and I don't have better things to accomplish than baking something we could buy at the store that will probably taste a million times better.

He measures out one cup of powdered sugar from a clear, blue canister. "*This time of year*? Dude, don't tell me you're a Hashtag Holiday Hater."

Hating Christmas is the one way I get to manage my familial expectations. I don't get my hopes up over silly traditions or false illusions of togetherness. It's safer than admitting that as a child I used to bleed red tinsel for this entire month.

"Speaking hashtags out loud should be illegal," I retort when I've regained my bearings.

"You're not denying it."

"What are you, one of Santa's helpers sent to see which list I should be put on?" My defensiveness fires up. "News flash: it's the naughty one! That's why I'm here serving my sentence. Can we drop it?"

"Just saying it's weird you're trying to throw a Christmas charity gala if you hate—"

"I said: Can we drop it?" I'm surprised when my eyes well up. I turn away quickly, blinking back the sudden-onset flooding. It's unnatural and unfair that my emotions get to pick and choose when they show up to the party.

"My bad, dude." And without another pause, we're back at it. "Egg?" he asks. I swipe one from the yellow carton in the fridge, tap it lightly on the side of the bowl, and watch the gooey contents land in what will soon be our dough. Not even a fleck of shell falls in. "Didn't know how to beat butter, but you can crack an egg no problem?"

"You haven't lived until you've had a cocktail with egg in it."

"Oh, I've lived a thousand times over thanks to my dad's coquito."

"What's coquito?"

"Puerto Rican eggnog with rum. It's coconuty and cinnamony and amazing. My family can't get enough of it." His expression grows pensive at the mention of his family, brows knitting together.

"What I wouldn't give for a strong drink right about now." My mouth waters. I'm thirsty. Both in the parched way and the from-looking-at-Hector's-thinking-face-too-long way. "I do—or *did*—plenty of entertaining, so I know my way around a cocktail mixer."

"You mean a shaker," he corrects.

"Whatever! Same difference."

I cut open a tea bag with a pair of scissors from a nearby drawer, getting horrific flashes of Mom going to town on my Amex card, while Hector adds the flour. To my dismay there's no comical mishap where the bag explodes and his face gets powdered. It would be nice to laugh at him for a change.

To avoid further conversation, he reaches for a clean bowl to start the icing in. He forces me to take the lead, telling me, "You can't possibly mess this one up."

Four ingredients get mixed together, and before I know it, the texture firms up into something resembling icing, stringy and sweet. By the time I'm done, we're scooping out the dough onto a baking sheet and sticking it in the oven. Fifteen minutes later, humming along to the Christmas tunes I'd forgotten I knew the melodies to, we've got cookies, lightly brown around the edges, a little burnt on the bottom. Not terrible for two novice bakers.

Thirty minutes later, the cookies are complete, iced and dusted with cinnamon. There's a bubbling in my stomach. Could it be pride?

"We did it," Hector says, giving me an impressed nod.

When we call the "judges" in, Grandma and Gramps are wearing formal attire. Gramps sports a fedora and Grandma is swimming in one of Gramps's blazers. They're taking this challenge far too seriously. Grandma sets her camcorder down on the island, framing themselves in an off-center shot. The red recording light is on.

"Bakers," Grandma begins in her best announcer voice, "we tasked you with completing a recipe for Chai Tea Eggnog sugar cookies. You had one hour, and we're pleased to see you were able to rise to the occasion without any major fiascos. We'll be judging you on four criteria: presentation, consistency, flavor, and creativity."

"Creativity?" I challenge. "Nobody said anything about creativity. We were following a recipe." Hector slaps my side, urging me to play along. I slap his side right back. He snorts, almost enjoying it.

"Bakers, please plate one cookie for each of the judges," Gramps directs, disregarding me. Grandma shuffles in her pink house shoes over to the camcorder and flips the lens around so it's on us. It's a whole damn production in here, and I can't help it. I preen, making sure the camera only gets my good side.

Thinking on my feet, I hand the plates to Hector.

"What are you doing?" Hector whispers.

"Getting those damn creativity points!" I race back to the fridge and grab the leftover eggnog. I fill two mugs full.

During my spree, Grandma produced two official-looking score sheets from the pocket of her tweed jacket. She hands one of two golf pencils to Gramps.

This couldn't get weirder, and for some odd reason, I maybe sort of secretly love it.

Hector obligingly takes the camera and records their first bites. Both of my grandparents wear their best unbreakable poker faces. Damn my family for never giving anything away. Covering their responses with their hands like they're taking the goddamn SATs, Grandma and Gramps circle their scores. Then, Gramps tallies up the total.

My pits let me know I'm nervous. Like full-sweat nervous, but I'm not anxious, which is both nice and new. Krampus must've gotten scared by all that Santa talk.

"For the viewers at home, the judges' verdict is the only thing standing between our contestants and the coveted prize—a chance to plan the Wind River Annual Holiday Gala. The team before us, the..." She pauses, so Gramps whispers something to her. "Yes, that's right. The team before us, the Bunk Bed Boys"—I groan—"need a grand total of at least twenty-four points to come out victorious. That's threes across the board from both judges. Contestants, do you have any final comments?"

"We did our best, and I think we had fun." Hector hits me with a genuine smile that spreads all the way from one ear to the other. Did he mean that? I'm so distracted by his one charming, slightly overlapping front tooth that I forget it's my turn.

"Matthew?" Gramps grumbles.

"Oh, um." Instead of saying anything sincere, inspired by that swoony smile, I revert to surliness. "Can we get on with it?"

"Fine." Grandma sticks her tongue out at me. "After careful deliberation and extreme feats of math, Team Bunk Bed Boys has scored..." She takes a Ryan Seacrest–style pause. "A 25!"

Seized with the success of barely scraping by, I'm tempted to shout, "In your face!" but that seems excessive. Instead, the energy bounds out in a surprising way.

Hector and I hug while jumping up and down like we just won an actual baking competition on actual TV. Bring in the giant check! Shoot off the confetti cannons!

His hands are hot on my back, and our chests are pressed together. There's a vibrant blitz of energy between us.

"You boys make a pretty good team," Grandma says knowingly.

Her statement bursts the bubble. When we realize none of that is really happening—there's no professional camera crew, just Grandma's camcorder—we shoot away from each other, finding our self-control on opposite sides of the island. "Cool," Hector mumbles, resetting while combing a hand through his hair.

"Yeah, thanks," I say, depositing the dirty spatula into the sink.

Grandma's expression has a perceptive gleam to it, sparking with something previously unseen. "Lunch in an hour. I'll give you a rundown of your duties then." She takes the rest of her eggnog and skedaddles with Gramps.

The game may be over, but the sense of play hasn't left me.

Coasting on that feeling, I steal a cookie from the sheet. It's been a while since I've had a proper, homemade Christmas cookie, and I'm curious after our previous conversation. But mostly, I just want to taste what they tasted. I mean, to see if we were fairly evaluated, obviously. What if I need to demand a recount?

When the first pleasing, spicy note of chai hits my tongue, I can't help but moan, loudly and with abandon. Hector peers over from the high-top chair in front of the island where he's resumed reading his book.

He looks studious, focused, handsome.

That hug loops again in my brain, and I'm hit with the same thought Grandma had: *We do make a pretty good team.*

CHAPTER 11

"You're throwing a gala for a bunch of geezers?" Bentley asks, utterly confused, as I FaceTime her from the service corner in the living room. I'm contorted into a pretzel, trying to keep the signal strong and steady. I have one foot on the fireplace ledge, one foot on an uneven ottoman, and my body is pressed into the window.

Outside, the snow has begun melting, the roads are cleared, and life is returning to normal after yesterday's storm. They're a well-oiled snow-moving machine out here.

"I'm only clarifying because the cousins and I hit the blunt pretty hard this afternoon," she says. "I take back everything I said about those little shits. Now that they're seventeen, they can totally hang. They brought the good stuff."

"Well, that's good," I bellow, trying to keep this conversation on course. My thighs are shaking from the sheer energy it's taking to stay put. "I'm just hoping if I do a good job, my parents might unfreeze my accounts and let me come home early. The event is on December twenty-third. I could be back in the city the next morning to resume planning."

Bentley's screen is paused, which can only mean one thing: she's checking her Instagram likes instead of listening to me. "Bee, can you give me your undivided attention for two seconds?"

"Ugh. Fine. My bad. A certain Hollywood heartthrob just posted a thirsty-thirsty thirst trap, and I had to see it for myself. Did you know he's still going around telling people we didn't really hook up in that hot tub in Saint-Tropez two summers ago? If only I had proof. I'm going to start spy-camming all my hookups for clout."

"Bee!" I say, both because that's a terrible idea and she's not even remotely keyed in.

"Right, we're talking about you." She says *you* as if she'd rather be talking about deranged sex cults or the dangers of Botox. "I was listening. You and Ax Guy are joining forces to save the small town and secure your ticket home. Though it sounds like you're trying to secure a ticket into his pants too."

"First off, you can't refer to him as Ax Guy. It was a wood-splitting *maul*, and his name is *Hector*," I say. "Second, I do not want to fuck him." Is she buying this? Am *I* buying this? I can't tell her the truth about that, so I tell her a different one. "There's no place in the universe less arousing than your grandparents' house. Gross."

"Epically gross." She laughs, breezy and forced. "I just needed to hear you say it. I didn't want word getting around that you were slumming it with some nobody in the middle of nowhere. Do you know how bad that would look for me?"

For me too, I guess. Bentley has made it abundantly clear that we only date and do boys in our social circle. It's almost incestuous, if you stop to think about it. In some ways, it makes sense. Power plus power breeds more power.

I always thought it lucky that Mom and Dad found each other. They got a good deal on all counts. Their individual successes elevate them as a couple into a greater echelon of influence. Their union, unfettered by the weight of life's expenses, has gotten them everything they've ever wanted.

Except maybe true love. But who cares when your joint net worth is in the stratosphere?

"Keep it in your pants until you come home. There will be plenty of fresh meat waiting for you on New Year's Eve," Bentley trills. "And if you need me to pick up some of the party organizing, I suppose I could do it."

"Aw, wait, really?" Bentley is not one to volunteer her time, energy, or money. Neither am I, usually, but look at me now. Maybe we're both learning and growing? This is the first true branch of friendship she's extended to me in quite some time, and I'd be an idiot not to take it.

"Yeah, well, don't get too excited. The Brazilian ski instructor I was seeing last holiday season went back home to 'be with his family' or some shit, so now I have no excuse to even hit up the slopes. I need something to look forward to. Marco won't even respond to my texts about…"

Just as she's about to monopolize the conversation once more, Hector barrels into the living room. "Sorry I'm late." Then he notices my precarious stance. "Dude, what are you doing?" I must look like some designer-clad cat burglar in my combat boots, black merino-wool sweater, and leather biker hat.

Bentley's voice rings tinny in my earbuds. "Oh my God. Is that him? Can I see? I want to know what kind of pauper could entice the prince." I end the call, lock my phone. Leave it to Bentley to say all the wrong things right when I have to spend the whole day with Hector—the supposed pauper with, dare I say, *princely* looks.

"Just finishing up a call." I carefully get down, red-faced, and retie my shoes. "Everything all good at school?"

"Yeah, I got stuck in my final. Three hours is not enough time to write three short responses and one full analytical essay. My thesis was so scattered, but it's fine. I'm almost done. That's what I keep telling myself."

His harried tone doesn't match the slight air of pleasure he seems to have gotten from overcoming the challenge.

Outside, as we approach Hector's car, about to embark on our very first gala-planning excursion, he arcs the keys over to me. "I'm exhausted. Do you mind?"

I'm stunned by this abrupt act of trust. The cookie challenge must have had as much of an effect on him as it did on me.

There's no time to ponder that thoroughly because panic zings up into my mouth, making my tongue go numb and heavy. "You want me to drive *your* car?" The metallic white monster glints in the streaks of broad sunlight.

"Sorry it's not one of the luxury sports cars—the Teslas or whatever—you're used to," he says before getting in.

Krampus slides out from the shadows of my brain folds, but I poke him back into place. I will not let my anxiety win today. Driving is a piece of cake. I might not have done it in a hot minute, but that doesn't mean I'm incapable of recalling the muscle memory.

I slip into the driver's seat. The keys shake in my unprepared hands. I inspect the gear shift and the steering wheel, trying to recall anything from that driver's ed course I slept through. I was probably nineteen the last time I operated a moving vehicle other than a golf cart around a country club, but shouldn't it be second nature?

I buckle my seat belt, feeling its constraints taut against my body. It reminds me of the almost-escape and the prank...

I should tell him the truth, but I'm locked into place, body working overtime to compensate for the crappy ways I've been acting.

The rattle of the beast beneath me ignites a fear inside me.

"We going or what?" he asks, expectant.

At the question, my hand maneuvers out of Park, but my foot slips too hard and too fast. The car flies forward, grumbling at the jarring velocity with which it's been thrust into action. Hector's shout is but background noise to my high-pitched screech.

Forward, we lurch and creak. This is it. This is how I die: attempting to impress a guy by doing a very simple task most adult humans can do without second thoughts. Sad in so many unique and humiliating ways.

Clearly not incapacitated by fear like I am, Hector pulls the emergency brake before we plummet into the ditch at the end of the driveway. The timing is impeccable.

The stop sends us both thrashing back into our respective seats. I try desperately to catch my breath. I realize there was no anxiety attack. Not that that's an improvement. I didn't have time with the whole life-flashing-before-my-eyes bit happening.

I'm a moron.

"Dude, what the *fuck*?" he asks. He pulls off his knit mittens and feels his face to check for blood or some other sustained head injury.

"I don't remember how to drive," I admit, which feels both good and bad. His eyes go wide with unmitigated shock.

"Seriously?" he asks. "Look, I know this is a heap of overused metal, but I don't want it compounded anytime soon. Jeez, it's like you think I have a death wish or something. Do you even have a license?"

"Yes," I say, patting around for my wallet. "But now that I think about it, it's probably expired…"

His jaw goes slack. "Okay, not only did you almost kill us, but you almost killed us *illegally*? You are seriously something else. Get out."

I do as I'm told, childlike embarrassment settling in my bones. We play a game of seat swap. I can't even look him in the face as we counter around the trunk.

We drive into town in tense silence. We take the same single road I've walked down, only this time trees, houses with brown roofs, and snow-covered fields flit by. Everything blurs together into a pastoral watercolor painting.

I hate the way I'm qualifying his worst ideas of me with one epic fail after another. Maybe my parents were on to something when they sent me here to sort out my shit.

Though I'd never in a million years admit that out loud.

I begin fake planning a Happy We Didn't Just Die Silent Disco.

Sponsored by Bose. Top 40 pop hits with themes of ephemerality and mortality. A laser light show and a massive disco ball presiding over the floor.

What I wouldn't give to dance away some of these worries right now.

My heartbeat settles back into a DJ sample-worthy rhythm, and my pulse drops down.

When we come to a stoplight in the Downtown District, I clear my throat.

"I thought it would be like riding a bike," I say softly. He cocks his head and grumbles something I can't make out. "You know, like, you never forget how to ride a bike. I kind of thought driving a car would be the same way. Obviously not…"

"No, obviously not, dude. One of those things we let toddlers ride and the other kills millions of people a year," he says, though there's some protectiveness in his tone. It's like maybe he cares about me...like he'd be upset if I got hurt.

Maybe, maybe, maybe. I'm brimming with so many maybes.

I'm overwhelmed with the urge to share that I didn't want to seem completely useless again after the wood-chopping and butter-beating catastrophes. But what would I gain from that? Any chances of impressing this guy flew out of my hands the moment that ax—*maul*, whatever—did. Now I've given him even less of a reason to believe in me.

On this end of our Odd Couple, I still have some serious damage control to do.

The Havensmith College sign in all its storied, stone glory comes into view. I'm thankful we're almost there because I can't stop sweating. Hector's radiating frustration like a furnace.

The campus extends out in all directions. The buildings are red brick with vines chasing each other across the facades. On the quad, a lone, newly made snowman sits. One twig arm waves in the breeze as if to welcome us. Students scramble up and down the winding pathways. It's finals week and you can see it in the hunch of their shoulders and the size of their travel coffee cups.

"How did you end up here?" I ask, hoping the question will quell some of the uneasiness between us.

"My dad grew up not far from here," he says. With a flick of his wrist, he kills the ignition in a nearby parking space. "He went to school here. Met my mom here." The cadence to his sentences slide together like he's singing an incantation.

"I thought you were from Texas," I say to his back. He leads us over to the main building. The looming doors spit out groups of students who sidestep us. This is nothing like the halls of NYU or any other city college with tight-squeeze hallways and heavily used elevators. This is old-school with spiraling staircases and weathered bulletin boards. History hangs from every railing and rafter.

"My mom's sister, Josephine, moved out to Texas when she got married, but then she had a miscarriage. It was right around the time my mom got pregnant with me, so my parents took my brother and sister, packed everything up, and moved out there to help my uncle and grandma take care of her and see what IVF treatments she could still pursue," he says. "Texas is the only home I've ever known, and Josephine is like a second mom to me, but my parents talked about Wind River so often, I felt like it was a part of me."

His boots make thumping echoes in the now-silent halls. Most classrooms have signs on them reading: QUIET PLEASE, TESTING IN PROGRESS. Just the thought of taking an academic test makes me twitchy. Thank God I'm not stuffed into a desk with a number two pencil in my hand right now. Scantrons are the work of Satan, I swear.

"This way," Hector says.

He holds the door open for me to enter the administrative offices. The waiting area with its plethora of fake plants is empty and the secretary is out to lunch, judging by the unoccupied swivel chair. Hector raps lightly on a slightly ajar door to our right.

"Come on in," a booming voice calls.

A White man with a full head of salt-and-pepper hair and a Pierce Brosnan–level smolder leans back in a rickety red chair, legs crossed at the ankles. He's a *daddy* (in the gay way, but probably also the biological way) if I ever did see one.

"Hector Martinez, always a pleasure," he says. "And you are?"

He stands and meets my offer of a handshake. "Prince. Matthew Prince." I guess the James Bond aura is influencing my speech.

"Ah, yes, Doug's grandson. How could I forget. Please take a seat. Make yourself comfortable," he says. "I'm Mark Graft, dean of Havensmith College. It's my understanding you boys are spearheading the Holiday Charity Gala this year. Always nice to see young people stepping up to the plate and helping the community. Especially with this year's cause benefitting small businesses. Wind River couldn't run without them. How can I help?"

I go to offer an explanation, but in the chaos of our near-crash, Hector never briefed me on what exactly we're doing here. I'm not used to taking a back seat in situations like this. Hard to believe, but I'm not one to ask for help. I like things done my way.

"Since Jack has come down with the flu, and Jack's shop desperately needs that renovation, we were wondering if the Great Hall was available for the event," Hector says.

Dean Graft gets on his computer and fiddles with a spreadsheet littered with electronic space reservations. "I can't see why it wouldn't be. This place will be deader than a graveyard starting next week. I only pop by on mornings like this to organize for the upcoming semester. And wrap my kids' Christmas gifts where their prying eyes won't find them." He nods over to a pile of boxes in the corner. "Speaking of the kids, Natalia is back from her trip abroad. I'm sure she'd love to see you," he says to Hector.

Hector freezes at the sound of the girl's name, but gives no more hints as to who Natalia is or why she'd *love* to see him. Instead of responding, he pulls up his own spreadsheet. It's a full budget breakdown.

"Where did you get that?" I ask quietly as Dean Graft puts on a pair of reading glasses (making him sexier, *kill me*), and does a closer inspection of his computer.

"Lorna sent it to me via Jack," he says.

"Why didn't she send it to me?"

Hector lightly chuckles. "Maybe because you might be creative, but when it comes to budgeting, dude, you tend to overshoot your shot." It's an Island Gate jab that I don't take lightly after nearly driving us to our untimely deaths.

"I can be frugal when I need to be," I say with a huff.

"Says the guy in a thousand-dollar scarf."

"This is Loro Piana."

"I don't care if it's Mario and Luigi." He reaches over to run his callused fingers over the loose knot by my neck. "It's too much."

Too much. I've heard that before.

I frown at him, still rattled from earlier, still certain he sees me as frivolously ridiculous. Even with his fingers inches from my face. Even as they caress the scarf in an almost intimate way, sending mini shock waves rolling across my collarbone.

"Sorry, I'm not used to us not bickering," he says, slight and sincere, pulling his fingers away.

"You're good," I tell him. Because he *is* good. Everything he does seems to prove Grandma right in that regard, and I don't hate it.

When we look back, Dean Graft is staring at the two of us, having caught our quasi-moment. He clears his throat into his large, hairy fist.

"Looks like the space is free. I can print you the pricing options if you'd like." He looks squarely at us. "Of course those won't include holiday fees for putting security and maintenance staff on. Not to mention the last-minute fee for reservations made within two weeks of an event," he says without any hint that he might be willing to waive those for a worthy cause.

Hector looks nervously at his spreadsheet again.

"It's not a holiday," I point out.

"The college observes Christmas Eve as a holiday, and it's the evening before, so it rolls in," he says, logic not landing.

"Seems like a bit of a stretch," I venture. Calling him out with the hope that it will throw him off his game.

He grimaces. "By all means, you can seek other accommodations at this late stage if you wish. I hear the inn has cleared out its storage shed. Might be worth a look."

I raise an eyebrow in defeat. "A price guide would be great," I say with a flashy smile.

Dean Graft goes out into the main waiting area where the robotic sound of the printer warming up becomes an added instrument in "Holly Jolly Christmas."

"Was kind of hoping he'd give it to us for free," Hector whispers. "We're on a tight budget as it is. When Jack does it, he hosts it in the basement of his record shop. They used to do concerts there, so it holds a lot of people. With the right lighting and tables, it's actually pretty fancy."

Thinking on my feet, like I did with the eggnog during the cookie challenge, I do a quick Google search of Havensmith. I want to see how much it's struggling as a private institution near no major city with no serious accolades afforded to it. It doesn't take too much digging to find the dirt I need as ammunition.

Dean Graft comes back with a printout, a few lines highlighted. The prices are reasonable to me, but staggering to Hector. I can tell by the way he sways back in his chair. I take a deep breath and boot up my best boss bitch attitude.

"Dean Graft, do you normally attend the annual gala?" I ask.

He looks surprised. "Of course. This town means the world to me." His sentiment sounds as hollow as a Christmas ornament. "My younger kids go to the public schools. My wife is a nurse at the local hospital. Anything to give back."

"And I'm sure the success of this school is of the utmost importance to you, yes?" Dad taught me that asking intimidating, big-picture questions in a negotiation always gets you a leg up. It also makes the person you're talking to think the thing you want them to do was their idea all along, leading to an easier agreement. Dean Graft just nods. "Well, unfortunately, we're on a shoestring budget this year."

"I can't imagine a Prince having a shoestring budget." He laughs. I cringe, but before he catches it, I lean back in my chair like this means nothing to me. In a way, it doesn't, but he doesn't need to know that. I slowly cross one leg over the other.

"Look, we're facing some hard times right now with the last-minute leadership change. Is there perhaps a nonmonetary arrangement we could make to get the Great Hall?" I ask.

The pads of his fingers come together in a steeple. "I'm not sure what that would entail," Dean Graft says. "Policies are policy for a reason."

Hector is shooting me uneasy glances. I ignore him and force my way forward.

"Listen, Dean. Can I call you Dean? Let me level with you. A simple search shows you're seeing low enrollment numbers and rising acceptance rates," I say. "How do you think those would change if I could ensure a visit and a guest lecture from my mother in the coming semester? Don't you think that would make a pretty great photo op for your website?"

Dean Graft's ears perk up. The dollar signs flash over his head. I know men like him. I've dealt with them all my life in Dad's rotating collection of colleagues. The bottom line is more important to him than anything else. He may purport family tradition and charitable acts, but at the end of the day, his business success is what helps him sleep at night.

"That's a very tempting offer. She'd do it? Sans her usual fee?" he asks. Oh, so now *he's* the one strapped about money. I've got him right where I want him.

"She may even deliver the graduation address if I ask nicely." My eyelashes flutter a mile a minute.

"I think that can be arranged," he says with all the smarmy smugness I expected.

I reach across the desk for another handshake. "We'll be in touch," I say, making it seem as if this is my office and I called *him* into this meeting. I can see the confusion on his face, so I nod for Hector to follow me out before he changes his mind.

In the hallway, Hector turns to me. "Can you really make that happen? Will your mom agree to that?"

"She stopped doing the college circuit when her TV show won an Emmy," I say. "But it got us the Great Hall, didn't it?"

That damn charming smirk creeps up on his lips again. I force myself to look away for fear I might give those lips a victory kiss. Not because they're *his* lips, per se, but because they're the closest lips to mine in this moment, and my lips have felt very lonely lately. That's all.

"So, you lied?" he asks.

"See you in hell, I guess," I say with a shrug. Though lying isn't a sin in my book. In Dad's *actual* book, it's a business strategy. "Not like he'll know any better before the gala. It's too close. Mom's got her publisher waiting with bated breath for her next project while they figure out this musical nonsense. The dean will never be able to get through to her people. I'll just yes him to death when he asks."

Hector says, "That's smart. I have to hand it to you, dude." He's the Cheshire cat of compliments—popping up out of nowhere to spring them on me while wearing a floaty, full-faced grin. It's endearing.

"Thank you." I revel in the first moment where I'm not being chastised for another stupid mistake. Doing something right feels good for a change.

"Now, I want to see this Great Hall I sold my mom's soul for," I add, before this awestruck Hector disappears into the mist again.

With an agreeable flourish, Hector ushers me down a corridor, giving major tour-guide vibes, all the while pointing out classrooms he's taken seminars in.

"Here we are," he chirps, minutes later.

The double doors swing open, and I'm completely confused. Whatever magic that moment in the office held has evaporated. I'm trying to figure out what's so *great* about this hall. There's a lecture pulpit, vaulted ceiling, and faux-marble floor. Aside from grandiose windows, it seems more like a typical hall to me.

"This is it?" I ask. I've seen old abandoned factories with more charm. Case in point: the one I booked for New Year's Eve.

"What were you expecting? The Plaza?" he asks.

I sigh a sigh so deep and loud I could've started a windstorm. I must figure out how to make something grand happen here, something show-stopping, something that if the people back home heard about it, they'd be clamoring for an invite to next year's soiree. But the more I look, the more my stomach sinks. The molding is chipped and the sound system seems like a relic of the eighties. The windows need a wash.

We've got our work cut out for us.

"Tomorrow I was thinking we can hit up Jack's storage space to see what decorations can be salvaged," I say. I tell him about the key and the location—the only information Grandma trusted *me* with. "Then, are there any home goods stores in town? Maybe a florist? Anything not totally tragic. I'm not above using my parents as bait again for a good deal."

He laughs. "I think I know a spot. Let's do the storage unit first. The less we spend on stuff, the more we can spend on food. Unless you think chicken fingers and fries from the diner are appropriate for serving."

I cringe. "Over my dead body."

"At the rate you're going, we'll both be history sooner rather than later," he jokes.

My shoulders go up in response. How did this come full circle to me being a walking disappointment? Our interactions are a roller coaster whipping over hills and careening off the tracks at breakneck speeds. I'm going to need an emotional barf bag when my time here is up.

He notices the change in my demeanor, so he lowers his voice as he says, "I'm sorry, that was insensitive. It's not you. It's finals stress."

I know he's trying to make me feel better, but that doesn't change the truth. "It's partially me. Partially that us-being-from-different-universes thing."

"I don't think we're from different universes. We're definitely from planets in the same solar system at least." He offers a small, helpful smile. "I think on your planet your capability and your image equal your worth. I also think you come from a planet of insane privilege and never-ending cash flow, both of which have sheltered you to the ways other people live in places that are strange to you, like, I don't know, Pluto..."

"I know you're an English major, but even I'm aware Pluto's not a planet anymore."

"Oh my God, dude." He face-palms and groan-laughs. "Forget the space metaphor. The people of this town are like...*unicorns*. They're accepting and kind and identify as all different races, sexualities, gender identities, nationalities. And this isn't some melting-pot bullshit, dude. This is like a little accepting oasis. I'm so blessed to go to school here. This place is special and this community is special. You need to be able to see how extraordinary they are if you're going to give them the night they deserve."

I nod. "I can vibe with mystical horned beasts. I just wish I had something to offer them. Something more than fail after fail after fail..." Throuple breakup. Island. Wood chopping. Near car crash. Maybe chaos does follow me wherever I go.

"You do have things to offer, Matthew," Hector says, using the voice that unwound me on the night of the not-so-great escape. A voice I'd like to press on vinyl and play from Grandma's record player. "You have charisma and event-planning experience. I mean, the way you worked Dean Graft into giving us this space for free. I couldn't charm someone like that."

Charm. He thinks I have *charm*. I know it shouldn't matter, but it feels like a massive eruption, lava spewing out of my dormant heart volcano, heating up my insides.

"I'm no you. You're, like, the golden boy around here," I say, deflecting.

"We have different skill sets. That's all," he says. "Mine's a tiny bit more practical—or *drab*, as you'd put it—but that doesn't make it any less important."

The bungle of our first meeting untangles us for real this time. The overwhelming urge to get back home doesn't hit so hard. I find a small sense of contentment in basking under his caring words, and I think maybe (*maybe, maybe, maybe...*) there's something in this town worth exploring after all.

CHAPTER 12

Hector doesn't wait for an answer when he asks if he can make a pit stop on the way back to Grandma and Gramps's.

That's how I find myself wandering Wind River Community Pharmacy, a cheery mom-and-pop shop that makes an average Duane Reade look like the Mall of America. This tiny storefront has four aisles, one fridge, and maybe two employees max, both wearing tragic mustard-yellow vests.

As Hector browses, I stumble upon an endcap that contains a series of stuffed holiday figurines on battery-powered stands. I press the hand of a disgruntled-looking Santa, and his hips begin to shake robotically. He bellows from a speaker sewn somewhere inside his abdomen, "Everybody out there been good or what?" à la Bruce Springsteen. I only catch the reference thanks to the holiday CD collection Dad used to break out when I was little.

Most of those have probably been lost to time—to dust or donations or the trash chute. I was probably ten or eleven the last time we listened to one of those together while baking Christmas cookies or preparing reindeer food.

Almost a whole decade of Christmases has come and gone without much fanfare. Dad dislikes the influx of tourists when getting to work. Mom can't pull herself away from writing to be bothered with the hubbub.

"Cute," Hector says, sneaking up on me as the song continues to play. It mixes in with another cover of "Santa Claus Is Coming to Town" that's playing on the radio; a female singer this time with a heavy pop production. Isn't anyone writing original songs anymore? It would at least break up the relentless drivel in the rotation this time of year.

I start away. "I guess, if you like that kind of stuff…"

"Come on, dude. Even if Christmas doesn't mean anything to you, don't you still have a soft spot for Santa?" he asks.

"Listen, if I'm going to sit on a man's lap, it's not going to be to tell him what I want for Christmas, okay?" I say, hoping my overtly sexual joke stuns him into backing off. However, his blush isn't all that bashful. His reddened cheeks pair splendidly with a smile and a laugh that are more wicked than I imagined he could muster. Is he picturing me…

No, he couldn't be.

"Nice one," he says, attempting a fist bump that I pretend I don't see. "But dirty jokes aren't going to get you out of explaining yourself, you Grinch."

"I'm not a Grinch!" I cry, but then I physically wince at the sight of an entire Christmas-themed aisle, and I'm a walking contradiction.

There are cheap polyester tree skirts with bears on them, and photo-frame ornaments with mistletoe hot-glued to the clay. How can this establishment possibly devote its already limited shelf space to seasonally specific *trinkets* nobody needs?

"You can run, but you can't hide, dude," he says. "Even the Grinch learns to love the holidays by the end. We're going to get the Christmas spirit into you one way or another."

There's a double entendre there I'm poised to point out, but currently I'm too busy brushing off his accusations to enjoy the saucy innuendo.

"Christmas isn't really a big thing in my apartment. It's just me and my parents. We gave up the Santa charade pretty young. We celebrate in our own way. I craft a complete design aesthetic for our communal rooms and have space architects come and fulfill the vision. We get two trees, one small for the dining room, and one full-sized for the family room, both trekked in from a renowned farm in Pennsylvania. They've done the Rockefeller Center tree before." Hector whistles, but I can't tell if it's an impressed whistle or a contemptuous one. "I give my parents gifts they pretend I didn't use their money to buy. They shower me with presents I pretend their personal assistants didn't pick out and wrap for them. Santa doesn't really have a place in that equation."

"Equation? It's magic, not math." He snorts.

"It's bullshit is what it is. Now, are we done here? Did you get what you needed?"

I notice he's got his hands hidden behind his back in an awkward manner, like he's about to master a card trick. Why does this guy give me so many amateur magician vibes? I swear he's probably got a beginner's kit tucked away in a closet somewhere in his childhood home.

Admittedly, he would look less than horrendous in a cape…

As if he's shouted "Alakazam," he produces a box of extra-strength Breathe Right nasal strips.

I'm taken aback, almost touched. He wouldn't get them when he was with his ex, but he's getting them for me? "I thought you said you didn't even know if those worked."

I mean, I shouldn't complain. Anything to avoid another sleepless night beneath the all-cylinders-firing lawn mower, but this is far too thoughtful to be fair. He shouldn't get to surprise me like this. When I'm off-balance, I let my guard down. I can't let my guard down right now.

"I still don't know if they work, dude, which is why I got"—out pops a six-pack of antimicrobial earplugs—"these."

My cold, microscopic heart warms at the sight of tiny pieces of silicone. How sad. My pulse quickens too. Damn my body for confusing his kindness for interest. And while I'm at it, damn my mind for wanting his interest in the first place!

I'm not here to meet someone, especially not someone who's my forced roommate and now planning partner. I'm here to lie low while Island Gate gets taken care of. Then, I can slink back into my old life.

But if that's the case, why does this handsome boy staring at me make me sweat so much?

He wears an infuriating sideways smirk, obviously taking my speechlessness as a good sign. My pits are puddles, probably ruining the delicate fabric of my studded crewneck.

I swear my perspiration isn't my fault. It has to be Hector's. He's got the kind of mouth Andy Warhol would've recorded putting on ChapStick or eating yogurt or kissing.

Kissing. Oh my God. That's something I need to stop thinking about in his presence. Except it's been so long since I've had a proper kiss. The kind of kiss that stops you in your tracks.

Since my breakup, I've stuck to hurried, only half-sober kisses in dark rooms at clubs. Where no one can see my neediness. No one can comment on my choices. There's nothing romantic or satisfying about those scratchy, grimy couches and the taste of cheap whiskey on some stranger's tongue.

"With these, we don't have any more restless nights," Hector says, shaking the boxes. Only, my mind runs rampant with erotic images of a different kind of *restless night…*

At the register, Hector pulls out the change left over from the fifty I rudely flipped him and uses it to pay for his items. Something in my chest hitches.

I need to keep him close—close enough to coast through the gala, yet far enough away so as not to catch feelings.

Because catching feelings would be far worse than being caught out wearing last season's shoes.

Trends in fashion come and go, but feelings? Those fuckers are forever.

·✳·✳·✳

"Do I look stupid with this on my face?" Hector asks sometime before bed.

That sliver of over-the-counter adhesive is treacherous. A tiny, sticky tipping point that I will not let sway me.

Hector squishes his nose and crosses his eyes, trying to see if he's placed the strip in the right place without the aid of a mirror, and I remain firm. Even if I'm the only witness to his soft brown skin creasing in so many weird and wonderful ways, I stop myself before I become play dough.

I'm sitting on my bunk, laptop plugged into the Ethernet cable after Hector's expert help, waiting to give a presentation on my gala theme idea, and he's making it impossible. In plaid fleece pajama pants and a washed-too-many-times Havensmith College T-shirt, he's a hunk of the month in a Christmas Cuties calendar, if people still owned calendars and I cared about Christmas.

Or him being a cutie.

Which I most resolutely do not.

"Yes, you look incredibly stupid. Can we get to my presentation now?"

He scoffs in defeat and sidles over to the rocking chair, slumping, still trying to keep the strip from pulling on his thin under-eye skin. "The floor is yours."

I flip the screen around to face him. The scheme for the slides is black-and-white, suave and elegant. A soft piano melody, reminiscent of something you'd hear in the lobby of a fancy New York City hotel, plays underneath. "Imagine for a moment the luxury and opulence of Manhattan in the middle of Wind River."

Hector snorts, breaking me from my concentration. At first, I think it's a side effect of the breathing strip, but nope. He's openly mocking my presentation.

"Listen, Hector, if you're not going to take this seriously, you might as well just quit now." I glare at him, which I've learned is a futile gesture, but I can't help it. It's my resting reaction face.

"No, no. Go on."

"Thank you," I huff. "After you asked if I was expecting the Plaza, I got to thinking: if I can't be back in New York, maybe I can bring New York here." I tap the right arrow and up pops my moodboard. "The tables will each be named after different New York City landmarks like the Empire State Building, Central Park, the Statue of Liberty, etc. Food will be cuisine inspired by famous New York City chefs." I've pasted in a picture of a famous, out-gay chef wearing only an apron, giving bedroom eyes over a sizzling pan of peppers.

"Seriously? You think some Netflix reality-show star is going to come here?"

Despite our cookie win and Hector's kindness today, I'm still not sure

Hector's up to the challenge of my perfectionism. His growing scowl concerns me even more. "He's a...*friend*." Not sure how I can describe to Hector that my exes and I once had a foursome with him after the launch event for his *New York Times* bestselling cookbook.

"I'm not an expert on this stuff, but what you're showing me are just colors and loosely related images. What do they even mean?" I hate that he's acting like this is rocket science. "Crystal snowflakes? Maroon?"

"That's vermilion!" His inability to identify basic colors is appalling, but I proceed. "May I continue? For entertainment, after careful contemplation, I've decided we have to go for classic crooning and BBE—big *band* energy." My joke jolts us back on track. I like when he laughs at me for being purposefully funny and not for being ridiculous.

"Okay. So, like, a local swing band?" he asks, engaging now. "I think the postal workers in town have one."

"Oh, Jesus, no. That sounds tragic." I cue up a jumpy clip of "Jingle Bells." "Let's think bigger. Nothing gets a party swingin' like the King of Christmas himself, Michael Bublé."

Hector's expression dims. "I'm pretty sure Santa is the King of Christmas."

"Agree to disagree," I mumble. "My friend's cousin is Mr. Bublé's manager. I can reach out about his rates and availability. My friend owes me big time after I bailed him out of jail for urinating on a national monument in Prague. I'm sure we can make it work." Hector's dubious expression gives me pause. "What's with that face? You think we should try for a Bing Crosby hologram? I know he's more *classic* Christmas, but the technology is confusing, the setup is probably a headache, and the licensing is a nightmare. Plus it's just so *dated*. I'm going for modern, not nostalgic..."

Hector shakes his head. "No, I don't think we should get holograms or famous singers at all. Everything you're saying sounds very expensive and over the top."

"Okay, well, *somebody* didn't share the budget breakdown with me, and *somebody* is making it seem like wanting to class up the place is an affront," I say, noting his sudden grumpiness.

"Maybe it is an affront, Matthew," he barks, but then walks it back. "Sorry, it's just... Not everything needs to be New York, all right?"

"I'm trying to make that abysmal Great Hall into something that doesn't completely suck. Something that's actually spectacular that people can get excited about, but go off, I guess..." Not like I spent hours putting this together only for him to dismiss it in a few sentences.

"Would it kill you to think for a second about the Wind River way? You should be planning for what the citizens of this town want. Not what you think they *should* want." His voice has a sharp edge.

"What theme did you have in mind, then?" I ask, giving it right back.

Collaboration is not my strong suit.

"Oh, I'm only the *action guy*. Action guys don't come up with themes. However..." He pulls open his Notes app. "Here, I made a list of vendors, community groups, and businesses we probably need to hit to get everything in order in a *realistic* way."

I moan, his words biting into me. "What? Ugh. I didn't know helping *people* would require interacting with so many...*people*."

Most of my event planning before this consisted of doodling and delegating. Back home, I'd hand over my sketchbook to a friend of mine who works in Broadway theater design, allocate a budget, and check back in on progress periodically. I'd give notes as needed. Everything would be as I envisioned it, and I wouldn't break a sweat.

This gala is going to be all my own sweat (and maybe some blood and tears too).

"I'm no doctor, but I think you'll survive it," he says. He takes his phone back. "One a day from this list, dude. That's what I'm thinking. If we do that, we should have everyone on board within a week or so and then the rest is just setup and execution."

He's only supposed to be in this for the plane ticket, and yet he's taking the lead. It's refreshingly optimistic, despite the annoying added superiority complex.

"And what about the theme? You can't throw a gala without a theme!"

Hector's Android lights up in his hand with an incoming call. A girl's photo flashes on the screen, but I don't get a good enough look to see if it's someone I've passed around town. Hector's posture changes, hardening in time with his expression.

"I gotta grab this, but let's meet at the storage unit tomorrow afternoon. We'll go dig around in there. See what we can find." His words slide into one another as he stands, eyes glued to his phone.

"And what am I supposed to do in the meantime?" I ask.

"Back to the drawing board, Party Prince," he says. "Hard work feeds the soul."

His words hang behind long after he's gone.

CHAPTER 13

"A Prince asking for a handout? That's rich!" the sole salon owner, Kendra, shouts when I explain to her about the donations necessary for the gala's silent auction. All we'd need is a free blowout or a cut-and-color to incentivize some bidders, but I guess that's too much to ask. "See what I did there? *Rich*?"

The other stylist, with hair so voluminous you could get lost in it, cackles, while I try not to cringe.

"Yes, I see what you did there," I say, summoning politeness with every fiber of my being. Everyone in this town is full of jokes and wordplay.

Kendra appears to be about Mom's age. Her last name is painted in swoopy script on the front of the salon: Cuts by Callihan. I wouldn't be surprised if she went to school with Mom, and the distaste for my family dates back to the year Mom refused to show up to the high school reunion after she landed her big TV deal. *I'm too busy for empty nostalgia*, she'd said.

Even the two women in the styling chairs—one with a head full of curlers, the other a head full of foil—glanced over at me with evident skepticism when the door whooshed closed behind me. Word of my presence in town has been spread like caviar over blinis. I'm an acquired taste. I know that.

But when I catch my reflection in one of the station mirrors, I realize I should've worn something less ostentatious if I was planning to beg for financial support. My Moschino coat and pants set covered in large hashtags and questions marks doesn't exactly scream *Take pity on me*.

I guess I didn't consider that when I decided to put Hector's advice into practice. *Hard work feeds the soul* replayed in my mind all night, taunting me. I want to show him that I can take the initiative. Wooing people is usually what I do best.

"It's for a worthy cause," I tell Kendra. "The Small Business Association helps establishments like yours stay…well, *in business*."

My joke is met with sudden silence. Tough room.

"Your mom could bankroll all the businesses in this town if she chose to. Why should I give her son free products for some frilly basket? Dip into your trust fund for us if you care so much," Kendra says, waggling her scissors semi-menacingly at me.

The elderly woman in Kendra's chair reaches a hand out from beneath her cape and places it on Kendra's elbow. "Go easy on the child. He's Lorna's grandson. He's just trying to help."

"We don't need outside help," says Kendra. "Jack usually takes care of all this. We're doing just fine without."

"It's the season of giving," says the woman with the foils on the other side of the room. A gentle reminder that I could give more of myself to win this woman over. "And the gala is to ensure we stay doing just fine."

"What if I could promise better than fine?" I ask. "After the New Year, I could promise an ad posting on my Instagram account. It reaches millions of people. I have a large following. Who knows? It could get you some New York clientele."

"Please, like your kind would come all the way out here for a haircut," she says, blowing me off.

"No, seriously. You don't understand the lengths the rich and famous will go to for the new, hot stylist," I say.

She shrugs, indifferent, but I can tell that's perked her up. "So why not post now? Show me you're serious."

I stifle a groan. "I can't. I'm locked out of my accounts."

"Likely story."

"No, I'm serious, but I promise"—I look her right in the eyes so she knows I mean it—"I'll come through." I'm surprised that I kind of want to come through.

"Fine." Kendra goes to her register and writes out a slip for one half-price haircut and a bottle of dry shampoo. "Best I can do for you right now," she says, turning her back as soon as I take it. She couldn't hide how light her till was.

I thank her and wish everyone a good day before leaving. I pocket the paper and check my list. Kendra was one of only two businesses I was able to convince to pitch in, and even so, *convince* is a strong word. The owner of the auto-body shop only gave me the free oil change and tire rotation slip because one of his mechanics nearly backed over me with a wayward Camry. My last name rang no bells for him, and the gala wasn't on his radar. He only cared that I could've been crushed on his watch, and that my outfit screams *I'll sue!*

Everyone else came back with *not this year* or *maybe later.*

I won't hold my breath.

A caffeine headache zaps across my eyebrow line. The sight of the neon Moon Beans sign across the street is a godsend. I don't even look both ways before I cross, checking my watch for the time. I have fifteen minutes before I need to meet Hector, so I can swipe a latte before our meeting. I'll need it.

Maybe Noelle will feel generous and can make an at-home coffee basket to donate.

The welcome bell to the café takes a different tone today.

There in the back corner where I'd talked to Mom only a few days ago sit Hector and some girl with curly brunette hair almost down to her hips. I've walked in on something I shouldn't have. Neither of them looks in my direction, so I stand there inspecting the situation like a documentary film-maker trying to examine his subject. Should I interject or leave myself out of the narrative?

The Hector holding court over his latte is not the Hector from the house. His chest is puffed out and his hair hangs down in shiny, well-groomed tendrils. This girl's hand dances dangerously close to his fisted one on the table, and for the second time I think about leaving.

"Hey, Matthew!" Noelle calls, coming out from the back kitchen, doors still swinging behind her.

Crap. I try to ignore the eyes that land on me that aren't Noelle's. Maybe I can pass it off like I hadn't seen them at all. But who am I kidding? My walk-in closet is bigger than this place. We're practically on top of each other.

"What *half-decent* coffee can I get you today?" Noelle's right eyebrow is arched so high.

"I see we're still not over that." I smile cordially. "Sorry, again. I'll take something—*anything*—strong and hot."

I'm hit with flashes of Hector chopping that wood. This is my punishment for letting my imagination get away from me with those damn snoring strips.

I should heed Bentley's criticisms more closely. Not for her reputation, but for my own emotions. If I didn't know if he was into me before, it seems like I have my answer now. He's clearly on a date, by the way he hasn't yet verbally acknowledged me. Crushing hard on a taken man is like being crushed by a boulder: inevitable if you put yourself in the wrong place at the wrong time.

Noelle smirks as she starts making me a drink. I claim a stool and take off my gloves. I make sure my back is to the lovebirds in the corner, even though I want to break out a pair of binoculars and dissect every micro-movement they make. I might be a teensy bit obsessive.

The counter is sticky, probably from the morning rush, so Noelle half apologizes before wiping down the space in front of me. A steaming cup of something sweet gets placed before me with a winning smile.

"Here, I'm giving you a chance to redeem yourself. Tread lightly. I'm trying my hand at foam art," she squeaks. "What do you think?"

I glance down into my mug at what largely looks like a giant white circle amid the rippling brown liquid.

"Is it…a Christmas ornament?"

"Try again."

"A snowball?"

"You're even colder now. Literally. You guessed a colder object," she says. "One last try."

"The…moon?"

"It's supposed to be a heart!" she shouts dejectedly. "You try to class up the joint and this is what you get. There's a whole lot of velocity involved in this. I thought I was a barista, not a physicist! Whatever. Most of our orders are to-go, anyway. Can't see my sad hearts under the lids. I'll keep trying."

After a beat, I ask, "Could you turn the music up a little?" Some Bing Crosby. She furrows her brow as if this is an odd request, but grabs the relic iPod Touch from the charging dock and does it anyway.

"Really like this song or something?" She rests her elbows on the display case with stale-looking croissants inside. I spot that she's wearing different holiday earrings. These are wrapped presents dangling from gold hoops. Her commitment to this season is intense.

"No, I wanted to ask you something, but I didn't want them to hear us." I nod behind me. She tilts her head as if to say *Proceed*. "Who's that girl with Hector?"

"You mean Natalia?" Noelle's on the brink of telling me something I already know: Dean Graft's adult daughter. "She's a beautifully trained opera singer. She studies music at Havensmith. She probably could've gone to a top conservatory, but free tuition can't be beat."

"Was she out of town recently?"

Noelle looks at me with confused amusement. "What's it to you?"

"Nothing. It's nothing to me." I must sound like a total creeper, so I reboot my coolness, attempting to appear aloof. "I just met Dean Graft doing gala prep and he mentioned his daughter was out of town and that she would probably want to see Hector, that's all. It's nothing."

I think she sees me sweat because she whispers, "Seems like someone might be jealous."

"Of him? Please, I'm gay." It's always weird being in a new place and meeting new people. The act of coming out all over again is exhausting, stripping away a little piece of yourself every time someone tries to get to know you. It's not that I'm not one-hundred-percent proud (okay, ninety-eight percent). It just took a lot of hard work to get there, especially with the media hounding my family.

Then I reconsider Hector's unicorn speech and recall the rainbow crosswalk. Maybe this town is more accepting than I initially wanted to give it credit for.

"Duh. I knew that. I was a fandom leader during the height of Dissension mania. It was all that came up when anyone did a search for your mom for a while."

At thirteen, when I was caught making out with Lukas, whatever privacy I'd thought I had disintegrated in my hands. My parents got Sarah Pearson involved and everything became clinical. That was the first time I realized intimacy wasn't really on the table for me unless it looked as good on the outside as it felt on the inside.

"I'm queer too, so it's no big thing," Noelle adds. I think she sees the complicated history entangled in my expression and wants to reassure me. It works. "Also, I wasn't talking about him. I was talking about *her*."

"You've lost me." I take a long, hearty sip of her handiwork.

"You're jealous that *he's* here with *her*. Hector is kind of a catch around town. I'll even admit I had a brief crush on him when he was a freshman and new to town. He'd come in here reading his Victorian-era novels at the table by the window, and I swear every passerby did a double take."

"Are you insinuating I have a crush on him? Because that's absolutely absurd." Noelle's wonky foam heart has morphed since I sipped, and now it really looks like a heart. A heart that's almost beating along with the music, mocking me and my silly emotions.

"Okay, Mr. Something Hot and Strong." Her sarcasm is off the charts. "Just because you're stuck here doesn't mean you're above Winter Boo syndrome."

"Winter what syndrome? Is that what they call a ghost with a cold?"

"Winter *Boo*, as in baby, sweetie, significant other. An offshoot of cuffing season," she explains like she's leading a TED Talk. "Come on, Matthew. Catch up."

"Fine." I take the bait. "What is this Winter Boo syndrome?"

She perks up. "I'm so glad you asked. Winter Boo syndrome is when you start catching feelings in the cold months for someone because you're looking for cuddles and cute dates and holiday romance magic."

"Yeah, no. That's not me. I don't subscribe to holiday romance magic. I don't try to live out Lifetime Movie taglines. I'm not about that life," I say.

She sighs. "I'm skeptical too. Trust me." A second, larger sigh. "Last year, I finally told my crush, Siena, that I've liked her for almost three years now, and we spent this amazing week together as winter boos before she got cold—ha, cold—feet about the whole thing, but here I am, choosing to believe again. Because, do you know why?"

"Why?"

"You're never too old for a Christmas miracle."

"Seriously, Hallmark should hire you to be their spokesperson."

"That network wishes," she says with a groan. "Anyway, this year I'm going to give my heart—and my foam hearts, once I perfect them—to someone special."

"Never mind what I said, now you're just loosely misquoting Wham!'s 'Last Christmas.'"

"Sometimes life imitates art, Matthew. That's not a crime!"

I relent, but still roll my eyes. "Why are you telling me all of this?"

"Because you're here for the holidays and he's here for the holidays, and matchmakers gon' match, if you know what I'm saying." She does a flirtatious shimmy to the beat of her own drum. It's clear she doesn't care what anyone thinks of her. I'm jealous.

"I have absolutely no idea what you're saying. Not even an iota."

"Matthew! The universe is clearly trying to set you up. The holiday romance magic is already at work." Her eyes sparkle and her voice jumps entire octaves like she's practicing a Mariah Carey riff. "You're from rival kingdoms. Big city. Small town. You're forming an alliance. The gala. Hello? This is just like when Prince Quigley and Princess Belinda joined forces to train those wild dragons in the second Game of Dark Dissension book. Even though they were born rivals, working together and almost dying helped them see all that they had in common and sparks flew."

I bypass her fangirling to say, "What about the sparks already flying over there between him and Natalia?"

Noelle shakes her head knowingly. "Even Quigley and Belinda had some baggage to overcome before they could fully tame Taregerton and win each other's affections."

I scoff at the mere thought of it. At the overly dramatic plot devices employed in Mom's books. The ones that make romance out to be an act of life or death. I guess in medieval times it kind of was.

The sound of the bell over the door rings out. Natalia walks by the front window wearing a caramel-colored, fur-lined parka that complements her skin tone.

Hector saunters over to the counter to settle the bill with Noelle. I look at him out of the corner of my eye to make him squirm.

"Good morning," I say with a bit of sass before sipping again. I feel like that shady Kermit the Frog meme from a few years ago. "Didn't mean to walk in on your date." I know I'm being coldly coy, but I can't help it. It's too tempting to pass up, running into him like this.

"That wasn't a… I mean, she and I, we're not…" He doesn't get a chance to finish because Noelle interrupts to hand him back his change. As he adds a tip to her jar, she flashes me an almost reprimanding glare before making herself scarce.

"Should we head out together?" he asks. His voice is barely audible underneath the caught-in-the-act discomfiture.

"Let's do it," I say. I leave a bundle of cash tucked under my saucer, and before I exit, I scurry back to add a little extra for all the juicy info.

CHAPTER 14

Movies and TV shows make storage units out to be grisly places where criminals and the testy elite hide their spookiest skeletons. Storage Unit Express is far from the kind of place you'd need to be scared walking around in at night. It's well lit and in a prime location for Havensmith students to store their twin XL bedding and wacky floor lamps over the summer months.

When we pull into the Havensmith Hollow business district, lanes upon lanes of bright-orange metallic doors fill an asphalt lot. It looks like a seaside motel, but only for your luggage.

The white tag on the key Grandma gave me reads C7. We follow the signs on foot as I regale Hector with talk about my morning. The businesses. The noes. The few hard-won yeses. I wait for his verbose praise, but he seems on edge since the coffee shop, so all he does is nod.

The sky is overcast, sending streaks of filtered light down upon us, as if the sun were a disco ball and the clouds were its refractors. Melted snow leaves behind pesky puddles I hop, skip, and jump over so as not to ruin the Chelsea boots I picked out for today.

Hector sets himself up for the pass, so I toss him the key and let him fiddle with the lock before sliding the door up and open.

It's like the Smithsonian of cardboard boxes inside. Aside from the stray, overly plastic standing snowman or the racks of folding chairs left in the back, there's nothing holly or jolly about this scene of decrepit winter wonderland displays.

"Did he leave a list of what's in these boxes?" I ask.

"Afraid not." Hector steps in, and I follow after him, only a bit afraid that the door will slide closed behind me, leaving us locked inside. I subdue my anxiety by inspecting the collection further.

"They aren't even all labeled." Whining won't do us any good, but there must be at least a hundred boxes in here. It'll take all day to inventory this garbage.

"Guess we're going to need to do this the old-fashioned way." He shoves his gloves into his pocket before hoisting a box into the center of the space. In a clear Boy Scout maneuver, he flicks open a pocket knife from his key ring and does surgery on the packing tape.

The flaps fly open like a jack-in-the-box. Tons of white foam and glittery fluff shoot out of the overstuffed box and into Hector's face. He does a near-perfect pratfall.

"Are you okay?" I'm concerned, but basking in the one moment where I get to laugh at *him* for a change.

"I'm good, dude." Though he sits there a couple seconds longer, bemused.

"Looks like you weren't kidding about being a scaredy-cat." I recall his horror at the SpectraLite mask.

"What? No. Not a scaredy-cat," he says, defensive.

"Fine. Wuss in Boots?" I ask.

He groans, shakes his head, and goes back to his box.

I wander toward the back. Some of the boxes weren't as expertly closed, so I dig around inside a few smaller ones. I find vases filled with tacky, transparent marbles and an assortment of snow-kissed fake flowers. In the next box, there's a strange, detailed ceramic cat with a pair of hand-knit mittens slung around its neck. I don't need to look further to know what I'd find: a bright copper kettle and brown paper packages tied up with string.

"Oh. My. God. Please tell me the theme was not My Favorite Things."

Hector chuckles. "Pretty sure the gala was for the town arts council last year. And come to think of it, in the spring the community theater group did a production of *The Sound of Music* so…I hate to break it to you, but it looks too perfect to be untrue."

"Is there anything we can salvage in here?" There's a box just marked Photo Booth that's full of bent phony props and a wrinkled wrapping-paper backdrop. It makes me sad that Jack even thought to save this stuff.

Honestly, I'd fund the event myself, like Kendra suggested, if I weren't locked out of my accounts. Mom and Dad wouldn't even know the money was missing. If I could spare no expense, my usual sixth sense would be kicking into full gear. I'd have dozens of decorative ideas, but I'm like a dried-up well surrounded by this much dust and so many depressing visuals.

"These will do." I look over my shoulder and find Hector tangled in a mess of Christmas lights. They remind me of the exact ones Gramps did up the bookstore with one year after visiting the town tree farm.

I make a mental note to check it out. I'm almost tempted to ask Hector to take me. Nothing like towering trees to make you feel the holiday spirit shoot through you, but I'm sure he's got better things to do and other people to see. Like *Natalia*.

"So, I guess Dean Graft was right. Natalia did *really* want to see you." I probably shouldn't be pressing this, but it won't leave my brain.

He goes from cool cucumber to ripe tomato in two seconds flat. Why do I like making him burn up like that?

"Yeah, she called. Asked to meet. We met."

"For coffee. In an empty café. Early-early," I say. "I wouldn't be caught dead meeting anyone early-early unless I was dating them. I once passed up brunch with a global pop star and her supermodel best friend because they wanted to get in a sunrise spin class before."

"You don't have to do that, you know?"

I shrug, pretending I have no idea what he's talking about.

"You don't have to try to impress me with who you know. It doesn't mean anything to me."

Okay, I guess I really didn't have any idea what he was talking about. I'm used to bringing up influential people as bids for social capital with my friends back home. I forget that this town runs on bad radio signals and a thriving indie movie theater.

"Got it." It's hard not to be a little offended.

"I like music, but to be honest, keeping up with trends is exhausting." He hikes up his faded jeans from the back belt loop. "I play Top 40 radio in my car since that's what the passengers around here like. I grew up listening to mostly Spanish language artists since I'm Spanish and Puerto Rican."

"Do you speak Spanish?" I ask.

"Hablo suficiente español para tener una conversación." It comes out choppy, but I still enjoy hearing it. I understand most of the words from various classes and travels. "I'm good with casual, low-key conversation, but heaven help me if my grandmother on my dad's side starts yelling. That magnificent woman speaks five-thousand words a minute, easy. Seriously, she should be in a record book."

"Sounds intense."

"Sometimes, but I love her all the same. Even if I can't always tell exactly why she's upset. My siblings made fun of me for not being bilingual all through middle and high school. I don't have a natural ear for picking up languages, but now I'm better at reading Spanish than either of them. It's been my mission to outpace them conversationally by the end of college. Just to prove something."

It strikes me how that sounds like something I would say. How I might motivate myself with the promise of besting others. Not sure it's healthy, but maybe it's working for him.

"Growing up in Texas helped a lot. There's a sizable Spanish-speaking Latine population in my city. I always saw the language as a source of pride and community. My dad was constantly looking for ways to make sure we felt connected to our roots whether it was through music or food or games of dominoes, but we pretty much exclusively spoke English at home. Learning the language is one thing I'm doing for myself, you know?"

"That makes sense."

"I'm lucky to have grown up where I did. Helped me come into my identity in a positive way." He pauses. "That facet of my identity, anyway."

I don't press any further about his queerness because after the bookstore conversation, it seems like slippery territory.

We return to perusing the utter mess left behind. I'm scared I'm going to turn and find a family of rats feasting on fake pine needles. Instead, I open a box and find a nearly crapped-out projector and a bunch of poorly wound cables.

Now this I can work with. I get a miniscule spark of inspiration. I could do something dazzling with this. Bentley's brother, Brody, works video-editing wonders. I make a mental note to text him for his rates.

I bring the box with the projector up near the doors and start a KEEP IT pile along with the lights.

"Did Noelle say something about Natalia and me?" Hector asks.

I don't say anything. I don't want to get Noelle in any trouble, but my face has been known to betray me.

He sighs. "She obviously said something. Jeez, that girl runs the rumor mill in this town, I swear."

"So it's a rumor, then?"

"That we dated? No. We did. We dated." It's clear he's conflicted about this, which I don't get since she's a goddess. "She just got back from studying opera in Vienna. We haven't seen each other since last spring, so we were just catching up." Though *just catching up* to me would end in something a bit more satisfying than just okay coffee. "There's nothing to read into it."

I don't know if he's said this for my benefit or for his own. Is he reassuring me that this push and pull I feel between us is something he's noticed too? Or is he just letting me know his guard is up with her and I shouldn't prod for any more answers? Either way, I feel a bit winded by the emotional volleying of it all.

"When I was a kid, I went to Austria," I say. I don't even know why I say it. Not like somehow Natalia and I are in competition with each other. "Ironically, my mom and I went on a *The Sound of Music* private bike tour." I hold up the kitten with the exaggerated whiskers and let out a cringe-worthy *meow*.

"Cool?"

"'How do you solve a problem like bad decorations?'" I half sing, wanting to hear that laugh.

He raises an eyebrow, but I do a final operatic-nun note and he breaks. The sound is infectious, melodic. It hits my ears and makes me vibrate with strange happiness.

"You're a weird dude."

I shrug, still giddy, even though I keep telling myself his opinion of me doesn't extend beyond the borders of this rinky-dink town. "So, how are we going to get all of this stuff to the college? Your car doesn't have enough trunk space."

"We're going to need a truck," he says. And then he sighs, realization falling over his expression. "I know someone with a truck."

He doesn't need to tell me who, and I'm already dreading that trip.

CHAPTER 15

You've reached Matthew Prince Sr. I am unable to take your call at this time. Please leave your name, number, and a brief message as to what this is concerning. I look forward to getting back to you.

God, I have that message burned into the back of my brain. I've heard it so many times. Never once has he called back with the excitement he so claims in that voicemail. The only things he looks forward to are golf trips and Rhode Island weekends. Talking to me is not one of his favorite pastimes. I'm sure of it.

I'm tangled up in the corner of the family room again. Gramps is probably still out shopping. Hector is back to chopping wood, which I now think might be his primary way of clearing his head. Grandma may or may not be back from the store.

I thought this would be a good time to tell Dad about my altruistic efforts. He's always been the more lenient parent. Not because he's soft—far from it—but because he's all business. He sees even personal interactions as transactions. If having me home served him somehow, I'd be out of here already. Unfortunately, that's not the case.

I shoot him a text:

I'm planning the Wind River Annual Holiday Charity Gala for Grandma and Gramps.

I almost add *Proud of me for taking the initiative?* But I don't want to be *that* leading.

From around the corner, Grandma comes hobbling into the room with red-and-green plastic boxes stacked in her hands. Items inside each clang and roll and bang, a discord of Christmas junk.

"In all the nonsense, I haven't gotten a chance to get up the rest of the ornaments." Her arms look so dainty, and her sharp eyes poke out over the top of the boxes. "Do you want to help? I'm never going to be able to get the angel up top."

The cookie challenge was enough holiday hullabaloo for one season. I'm already waist-deep in designing this gala. Trimming a tree would be a step too far into mushy sentimentality for my taste.

However, Grandma's tree is somewhere between a Charlie Brown travesty and a bad department-store display window. It's nothing compared to the gorgeous ones I pick out for the apartment. They have to use the service elevator to get them inside.

I hardly noticed this one in the corner up against the window. On closer inspection, I realize it's fake. The smell, which is far more pungent than I'm used to, comes from a pine-scented hanging stick hidden in the branches. Shameful.

"When did you and Gramps go plastic?" I may not care about Christmas, but I do care about design aesthetics. Faux plants can kill ambiance and flow and make everything surrounding this holiday even falser than it already is. Too much of Christmas is kitsch. High straight camp with no concept. This place desperately needs the Matthew Prince touch.

"A few years ago, when Gramps threw out his back. Going to the farm, tagging, chopping, lugging it home… It's a whole ordeal. Too much for our old bones." She slumps like a marionette to prove her point.

"This is…kind of depressing." The cringe factor is off the charts. I want some sense of regularity here. If I can control one thing, it's the merriment I make for myself. Even if I'm not looking to be merry at all.

"I don't think it's so bad." Her conviction could use some coaching.

I get a sudden second wind after a day of documenting sad, soggy boxes. "Let's get a real one. Hector and I can help. Hector says he knows someone with a pickup truck. We need to borrow it to get the decorations to the school anyway. Maybe he can get it tonight. The farm is still open, right?"

I check the clock blinking over the stove. It's only a little past six. The sun has gone down, but my hopes have shot up astronomically. I recall what Hector said about getting the Christmas spirit inside of me one way or another and, double entendre aside, this is one way I can stand to stomach.

I don't know that Grandma loves the idea of tearing down the tree she already has. I'm about to suggest we could put the new one down in the basement because selfishly that's where I'd want it anyway, but I think she notices the shift in my demeanor and doesn't want to kill my buzz.

"Let me give Gramps a call." She picks up the landline and begins to dial.

Downstairs, Hector is nowhere to be found. I search outside, but he's finished up and put his tools away. Most of the rounds that had been left in the woodshed are split, stacked, and ready to be burned.

Returning inside, I'm about to give up when a lock clicks and a door opens.

Hector steps out of the bathroom. A cloud of post-shower steam billows around him. He's dressed in only a maroon towel. His torso is taut and rippling. Still-wet dark hairs are dashed across his chest. He runs a second, smaller towel through his black locks, not seeing me at first.

Blood rushes north toward my face and down south. *Whoa*. It's been a minute since I was alone in a room with a half-naked hot guy like this. And the fact that the half-naked hot guy is Hector Martinez only makes this moment more invigorating.

When he finally notices me, he jumps. He uses the hair towel to try for modesty, but fails spectacularly. "Shit, dude. My bad." He rushes over to his bed and brushes past me on the way. That moment of contact sends a scintillating shiver down my spine. "I thought you were upstairs. I would've brought my clothes in with me."

Would it be weird if I said I didn't mind? The alarm on his face says: *Yep. One-hundred-percent weird.*

"It's fine." I'm hoping to sound as nonchalant as possible to disguise any and all arousal that may have sprung up (*kill me!*) from this surprising scene.

One foot at a time, he slips the black boxer briefs up under his towel, and I train my eyes on his collarbones. That seems like the least compromising and safest place to look, while I ask in a landslide of excitement (tree-related excitement *only*), "Do you think you can get Natalia's truck tonight?"

He grabs for his T-shirt, his worked-out shoulder muscles flexing, and I realize I've horribly miscalculated. I'm even more enthralled than before.

"I thought we agreed we weren't going back until tomorrow morning?" he asks.

"I want a tree, *a real one*, for the living room. I hate that fake stuff. My grandma said they stopped getting one from the farm because of Gramps's back, but they've got two strapping young men living here now, so I figured we could do all the heavy lifting. What do you think?"

"I think they have *one* strapping young man living here now and one *semi-strapping* young man who can supervise." The word *strapping* sends my gaze lower and then right back up. I'm beyond flustered, eyes bouncing around, pulse spiking.

I swallow hard, avoiding other inconvenient hard things.

"So, can you get it?" I ask, angling away.

"I can ask. I'm sure it's no big deal. They don't use it much anymore." It knocks me that he knows this fact. That means there is a whole book full of other facts he could spout off about Natalia and her family. He knows her. Not in the way I want to know him right now, sweaty and with no strings, but fully and intimately.

There's a beat. A heated look. An urge to fill the gap, but nothing comes.

"I'm going to finish getting dressed and call. Do you mind?" Of course, he'd want privacy. He nods toward the stairs. It's clear he's directing me to go before he undoes the knot in the towel.

"Sounds Gucci. I mean, good. I mean, uh, yeah, sounds good." I shoot him finger guns before hurling myself up the steps.

Sounds Gucci? Finger guns? Fuck. My weird side—the one Bentley makes me coat-check on the way into clubs—is showing just like it did when I sang from *The Sound of Music*. He's getting to the core of me, and that's cause for concern.

Even so, I think about his collarbones all the way back to the kitchen.

Why is it that I'm always losing my chill around him? I know it's shallow, but in the city, people clock me from across the dance floor and don't think twice. Even in profile, they know who I am and who my parents are. It doesn't matter if I'm a sweetheart or a major asshole. It doesn't matter if I'm wearing the right cologne or the best pants that show off my ass. Guys want to sleep with me for the story.

Do I love that? No. Do I love a chiseled jawline and biceps that could crush me? Absolutely. And I can't blame these boys. I've done the same with more than my fair share of semi-celebs and models. Falling into bed with someone isn't falling in love. Casual sex is a hobby you pick up whenever the fancy strikes.

Here, right now, the image of Hector's bulging towel swimming in my mind, the fancy is striking hard and hot. I don't know if I'm looking for a distraction and seducing him will do the trick or if I expect some sort of mind-blowing orgasm out of this whole ordeal. Either way, he needs to stop looking the way he does because it's dangerous.

Grandma hangs up the handset. "Gramps is on his way home. He sounds excited." She starts riffling through a chest underneath a bench seat by the door. In it, she stores her winter accessories. She picks out a purple hat with a ridiculous pink puffball on top.

"This is going to be fun!" she squeals.

And for the first time since I got here, I think the same.

CHAPTER 16

Gramps pulls his sedan up to Natalia's house in Havensmith Hollow, just south of the Downtown District.

It's a sprawling Victorian home settled upon an estate. It has a grandiose off-white exterior and forest-green shutters that are stark in bright landscaping lights. Electric candles sit proudly in every window, welcoming the holidays with their persistent glow.

An ominous, pointy tower punctures the night sky on the far right, a story or two above the bay window. I devilishly wonder if that's where Natalia's parents hide her away from the world. With long hair like hers and an operatic voice, she couldn't be more like Rapunzel if she tried.

I don't know what I expected, but of course this is where she lives. Her father is the dean of a college, and she just studied abroad in Vienna. This must be campus-owned housing since it's only a short walking distance from the main lawn, but the decor and level of care scream wealth.

Hector and I hop out from the back seat. A light snaps on near the front door. Natalia appears in that same fur-lined parka, just in a different color—a sensible olive green. I didn't notice how short she was before, the two of them having been sitting and no one to compare her to when she walked by the café window. A big smile takes over her face and her prominent cheeks puff out.

"Twice in one day, huh, Hector? Just can't stay away from me, can you?"

Hector shifts. His hands dig further into his pockets almost in search of something that I know isn't there. Something that doesn't exist. Tangible closure.

"Thanks for loaning us the truck," Hector says like a shy schoolboy. I can't blame him. This girl has a strut that could rival a supermodel on a catwalk. Must be all that time spent onstage.

"It's no problem at all. We've had absolutely no use for it since we sold the horses. Plus after Matthew agreed to get his mom to come to the college, my dad would do just about anything for that family," she says before turning to me. "Matthew, it's so good to meet you. I'm Natalia, in case you didn't catch that."

As if I haven't been thinking about her incessantly since Noelle gave me the inside scoop.

She doesn't offer a hand, so I smile and nod.

"Sorry for being the rudest little thing this morning. Hector didn't say that was you at the counter. Otherwise I would've introduced myself." She nudges Hector as we walk around the back of the house, off the driveway. I expect to see two or three vehicles, but they've got seven, all scraped off and shoveled out after the latest storm.

Now, I'm not one to talk when it comes to excess, but being a city boy my whole life, and only learning how to drive on Dad's Mercedes at the Rhode Island house as a rite of passage and sheer formality, I'm a little taken aback.

Natalia hands a gray and red Havensmith College lanyard over to Hector. "Take care of Perdy. She's an older gal, but she runs good. My dad doesn't care when you have her back by, just vacuum out the bed before you do."

"You got it."

They catch each other's gaze, and in that instant, I'm a voyeur. Whatever's coming to pass between them is both intense and almost melancholic. It's the kind of look I might share with my married exes, should I ever dare lay eyes on them again. I'm still reeling from our last run-in, the loaded encounter that spurred the island purchase.

A honk comes from out front. Gramps wants to get on the road. We are under a time crunch. He called Arthur at the farm to let him know we were coming, but he has a strict closing time. No exceptions. Not even for old friends, apparently.

"Thanks again." Hector leans down to give her a hug. When Hector pulls away, before he's out of reach, Natalia presses her glossed lips to his cheek.

Suddenly, I'm jealous. Irrationally so. I wonder what his stubbly skin might feel like under the weight of my own lips, how he might react should we share something so intimate.

But we won't. Not even that—we can't. Not under my grandparents' roof. Not with my circle back in New York privy to anything and everything that goes on in my life. Not with my heart still on the mend.

His green eyes flick over in my direction, perhaps to see how I'm reacting. After years of dodging paparazzi, I've learned to put on an expression that is stone-cold, unreadable.

Natalia wishes us a good night with a cute shiver before skipping up the back steps of the wraparound porch and into what seems to be the kitchen. She's like a pixie, there one minute, vanished the next, leaving behind a cloud of sparkles in her wake.

The inside of the truck has a weird smell, like it's brand-new even though it's at least six years old. Hector seems to know the layout by heart, and I wonder how many times he's driven Natalia around town in this rigged-up ride.

I imagine her bare feet on the dashboard, midsummer, the radio on full blast. It's like a Taylor Swift song come to life. I bet the back bed even makes a good place to lounge during a movie at a drive-in. My mind runs rampant with visions of the two of them together.

I fall into infatuations easily. And I know that's what I'm doing here. I'm overanalyzing Hector's every move to somehow save myself from thinking about the real shit going on in my world: Mom and Dad sending me here and the secret thing between them that Grandma seems to be in on but I'm being excluded from.

To avoid thinking too hard on that topic, I launch into conversation.

"How long were you two together?"

We begin our ride to the Wind River town line. Twin taillights cut through the night up ahead.

"Like, ten months, almost a year." The way he says *like* sounds as if he's trying to remain casual when really he knows how long the relationship lasted down to the nearest minute. "I went back to Texas this past summer to help out my dad   right after everything blew up with his business—and she was leaving for Vienna in August, so we broke it off. Or she broke it off and I agreed it was the right thing to do."

"Did you really think that it was the right thing to do?"

"Honestly, I don't know, dude." His voice is bogged down, almost soupy. "I knew my dad was in a lot of trouble and my sister was calling every other day crying. For some reason, I couldn't confide any of that to Natalia. Her family is just so…put-together? I was afraid she'd judge me and my family and it seemed like the easy out, not to have to drag her into it."

His grip tightens around the gearshift, veins fanning out on the back of his hand. I'm tempted to use the pads of my fingers to chart them each like tributaries flowing into the river of his heart. Does it still beat for her?

"Do you think you'll get back together?" I don't even know why I ask because I know I'm not going to like the answer. I plunge my hands underneath my thighs to keep them from shaking.

The grandiose homes fade away into farmland. We stop at a red light just beyond Havensmith Hollow. His profile is a display of uncertainty in the illumination. "No. We're friends now. She met a guy while she was at her program. Another opera singer. He's all over her Instagram."

"Wow. A European romance. What a whirlwind fantasy." He shudders when I say it. "I'm assuming they also broke it off before she came back." That would account for why she wanted to meet Hector this morning. The classic *I'm just out of a relationship and vulnerable, will you hold me until I feel better?* It's the oldest play in the book.

"Nope." His jaw locks. I can almost hear his teeth grinding. "They're doing long-distance."

I suppress a gasp. That right there is why I don't open myself up to people on the reg. They can show you their true colors with a single change of heart. She couldn't do long-distance with Hector, but this Austrian opera buff gets what Hector couldn't have? That must hurt.

I want to do something to show him I sympathize. Or empathize? I don't even know what's appropriate in this situation or what the difference is really. My own emotions have always taken center stage.

Plus we haven't really set boundaries. We go from hostile to vulnerable in two breaths. We go from banter to heart-to-heart in three. Six days gone, and we're in so damn deep. I guess that's what sharing bunk beds and a shower can do to you.

"What happened with your dad?" I ask, thinking the change of subject might do him good, but I may have struck a second even-more-exposed nerve.

"He made some bad calls. His business partner was pushing for their contracting company to take on more remodeling jobs before they were ready," he says, probably reliving the heartache all over again. "Business started booming when I was in high school. We were never a family with tons of money, and suddenly we could afford an above-ground pool. My dad paid for my sister's beauty school. He started a college fund for me. I mean, it was almost like a dream."

"Until?"

"Until while I was away at college the growth got away from him. Shoddy pipes, exposed wires, faulty door hinges. Hack jobs that completely ignored code that could've been avoided had they slowed down enough to notice, but the backlash was immediate," he says, wiping a hand down his face. "Complaints were filed with the contractors' board, and when my dad and his business partner couldn't find the funds to foot the repairs, they were staring down the barrel of a lawsuit. That's when I said goodbye to the rest of that shiny college fund, and my dad said goodbye to the business he fought tooth and nail to start."

"That's terrible," I say.

"My mom was so mad at him for being so careless. His employees too. It sucked because I worked with those men and women over the summers to help out. I met their kids. I took lunch breaks with them. They were good people who were out of work because my dad got greedy and thought he could cut corners."

God, I really should say something profound. Especially since his intense distaste for me probably stems somewhat from my flamboyant shows of material wealth. For his family to lose everything in pursuit of that must suck. As we drive, I can't think of anything that feels right other than: "I'm sorry it went down like that."

Wow. There it is. Another fully formed apology born from the ashes of my old habit. My chest blazes.

"It's okay," he says, even though it sounds like it's anything but. "It taught me an important lesson."

"What's that?"

"You can't count on good things to last," he says. The burning inside me becomes a scorch, singeing my rib cage with blistering sadness. For him. For the hope he lost over someone else's mistake.

Instead of harping on that, I gaze out the window, focusing on how such a small town can seem so infinite. We've only gone about eight miles from Havensmith Hollow, but the charged silence makes it feel more like eighty.

Finally, we pull into the farm, a dotted field of festive treasures. Hector kills the engine and sits there for a second. He stares out onto the rows and rows of trees lined with lights. An unexpected childlike wonder turns on inside me. I hope the sight does the same for him.

"This was a good idea." A small smile forces its way onto his face, allowing me to relax. "I can't think of a better way to get out my aggression."

I can. It involves him, me, less clothes, and shaking bunk beds. But I shelve that thought and replace it with the wholesome, family-friendly one this place demands.

With a deep breath and a pep in my step, we join Grandma and Gramps at the small red barn wrapped in garland. Families stand in line. The kids race in circles around their parents' feet, fueled by candy canes and hot chocolate from the snack bar.

The night is dark, the wind is cold, but I'm warmed by the prospect of bringing home the perfect tree to sit around on Christmas morning.

If I'm still here by then...

CHAPTER 17

"Let's bring home a winner!" Grandma shouts when she sees us.

We move to meet Arthur inside, where chatter mixes with the sound of a model-train whistle. The train zooms around a toy village on an expansive table. I recognize it immediately as the collectible Dickens village with carolers, robotic ice-skaters, and Scrooge himself stalking through town. My inner child breaks through again, and I rush over to inspect it closer.

Arthur is a tall Black man with a bushy mustache. He wears layers upon layers of wildly contrasting flannels, which appears to be the dress code in these parts, and a Santa hat with Mickey Mouse ears sticking out the sides.

"Greetings, Winstons. What brings you out here tonight? You broke my heart when you went fake a few years ago. Come to mend it again?" His smile looks familiar, but I can't place it.

"Don't be such a softy," Gramps says. "You know my back can't handle all that upkeep. Good thing we've got these two boys to do the brunt of it."

Hector and I smile sheepishly.

"Matthew, you look so much like your mother. She and I went to school together. She was voted Most Likely to Succeed in our senior yearbook. She *far* surpassed that expectation."

I nod with a strange surge of pride. Hearing about Mom when she was young has always struck me as odd. To me, she's forever stuck at whatever age she is now. Photos of her, even the ones around Grandma and Gramps's place, come across as if they're of someone else entirely. Her world then wasn't the world she inhabits today. She really made something of herself.

And, not for nothing, she made something of herself *before* Dad. She wasn't riding on his expensive coattails until she was well on her way to selling a book. She worked her MFA program, got an agent, and then met Dad. I was only eight when she signed her first book deal. How she balanced being a mom and writing full-time is beyond me because, let's face it, I'm a handful. Thankfully she had Oksana for the playdates and temper tantrums.

"Everyone warm enough? Need any hot cocoa before we head out? I've tagged a few of the nicer ones we've got that will fit in your family room. Sound good if we start there?" No one objects.

Hector and I hang back a little. He's got a wandering eye, scoping out trees but not fully buying into the infectious energy yet. I can tell he's still thinking about Natalia and his dad. He sniffles.

"For someone so 'bah humbug,' you sure seemed excited by that winter village display back there," Hector says, coming back to earth enough to poke at me.

I experience a pang for those easier days with Mom and Dad. Movie marathons and bedtime stories and letters to Santa.

"We used to have one just like it at the apartment," I say. "My obsession with *A Christmas Carol* started young with the Mickey version. You know the one with Scrooge McDuck? Every year, my parents added another movie iteration of it to our rotation, I read the book, and eventually it leached its way into our Christmas decor. We dedicated a whole room in our apartment to tables of those figurines. Every morning I'd race into our sitting room and plug it in, waiting to hear the gears whir and the lights flash on." I sigh, wistful. "It's the kind of classic story you can't shake."

This makes him smile. "I love it too, dude. It's why I chose it for my paper. Cherry and I are doing cross-analysis with some of the movies. Which one do you think is the best?"

"Oh God. No. I can't say. You'd judge me so hard." My choice hasn't changed since I was six. It's the one I keep coming back to.

"Dude, try me," he says. "Wait, how about this? I count down from three, and we both say our favorite at the same time."

I accept his deal with reservations. As he starts the countdown, I think about lying, but what would be the point? Christmas is all about sharing and giving. I conjure my childhood self who would be unbothered by a non-Criterion Collection opinion of movies.

Right after three, we both shout, "The Muppets!"

Our eyes go wide with pleasant surprise. We stop to be sure we've heard right.

"Kermit is by and large the best Bob Cratchit *ever*," I say.

"And Fozzie Bear as Fozziwig?" he adds. "It practically wrote itself."

We laugh, our breath appearing and disappearing in front of our faces like the ghosts in the movie. Half of me thought I couldn't have anything in common with Hector Martinez. Maybe I wouldn't let myself look hard enough.

We catch up to Arthur, Grandma, and Gramps, all gathered around a handsome, six-foot-tall Douglas fir. I'm well versed on Christmas trees due to my insistence on the strongest and best for the apartment back home. I have our farm in Pennsylvania send me pictures starting in infancy. I like to see our trees from the very beginning. It makes me appreciate them even more when they become the centerpieces of our home for that brief period.

I wonder what Bart and Bev (I like to name my trees, so what?) look like in our apartment right now. Hopefully, Oksana has been watering them properly. Did Mom and Dad allow the decorators to go ahead with my design concept—gold poinsettias and old-school strung popcorn for a traditional vibe? It seems like ages ago that I drew up that idea in one of my many sketchbooks. Bart and Bev may be brittle and barren by the time I make it back, ready to be dumped out on the curb to be cleared away and forgotten about.

"What do we think?" Grandma asks.

"I like it," says Hector.

"So do I," I add, but I'm not looking at the tree. I've got my side-eyes shifted toward Hector's face, which has transformed, become sweeter. I can't rip my gaze away from the deliciousness of his exquisite jaw.

"I'd normally say let's keep our options open, but…" Gramps gives the tree a good shake and then runs his hands along the needles to test its durability. "I think this one will more than do the job."

Arthur disappears and returns with a bow saw. "Who wants to do the honors?"

I take a step forward before Hector's gloved hand wrenches my shoulder. "Don't even think about it," he says with a playful eye roll. I can't help it. I swoon. And he sees it, spotlighted by the swaying amber bulbs above our heads.

"Give me a chance," I say, stepping up to the task.

The hesitancy in Hector's expression shuts off when he sees how hard I'm trying, and that seems to be enough for him.

Instead of backing away for safety, Hector helps me see to it. Together, we switch off sawing with Arthur's strict guidance. Sweat collects under the wool of my hat. But it's all worth it when the tree teeters and then tumbles into the waiting hands of some of the farm workers. Our perfect pick gets carried back to the barn by two high school boys, to be netted and paid for.

"Nice work," Hector says, offering me a lingering high five before trotting ahead. He insists on helping because, as I've now realized, that's the kind of guy he is.

Gramps ropes Arthur into a conversation about his back, which Arthur nods through. I fall into step with Grandma, who's playing with the pompom on her hat like she's deciding whether to say something.

"We've already chopped it down. There's no going back now," I say with a laugh.

"No, no. It's not that. I just remembered that your mother…" Her voice trails off.

"What?"

"Your mother and Arthur used to date back in the day. They went to the senior prom together." I'm not all that shocked by this news, but it does unearth a layer of Mom I didn't know existed.

Obviously, she dated men before Dad, but Arthur is rugged, open, and inviting. He's like the antithesis of Dad. Where Dad is facts and numbers, dress slacks and designer cologne, Arthur smells woodsy and dresses like he shops exclusively at L.L.Bean.

"There was a while there I thought she might change her mind about the big-city school for college and stick to Havensmith just to stay with him, but you know your mother. She's got dreams bigger than her ego." She covers her mouth like she burped. "Oops, I didn't mean that to sound the way it did. I love your mother. Her strong sense of self is what got her to where she is. I'm proud of what she's accomplished."

It's clear that even in her seventies, Grandma is still figuring out her own family dynamics. It makes me think that's the kind of work that never stops. Sometimes I wish relationships could just be simple. Simple as in Mom doesn't subject me to weird punishments, Dad answers my phone calls, Bentley sees our friendship as the two-way street it should be, and Hector wants to sleep with me.

Maybe that last one is a bit heady, but can I be blamed?

When we return inside the barn, I put together why Arthur's smile looked so familiar. Noelle stands behind the register talking with Gramps while counting his change. What is with the people in this town taking on twenty-seven jobs?

"Matthew! Hey!" Noelle waves, excited to see me in a setting where she isn't wearing a stained apron that smells like burnt, *more-than-decent* coffee, but there's also an undercurrent of urgency.

"Fancy meeting you here. Do you ever sleep? Barista, cashier, Christmas earring craftswoman…"

"Oh, no. The earrings are all my mom. She sends them to me from Chicago. She's a jewelry maker." She shoves back her hair to showcase the glorious silver angels, tiny horn-playing heralds. "I didn't get that gene. I'm not that crafty. You saw my foam-art disaster."

"There was definitely room for improvement, but you seem like the kind of person who doesn't give up easily."

Noelle nods, sneaks out from behind the counter, and sidles up beside me, leaning in conspiratorially. "Do you see the beautiful girl with the space buns and the brown toggle coat, talking to her sister in the corner?" There are two girls a few years older than me by the Dickens display. The taller of the two sports ratty Ugg boots and a striped turtleneck that peeks out over the lapel of her coat. "That's Siena. The girl I was telling you about in the shop." I remember. I can't believe how quickly I've become entrenched in small-town gossip. And to think I actually care. Something must be seriously wrong with me.

"She's cute," I say, and then remember what Noelle told me about her and her broken heart. "I mean, if you're into that tried-hard-to-look-like-I-didn't-try-at-all thing."

"I am," Noelle says, deep-seated longing in her voice. "I so, so am. Anyway, I just sold her a tree and invited her to the Lights of Wonder Spectacular at the park this weekend and she agreed." Her eyes are dark twin disks of stricken panic.

"That sounds like a date. Isn't that a good thing?"

"No. No, Matthew. It's not a good thing. I made it sound like it *wasn't* a date. I told her a *group of us* were going. I mentioned it would be chill and casual and low pressure. When it's entirely not chill or casual and now *I'm* under a lot of pressure," she says, gripping my arm.

"So you lied to her?" Wow, I sound about as self-righteous as Hector did when he found out I lied to Dean Graft.

"No, I did not lie. I bent the truth," she says. "Which is where you come in. I need you to straighten out the truth for me."

"Nobody has ever come to me for *straight* anything."

She bites back her smile, swallows her laugh. "This is not the time for jokes, Matthew. I need you to get a ticket and come with." Her eyes flit over and land on Hector across the way. Arthur tells the boys to bring the tree out to the truck. Hector grabs the bungee cords Natalia left in the glove compartment for him and heads out. "And bring Hector too, if he's up for it."

"I'm not sure about that." Inviting Hector on a non-gala-related outing might also sound like a date, and it can't be a date. The only date I'm interested in is the expiration date on this repugnant punishment. This is an alternate timeline, a blip in my real life. A romantic date would be serious business for something I'm taking entirely unseriously.

"You owe me. Besides, what else could you possibly be doing in Wind River on a Sunday night?" She's got a point, and she's pinning me with her questioning stare.

"Fine, fine. I give in." The train whistle blares and the Christmas playlist starts back in on its loop. I nod and get an idea. "On one condition: Donate a few trees to the charity gala? Or just one big one? With that high vaulted ceiling in the Great Hall, we're going to need some kind of immaculate showpiece."

Her face dims, but then grows ten times more cheerful. "You drive a hard bargain, but we do have a particularly tall babe out back that was rejected by the mayor for the municipal center tree. Nobody's bought it since nobody has a home big enough to fit it. Let me talk to my dad and see what I can do."

"You're a saint."

"My parents didn't name me Noelle for nothing." She makes a halo with her hands over her head. "But even if Hector says no, you're in. Got it? It'll be too painfully awkward if she shows up and it's just me."

I laugh. "Okay. Got it."

Weekend plans? Friend groups? It's like the old Matthew is recalibrating for his new surroundings. It's an adjustment, but I suppose not an altogether unpleasant one.

Noelle hugs me good night and the physical affection doesn't feel labored. Instead, for a change, it feels nice.

I could get used to this.

CHAPTER 18

Hector and I guide the winning tree inside the house. It only takes a few tries to get it into its stand. Grandma and Gramps successfully deconstructed the fake monstrosity and stored it away where no one will have to look upon its garish greenery again.

Once the new one is wrapped in classic white lights, the four of us stand back to inspect our work. For a quick turnaround, we made something quite beautiful to behold. A Christmas calm washes over me for the first time this year. I don't feel the urge to run.

"Tree-trimming party. Tomorrow night. Attendance is mandatory," says Grandma right before a big yawn.

My heart does a funny dip. I half expected this to be a one-and-done scenario that would prove to Hector I've gotten bitten by the holiday bug, but alas, the spirit of Christmas keeps tugging me along on a tinsel leash. I'm practically radiating emotions of olde or some shit.

I kind of like it—okay, I *love* it—but I'm afraid that if I fall too hard into the jolly and joyous feelings, I'll end up crushed when they go away again. Next year will only wallop me harder when my life returns to normal.

But Gramps is smiling so widely at me right now that the future anxiety fades to black.

"I'll make my famous spiked eggnog and we can get all these ornaments up," Gramps says.

"I expect all hands on deck," Grandma adds.

Hector and I nod in time with each other. Gramps finds Grandma's hand at the inlet to the hallway. The tenderness nearly repairs my rusted, mechanical heart. Together, they withdraw to their bedroom for the night, and we do the same.

It's only a little past ten and Hector's slipping into sleep clothes, but a second wind has overtaken me. Hector, however, seems to be crashing hard after the distraction of the farm. The open wounds he shared with me in the truck are still stinging, and, surprisingly, I want to soothe them in a special way.

"Any chance you want to watch *The Muppet Christmas Carol*?" I ask, trying not to make the offer sound as awkward as it is. Two grown men watching a children's movie together.

He sighs with a volume that could knock down a little pig's house of straw. I'm all for dramatics, but even this display is too much for me. It's not like he's the first person to ever get his heart broken. I offer him the best I've got: "I'm freshly out of a relationship too, so I know how you're feeling. Probably worse because I got doubly dumped."

"You were seeing more than one dude?" he asks after an excruciating beat.

"Well, those *dudes* were married to each other. We were a throuple. It was nice...for a while." Though maybe that's no longer the whole truth.

The truth is that saying how it really was makes it sadder than I want it to be. That mistrust, a lack of boundaries, and a need to *sell, sell, sell* social content for clout killed whatever chances we had at building something that could last. I never could quite tell if my heart was the only one on the line or if we all had something to lose in the end.

"Seriously?" Hector asks. "You don't have a valid driver's license, but you had two boyfriends who were already husbands? I'll say it again: You're a weird dude, dude."

I laugh, both at the repetition of the word *dude* (which has waned away into semi-charming at this point) and the fact that he's right. In my protest of "traditional" relationships, and in defiance of my parents, I jumped at the chance to play house with people who already had their home and garden in order. They were thriving, not just surviving like I was.

"Yeah, Baz is an indie singer. He mostly writes autobiographical lyric-driven songs about growing up Black and gay in the Bronx. Spencer is the heir to a particular microwave breakfast sandwich company. The optics were optimal. That's kind of how high-profile relationships are."

"High-profile relationships are about optics? What about attraction and emotion and trust?" he asks, like they're essential ingredients in the recipe for perfect romance.

I shake my head. "Those things come later if you're lucky. Relationships on the planet I'm from have a lot more to do with mutual advancement. First comes lust. Then comes capital gain. A perfect fairy tale."

He's not buying it. "That's messed up."

I'm thrust back to the night I met Baz at a fancy party. Mom's publishing house was throwing it to honor career achievements. Mom was accepting yet another ridiculous award she would no doubt cram onto our overcrowded mantel. After the mandatory photo op of the two of us for the press, she ditched me by the massive display of shrimp. I knew no one else in the room.

I talked my way into a cosmopolitan from the cute bartender who totally forgot to check my ID after I complimented how dexterous he was with a cocktail mixer—*shaker*, whatever.

The buzz was setting in and Baz was eyeing me across a very crowded Upper East Side members-only club. His hair was in waves and a low fade, and he sported a well-groomed beard, clipped close.

He'd written the title theme for Mom's TV series. It became a big hit, and they'd gotten him to come and play the acoustic version as part of the celebration.

I'll admit I had stalked him once or twice, watching his music videos and scrolling through his Instagram. I knew he was married to a very hand-some, wealthy, White, Jewish businessman. Also that they both looked exquisite in matching Speedos.

His first glance turned into a long chat over the state of the music busi-ness, the benefits of connecting with fans over social media, and the even better benefits of an open relationship. Obviously, the last one was why he'd come over, and as soon as he performed and I joined Mom up onstage to accept her award, we slipped out the back doors and rushed to his place for a nightcap and a night of uninhibited fun.

We exchanged numbers and when we moved on from a one-night stand into two-night sleepovers, it seemed like the logical next step was to meet his partner. Spencer was returning from a meditation retreat in Bali that night. Over bottles of Bordeaux, we all got to know each other in the kitchen, in the dining room, in the living room, and finally, and quite climactically, in the bedroom.

I was violating so many of my own rules. I say *my own*, but I do mean rules Bentley laid out for us over a long and turbulent friendship. We weren't supposed to get into anything serious. Serious was for old people. Serious was for status.

But with Baz and Spencer, I was getting status, so with that box checked, I gave myself the green light. Our relationship was like driving a Corvette on an open road with the top down. That is until I missed the yellow light and they suddenly flashed me the red.

"You okay?" Hector asks.

"Totally," I say, even though I don't believe it. It's not a feeling I've sat with in a while without making a joke of the whole thing. Now it's almost suffocating.

"What happened?"

I go back and forth over whether to tell him the version Sarah Pearson sold or the truth. We're in pretty deep at this point. The truth seems like the better, kinder option. "I got very drunk and very high at a Fire Island party. The three of us had been fighting earlier in the month over Baz's latest music video. His team had been having difficulty casting his love interest for the shoot, and Baz got the idea that one of us could do it. I suggested *both* of us could be in it to avoid any hurt feelings and put some positive polyamory-representation out into the world.

"Well, Spencer made this whole case about how *he's* been around the longest and how *he* fit the casting breakdown better and how *he* was the only reliable one. He made me feel worthless. Like I meant nothing in the relationship. Jump forward to our trip, and it comes out that they'd decided without me and filmed it behind my back. Completely betrayed my trust. And, well, I spiraled." I clear my throat. "The way I did the other night..."

"You had an anxiety attack?" Hector asks in plain language that shocks me. Nobody in my circle says it outright.

I hesitate, but ultimately nod, words like marbles in my mouth. "I have a...um, generalized anxiety disorder." He doesn't flinch. For some reason, I didn't expect him to. It confirms something unnameable for me. "Confrontation of any kind can set me off. Neither of them felt they did anything wrong. My mind was tunneling. I was sweating. It sucked."

"Did they know?" Hector asks, totally calm.

I shake my head. "No, I never told them. It's not something I talk about with anyone except my therapist."

He half smiles. "Thanks for telling me. You don't have to say any more if you don't want to."

"No." I press on. "It's fine. I was feeling mad and impulsive, and the ecstasy I stupidly took to combat the anxiety was really kicking in. So, while wearing only a white jockstrap and matching harness, I got up on the DJ dais and stole a microphone." I imagine myself back on that stage, vision hazy, hundreds of eyes cast upon me in confusion.

"This can't be going anywhere good." Hector's enraptured by every word.

"Hold on for this story. It's going to be a bumpy one," I say. "I called everyone to attention and then announced to the crowd that the sausages in Spencer's family's breakfast sandwiches were made of baby horsemeat. Out of nowhere. No pretense. No context. Just me, cross-faded, shouting a bold-faced lie: 'The sausages are made from baby horses!'" I sigh, realizing that the boy I'm talking about is a different iteration of myself from a separate past life, removed from who I am here. All the previous me's have been chunked off, lopped into little figurines in a Dickens-style display that represent old hurts. Oh, how I want to take a bat to the table and smash them all to smithereens.

"How did this not get out online?" he asks, trout-faced.

"The saving grace was that it was partially a sex party, so they made us check our phones with our clothes in locked pouches at the door. Nobody was able to record it and make it go viral, but word of mouth still spread, and Spencer was pissed."

"That's some seriously messy shit."

"I know." I palm my face. "Thankfully, Spencer's family did not sue for defamation. Instead, my parents paid Sarah Pearson, our publicist, to make the story go away. She planted an article about our three-way mutual parting, and I begrudgingly moved back in with my parents."

"And what happened with the music video?"

"It was a moderate steamy hit on gay Twitter." I crack an uncomfortable laugh, remembering a time when I wouldn't have thought twice in engaging in that kind of online exposure. "It's funny because I swore I'd finally gotten something right. That we three were meant to be." I force a feigned smile. "So, as you can see, we're sitting in the same sinking boat. Can't get home. Can't fix our past relationships. Can't figure out a goddamn theme for this goddamn gala. I could use some movie comfort right now."

"All right, let's do it then," Hector says before helping me get my laptop connected to the Ethernet cable and the movie rental pulled up. The cable still doesn't reach far enough to situate the screen anywhere for us both to have a good view. We end up pulling the rocking chair in front of my bunk and placing the computer on the seat. That means Hector and I will have to both sit in my bed to see.

"Is this okay?" Hector asks, taking the end opposite my pillow. I nod, curling up into a ball so none of our extremities touch. If we make any kind of contact while in a bed, I might go full Frosty the Snowman and melt. My hot and heavy fantasies of him and me together can only be quelled by firmly maintained physical distance.

The opening song brings back memories of Christmases past. Of parents bracketing me in on a comfortable couch. A refrigerator door covered with holiday cards from all over the map. A world that felt small at the edges but infinite in possibility.

As the movie plays, Krampus threatens to rip through, but I beat him back. Not now. Not next to Hector, who's looking at Kermit with so much childish glee. I hope he can't see that I'm looking at him the same way.

Except the side of his mouth hitches, and his eyes flick over. He's caught me. "Thanks for telling me that stuff. And for tonight in general. I, uh, yeah. Just thanks." Scrooge appears on screen again and my miserly ways fall to pieces.

There's a hint of bashfulness on full display in Hector's expression. It's the same hint I saw after Natalia kissed him. Do I have that effect on him too?

"Of course. And if you ever want to talk about anything—related or not—I'm willing to listen," I say. He nods, but it's long and languorous, like he's contemplating even more.

"Was staying with those dudes really what you wanted?" he asks suddenly.

Want. Another wishy-washy word with too many meanings to know for sure.

"I don't know what I wanted. I dropped out of NYU first semester because I didn't know what I wanted. I started dating them because I didn't know what I wanted. I bought that island because I didn't know what I wanted." It hadn't occurred to me what a pile of untended-to feelings I've been hoarding.

"I'm sorry, dude, but it's still wild that you bought an island," he says with only a little judgment. "Can you please tell me what you were going to do with it?" He's asking in earnest, I can tell.

I press my head into my hands. "Throw a music festival called Prince-a-Palooza." Saying it out loud magnifies my utter misjudgment. It was supposed to be my special thing. How had it all backfired and turned me into the family menace? I feel meek and dumb.

"That name is pretty fire, at least," he offers, which incites me to go on. Getting this all out, finally.

"I thought with the right investors and musical acts, it could be the next Coachella. I wasn't thinking of the work that would need to be done. Nor had I done *any* research into the field, but my intentions were good. I swear." I hug a pillow to my chest. "Baz and Spencer had conceptualized it with me. It was this running conversation we had, but the problem is that I didn't realize it was a running *joke*. I was taking it seriously, coming up with all these wonderful ideas and reaching out to contacts. I was knee-deep in yurt styles. Then when we broke up they made it clear how naive and stupid I was about the whole thing."

"That's shitty of them," Hector says, coming to my defense. I nod in appreciation.

"A new LGBTQ club opened in Midtown last week, and I went to the opening with my friends. Baz and Spencer were there. I didn't go over and say hello or anything, but I saw them flirt hard with and take home another guy. Cooler, fitter—*if you can imagine*—richer. Something inside me splintered. I felt full of wood chips." My voice trembles as I tell it, the emotions still fresh. "So, in the heat of the moment, high off my ass, I called my real estate contact and told him to pull the trigger on the island purchase. The next morning, I woke up the proud owner of an entire piece of land surrounded by water." That's exactly how I feel right now. Drowning in a sea of my own making.

"I mean, dude, don't get me wrong, that's an extreme reaction, but sometimes people hurt us and then we hurt ourselves as some twisted form of punishment for not seeing it all sooner," he says. The words wash over me in lapping, salty waves. I was trying to soothe him, and here he is doing it for me. And I know he means it, which means a lot.

"Thanks."

"Making a bad decision doesn't make you a bad person."

"It was more than *one bad decision*," I confess. Most days, I'm a teetering trash tower of them.

He shakes his head, hair swishing. "You know what I mean. You might not want to own up to it, but you're human. Humans make mistakes."

His sweet words assuage some of the hurt. If only for tonight. If only while he's next to me and his presence can ward off the unhealthy thoughts. I'm beyond grateful for that.

"You're right," I say after a beat. "And I never like admitting someone else is right, so…" My joking smile morphs into an appreciative smolder so intense it ripples heat straight down to my toes.

The movie is but background noise now. He's got his eyes trained on me, watching like I'm more interesting than any film could ever be. "Even if they didn't know what you were struggling with, you didn't deserve to be treated like that." Hector's declaration is firm; his protectiveness blankets me. Rarely has someone defended me unless it was Sarah Pearson, someone *paid* to do just that.

Hector's saying this out of kindness. Not obligation. It's sad, but it's a first for me.

"Thank you," I say with heart-stuttering breathlessness. I'd say it a million times if I could, which hits me square in the heart.

I watch him swallow, his throat bobbing. His eyes dip to my lips, and I take that as my cue to thank him in a different way. A way I've wanted to for a while now.

Boldness broadens my chest as I inch closer, lean in, let my flights of fancy come to fruition.

Except the sound of rattling chains and ghostly roars from my computer speakers make me realize: these *are* only flights of fancy. His eyes landing on my lips might've been a trick of the flickering screen. I was just seeing what I wanted to see.

I stop before I make an ass out of myself.

Only then he surprises me by whispering, "Please?"

And I don't dare second-guess this Christmas miracle.

One hand finds his face. The other finds his waist. Our lips find each other's for the very first time in a kiss that can only be described as overdue and yet still right on schedule.

Those thank-yous pass from my lips to his—for listening, for caring, and for, *fuck*, for kissing me back with so much enthusiasm. He tastes like peppermint gum and Yuletide cheer. His hands are big and rough yet warm and reassuring as they move from my neck to the sides of my face, tenderly cupping my cheeks. Somehow, cradled, I'm both breakable and indestructible. I want this feeling to last forever.

It goes on for minutes like that, the intensity rising. Silken locks slide effortlessly between my fingers. His scent is clean shampoo mixed with a heavenly musk. I harden with each brush of our eager bodies. His flannel rides up a tad, revealing that tantalizing line of skin, and my pulse jolts into my core.

Abruptly, I realize what those drunken rebound kisses on club couches were missing: *connection*.

That's what I've been holding out hope for.

And here it is. Miraculously. In the flesh.

I lean back, slightly overcome and afraid he's not willing to go farther.

Am I willing to go farther?

He looks stunned, but euphoric in a rumpled way. It would be so easy to push him back on the bed, to consummate this in the way I so desperately want to, but a creak upstairs caused by shuffling footfalls brings the reality forward. It's probably Gramps getting a late-night snack—leftover cookies from the other day.

Our eyes lock once more, but the passion has fizzled, and understanding settles.

This isn't the place to do anything more. As much as I wish it were. I could use the release to de-stress and let those old hurts ripple out of me at least for a hundred hiccupping heartbeats, but—

"Sorry, but we should probably stop," I say, disheartened, training my eyes onto the movie. It's a sad part—thank God—that snuffs out the mood entirely.

"Yeah," he agrees, doing the same. "For sure."

But neither of us moves away. Instead, we sit there on my bottom bunk, hands touching, shoulders brushing, energy sparking between us, until the credits roll.

CHAPTER 19

The house is empty when I emerge the next morning. There's something striking about the silence here. Back in the city, I'm lucky if there's a moment when I don't hear someone shouting down the avenue or a siren blaring in the distance or a dog barking a mile a minute. Living on top of Central Park, there's plenty of foot traffic, and no matter how high we are, the world down below always seems to creep inside.

Here, I could drown in my own thoughts. If I were as hell-bent on getting out of here as I was a few days ago, that would be dangerous. Now, I'm still holding on to last night's calm, admiring the tree in the corner with a full heart.

My lips still tingle from last night's kiss as well. I can almost feel the phantom prickle of Hector's stubble against my cheek and his hot breath ghosting up the side of my neck.

I hope he doesn't regret it. Even if I'm unsure of where I stand on the regret continuum myself.

I turn on the teakettle and grab a mug. I find some instant oatmeal packets in the pantry, deciding that this is the best my nonculinary self is going to get for breakfast without Oksana here to whip me up one of her homemade sausage-and-spinach omelets.

Once I'm settled at the kitchen table, I open one of the Moleskine notebooks I brought with me and uncap the fountain pen I got as a gift from Nan, Dad's mom, a few years ago. I've been known to doodle. I'm good at it. I could never be an artist, but I do have a designer's eye.

I flip fast past the pages covered in notes for Prince-a-Palooza. After talking to Hector, I realize how childish that whim had been. Just because I know a lot of people doesn't mean I have the connections to enter a thriving market. Yet another poor decision born of a bad bout of the *look-at-mes*!

To scrub myself clean of it, I take the next hour to envision the Great Hall in a few different ways. All of them feature the promised tree at its center, circular tables spiraling out so everyone can get a good view. I draw in garland centerpieces with gold-embossed candles. Winter floral arrangements sit on stands near the doors.

I think up a clever way to hide the projector in the winter wonderland display that's been a decorative staple for decades. You can tell just by looking at it, all that wear and tear, but I'm not about to argue with tradition. Not anymore, anyway.

Maybe we can fashion it into a living art installation, a video photo op with virtual snowfall and a snowman that winks back at you. We could merge the physical elements with the technological ones.

That's when the idea strikes me: the theme should be Past, Present, and Yet to Come. Like the ghosts in *A Christmas Carol*. The My Favorite Things theme felt too tacky, but this could have real emotional resonance with the guests. I'm sure plenty of them have connections with the story like Hector and I do.

My hand can't quite keep up with how fast my thoughts are spilling out of me. It'll be a miracle if I can decode this gibberish when I'm finished.

We do a Past section where we dig up old guest ledgers and photo albums from galas past. We have a Present exhibit, which is the centerpiece tree surrounded by *literal* presents with platitudes about *living in the moment* and *breathing in the now*. (Suburban women love that shit.) The last would be Yet to Come, the technological wonderland where we lead people into the silent auction to remind them that they're giving for the future good of the community.

I'm impressed with myself. Sure, it's not the subtlest design I've ever come up with, but I must admit that it's good. That kind of journey would make people open their purses to reach for both the tissues and their wallets.

The sound of a key in the front door jars me out of my cone of creativity. When I check the time on my phone, I realize two-and-a-half hours have passed. Time flies when you're having an epiphany, I guess.

I'm surprised to see Hector a bit disheveled but happy to see me, pink stripes stitched over his cheeks. His brown canvas backpack gets dropped by the coats. He raises his long arms in triumph.

"I'm a free man," he says, bypassing what I assumed would be an uncomfortable encounter after last night's full-on Frenching.

"Papers all finished?" I ask, thankful our ease is intact.

"I just left the library, where I submitted my very last one. It feels freakin' amazing at the end of finals week," he says. "Can't survive on coffee and carbs alone for any longer. Seven down, just one more standing in between me and that degree." He catches his overzealousness and scales back. Maybe from my mention of dropping out of NYU. Maybe from remembering that we kissed last night. "What are you working on?" he asks.

Instead of explaining, I hand over my book, which is an act not to be taken lightly. It's rare that I let someone see the gestation period of a work in progress. He flips through the pages, taking in every sketched line and purposeful annotation. A hitch in my chest lets on that I care about his opinion. I want him to approve.

"How very Dickensian," he says.

"But in a good way, right? Not like a sad way?" I ask.

"No, not like a sad way," he says. "We've definitely got our work cut out for us if we're going to get that done."

"Good thing I have plenty of time on my hands," I say.

"I do too, now. Lorna says she doesn't need me at the store until after the gala. I can devote my time and energy to the project. Speaking of, we've got a band to secure," he says, rattling his keys around.

I follow him out the door without hesitation.

·*·*·*

"I'm only twenty-one. I'm not old enough to be dumped in one of these places already," I jokingly protest.

We pull into a parking spot outside of Whispering Willows Nursing Home. It's all crisp lines and beige windows looking out on the park where the Lights of Wonder Spectacular is housed, the architectural walk-through Rosalie had told me about at the inn. The one Noelle is coercing me into.

The one I want to invite Hector to…

"You're never too young for a swing dance and dine soiree," he says. I can't believe all those words mashed up into one sentence came out of his mouth.

The inside is all dingy wallpaper matched with scratchy-looking carpets. The receptionist is a man with pointy black hair. He wears a light-up wreath pin yet doesn't smile when he sees us.

"Welcome to Whispering Willows. What can I assist you with?" he asks drily, not living up to the playfulness of his pin.

"We're here to meet with Bruce Harlan. He's the leader of Swingin' Six, the band playing at your event today," Hector says. "He's expecting us."

Wreath Pin gets out a guest sheet and makes us both sign and date it. He begins filling out name tags.

"Oh, no, thank you," I say in a chipper tone to save him the trouble.

"Every visitor must wear a name tag," he says.

"But you can't stick adhesive on cashmere." I motion to my AMIRI intarsia-knit cardigan.

He raises his eyebrows as if to say *That's my problem?* Hector shifts from foot to foot.

After a moment of internal struggle, I say, "I'll happily take the sticker." I own enough cashmere cardigans to outfit an entire professional football team. I can stand to sully one for a good reason.

He leads us toward the ballroom. We pass women sitting in armchairs flipping through magazines and men with walkers flapping their gums at one another. It's like a hotel lobby exclusively for AARP members. They seem happier when they see us, so I wave and smile like I just won a pageant.

The ballroom is decked out for the day. The volunteers and workers strung the place up with a few odd streamers and a bunch of balloon bouquets.

It's a solid attempt at making the space festive, but none of the residents seem to be into it. They pick at plates of soggy food, not even tapping their toes to the beat of the music.

Our guy Bruce is in the corner, crooning his way through a Christmas tune. He's not half-bad, but he hasn't inspired anyone to hit the dance floor yet. A major disappointment.

A kind woman in blue scrubs comes over to greet us and offers us some punch.

"Is this how you thought you'd be spending your time when your parents told you they were sending you here?" Hector asks me. There's a hint of yesterday on his tongue. Is he asking about what transpired in our bunk beds, or genuinely curious about this? I choose to answer the latter.

"I do love being the youngest, prettiest person in the room, but this might be taking it a little too far," I joke. "At least I'm here with you."

Oh no. I'm a magician who's pulled the rabbit out of his hat too early in the act. For a long moment, he looks at me funny. As if at any moment he might drag me close and kiss me again.

But instead of harping on that, I get a fresh idea to change the subject. "Dance with me," I say, setting down our punch and holding out an open hand to him.

"What? Are you serious?"

"Looks like these people could use a little nudge," I tell him. Nobody even gets up as Bruce switches to a slower standard they could shuffle about to. "Let's face it, they're not getting any younger."

Hector laughs off his inhibitions. Thinking back on the rainbow crosswalk, the unicorn speech, Noelle coming out to me, I assume these folks won't bat an eyelash at two guys dancing together, so I bring Hector to the center of the room and walk him through the *one-two-three* footwork.

"Where did you learn to dance like this?" he asks, catching on easily. He's got natural rhythm and good timing. He doesn't even question it when I lift my arm and allow him to pass under. I like that he's letting me lead for a change—twirling about, carefree.

"I've been to enough black-tie functions to be able to do this in my sleep," I say. "It's basically a developmental requirement. At seven you get fitted for a tux with tails, at eight you learn to waltz, and by nine you've become entirely dependent on Dom Pérignon in social settings."

"Is Dom someone from your past I should be worried about?" Hector asks, eyebrow cocked.

"No, Hector, Dom Pérignon is—"

He stops my sentence by dipping me in his strong, sturdy arms. It takes my breath away. "I know, dude. I was just teasing you."

Our laughs get interrupted when we notice the other couples stepping out onto the floor, putting those new hip replacements to good use. There's a saucy, big-haired woman in a frumpy red sweater who locks eyes with Hector as we continue to sway. With a lick of her lips, she gets up and approaches us. She's got gusto, that's for sure.

"Mind if I cut in?" she asks. Hector looks at me with uncomfortable eyes. "You don't mind, do you, young man?" she asks me.

"Not at all," I say, knowing I'm about to get far too much pleasure out of this.

She drags him away by the hand, leaving me partner-less. Hector keeps looking back at me over the heads of the other couples who've shrunken in their old age. I playfully wave.

"Thanks for doing that," Scrubs says upon returning. "It's hard to get the residents up and moving these days. I really appreciate it."

"Don't mention it," I say, picking up my cup of punch and taking a sip.

"Looks like Greta stole your man. She's a minx, that one."

"We're not... He's not *my man*," I say, flustered.

She scrunches up her face. "Yikes, sorry. I don't know why I assumed that. I guess he was looking at you a certain way while you were dancing, and I just thought... I don't know. Sorry." She scurries away to assist a woman struggling with her cane.

Alone again, watching as Hector dips Greta like he did me, I think about what a relationship with him might look like. It's not the portrait of power you frame for the wall of a legacy mansion, but it might be the kind of candid photo you place in the living room of your shared apartment. I don't hate the idea of the two of us together. What started as sexual tension could be something more if I let it.

Jeez, we haven't even talked about yesterday and I'm practically picking out vintage china patterns over here. I need to calm down.

Except telling myself to calm down always does the opposite.

My breathing picks up. My thoughts pick up too. Krampus lets out a piercing cry only I can hear, but I shush him with an event. Not an imagined one though. Instead I picture the Wind River Charity Gala.

The photo booth. *Inhale. Count to ten.* The Christmas tree centerpiece from Arthur's farm. *Exhale.* The *vermilion* tablecloths. *Inhale. Ten count.* A walk-through mobile of images from galas past. *Exhale.*

It doesn't take as much to resettle, which astonishes me. I make a mental note to ask Grandma for help sourcing old gala photo albums. I need to get a move on that Past exhibit. Still so much to accomplish before the big day.

Swingin' Six announces they'll be taking a five-minute break.

"You're lucky they stopped playing or you would've been next, sweet cheeks," Greta purrs, handing Hector back. I'm momentarily concerned by which set of cheeks she's referring to.

"That's too bad. Maybe next time," I say. She stalks off, still snapping her fingers to an unheard beat.

Hector glares at me. I can't help but chortle right in his face. It was fun. Being with him is always fun. In surprising ways, every time. I want to extend the fun for as long as possible.

Bruce Harlan comes our way, and before he hits the food table for intermission fuel, I call out to him.

"You the gala guys?" he asks. He's got big eyes and short blond hair. He picks up a loaded piece of bruschetta. We nod. "What do you think of the set so far?" Tomato bits fly out from between his teeth.

"I certainly enjoyed myself," I say, nudging Hector.

"Glad to hear it," Bruce says. "We've got an arsenal of Christmas classics we can do for your event if you're into us." To avoid another spit shower, Hector and I both move a few inches to our left and hope he doesn't notice.

"That would be great. We would just need to figure out a rate," Hector says, pulling up the budget again on his phone.

Bruce shakes his head. "We don't want money. This is a hobby for us. We're all nine-to-five guys—mailmen and delivery drivers—who do it for the fun of it. Any chance to play is pay enough in our books." He laughs. "Plus then we don't have to go home to our wives that night."

I fight the urge to cringe. Heterosexuals have no sense of humor.

After a painful beat, he asks, "We get the gig or what?"

Bruce and I shake on it to seal the deal.

CHAPTER 20

Grandma wasn't kidding about the tree-trimming party. As soon as we return from our full day of planning, we're adorned with jangly felt reindeer antlers and slugged with barf-worthy polyester blends. My grandparents stand before us in matching crewnecks. My eyes are almost burning from the repeating bright colors and mismatched patterns.

"Don't fight us on this, Matthew. Everything's more festive in an ugly Christmas sweater," Gramps says.

I ruined a cashmere cardigan today, so with the fashion overlords already angered, I heed his advice. I slip out of my jacket and slide the monstrosity over my head, hair going all staticky.

I check myself out in the mirror without cringing. I think I wear such expensive designer pieces because if I can cover myself in beautiful clothes, maybe I'll start seeing what's underneath as beautiful too. Even the imperfect parts.

Hector's seen through the armor since day one, calling it exactly what it was—a way to keep people out. I think I might be ready to let people see me in all my messy glory.

In many ways, I already have.

"Gramps set aside all the little ornaments you made for us back in the day," Grandma says.

"You kept those?" I ask. The silly pipe-cleaner and Popsicle-stick creations fill me with nostalgia. I had teachers at New York's most prestigious preschool who emphasized the homemade gift as a tiny piece of the heart. Mom and Dad were not the types to appreciate a portrait done entirely in eco-friendly crayon and plant-based glue. Grandma and Gramps, on the other hand, would display any Daliesque product of my imagination. So, come Thanksgiving every year, I'd pack up all my crafts in a box and I'd trek them to Massachusetts.

I place my boots on the shoe rack and come over to the couch. Gramps has made a neat collection on the coffee table. There are snowflakes and mini sleds, pom-pom snowmen and a clay reindeer that looks more like the poop emoji than an animal capable of guiding Santa's sleigh.

"Matthew was quite the artist when he was a kid," Grandma says to Hector, who hangs back.

I can't tell for sure why he's hesitating. Maybe it's because he's not sure if joining in is overstepping. Or maybe it's because we haven't spoken candidly about our kiss yet.

Either way, I can tell he's missing his own family, his own Christmas tree, and his own traditions that don't involve his professor, his professor's wife, and the rich boy he's tolerating—and *tonguing*—for the time being.

I hand him the clay reindeer turd as a peace offering.

"Not my finest work, but deserves a special spot anyway," I say, imbuing my voice with a saccharine quality. He takes it with a slight, squished smile.

He inspects the open branches like a scout on the hunt for a perfect camping spot. His commitment to getting everything right is immeasurable. I'm starting to see how it benefits him.

Baz worked hard when inspiration struck. He'd spend whole days holed up in his studio with his instruments and innumerable energy drinks fueling his creativity. Spencer was a delegator—the big boss to the little bosses. When there was a fire, he wasn't the one to put it out. Bentley is an influencer and makes most of her money through YouTube partnerships and Instagram sponsorships. Not like I learned the value of a dollar from any of them.

Now, my parents work hard. I know that. But they are at the top of their fields respectively. Hard work looks different when you're standing at the summit. You make your own schedule. You choose your deadlines. The world realigns itself to spin when you say spin and stop when you say stop.

The three people standing before me are prime examples of hard workers. I know it sounds overdramatic, and I haven't been here that long, but I'm starting to see the upside of humble pleasures, of the joy that comes from setting your mind on something and successfully completing it. I know the gala isn't finished yet, but the work we've done so far is worth being proud of.

Full of festive glee, I bite the bullet on Noelle's request. "Do you want to go to the Lights of Wonder Spectacular?" I ask Hector quietly as Grandma and Gramps ready the spiked eggnog in the kitchen.

"Together?" He holds one of my misshapen ornaments at a standstill.

Our eyes meet over the pom-pom snowman. "Yeah. Sunday night. With Noelle and Siena."

He must have some inkling about what Noelle and Siena are to each other because his cheeks turn rosy, and it's not from the fireplace blasting. "Oh, uh, we've got auction baskets to arrange and name cards to fold…"

It's like he hasn't noticed I'm a walking checklist of responsibilities these days. "I've planned out our schedule, and if we pull some late nights next week, we can afford to treat ourselves." A new idea sprouts up. "Maybe we can even get the manager to add some sparkle to the gala!"

"Are you sure, dude?" he asks.

"You know, for someone who studies English, you sure say 'dude' a lot."

That helps him crack a smile. "My dad and brother say it all the time. My sister picked it up from them. I picked it up from her. I know it's a bad habit. Some families have a swear jar. My mom keeps a dude jar in the kitchen. A dollar every time it comes out around her." He laughs.

"That's not a bad idea. From now on, I'm going to Venmo request you every time you say it around me." I take out my phone to show him I'm serious.

"Don't you dare, *dude*." He smirks, pushing the phone away, pressing closer to me. There's the Hector I've come to count on.

"Fine, I won't. If you agree to come," I say slyly.

"Fine," he says. "But only because I don't want to decline forty payment requests a day."

"Forty? That's a pretty low estimate, dudemeister."

"Dudemeister? Do you want me to come or not?"

My face heats. God, I'm Matthew Prince Jr. I shouldn't be *blushing*, but I am. Because I think we've solidified a date, and I haven't had a date—one not for a photo op—in forever. "I do."

"Then it's settled," he says.

We both reach for the same branch to hang our respective ornament on, causing our hands to touch, sending a tingle through my body. Our moment is only interrupted when someone clears their throat behind us.

"Eggnog anyone?" Grandma asks, holding two boozy mugs.

"Before we start drinking, who wants to put the angel on top of the tree?" Gramps asks. He's not about to brave the step stool with his back.

I nominate Hector since I know he needs it more than I do. He glows brighter than the tree at the suggestion. I file that away for safekeeping. I can make him blush and I can make him beam. I'm excited to see what other emotions I can make him feel.

With steady assurance, he climbs up, sets the heavenly host in its rightful place, and we all step back to take in our creation. "Silent Night" starts playing. I can't help it. Tears begin to form.

"A job well done, I'd say," Gramps announces.

We all settle in on the couches, eggnog refilled and the clock ticking into the wee hours of the evening. Hector tells us about his family traditions— the Nochebuena feast with his dad's family featuring pasteles, rice, and pork, midnight mass with its own pageant (where he once played Joseph and nearly dropped the fake baby Jesus), and the Christmas morning breakfast with his mom's family where his grandma serves chorizo and omelets before anyone can open a single present.

I snuggle further into some throw pillows and a fleece blanket. The world fades in a bit at the edges. I guess moments like these are what this season is all about. It may not be as glamorous as I'm used to, but it feels right, the way it once did, and that's all that matters right now.

CHAPTER 21

The storage units are as desolate as they were the other day.

The next morning, we find our target and undo the padlock. We lug boxes, assembly-line-like, into the back of the truck with only brief breaks for flirtatious eye fucking that's riling me up.

Last night brought about a loaded good night. Should we kiss again? Should we talk? Should we shed our clothes and figure it out later? We ended up giving each other an awkward hug, shutting off the lights, and lying in silence until sleep overtook us both.

"Were you studying art or something at NYU?" Hector asks out of nowhere. When I look over, he's flipping through my planning notebook, full up with sketches. He's searching for our last-minute list of items that need to be ferried to the college, but stopping every few pages to inspect my art.

I slide the projector onto the floor in the front of the truck. We don't want that rattling around with everything else. It already looks moments away from combusting of its own accord.

"Uh, no. I was just in the school of general studies. I never declared a major or anything like that," I say. "I wasn't there long enough to even contemplate any of that. I sometimes like to think if I had stayed, I would've created my own major, but even in my fantasies I can't figure out what it would contain or be called."

"I was only asking because these drawings are really good. Like, *really* good." I glow in the radiance of his compliment, even though he seems shocked I could possess a talent beyond a rigorous beauty regimen.

"I wanted to take a gap year. I told my parents that. They claimed I couldn't just do that because that's what all my friends were doing, but it really wasn't that. I didn't want to tour Europe on their dime or anything. I just didn't feel ready to make any big decisions. Probably because I'd had so many big decisions made for me by them for so many years." I let out a sigh. "It's unfortunate that society expects young adults to make good, life-changing choices. What kind of system is that?"

"I hear you, dude," Hector says. He unrolls the tarp we're going to lay over the boxes in case a flurry or rainstorm rolls in. I grab the other side and spread it evenly over the bed.

"What about you? Why English?" I ask.

"I think because that's what my mom studied when she was here. She wanted to get an MFA, do advanced research in early Spanish literature, the baroque masters—Cervantes and Lope de Vega—or sometimes she'd say she preferred the Italian-inspired Renaissance stuff—León or Cruz—because of the heavy religious themes. She's the smartest person I know. But during senior year of college, she got pregnant with my older brother. She and my dad rented an off-campus apartment above some of the shops in the Downtown District after graduation and she traded the graduate degree for motherhood," he says, fastening the tarp to the sides of the truck bed.

"So, you're completing it for her?" I ask.

"Kind of," he says. "She instilled a passion for reading in me at a young age, and studying English just kind of made sense." I add an early love of literature to our growing folder of shared interests. He continues, "Plus I had Dr. Winston for my freshman writing seminar and I fell in love with the way he teaches. His excitement over words is infectious. It's quiet, but it's strong. It's not even what he says exactly. It's in the way he moves while he says it. Like a metaphor is a piece of candy to him, waiting to be unwrapped and savored. I had my mind made up by the end of that first term."

I enjoy hearing about Gramps this way. My most vivid memories of him are his long-winded stories when he's gorged out on dark meat at

Thanksgiving dinner. They aren't him poised in front of a lecture hall, teaching the next generation of thinkers. It's such a noble profession. Underappreciated too. Even if their work isn't for me.

"Did you come back here to see where you would've grown up had things been different?" I ask. I know it's a loaded question, but we're at that level now. At least, I hope we are.

"I think so. When I got my acceptance letter, I was worried at first that maybe this place had changed too much in the time since my parents were here, but I decided I had to find out for myself. I didn't connect well with the people I went to school with back home. That world was sports, marching band, rowdy parties, and not much else. My brother did the sports thing. He played basketball before college and then the fire academy. My sister was in with the out-and-indie crowd. Like, full-on head of purple hair and multiple cartilage piercings, making my mom furious. I never really found a group that got me. I wasn't a drama kid and I didn't want to do debate, so I escaped into books," he says. "Plus the humidity gets to you after a while. I wanted to experience a different climate. I love the snow now."

"Snow is pretty coming down over New York City, but disgusting once it's settled. Blackened slush is probably the saddest sight around the holidays," I say. "Though, I do miss my January strolls through Central Park. I used to pretend I was somewhere far-off, isolated in my own world of freshly fallen crystal. It's the closest to inner serenity I've ever found."

I pick up one of the leftover light strands and start detangling it. We might need the extra glamour at some point before we're done.

"Technically, I grew up in a suburb of Dallas, but it's basically a city of its own accord. So this small-town change of pace is nice," he says as I struggle with a stubborn knot. "I feel calmer here. More *me*. I like knowing people and being known. Especially by people who accept me for who I am."

"When did you come out?" I ask as he takes a seat atop a plastic tub and joins me. His nimble hands have better luck than mine do.

"When I moved out here, I just decided I'd be open about who I was. There wouldn't be any pretense about who I had been or who I wanted to be. I never formally came out to anyone on campus, but when I started exploring my bisexuality freshman year, going to club meetings and stuff, I would talk to my sister about it during our weekly FaceTime calls. She was working toward her beautician's license, and not to be super stereotypical, but there were quite a few queer dudes in her program, so I knew she'd get me."

"I'm glad you had that kind of support."

Hector says, "My parents know now too. They're devout, church-going Catholics, so I thought it would be an ordeal, but surprisingly it wasn't. I think it helped that I have a cousin on my dad's side who's a lesbian. And that my mom loves Ricky Martin just a *little too much*."

"I don't blame her," I say. And then I blush because I realize Hector does share some of the talented performer's brooding features. He catches me trying to hide it, and I decide after the other night what's the use? He knows I crave him.

I smile a flirtatious smile, wishing he'll pick up the baton and make mention of our steamy, pulse-spiking make-out session during the movie. Maybe start a second one to rival it.

"What about you?" he asks, killing my hopes and prolonging this conversation about everything but the kiss in question. I drop the smile, deflated a little. "I mean, you've been out for a while, right? What was that like, being a young poster child for the LGBTQ community?"

"Poster child? I don't know about all that." I swallow some of the hard, jagged feelings scratching up my windpipe, but I tell him what I can. The sentiments that won't choke me. "It was not as glamorous as the GLAAD awards make it seem. I didn't do it on my terms, nor was it my choice."

He plays protector again. "Somebody outed you?" There's anger in the way he drops his task to focus his attention on me.

"No, not like that. I was caught kissing a boy I shouldn't have been." I leave Lukas's name out of it. Despite the trust building between us, it's only half my story to share. "After confirming I was gay, my parents and our publicist kicked into high gear, deciding how and where and why to tell the story."

"They didn't even ask if that's what you wanted?"

"I was just over the moon that they accepted me. That they wanted to shout their pride from the rooftops. It didn't occur to me until I was working with my therapist that it was mostly a PR stunt." I kick aside a stray box. "Lo and behold, I come out and queer side characters pop up in the Dark Dissension series. I should've seen it."

"You were young," he says, as if this makes it absolvable.

"But old enough to process the feelings and know how I felt about that guy. We were barred from seeing each other again." Hector doesn't ask who. It's a small detail, but an important one. In New York, listeners would be hungry for names so they could regurgitate the story to the first person who will care, but Hector's not like that. He's more interested in my hard-held emotions than who brought about my sexual awakening. "I thought about that last kiss a lot." The admission is freeing.

"I've been thinking about our *first* kiss a lot." Such a suave pivot. Such sweet words. I could shatter for him, right here on the cement.

"Me too." Another equally freeing admission considering how scared I was that it would become another bunk-bed fever dream.

"Replaying it has kept me up the last couple nights." So I haven't been imagining that frantic tossing and turning over my head. The sound of an elastic waistband slapping back into place minutes after.

"Same for me." It's winded me and wound me up, making sleep impossible even though Hector's snore strips have been working.

"Can I ask you something personal?"

"Go for it," I shoot back, realizing my guard isn't just down. It's not here. I lost it while dancing with him yesterday. Maybe even before that. I stand, stretching out my strand of lights, using it as an excuse to edge closer to him.

"Have you been with anyone since your exes?" he asks. His question is brazen, forward, and fills me with a million swooping bumblebees. I rumble and buzz with expectation of what he might say or do next.

"Are you asking if I've had sex since my breakup?" I raise my eyebrows, preen a little bit.

He lets out a pleasing, barely audible "Yes."

"I have. Once or twice. Nothing to write about in my diary, that's for sure," I joke, liking where this is going. I back myself against the wavy metal wall in anticipation. Isn't this what actors in Baz's music videos do to signal they want to be kissed deep, pressed hard, taken somewhere exhilarating? "Why do you ask?"

"Because I haven't. At all. And I…" He clears his throat, growing shy as I grow fuller in my jeans. "I was…"

"And you were hoping we would…"

"Yeah, dude." His voice cracks in a sexy way. "I was hoping we would. The other night."

"We still can." I let my voice trail into a tantalizing place.

"Here?" he asks, looking around, uncertain.

"Why not? It's secluded. It's private. Nobody around to interrupt us…" My list could go on, but I can't take it anymore. From the moment I saw him, the second he needled me like nobody else ever has, I knew I wanted him, and now he's here, offering himself. I can't let this moment pass. A drive back in the truck could change everything. I won't let the fragility of what we have smash to pieces in transit. Pressing pause, like we did that night, isn't an option any more.

I want this. I need this.

"Are you sure?" he asks.

I nod. "I'm so sure."

Without further prompting, he's locking the truck and hauling the gate down. In only the glow of an electric lantern that's on its last leg, he finds his way back to me, stopping inches from my body. He's radiating pheromones and full-throttle heat in these freezer-like temperatures.

A single hand reaches out, hesitant, and strokes the side of my hair, tracing the divot of my ear. My whole body shivers. "Is this okay?"

"Yeah, your fingers are just cold," I say, panting. He turns into an ice sculpture, uncertainty magnifying in his eyes, but then I whisper, "It's okay. I want this. I don't care." Cold fingers can go to hell. "*I need you.*"

That's all he needs to hear.

"Warm them," he instructs, presenting his fingers to me, using the bratty tone from the day we met. Except this time, it's fucking sexy. So fucking sexy that it shakes up my insides like a snow globe.

Without hesitation, I take his forefinger in my mouth. My tongue wanders over the ridges of bone, tasting his calluses, before I do the same to the next finger and the next and the next. Then, he's presenting me with his other hand, and before I know it, I'm blowing hot breath up their sides, so entranced by this strangely erotic act. So in the moment that it scares me.

He goes to touch my face again, but I flinch. "Still cold." The straining denim below my waist gives me an idea. "Try this." I undo my belt and slip his hand into the deep warmth there. I cringe at first, sudden shock, but settle into the firm press of his palm.

"Much better," he whispers in my ear before pushing up against me. I do the same for him and allow our mouths to meet. This initial kiss isn't tentative. It's sumptuous, toothy. Hurried, matching my rocketing heart rate.

We're on it—on each other—like that for a while. Our thumping bodies working hard toward the desired result. His pants fall completely down to his ankles, so I pull him closer, gripping his now bare ass. He gasps into my mouth, sweet hot breath, as the pads of my fingers massage the soft flesh there.

"I love that. Keep doing that," he groans, commanding. I knead him more, making his goose bumps disappear.

My brain is flashing, pleasure centers spiking as he slickly strokes me, kisses me, brings me to the brink of orgasm and then walks it back. Over and over. He's an expert at teasing me, both with words and his hands, apparently.

I'm seeing stars in the shadowy dark. "That's it, Matthew."

Time starts skipping like a jumping needle on a record player at his praise. We find a steady rhythm that satisfies us both and sounds like music. It's all too real and utterly dreamlike.

By the time Hector's hand has fully defrosted, I'm frantically whispering, "I'm close. Please, *please*. I'm close."

We both moan into each other's necks, gasping for air at the flood of overwhelming relief that comes when we topple over the edge one right after the other.

Finally. When the shuddering ceases, I can breathe again.

"That was—" I start.

"Yeah," he finishes, half-pensive, half-sighing. "Wow."

"Yep. Wow."

We look at each other. Freezing yet overheated. Satisfied yet yearning for more. The charged awkwardness gets broken by a breathless, necessary laugh. There's no more left to be said.

We're both too spent to speak.

We find old napkins in a nearby box, clean ourselves up, and see ourselves out, lighter and somehow more weighted too.

As the truck rolls out onto the road, the carnality of coming together presses into my breastbone, makes me question my motives.

I need you. Had I really said that? And more importantly, did I mean it?

It's not until we're at the college, unstacking folding chairs and unfolding linen tablecloths, that I begin to see the progress we've made. The space is starting to take shape—look special, *feel* special.

Something else in this room feels special too.

I glance over and soak in Hector's profile as he sets up the plastic snowman, tracing the sloping bridge of his nose with my eyes. When I reach his lips—his perfect, still-swollen lips—I find my answer in his glimmering, sparkling smile.

I do need him.

And I don't know how to feel about that.

CHAPTER 22

I'm a bundle of anxiety by the time the crew from Bishop's Family Farm arrives with the tree.

Noelle's text was a welcome respite from the uncomfortable silence surging through the Great Hall post-sex, post-revelation, post, well…*everything.*

The mutual masturbation was electric, all-encompassing, soul-baringly awesome, but it also struck a strange nerve in me. I'm on the fritz, finding it hard to focus with him nearby. I have no space to sort through my twisted yarn ball of a brain.

Tunnel vision holding strong, I texted Noelle back, telling her to come ASAP.

Now, the twelve-person team erects the spectacular tree in the center of the space. It was a series of serious trial-and-error moves to get the marvelous beast through the door, but now it stands tall and proud, ready to be decorated.

I step aside as ladders get carted in, and everyone works overtime to wrap the branches in the twinkling lights Hector and I unraveled in the storage unit. Before we unraveled each other, that is.

Gah. Stop thinking about that, Matthew.

Popping the top on a box, I sort through Jack's old ball ornaments, separating them by shininess. Only the brightest and the best deserve a spot on my centerpiece.

This mindless task is enough to distract me for the moment. The kiss led to the realization that Hector and I have a connection. But this afternoon solidified something scarier. That this connection could lead to something more. Something probably incompatible with my life back in New York. I'm not in the market for untenable.

I don't get a moment to parse this out because Hector appears beside me, bundled up and worried. "Is everything all right?" he asks.

"Fine," I lie. I need him to leave me alone before I do one of two inappropriate things: jump his bones again or freeze into an icy snowbank of emotions. Neither would be good when we have an important gala looming.

Admittedly, a little while ago I escaped to the bathroom. I reached for my phone on autopilot, in search of Bentley's contact, but I realized she wouldn't understand. She'd scold me for even entertaining these whims. That's not what I need with feelings this fresh and conflicted.

"You know you can tell me if it's not," Hector says, caring eyes becoming almost *too* caring. And while I know he's right, I don't want to be *too much*. Overshare here. In public. With a twelve-person crew, including Noelle, nearby.

Noelle's presence inspires me. "I'm good. Seriously. Just need to get this done quickly before Noelle and I break for lunch."

The barista herself sweeps over. "Did I hear my name?" She looks like she's on a mission: Operation Save Matthew from Himself. She's overheard everything as she fluffed the branches.

"Ready to head out for our lunch?" I ask, signaling with my eyes for her to play along even though we didn't have any prior plans.

"Uh, of course. Let me just grab our coats," she says.

"It's to, um, thank her for the tree and everything," I say awkwardly when I'm left alone with Hector.

He appears disheartened to not be invited, but what am I supposed to say: I need to talk about you to someone who's not *you*? I don't think that would go over very well.

"Just text me when you're on your way back, I guess," he says.

I hang my head; it feels too heavy to keep upright.

What even is this I'm *feeling*? I used to be able to tamp this inconvenient stuff down with tequila, shopping sprees, spontaneous vacations. I guess without the spendy distractions I have to face my dilemmas head-on. Unfair, but necessary.

For a second, I think about shooting off a text to my therapist, booking a virtual appointment like they suggested when I left town, but before I can find their contact, Noelle is back.

I put my phone away.

It's fine. It can wait.

"What was that car crash of a conversation?" Noelle asks, smacking me in the stomach with my own jacket. I stutter, but she holds up a hand. "You know what? Tell me on the way. I really am starving."

* * *

"You did what, where?" Noelle shrieks from the opposite side of the booth.

It's been ages since I set foot in a diner.

Where are the tasting menus, the required dining jackets, and the waitstaff dressed in matching cotton blends carrying full trays of gin and tonics, speared olives on the top of the glasses?

Here, gruff-looking gentlemen are hunched over poached eggs and steaming mugs at the counter. They grumble to one another about the news or the daily crossword. An out-of-service jukebox sits near the door and the vinyl booths, all done in a deep red, have seen better days. Tinfoil snowflakes hang from the ceiling by flimsy paper clips, and I nearly smacked my head on them when we came in.

In my leather Tom Ford jacket, black turtleneck, and Givenchy baseball cap, I turn heads. Even more so due to Noelle's volume.

"Lower your voice. The whole damn town doesn't need to know about it," I say. Funny, considering back in New York I'd be worried about the whole world knowing. Now, I'm concerned about my reputation among the locals, needing—*wanting*, really—them to remain on my side for the gala to go off without a hitch.

"You just spilled some seriously hot tea, and you expect me to lower my voice? Matthew, get a grip! The holiday romance magic is alive and well!" She beams at me as if her psychic abilities have all been confirmed.

As usual, I roll my eyes at her.

Our waitress arrives in a frenzy of flipping order-pad pages. She's got a weathered smile and chipped green fingernail polish. "I'm Ella. What can I get you both?" she asks, red pen at the ready.

I was so busy dishing out gossip that I didn't even get a chance to open the comical, infinite accordion fold of the menu. Noelle reaches out a hand and snatches the laminated tome from my grasp before I get a chance to.

"We'll take an order of Bedrock pancakes to share and two Cokes. We're celebrating!" Noelle says.

"You got it, hun."

Ella starts away and Noelle adds, "You're going to love these. Just as much as you love Hector's sweet, sweet kisses." Her teasing is next level. Both annoying and lovely.

My nose twitches. My mind races. I'm back inside that storage unit. "It only happened twice."

"Is it going to happen *again*?" she asks, leaning in and batting her eyelashes. I suppose I owe her some juicy details after she shared the Natalia stuff.

"It shouldn't, right?" I ask, exasperated. "I need to get this gala off the ground in exactly a week. I still need to call my contact in New York about the special effects for the Future exhibit. Grandma and I still need to sort through old gala photographs for my Past exhibit. The only present I should be concerned about is getting my Present exhibit finished."

"You didn't answer my question," Noelle says, toying with a ketchup bottle.

"Short answer: I don't know."

"Okay, fine. Long-answer me this: Do you *want* it to happen again?"

It was heart-stoppingly surreal. Of course I want it to happen again. I haven't felt this way with a guy in so long. Yet the more I contemplate the idea of kissing and touching him again, the more I fear the drama of it all would consume me.

I mean, he's hung up on Natalia. I'm still nursing the wounds from Baz and Spencer. He's hurting because he's away from his family. My family is on the fritz. Insert romantic and definite sexual attraction into the mix, and you've got a recipe for major disaster. I'm already a walking, talking, bumbling hazard.

"What I want is kind of irrelevant right now. I'm leaving after this gala. That's all I know for sure," I say.

Noelle sighs, almost like she'll be bummed when I leave. "Look, Hector is a snack and a half. He's also a sweetheart. You better get your emotional ducks in a row because I may like you, but if you hurt him, I will rain down the flames of hell upon you."

"Wouldn't the flames of hell rise up?" I ask. She lunges across the table, spilling the pepper shaker in the process, and punches me on the shoulder. It's a pain far worse than Grandma's cheek pinches.

"You know what I mean. If you like him like I think you do, now is the time to shoot your shot. Like I'm doing with Siena! You are capable of genuine human feeling, aren't you?" she asks.

I glare at her with the intensity of a thousand suns. Of course I'm capable of genuine human feeling, but do I really want to be? Out here? Where everything has a flashing countdown clock attached to it?

"We're too different. It would never work. I'm going to open myself up for something that can't and won't last? Seems like a waste of time and energy," I say, hoping she'll tell me I'm right. That the warm, fuzzy emotions I'm snuggling up to are not worth the heartache of losing him when I leave.

"Matthew, I say this because I care, but you need to stop obsessing over what people are going to think of you. I can't pretend to know what it's like to have every move I make taken out of context and splashed across a trashy website, but I do know what it's like to get over other people's perceptions of you." With her hair spreading out like wavy, black vines on the back of the booth, she closes her eyes. "When I graduated from Wind River High, my friends were leaving for big cities, fashion institutes, and state schools. They had prospective majors and interesting career paths. I struggled in school. I was a middle-of-the-road student, with middle-of-the-road test scores, and more school just felt like a punishment rather than an investment in my future."

Our stories sound similar. "What did you do?"

"When I told my dad that I wanted to stay in Wind River, keep working at Moon Beans, and maybe try a Havensmith online class in entrepreneurship at some point, he supported me. And when I walked across the stage on graduation day to collect my diploma in front of my other classmates, my friends, and my girlfriend at the time, they all whooped and cheered when they heard my name. I realized that it didn't matter. Following expectations doesn't make you a better person. Being the person someone says you should be doesn't always make you happy," she says.

I can tell she's been sitting on this pile of pent-up frustrations for a while. Surprising myself, I offer her my hand on the scratched tabletop, and she takes it. We really are kindred spirits. An unspoken understanding passes between us.

In all my years of friendship with Bentley, never have we had a bond this open or true. I barely know Noelle, and she's already accepted me, flaws and all. She may be pushing me toward a devastating ending, but at least she cares enough to see what's good for me when I'm too nearsighted to.

Ella comes back with our Cokes, lemon wedges affixed to the rims, and a plate of pancakes with Fruity Pebbles baked into them. On top is a huge dollop of whipped cream, more cereal, some fresh berries, and a bit of powdered sugar. I'm both disgusted and pleasantly excited.

"You're about to see God, I swear," Noelle says. She takes a forkful and a blob of whipped cream disappears down her sleeve. She doesn't even care. Her eyes light up with intense pleasure at that first bite.

CHAPTER 23

The Blacktop Tavern is a hole-in-the-wall townie bar.

On Sunday night, the crowd is sizable, and the floor is littered with shucked peanut shells. The air is tinged with the smell of burning thin-crust pizza dough.

Hector spots Noelle and Siena at a high-top table in the corner, just far enough away from the rowdy game of pool happening in the back. I follow him over to it, and something snags in my brain.

This is my first date since Baz and Spencer.

I wonder what Hector's thinking right now.

"You made it," Noelle cries, already one drink deep and happily tipsy. Her tolerance must be low. She jumps up and embraces us both. "Sit, sit. We ordered already, but the server said he'd be back when you arrived. Hector, you know Siena."

"Sure, hi. Good to see you again." Hector slings his coat over the top of a stool and sits on it.

"Siena's sister owns the hottest restaurant in Wind River, A Very Fine Vine. Siena works there too. It pairs tasty, Italian-inspired dishes with imported wines. It's the perfect date spot," Noelle says, and then shrinks back, her multicolored sleigh-bell earrings jingle-jangling as she goes. She's said the d-word out loud, making what might have passed as a group hang into a certain setup.

"Pleasure to meet you," I say, sitting across from Siena and trying to move past that. When I glance over to Hector, it appears as if he's chewing on the word as well, biting his bottom lip and pretending to be into the football game on TV.

A handsome guy somewhere north of thirty approaches our table with a pencil behind his gauge-pierced ear and an empty tray in his hands. "'Sup, boys?"

I give him a smile as he produces two menus for us. It's all standard bar fare from wings to fish and chips. The craft beer specials are listed in big bubble letters on a dry-erase whiteboard hanging above the bar.

Once we've put in our orders—a hard seltzer for me and a lager for Hector, a sad-sounding salad and a ribs basket—Gauges leaves, but not without flashing me a toothy smile. It glints in the reflection of the sign behind my head pointing toward the bathrooms. Classy.

As I push up the sleeves of my Fair Isle crewneck, the humidity registering at sweat-inducing levels, Siena looks at my forearm.

"Sweet ink," Siena says.

I flush hot. On my eighteenth birthday, I insisted on getting tattooed. Bentley took me to the best tattoo artist in Williamsburg. She was a bombshell Amy Winehouse type with droves of jet-black hair and a colorful picture book tastefully curated across her body.

We'd emailed back and forth for a few weeks, trying to decide which one of my amateur sketches I'd like inked on me for eternity. This was a hard decision considering I waffle on almost everything. We decided on an open, ornate birdcage. Left inside is a bouquet of colorful flowers. In the distance a lone blackbird is flying away.

"Any significance?" Siena asks.

"Just pretty, I guess," I say, not wanting to get into it. Though from the look on Hector's face, it's clear he might've deduced it's one of my own drawings. I start to slip it back into my sweater.

"Wait, wait," Siena says. She stops me with a hand that's wet from her glass. "I like to play guess and go with new friends and their tats. Is that cool?" She lifts an arm and shows off her own tattoo sleeve.

"Go for it."

Siena leans over the table a bit, her hair falling around her face, to get a closer aerial view.

"All right, well, you got money, that's for sure, because this is some detailed shit. That *shading*. You must've sat for a while for this." Her thumb brushes over it. "And it must've hurt like a motherfucker if you're that sensitive," she adds, noting how that tickled me. "Birdcages suggest some kind of confinement, but the open door and the soaring bird make me think you're escaping something. The flowers left behind feel like what you do at a gravestone. You're mourning a past you? Some self-care shit?" Her hot-chocolate irises, made larger by her glasses—which may or may not be prescription—meet mine again. All I can do is nod. "Then there's the movie *The Birdcage*. Plus that Maya Angelou poem… Now, I'm just free-associating here, but I'd say you got this tattoo at eighteen or nineteen to represent your newfound freedom." Her words land with finality and an impressive sense of authority.

"You got all that from my forearm?" I ask.

"Don't tell me if I'm wrong or we'll be here all night." Siena's laugh is light and charming.

"No, you pretty much nailed it."

"She's like a palm reader but for tattoos," Noelle says.

Siena nudges her with an elbow. "Too bad this one is afraid of needles, so I'll never know what's going on in that pretty head of hers." Siena blushes when she realizes what she said, and now I'm starting to think Noelle didn't need us here at all. Maybe Siena's been harboring feelings for Noelle since last Christmas as well.

"Have you ever thought about getting a tattoo?" I ask Hector.

The table is wobbly, much like my insides, but I lean forward. The tart, acidic hint of cranberry in my seltzer goes down smoothly and turns my stomach into a kiln.

He looks away. "I have one."

"Well, now I have to see it," I say. My eyes scan over every inch of exposed skin.

"It's not exactly in a bar-appropriate place."

"I would argue pretty much any place is appropriate in the right bar."

He raises his eyebrows. "Surprised you haven't noticed it already."

Siena and Noelle laugh with abandon at Hector's relentless read of my open admiration. I knew I wasn't being subtle about my thirst, but his call-out still tickles me. I finish my drink to hide my grin.

At least he can joke about our sexual chemistry. That's a good sign.

The food comes right on cue. I push the soggy lettuce around on my plate. It's drowning in unidentifiable dressing. The smell of Hector's meal makes me wish I'd made a better choice.

"How is gala prep going?" Noelle asks.

I swallow a bite. "Prep is good. We're still on the hunt for the perfect caterer. I'm woefully inexperienced in Wind River cuisine, and I'm sure this place doesn't do events."

"I can see it now. People trying not to get BBQ sauce all over their evening gowns," Hector says.

"Just stock up on napkins. No, no! Better yet, get custom bibs. They can be commemorative," Noelle suggests.

Hector's already sporting a BBQ sauce mustache himself. Without thinking, or at least fully thinking, I lean over with a napkin and clean him off. He lets it happen, the Cupid's bow of his lips revealing itself from beneath the brown sludge, and I get this strange feeling that he might even like it. "Dude, either you've got a strong paternal instinct or you can't stand looking at messy eaters."

"That's it! I have had it up to here with these 'dudes.' You definitely owe me a dollar," I say. I playfully pull up Venmo on my phone.

Siena clears her throat, breaking up the banter. "My sister is one of, if not *the* top chef in town. Why don't you give her a try? She's always wanted to attempt catering. Jack had a family friend from out of town do all the cooking for the gala and imported it on trucks, but with the dining hall kitchen available for use at the college, it might be nice to get an in-house chef and a staff."

In my experience, I remember the excellent crab cakes or the signature cocktail over anything else when I attend one of these philanthropic social functions. The conversations held over side salads and fresh focaccia are what stay with me. My taste buds hold on to my memories.

Siena is showing me food photos from the restaurant. My mouth is already watering over the cacio e pepe as I pick at my pathetic excuse for a salad. "She'd totally let you two come in for a tasting to sample the goods."

I'm about to accept when Dad's caller ID appears on my phone, lying face up on the table. I stall, but ultimately send the call to voicemail. It's his turn to memorize the sound of my prerecorded voice. Let's see how he likes a tiny taste of his own medicine.

At the bottom of our fourth round, we all chip in to close out our tab.

When we hit the parking lot, woozy in all the best ways, the bouncer wishes us a good night. I swear I'm seeing two of Hector's car, one parked on top of the other.

"Crap," Siena says.

"Yeah, we can't drive like this," I say.

I gaze up at the dark night sky. Not a cloud in sight. The moon is huge and hangs over us like a painted scenic prop in a play. The lights of the walk-through can be seen in the distance.

"I'd say we could call a RideShare, but..."

"I'm kind of the only game in town right now," Hector finishes for us.

We all laugh.

With Google Maps pulled up, Hector leads us on the shoulder of the road toward the promised land of lit-up delights.

CHAPTER 24

If someone had told me that looking at a massive Christmas light display while properly buzzed was this fun, Bentley and I would have been doing it a long time ago.

I can see fine and walk in a straight line, but the fun-drunk haze washes over the extravaganza around me. Dangling fish flop into waiting penguin beaks. Santa crashes his whip in the direction of eight athletic reindeer on an endless loop. Lights blink and run and dash around me.

I do a three-sixty spin, which I regret immediately. I lean into Hector for support. His strong arms and tight grip keep me upright. We enter the front gate, purchase our tickets, and join the growing throng of excited families.

Noelle and Siena are cutely cozy, clinging to each other's arms. I wonder if this is a friendly show of affection or a full-blown rekindling of what they had last year.

We hook a right, following a sign toward Santa's Workshop. It's amazing how many niche and probably expensive lighting pieces there are out here. Elves made with weatherproof wire and string lights do a jig in various green outfits, their pointy ears cartoonish. There's a rope keeping us off the grass so as not to disrupt any of the complex wiring being concealed by tape and darkness.

Things like this happen in the city all the time, but there's something touching about the homemade nature of this small yet impressive collection. It's special. I'm becoming a softy out here, aren't I?

This is months of planning, purchasing, designing. All to ensure a good customer experience. It clearly took a village.

I must admit I love this stuff—putting together an experience that people can attend and make memories within. I saw the gala as my ticket out of here, but now I see it more as a chance to prove to myself that I can be an event planner without my ego taking center stage. Hector sure knows how to reel in that monster for me. Unlike Bentley, who feeds that monster if only to match the size and grisly shape of her own.

I shoot Hector a sideways glance. He's awestruck by the LED screens in the distance projecting Elsa's big song in *Frozen*. Or the sequel. Who can keep up anymore? Either way, Hector looks adorable as hundreds of light trees do a coordinated, choreographed dance in time with the music.

Moving on with the crowd, we notice a line snaking into the opening of Santa's Workshop. A camera is set up, facing a throne where Santa himself sits. A child in a white puffy coat wriggles around on his lap.

I yearn for those pressure-free days where looking cute for a Christmas card was enough. When looking cute for the *entire world* wasn't an issue. Little did I know my obsession with image would lead me to buy an island, to here...to *him*.

Which makes me ask in a daze, "Do you want to get our picture taken with Santa?" I need a physical memory of this night. A vestige to cherish when I'm gone.

"Sure," Hector says, full smile.

Noelle glances back at us with a sneaky expression. "You two have fun with that. We're going to...*explore*."

Explore sounds like it means *find a shadowy spot to make out*, but I don't question it for fear it might scare Siena off again. I enjoy seeing Noelle so happy.

"Meet you at the exit at closing?" I ask. She shoots back a thumbs-up.

"Say hi to Santa for us!" Siena calls before they get eaten up by the bustling crowd.

Hector grabs my chilly hand and drags me to the end of a line that is far longer than it needs to be. But I will wait. I'm excited, so this will be worth it.

The alcohol and my layers are keeping me toasty. So is the way Hector looks at me with a big, goofy grin.

To avoid an overt blush, I start reading the pamphlet Noelle handed me on the way in. The organizer and mastermind behind it all is named Wendy Samson, a White trans grassroots organizer with a love for all things Christmas. She owns a garden architecture business, which explains her exquisite use of the town's one-and-only recreational park.

I share my findings with Hector.

"Dude, that's awesome," he says. "Wait!"

"What?" I ask.

He points to a photo of Wendy in a Mrs. Claus costume, holding a pair of those extra-large scissors. "I know her! She runs weekly meetings at the Wind River LGBTQ Center. The Havensmith Queer Advocacy group holds joint events with them sometimes. I met her during one of the sexual health fairs we did during my freshman year."

"Wow. The people in this town really are unicorns."

"*Badass* unicorns," he corrects.

When I look up, I spot a person walking around in a yellow jacket with Lights of Wonder Spectacular stitched on the breast and EMPLOYEE stamped on the back. I wave vigorously at them and they come right over.

"Anything I can help you folks with?" the person asks, face still obscured by the overwhelming backlight.

"My name is Matthew Prince and this is Hector Martinez. Do you happen to know where we can find the organizer of this place?"

"I do because you're looking right at her." The woman steps closer to us. The lines of her kindhearted, round face come into focus. "My name is Wendy Samson. She/they pronouns. This is my special spectacular you're looking at."

"Wow, okay, um, that was easy. Again, I'm Matthew. My pronouns are he/him."

Wendy's eyes land on Hector as he says his pronouns. "Well, hello there. I know you. Aren't you a Havensmith student? You struck it big at that sex-toy bingo I organized for your gang a few years back!"

"Guilty," he says, looking bashful. And now I'm fantasizing about the arsenal of toys he's been hiding from me in our room.

"All eyes were on you that night, that's for sure," she jokes. "This must be your partner." She gestures to me and he freezes up.

We are planning partners. That much is true. Correcting them seems unnecessary given the circumstances, so instead, I jump in to save him.

"We were just hoping to see about getting some of this light artistry assembled near the entryway of Havensmith to welcome guests for the annual charity gala. Is there any way you and your team could swing that?"

"We know it's short notice," Hector adds.

"Oh, that is a fabulous idea. We have a bunch of lights left over that we can repurpose. I'd love a side project to keep the cheer going."

"The event is on the twenty-third—this Friday—so the turnaround will be quite tight," I say.

"I work fast, but I don't work for free," she says, getting right to the point. I appreciate their business acumen and can tell she'd be a strong supporter.

"Right," I say. "What if we promised you prime advertising space at the event? Maybe we print and lay table cards on each place setting? No cost to you, of course. You own a business, right?"

"I do," she says.

"We're expecting a sold-out event," Hector mentions. "And it's all to benefit the SBA."

"I'll tell you what. Since you two seem very sweet, throw in lunch for my crew and a donation to the Wind River LGBTQ Center, and I'm in."

"Done and done," I say. "Is the LGBTQ Center responsible for that rainbow crosswalk downtown?"

"Yes! It was a Pride Month project about four or five years ago. Our organizers are always thinking of fun ways to uplift the community in such a small town. Our meeting space is in the studio apartment above Moon Beans," they say.

It's funny Noelle has never mentioned this, but I guess it never came up. My mind is already thinking about how next year's gala could aid the LGBTQ Center. But I really shouldn't be getting ahead of myself.

I give her my email address. I'm a bona fide professional as we talk shop. She makes suggestions for what fixtures might look nice along the main circle.

"Wendy, we need you over by the snack stand," says a young boy with a walkie-talkie glued to his hand.

"A woman's work never ends," she says with an exaggerated eye roll. "We'll set this up ASAP."

Wendy leaves us to wait. For the first time, that sense of connection I was craving before coming here doesn't just extend to Hector. It extends to this community too.

Even half-drunk, I'm committed to making this gala great for citizens like Wendy who give so much. She deserves to get a little back.

I'm about to say that to Hector when I notice a shift in his expression. He grows quiet as the brunette elf girl ushering the lineup looks at us funny. I choose to ignore her. Shouldn't elves be all smiles and no sass? But it is cold out here and maybe she's had a rough night. It can't be easy wrangling a bunch of overtired children into smiling for a camera with parents insisting on retakes.

That's when I realize it's not just any brunette elf: it's Natalia.

Nothing like running into your maybe-date's ex while drunk and giddy off your ass.

"Hey there," Hector says, his quietness qualified. Only this time I don't see him self-consciously digging around in his pockets. He's standing tall, broad shoulders pulled back. It's a sign that maybe this won't kill our evening.

"Hello," she says, high-pitched and elf-like. Not letting on that this is awkward.

"Good to see you, Nata—" I start.

"It's Twinkle the Elf," she proclaims with a curtsy, and then leans in for a whisper. "Can't spoil the illusion!"

"Right," I say, nodding.

Hector clears his throat. "Didn't expect to see you here."

"Santa always has to travel with a few elves for holly-jolly support," she says, really committing. I don't know what to say to that. "Speaking of, it's your turns to see the big man!"

Slightly uncomfortable and totally off-balance, we shuffle over to the throne.

Santa welcomes us with open arms, *ho-ho-ho-ing* and all that. Hector and I step around to opposite sides of his chair.

"I remember you both when you were *this big*," Santa says, gesturing with his hand to a height even I can't remember being. "You were both cuter then."

"Not all of us get to stay the same age forever," Hector shoots back.

"Magic will do that for ya," he says. Upon closer inspection, the beard is real, the belly is real, and so are the rosy-red cheeks. He's a perfect Santa, all suited up. "Have we been hitting the eggnog this evening?" he asks. He must smell the alcohol on our breath.

"Hope that doesn't get us put on the naughty list," I joke. Hector looks at me conspiratorially. My heart does a spin, a twirl, and for the grand finale, a cartwheel. Perfect tens all around from the still-drunk judging panel inside my head.

"Oh, please. What do you think Santa does in the off-season?" he asks. "Now, what do you boys want for Christmas this year?"

Hector doesn't even hesitate before saying, "I'd really like to get to see my family before the spring semester starts. I'm away from them right now, and I'd just…really like to be with them for at least some of the holiday." I can hear the complicated emotions fighting for dominance in his voice.

Santa reaches a white-gloved hand out to him. A moment passes before Santa replies, "There's no greater gift than family. I'll do my best." He turns to me. "And what about you, young man?"

I puzzle over this, wondering how I can follow that up without sounding shallow, materialistic, or jaded. Quickly, I decide on: "I'd like to feel settled and sure of my future. Be able to find my own way for once." Vulnerability knocks the wind out of me as Santa winks. That was more truth than I intended to share, but I suppose alcohol will do that to you.

"That gift," Santa says, oozing sage warmth, "has always been inside you." He taps his nose as if to illuminate his magic.

Unsure what to say, I smile and nod at Santa before we all turn in toward the camera. Natalia counts down from three and snaps a photo that prints out immediately.

Still sorting through Santa's cryptic yet reassuring message, I watch as Natalia inspects our picture for a tenuous moment before handing it to Hector.

I'm surprised to see her doe eyes filled with something akin to sweet understanding. She leans in again so no one else can hear. "You two look very nice together." She angles in to Hector, squeezing his elbow through his puffy jacket and dropping the act. "I'm happy for you both."

It's clear she's seeing what we've been avoiding. What Scrubs saw at the nursing home. What Wendy assumed moments ago.

There's no more time for denying the obvious. I think Hector feels the same because he says, "Thanks," before smiling shyly at me.

A newfound sobriety comes over us. We walk slower now, slipping into the Candy Cane Forest that loops and turns at various intervals. It's getting later and later and the smaller children are filtering out.

Hector pulls his beanie tighter over his head as a fake-snow machine pumps bubble bath leftovers into the air around us. A little movie magic sprinkled into real life.

We're more keenly connected than we were earlier today. I can sense our chests swelling and shrinking with the same anticipatory rhythm. Our heartbeats add a drum-line remix to the swinging jazz staple coming out of the plentiful speakers.

Once I build up the courage, I say, "Santa can only do so much, so I hope we pull this off and I can help you get home to your family." It's a full honesty bomb dropped between us.

"Thanks, but if it doesn't work out, it won't be the end of the world. If this is where I'm supposed to be right now, then this is where I'm supposed to be." He sounds settled, certain, and not bitter.

"My grandma said the same thing to me the night after I got here. If my parents think this is where I should be, then maybe it *is* where I should be."

At the time, it sounded like a cop-out, an easy bandage to put over the gaping wound of my neglect. But standing here, drinking Hector in, I believe it may be true. My parents, unlikely conduits through which some higher power works, sent me here for a reason. To learn something, maybe, but also to bear witness to whatever this is between us. Weeks ago, I never would have believed this to be possible. I'm not sure I would've even *wanted* it to be possible. Now, it feels…inevitable, almost.

"Maybe we're both where we should be, even if it's not where we would be if we could be where we wanted to be," he says.

"Wait, *what*?" I ask. My brain is still blurry. "That's too many similar words smashed together to process at once."

He stands up straighter and says, "This should be easy to process since everyone else sees it… I have feelings for you, dude."

I'm taken aback by his bluntness, but before I lose my courage, I blurt out my own piece. "I have feelings for you too." The heaviness of that truth becomes a third person standing beside us, an omnipresent observer.

"Okay." He breathes out, relief loosening his shoulders. "Well, what I'm saying is that—God, I hope this doesn't sound horribly cheesy, but I think we're both stuck here for a reason. At first, I thought it was a bad reason. That you were some sort of punishment in a pair of hot-pink pants, but then we talked and kissed and you were *not* what I expected, and suddenly it was a good reason. A really good reason. But then, I don't know, we hooked up…" There's a long fragile silence where his flighty fingers fiddle with the drawstrings on the purple hoodie beneath his coat. "It was my first in a long time. It meant something to me. I didn't expect it to, but it did. It *does*."

I sigh, wistful. "It means something to me too."

"Okay, well, it didn't make me feel great when you ditched me at the college afterward," he says, voicing an upset I should've seen. "I know I should've said something sooner, but…"

"No." I stop him. "Full disclosure, I was anxiety spiraling after what happened in the storage unit." His eyes are glistening coins flipped over to show his concern. "Not like that. It's just because of how overwhelming and amazing it was. I needed that alone time with Noelle to calm down. It wasn't you. I promise."

My unfiltered explanation reassures him enough that he reaches out.

Just a light touch, enough to brush a hair out of my eyes, but it cracks me open a little more.

I don't know if it's the honesty or the alcohol or that I'm finally letting myself buy into the infectious jolliness of Christmas again, but whatever the case, I unwrap my sweeping feelings. The best gift I could give this year. "This—what we have—feels real and I don't want to let that go. Not for a second. So, if you're willing to be patient with me, I have a *proposition*," I say. He meets my gaze with curiosity and a dash of underlying seduction. "I'm going to kiss you again now, and if this kiss still feels like the last ones, I think we should make a deal right here that we forget about our past relationships, our parents, the whole works, and we have fun with this."

"Do you really mean that, dude?" he asks.

"I really mean that, *dude*." God, how has *dude* become the sexiest term of endearment ever?

He shakes his head as the song changes to something by Ella Fitzgerald. I think he might dismiss this, dismiss me. Instead, he does something entirely off script. He grabs each of my elbows and pulls me in.

It catches me off guard, but I settle into it. My lips are slightly chapped and my cheeks are ice cold, but the heat that shoots through my body is stronger than any drink could ever be.

His palms slide down my arms and into my waiting, cradled hands.

His breath tickles my lip for a second, dangerously close.

"Let's do it," he whispers, and then we crash together.

With the music blasting and my heart racing, his lips part, allowing my tongue to slip inside and taste the salty sweetness of his mouth. It's like we're trying desperately to merge on the molecular level, any space between us wasted. His five-o'clock shadow is soft from beard oil underneath my touch. My stomach swoops.

"Just as good as the last ones?" he asks of the kiss, pulling back and searching my face for confirmation.

I shake my head. "*Better.*"

CHAPTER 25

"Welcome to A Very Fine Vine. We're so glad you could join us," says Christina, Siena's older sister and the head chef. She's got wavy hair that's pulled back with a sleek black scrunchie and a professional, close-lipped smile.

The place is mostly empty since this is a dinner-only establishment and it's barely noon. A couple of employees leisurely prepare for the nighttime rush, restocking stations and folding napkins into fancy four-point masterpieces. Though this outing is under the guise of planning, we both dressed up nicer. Hector even smells like a woodsy spritz of cologne.

I believe this is our second date, and I *believe* I'm giddy about it. God help me.

The decor is exposed concrete walls with cracks painted on where glorious vines slither out in different directions. It's not all that different from the kind of award-winning, month-long-waitlist place you can find on nearly every street corner in the Village.

"Hello again." Siena sets the tasting menu on the table: three starters, three entrees, and two choices of dessert. Siena has taken the liberty of bringing us two wooden flight paddles of the corresponding wines, which she assures us are all imported from the rolling hills of Tuscany where their family originated. "Thank you for considering us for this opportunity. We've always wanted to work the gala, but Jack was very set in his ways. It's nice to have this chance, especially since they're honoring the Small Business Association, which is imperative to the support and growth of our restaurant." Siena pivots to Hector. "Have you dined with us before?"

"I have. Always delicious," Hector says. He flushes a little. He's probably remembering meals he shared with Natalia here. After last night and her quasi blessing, that's more than okay. We both have our histories. Pretending won't make moving forward any easier.

When the sisters vanish into the back to prepare our plates, Hector reaches for the first mini glass from the walnut tasting tray before him, so I do the same.

"Who decides what the cause is?" I ask. Plates of to-die-for calamari, a risotto ball, and some sort of micro-green salad with a pleasing pink dressing get placed before us, all so fragrant. Siena tells us to enjoy.

"There's a committee that chooses. SBA provides grants, loans, help with filing incorporation papers, stuff like that. I think they do seminars and workshops too. One of the higher-ups teaches a personal finance class at Havensmith," he says.

When I came around to volunteering, the Small Business Association was a minor detail in my major escape plan. Now, I realize that it's an imperative part of the makeup of this town. It's wild how much I can overlook when I'm so engrossed in my own ego.

"Your grandma would know more about all the ins and outs," Hector says.

"What do you mean?" I ask. I take my first bite and can't help but moan.

"Well, this year's gala is mostly to pool together grant money for struggling businesses. Lorna's place is on the list of recipients."

I stop midchew. This is the first I'm hearing of definite hardship. Sure, the place isn't a revolving door of spending customers, but it has its charms, its town significance, and one of the savviest business ladies running its operations.

"Why doesn't she just ask my parents for money?" I ask, confused.

"Pride, probably," Hector says, mouth hung up on something else. "Maybe other reasons. I don't know. Everyone loves your grandma, but love doesn't always mean spending money."

I'm learning that the hard way. It's weird how almost every conversation Hector and I have comes back to the green menace in the room. Dollar signs roll like slot machine reels above our heads. I wish their incessant clanking would stop. There's no jackpot at the end of this rainbow.

I wonder what Siena and Christina see when they look at us. There are stark contrasts in the way we dress, but does the class disparity show? Am I a shallow asshole for even thinking that? It no longer feels like a deal breaker, but it's still a serious consideration especially with my friends back home. Not to mention the media that sometimes circles me like a hawk.

I don't want to cause Hector any extra hurt. He carries enough as it is.

I can never pretend to know what his journey to self-acceptance was like. In any case, he's probably negotiating that every day. Being White and rich, even identifying as gay rather than bi, allows me mobility he doesn't have, more privileges I've yet to fully take stock of. I've got work to do, personal work. Loads of it, I'm realizing.

Over tiramisu and our last glasses of wine, we drop talk of town-wide struggle and focus on the gala. The only way we can help Lorna's Used Books & Beyond and the whole of Wind River is if we throw a gala where people are ready to throw around their cash. We think A Very Fine Vine should be a part of that success.

Christina and Siena are thrilled when we tell them the news. We discuss logistics: the college kitchen and the presentation of the food. They spit back numbers, both price and staff considerations. The ballpark is hefty, but Hector excuses himself to the bathroom to do some calculations.

Siena twirls her ponytail with her index finger while we wait. "I don't mean to switch gears, and I hope this isn't unprofessional, but do you happen to know if Noelle has a date to the gala? I was going to ask last night but..."

My attention piques. "Your mouths were a little busy?" I wink. "But, no, I don't think she does."

Siena's face lifts. I never thought I'd be plugging a love connection today that wasn't my own, but I'm happy to do a bit of matchmaking for a friend as good as Noelle.

"Glad to hear it," Siena says, nearly giggling.

When Hector returns, he shoots me a thumbs-up behind their backs. We uncork another bottle of wine to celebrate. Hector and I leave full, a little drunk, and happy to be bringing some good to this town.

We decide it's best we take a walk before we head back to the college, and my heart flutters when he discreetly slips his hand into mine. His mittens are soft; my emotions are softer.

At the end of the street, I pull Hector into an alley between two stores. I press him against the wall and kiss him. There's something so hypnotic about his lips.

He tastes like garlic and red wine as our tongues brush together. I become aware of all the layers separating us, and while I want to do this right, I'm really looking forward to the moment when I can slip him out of his clothes.

The storage unit was fucking hot, but seeing him in all his naked glory would be beyond hot. It would be a downright inferno.

I stiffen in my briefs at the mere thought of our sweaty, heaving bodies. It's not until Hector is whispering, "Easy there, dude," into my ear that I realize I'm toying with the elastic of his underwear.

"My bad," I say, taking a step back.

"You *are* bad," he says seductively. He takes my hand in his again and we head back onto the sidewalk. "Stop for a coffee? That will sober us up."

Not to mention giving us time to cool down. I take a cleansing breath.

"Noelle would love an eyeful of this," I say, holding up our waffled hands.

"Let's make her day then, dude."

Little does he know he's already made mine a million times over.

CHAPTER 26

FaceTime from Mom blinks on my phone screen.

It's late afternoon and I'm reading over my to-do list. Hector went out on some rides, noticing his dwindling bank account thanks to the time off from the bookstore. Gala prep has been pushed back to the evening. With the stage dressing set, the tables placed, and the lights in progress, we need to make headway on my special exhibitions.

I press Ignore. It's not like me to avoid Mom, but Hector and I promised we'd keep our focus squarely on us and the gala. No family drama. I'm sticking to that.

Grandma rolls in, a blustery wind whipping at her backside. She slams the door to keep the draft from invading the snug warmth of the house. She looks swept. Her hair is pointing out in all different, funny angles and her tote bags are stuffed to the point of overflowing.

"Do you need some help?" I ask. It's early for her to be home.

"Winter up here is always so persnickety. You're walking a hiking trail midspring and it's like your mind wipes the slate of all the chilly winter memories and then you're hit with a snow squall in December and it all comes rushing back to you," she says. I take her multitude of tote bags and bring them over to an empty chair at the table.

"What is all of this?"

"Take a look," she says knowingly. Inside is a plethora of old photo albums, pharmacy one-hour photo envelopes, CDs, and flash drives. "Jessica at the library helped me. Jack had some at his place too. I collected them for you."

"You didn't have to do all that," I say, touched.

She pats my back with such tenderness. "Least I could do for how hard you're working."

When I sprawl the contents across the table, I'm faced with a multitude of photographs from galas past. What I assumed was some sad town affair turns out to be an elegant celebration. You can tell the decade by the haircuts and outfit choices—colors, dress cuts, tie-and-cummerbund combos. One of the photos, dated from the nineties, even has the look and feel of my masquerade fantasy. Everyone is wearing a red or green mask.

"That year's theme was a literal Secret Santa," Grandma says with a laugh. "Hard to keep up the mystique when you know all your neighbors." She plucks a weighty scrapbook from the bottom of a bunch. "Thought you might be interested in this one."

On one of the back pages is a photo of Mom at twelve years old standing on a stage in front of a microphone and holding a small spiral-bound note-book in her hands. "She'd written a story about a Christmas heist. A jolly, Grinch-like thief was stealing all the Christmas decorations around town."

"I didn't peg Mom for a plagiarist," I say. Her books may be full of well-loved fantasy tropes, but they always have original twists. Creativity is the one trait Mom possesses in droves.

"Oh no. The thief didn't steal them to cancel Christmas," Grandma clarifies. "The thief felt the townsfolk had become disconnected, so they took it upon themselves to create a massive Christmas celebration for everyone as a surprise. The decorations had been repurposed for the good of the many."

"That's sweet."

"Sounds almost prophetic, doesn't it?" Grandma asks, pinching the cheek closest to her. I don't pull away. The pain is worth the closeness curling up inside me. "Your help has been a blessing."

Who am I right now? If I'd had a LinkedIn before coming here, *helping* would not have been on my list of special skills. Now, it seems like it's all I want to do. Maybe the indestructible self I thought I'd cultivated back in Manhattan was just as breakable as every other person's.

I glance back down at the photo, take in Mom's short stature and dark-blond hair. "Do you miss her?" I ask Grandma.

"Haven't seen her in ages, but she calls on occasion." It's obvious from her answer that she's not understanding me.

"No." I point to the girl in the picture. "Do you miss *her*?" I realize I was right. When I arrived and saw Mom's faces in the dusty photo frames, I couldn't reconcile her with the woman I know from New York. The woman who raised me. That's because they're two halves of a whole person, one whom I've never met.

Grandma's mouth is immobile, but her eyes are cast downward. "Sometimes, but that's what being a parent is—watching a person grow and learning to accept them for who they become." She grabs my hands over the book, squeezing them. "When your mother asked if she could send you here, I felt hope for the first time that a door—no, maybe not even a door—maybe a window into our life was reopening." She swipes away the tears before they fall. "Here," she says, reaching for another book and changing the subject.

The next photo she produces is one from a dirty paper envelope. She shuffles until she sees the image that erases any evidence of upset. Upon peeking, I spot an unforgettable face. It's young me—probably eight or so, pre–Mom's books—wearing a wrinkled white robe, holding a folder of sheet music.

"I convinced your mother to come home for one Christmas before her book was published. She'd signed her deal, and I had this inkling that everything was about to change. Call it mother's intuition or what have you." She hands the photo to me. "Gramps and I would never miss a gala, so we got the three of you tickets and when we arrived early, you bawled when you saw the children's choir rehearsing. You wanted so badly to take part. You were sensitive, and it was sweet, so I convinced the director to lend you an extra robe and stick you in the back. You joined the rest of the kiddos for 'Jingle Bells.'"

A hazy memory blooms in my brain.

"You only knew the Ella Fitzgerald version of the song, and since you didn't have time to look over the sheet music with the group before the big performance, at the end you shouted, 'I'm just crazy about horses!' Like she does in her rendition," Grandma says with utter joy. "The whole place was roaring with laughter. You got so red and slipped right off the risers. Your mother nearly had a heart attack thinking you'd hurt yourself. It was the very last Christmas you and your parents spent up here."

The heat of embarrassment is outweighed by the burden of an uncovered past.

That boy in the photo is not a boy I've faced recently. Working with my therapist, it's almost hard to see something like this and not immediately wish I could reach through the paper, shake that boy by the shoulders, and give him all the tools he needs to survive what's ahead. To make better choices. To build better relationships.

I never want to hear Grandma say she'd settle for a window over a door into my life. There shouldn't even be a door. No wood or keys or hinges between us. I want to leave all that in the past. There should only be a clear pathway from now on.

Maybe those lesson-bringing ghosts I summoned when I arrived weren't as literal as Scrooge's, but it seems they've come all the same. Showing me important forgotten moments to inform my present and illuminate my way into the future. Whatever that may hold.

I'm about to ask Grandma about her struggling shop when Hector arrives in the hallway, breaking up my revelation.

The squall must've died down, though remnants of it linger on his coat and his long eyelashes. He smiles at the two of us, as usual, clad in plaid. That smile deserves a shrine, I swear.

Looking at him, taking him in, my future unfurls in a mental scrapbook of memories not yet made. To my delight, Hector's featured in every perfect shot.

Maybe Santa was right. The power of foresight was inside me all along. It just took a provocative nudge to knock it loose.

"Hey. I'd like to get over to the college before another patch of this snow comes through. Wendy's team has been working all day. Can you be ready to go in five?" he asks me.

"Sure," I say, smiling. "Thank you for these. And for this," I tell Grandma.

"Of course, dear. I can't wait to see what you create with them," she says and kisses me on the forehead.

CHAPTER 27

My fingers cramp from all the cutting, taping, gluing, and hanging.

All the photos from Grandma's helpful collection were sorted into piles and tagged, and each given a special place among my Past exhibit. My sketch comes to life one trip up the ladder at a time.

The entryway walls are a collage starting with the oldest at the exterior doors and leading to the most recent, almost like a time machine. I pasted some onto glittery snowflakes, inspired by the ones from the diner (only classier), and hung them from the ceiling using fishing wire to make a magical snowstorm of memories floating down on the guests as they arrive. The snowflakes will sway with the passing breeze. With the right lighting, it'll be an exquisite scene.

Before I pack up my supplies and move to my next task, I notice the photo of me in my choir robe from all those years ago. There are so many reasons to be embarrassed by this. Chief among them my tragic bowl cut and my chubby cheeks, but there's a gentleness about this boy that I miss.

That's enough to send me back toward the 2010s section. I find one spot on the wall where my picture will fit without looking out of place, and I tack it there without another thought. Most people won't notice it, and even if they do, they won't be able to identify me from the missing baby teeth and unruly smile, but I'll know. I'll remember. That's what matters.

"Is that you?" comes Hector's voice from behind me.

I turn to see him standing there, shivering a little. Cute as hell in a hat with fuzzy flaps that fall over his ears. I don't even think about lying to save myself the embarrassment. I'm proud of who I am and where I've been. "Yeah."

He steps closer to get a better look. "You were adorable."

"*Were*?" I scoff.

"Are." He smiles back at me. "You did an incredible job, dude."

"Thank you."

"Even better than your sketches. People are going to be blown away." While I love the compliment, the fact that I've impressed him means more than anyone else's opinion. The awe in his eyes as he tips his head upward to take it all in makes my heart swell. "If you're all finished, you're needed outside."

"Lead the way," I tell him, snatching my coat from one of the nearby folding chairs. He extends a hand, and I happily take it.

Outside, Wendy and the team are joined together on the lawn. Boots crunch in the leftover snow. Everyone tugs their scarves tighter to their necks. Now that they're not working and moving, the cold is creeping in, and everyone is antsy to get home.

"We wanted you to be here when we did this," Wendy says, holding the ends of two different wires. The plug and the receiver. "We've still got some taping down and weatherproofing to do, and the carpet can't be rolled out quite yet, but the majority is done."

Hector tugs me forward. I stand next to Wendy, peering around at all the dormant lights. I'm bouncing with excitement.

"3…2…1!" she shouts.

The college comes alive, shining out for all to see.

Lights race around the archway of the entrance, pulsating. A fence of garland loops around the main parking lot. The stone clock face above the double doors is surrounded by a beautiful wreath that's winking blue and white.

The last of the lights lead like bread crumbs up the steps and through the doors, which are still propped open. Through them, I can see my exhibit swaying in all its fantastic glory. I get choked up for the millionth time since coming here.

"It's better than I could've imagined."

The crew, including Hector, all cheer with approval.

Right on cue, a honk rings out. Noelle hangs out the passenger-side window of the Moon Beans truck, waving her hands and smiling as it rolls up the drive. The owner, a man who may or may not have played Santa at the Lights of Wonder Spectacular the other night, puts the truck in park. Two back flaps fly open.

"Get it while it's hot!" Noelle calls. She begins pouring steaming cups of hot chocolate for the workers.

"My treat!" I shout. Everyone charges over to form a line. Noelle can barely keep up with the demand.

"You did this?" Hector asks.

"Of course," I say, beaming. "I texted Noelle this afternoon, and she said they could swing by after they closed for the day. It's just a gallon or two of hot chocolate." He gives me a worrisome look. "Don't sweat it. I cross-referenced the budget sheet to make sure we had the money for it. They worked out here in the cold all day, while I was inside. They deserve it."

"Cross-referenced the budget sheet? I love it when you talk responsible event-planning to me." Hector puts a proud hand on my waist.

"Oh yeah?" I ask, toying with the drawstrings on his fur-lined hoodie. "Then you're going to love it even more when I say, 'We've got projections to set up.'"

He knocks my elbow with a funny growl. "Of course. Hey, uh"—he glances over at the truck, stalling for a second—"grab us two hot chocolates and meet me in there?"

"Sure."

The line has dissipated, everyone broken off into groups to drink and start to clean up, so Noelle is chatting with Wendy when I step over to place my order. She doesn't miss a conversational beat as she whips up two over-flowing cups with extra marshmallows and candy cane bits.

"Don't dawdle too long out here," Noelle says. "I've heard tell there's something special waiting for you inside."

I squint back at her. "More work?"

"All work and no play makes for a very sad day," says Noelle. Wendy chuckles. I shake my head and slip the agreed-upon amount from my pocket to pay for her services.

"Your money's no good here," Noelle tells me.

"What are you talking about? When I called—"

"Consider it a present from Father Christmas," she says, winking back at her boss. "It was the powdered stuff anyway, so I may have overshot the price. Now, get those cups inside before they get cold!"

Wendy pats my shoulder. "We'll be heading out in ten. I'll send a few people by tomorrow to make sure the finer details get done."

"Perfect. Thank you again," I say. She offers a hug, and I take it.

When I walk in from the cold, the hallway has been transformed. Hector has set up blue lights in the hallway that make my exhibit look like a winter wonderland. A small wind machine makes the snowflakes dance even more. I'm almost tempted to stick out my tongue and try to catch a memory, let it melt there and sink in.

The leather-bound guest book I secured has found its way to the podium next to the door.

Just past those doors, the tables, all covered in lovely vermilion linen, are in a circle around the monumental tree that presides over the place. Fully decorated, it's dazzling. Awe ripples through my abdomen at everything laid out.

I do a lap around the perimeter, looking for Hector. In one corner, the plastic snowmen, refurbished with new smiles, sit up against the white draped backdrop where we will project the snowfall and Santa flying over-head created by Bentley's brother, which I have saved on a flash drive tucked into my pocket.

Down comes an overhead screen, probably used for guest lectures and the likes, to my right. Hector appears around the side of the tree holding a remote. The projector takes a moment to turn on, but when it does, the home menu for the DVD version of *Home Alone 2* comes on the screen.

"Figured you could use a little reminder of Manhattan since you can't be there," he says. Then, I notice that on the far side of the tree he's repurposed one of the tablecloths as a picnic blanket. A wicker basket sits half-open. Inside is a collection of cookies.

"This is super sweet," I coo. I can't think of anything more escapist than watching some kid brutally beat up two crooks trying to track him down in the greatest city in the world. I never quite understood the Christmas component, but I enjoy it nonetheless. "But weren't you the one complaining we had so much still to do the other day? I still have to align the projections."

He holds up a hand. "Hard work feeds the soul, but rest fuels the body." He wheels a cart out from behind one of the tables. On it are rolls of wrapping paper and stacks of card stock. Each page has script names and table numbers on them. "I figured we could multitask. We still have place cards to fold and decorative boxes to wrap."

I set down the hot chocolates while he starts up the movie. The gala may be the literal project, but getting to know him feels like the real race to the finish line. This sweet gesture tells me a lot about his romantic side. Hints at what he might plan for a big anniversary or Valentine's Day.

I hand him a dark-chocolate peppermint cookie, and he hands me a box to wrap.

We work in silence for a while. The movie provides ample entertainment after a tiring day, and the pleasing satisfaction of scissors gliding along paper rolls is soothing.

"Do you ever wonder what happened to Macaulay Culkin?" Hector asks. "Child stars must have to go through a lot of nonsense. But on the plus side, he's probably still making major bank from this movie. It's iconic and on almost every cable channel this time of year." It must register to him that my own upbringing in the public eye may not have been Culkin level, but it was still very intense. "Sorry."

"Don't be," I say, taking a second cookie, hoping the sugar rush overrides my nervous system.

"What's it like, *the Big Apple*? Is it everything the movies say it is?"

"It's fabulous, lively. It's actually better than the movies make it out to be."

"I've never been. Between school and work and the other nine million things there are to get done, I don't have the time or the money to travel. I've never seen the appeal per se, but I've always been curious." He casts his eyes away, growing reserved.

I think about extending the invitation for him to come and visit me there once we succeed with this gala, once we've both fulfilled our ends of the deal, but is that what he's insinuating? Our time together here has been wonderful; however, I fret over whether he'd fit in on that island. Jeez, why is everything about *islands*?

He'd hate the bustle, the crowds, the attention. My life is only bustle, crowds, and attention.

Here, I got to adapt to a different pace, but I don't think I can stay moving this glacially forever, so I keep the offer to myself. For now.

"Could've fooled me. All those times you dismissed it as a cesspool of people in objectionable pink pants." The joke acts as a buffer between this perfect moment and the real stuff to come. The inevitable juncture when I will return to the towering skyline and busy sidewalks.

"I've seen the error of my ways, dude," he says with a snort. "First perceptions aren't always right." His eyes flick back to me with clear intention. "I've been pleasantly surprised before."

I let that sentiment sink in for a second, happy in the knowledge that he sees me differently now. That I'm not the bitch behind the sunglasses who blew into town with no regard for anyone else.

"Does that mean you'll try on the pink pants for me?" I ask, dying to see Hector in a piece so out of his comfort zone.

"You wish, dude," he says, focusing again.

His nimble hands begin grouping the cards together and cutting them up, but his gold-flecked eyes keep glancing over at me. I tape with crisp precision, trying not to let him distract me too much from the task at hand.

"Did the present platitudes get done too?" I ask.

He nods, handing me a plastic-wrapped deck of calligraphy cards. They say things like *Drink in the moment like a cup of eggnog* and *The Present is the greatest present of all*. Corny, but in a cute way.

I pass him another cookie, a caramel one this time, and our fingers brush. A frisson of heat traps us there.

Wrap three boxes and then you can kiss him, I tell myself. *Wrap six boxes and you can make out a little,* I add. *Slap the golden phrases on all six, and you can do even more if he's in the mood.*

I work fast with my new incentive system. The caffeine and my hormones mix into a dizzying cocktail coursing through my veins.

A little before the halfway mark of the movie, Hector's hand inches toward my thigh. The heat of his palm through my jeans is titillating. We begin creeping our mouths toward each other. I'm desperate for him, so we kiss with an openness that thrills me.

One of his hands goes up under my sweater and onto the bare, sensitive skin of my stomach. The tickle causes me to balk, but on the exhale, I press into it. I allow his fingertips to trace over my belly button.

We recline so that he's nestled into my side. He fits so well there.

I reach for the zipper of his pants, overeager to please. We begin to undress each other, piece by piece, really seeing each other this time, taking extra care to kiss and lick every inch of revealed skin. We're both glistening in the low lighting.

That's when I see it. The tattoo is on the inside of his left bicep. It's a small depiction of Don Quixote riding Rocinante while holding a sword and a shield, done to look like one thin continuous line of ink. Hector flexes at my sudden touch, and I swear I watch the horse take life and gallop toward the crook of his elbow.

"It's…" he begins, but I cut him off.

"I know."

I'm overcome with the urge to absorb him. I kiss him hastier, hungrier.

We fumble awkwardly as the shiny cloth slips underneath us. Our heads crash together at one point, knocking our teeth, but it elicits nothing more than a laugh, a repositioning, and a further opening of ourselves to each other.

Yes, yes, yes…

Just as I'm about to undress him fully for the first time, a flashlight flicks into the space.

No, no, no!

Thank God this ginormous tree is covering us. There's a moment where neither of us knows what to do, but then Hector collects himself with the speed of a quick-change artist, pauses the film, and steps out into the light.

"Who's in here? What's going on?" a gruff campus security officer calls into the semidarkness. My half-naked body shivers at the sudden gust of cold air invading the hall.

Hector waves a hand. "Hi, sorry, sir. I'm planning the holiday gala and we were just doing a little late-night setup. We can clear out if it's too late." His voice is impressively even and calculated. I never could've done that.

"Oh, uh, we thought everyone went home already. Well, no rush, but we want to lock up, so once you leave, you can't reenter. Make sure to shut this all down and unplug everything," he says. I hold back a laugh because he sounds young and new at his job, probably hapless in any situation but this one especially.

"You got it. Have a good evening," Hector says.

"You too."

When the door is safely shut, Hector returns to my side. We look at each other and crack up. The mood may have passed, but the intimacy is still there, dancing around us like sugar plums in the silence as we continue to work.

An hour or so later, after we pack up the picnic and the presents, lock the doors and shut off the lights, we step out into another light snowfall that's dusted the walkways. The flurry looks like the one I made in the hallway, trickling down in twirling, skittering flakes. The soft wind knocks them every which way.

Hector goes to unplug the light display like Wendy taught him, but before he can reach the extension cord, I tug him back by his sleeve, overcome and needing him to know it. His gesture tonight was beyond adorable. I've never known this kind of care.

"Kiss me first," I say to him. "I want to remember us like this." Snowflakes collect on his shoulders and the edges of his scarf. He's a winter dream as he steps closer, closing the gap between us.

"Who knew a little snow could turn a Scrooge into a romantic?" he teases.

I roll my eyes, shake my head, and kiss him like I mean it.

Because I do. I mean it with my whole damn heart.

CHAPTER 28

Morning clarity comes with the first rays of sunlight: Hector and I are getting serious.

I brush my teeth in the bathroom and brace for panic, but no Krampus charges through my skull. Instead, my heartbeat and breathing remain steady and even. I spit spearmint foam into the sink, stare at myself in the mirror, and realize that falling for the guy in the top bunk might be the healthiest decision I've made in a long time.

Back in the bedroom, Hector can be seen through the sliding door. He's chopping wood again, his mouth in a tiny, puckered O. He's whistling a happy tune, I can tell.

I slip into different clothes and run up to the main floor with a newfound joie de vivre. I'm replaying last night on repeat, dissecting all the little ways Hector lit me up with his comfort, care, and roaming caresses.

That's until I see a familiar face sitting at the kitchen table, makeup done, French-tipped nails resting around the brim of the gingerbread coffee mug I've been using since I arrived.

"Mom?" I ask, skidding to a stop. "What are you doing here?"

"A hello would be nice," she says, getting up, crossing the room in four strides, and then hugging me with all the warmth of a blast freezer. "You weren't answering my calls and I was worried about you."

Grandma catches my eye from across the kitchen. The way she scrunches up her mouth means she wants to say *I'm sorry*, but she can't right now. Mom leans back, looking me over.

"Are you just here for the day? Did someone drive you? What's going on?" I have twenty-seven more questions for her, but these are the only ones I can formulate because right outside, Hector is hard at work. Despite my better instincts, I'm uncertain what Mom will think of him. I'm even more uncertain how to introduce him.

We've surpassed sharers-of-bunk-beds and odd-couple-working-together. We've even surpassed casual friends. We made a pact, but I don't expect Mom to understand any of that.

"I thought it would be nice if we could go somewhere to talk," she says. Her expression hasn't changed from the straightforward stare she plastered on when she greeted me.

She's not some monster of a mother. I know she cares. I know she loves me. But she has this habit of acting like Anna Winston-Prince the author instead of Anna Winston-Prince the woman who raised me whenever we've been apart for a significant period.

I hate it. It makes me feel like some fan who's waiting for her to sign my books. There are few moments in my life where I have felt like just her son, plain and uncomplicated. The last was when I got into NYU. Look how that worked out.

All the other moments on the timeline of my life have fluctuated somewhere between a priority that needs to be dealt with or a hindrance that needs to be dealt with. I'm curious how she sees me now.

"There's that cozy parlor in the B and B that does afternoon tea. Wouldn't that be nice?"

"Sure," I say, not in the mood or mindset to argue. "Let me just grab my coat."

"Perfect. Maxim already left. I'll call us a RideShare," she says.

It's not until I'm halfway down the steps that I realize what that means... but it's too late.

··*

The awkward in this car could be cut through with a knife.

I vacillated at the passengers' side between the front seat next to Hector and the back seat next to Mom. I decided the safe choice was the back seat since that's what Mom would expect of me, but when I try to catch Hector's eyes in the rearview mirror, he either won't meet mine or he hasn't noticed.

Never has our disparity been more pronounced.

"How serendipitous that you're staying with my parents, Hector. Thank you for the ride. I do appreciate it," Mom says, making herself more comfortable than necessary for such a short ride. We're only going down the hill and into Havensmith Hollow.

"When duty calls," he says. There's a clipped rhythm to his words. I bite my lip.

"How are you two getting along?" Mom asks. "I know my Matthew can be a bit of a handful."

"We're getting on all right. We've been planning the gala together, so we've been seeing a lot of one another," he says. I blush, thinking back on last night and just how much of him I got to see. I'm still craving more, even though thoughts of satiating that craving are the last ones I need right now.

"Matthew, you didn't tell me you were collaborating. That's wonderful. Back home, he refuses help with any of his lavish parties. Aside from the hired help, that is. If there were something above type A, that's Matthew. He gets that from me," she says, as if this were a point of unadulterated pride.

"I didn't tell you a lot of things," I mutter under my breath.

Before she can ask for an explanation, we pull up outside of Rosalie's inn.

Mom makes a big show of tipping Hector and gives him a five-star rating on the app before leading the charge inside. I mouth a thank-you to him. He swipes a don't-worry-about-it hand through the air, but his mouth doesn't tip up into a perfect crescent moon. Instead, it stays stern like it was on that first day, and a scared feeling rushes through me.

Last night, I could tell he was on the verge of asking what will happen when I return to New York. How sturdy we are. Whether I'll do what Natalia did. I wanted to reassure him. I wanted to stroke his hair and tell him this good thing *could* last. But I didn't want to disrupt the moment. Speak a possible false reality into existence.

Has Mom's abrupt appearance scared him now too?

Should I tell her the truth about him? It's practically all I keep asking myself as Rosalie escorts us into the reading room where lacquered tables sit picturesquely up against rows and rows of weathered books, probably from Grandma's store. The bindings are arranged by color and the bookends are small busts of literary authors.

"Back so soon, huh, Mr. Prince?" Rosalie asks, a shady note to her voice.

"So soon?" Mom asks.

"It's a long story," I huff.

There's only one other couple in here, two elderly gentlemen wearing newsboy caps and worn-out loafers. They don't look at each other over their unfurled newspapers as they nurse their hot tea with shaky hands.

Rosalie places the extensive tea list down before us, along with a pair of flowery saucers.

Mom wants the deluxe afternoon tea, which comes with champagne, naturally, and since she's the one who traveled all morning, I don't protest that it's not even one in the afternoon.

We settle on a pot of the Christmas blend to share. My stomach rumbles to remind me I haven't eaten anything. This impending conversation is seriously testing my appetite, an unfortunate symptom of my anxiety.

"What are you doing here?" I finally ask.

"I'm going to be in town through the gala. Had to see your handiwork for myself. I'm staying in the suite here," she says. Of course she could swing the suite at the last minute while I was on my hands and knees begging for a cot in the back garden. "I think it's best to be away from the city and the chaos for a while. To catch up with everyone."

"What about all the meetings and the parties and the musical?" I ask.

"I had my people scrub my calendar. I wrote handwritten apologies on the drive over to everyone I'd miss. Don't worry about that. I'm here for you," she says, affected in a way I'm not used to. She grabs my hand in hers. It's a tender moment that I want to be true, but can't be sure about. "I hope you don't hate me too much for sending you here."

There's a frightful forwardness and uncomfortable intensity to the statement. She either wants to evoke the right reaction or she means it. I can never tell with her what's real and what's fiction.

"No, it's been…" I fumble over what to say. "It's been good, actually." And I mean it. From the bottom of my heart, the sentence resonates with a truth even I'm surprised by.

She gives me a satisfied smile from behind her teacup. Does she suspect something, or is she relieved?

"That's *good*." She sips for a while, putting us in a holding pattern. Does she want to say something else? "I won't get in your way these next couple of days. You'll be able to finish planning the gala and getting everything in order. I'm going to relax for the first time in what feels like forever. No writing and no calls. I'm going completely dark as well."

"That's not like you," I say suspiciously. Mine was a punishment. Hers is elective? To prove her point, she sets her phone on airplane mode and slips it into her bag.

"Planning a gala for someone other than yourself is not like you either, but perhaps we're all due for some growth." She clasps her hands in front of her. "Speaking of which, your father and I have agreed that should all go well at the gala, you're free to return home and throw your New Year's Eve party."

Her words rock me to my core. Leave? So soon? It's hard to consider, even though that had been my original goal from the start. So much—*too much*, maybe—has shifted.

"You're serious?" I ask. Amid all the planning, I forgot to even check in with Bentley to see if she's completed any of the urgent tasks from the brimming folder I sent her.

"We're impressed with the initiative you're taking. Christmas cookies? Light walk-throughs? It's all very unlike you, which was the desired outcome," she says, though I'm unsure whether she knows how much like an insult that sounds.

I'm confused. "Is Sarah Pearson in on this? Was she consulted?"

"Miss Pearson is not your mother. I'm your mother. And I think I can make whatever decisions I so choose as such," she says. "Unless you'd rather stay, which by all means go ahead and do so if you don't want to spend the holiday with your father and me, but—"

"No! I do. It's just…" It's all I've wanted since tradition slipped through our fingers. It's why I've tried to convince myself I hate Christmas. Create distance to avoid the colossal letdown. "I wasn't expecting that." My whisper nearly gets drowned out by the clanking of cups and the incoming of a new, chatty group. Processing is impossible, especially when I was hoping for this outcome all along. It's like a fever dream, yet it churns like a nightmare. Never did I imagine having something—someone—here that would make leaving unimaginable.

Any second now, I'm going to wake up in my bottom bunk with a dewy forehead and a backache. I'm sure of it.

Except there's Mom, in the flesh, sitting across from me, squinting over her strawberry jam sandwich. "Again, impress me with the gala, and the Town Car will be waiting." I don't need her to lay out the alternative, which is that I'll finish my sentence here and then come back to New York quietly in the new year.

Hector swims into mind. I don't think I'm ready to leave him, and parsing that out is going to take time, time that I sincerely don't have.

The conversation pivots away from the heavy stuff. She asks about the gala and about what embarrassing stories Grandma and Gramps have told me about her. I tell her about getting the tree, Noelle, and Arthur. There's a massive shift in her expression at the mention of his name. I file that face away for later and finish my tea.

By the end of our time together, both my heart and stomach are overstuffed.

CHAPTER 29

When I return to Grandma and Gramps's place, the two of them head back out to meet Mom in town. She's treating them to dinner at A Very Fine Vine, a nice gesture that feels more genuine now that I've come around to the idea of her here. Even if she was acting slightly strange.

The house is silent, a calm I've finally gotten used to. I wonder if Hector is in our room, out back, or on a ride. I haven't heard from him since he dropped me off this afternoon, and as the day ticks away into darkness, I realize we have the place to ourselves for at least a few hours.

When I skip downstairs, I find Hector's bed made, his books all arranged, and not a single piece of clothing lying on the brown carpeted floor. It's uncharacteristically clean.

Hector's perched on the edge of my bunk with a copy of *A Christmas Carol* open in his lap. It's the copy I haphazardly pulled from his stack on the night of my not-so-great escape. He's running his fingers over my liner notes like he can decipher more through touch than sight alone.

A floorboard creaks below me, giving away my position. He snaps the book shut.

"I notice you've cleaned up," I say.

"Oh, yeah. Nervous habit."

"What are you nervous about?"

He makes a *pahpahpah* sound before admitting, "Something stupid."

"Doesn't sound stupid," I say, remembering how he made my coping mechanism feel like the most normal, natural thing in the world not so long ago.

"I was afraid your mom was here to take you home and that you'd leave tonight," he says. I shift my weight. The heat of his care crackles between us. I'm tempted to poke the embers and see what other feelings might spark. Instead, I reassure him the way I'd want to be if I were in his shoes.

"Nothing to be nervous about. She's here through the gala. You've got more days of me," I say, going over to sit in the rocking chair. I know I should tell him about Mom's offer, but it doesn't appear to be the right time.

"Is that a threat or a promise?" he asks.

God, I could stare at that smirk forever.

"So, what was your plan if I *was* leaving? Did you come down here to hide all my stuff? Steal my suitcases like you could've on that second night?"

He dips his head, hides his blush. "No, nothing like that. It's just that I realized when you go back to New York, I'll be here or in Texas and you'll be there or jet-setting around the world and, I don't know, dude. Distance and I aren't exactly good buddies."

He says distance, but I think he means *long distance*. He may be over Natalia, she may be over him, but the distrust she left behind lingers in the depths of his heart. Now I really can't tell him about what Mom said. There's no use letting him worry about it.

I have too much to think about. On one hand, with my accounts unfrozen, I could easily get him into the city for my party before having him fly home on New Year's Day, but… Again, what would Bentley say? What would the internet trolls say? I don't want to bring him under the lens of scrutiny.

We can't hide behind the excuse that we're in it for the social and commercial gain. I can't pretend I'm removed from it somehow. We're a bundle of raw, hot emotion.

There's a fantasy world where I stay and celebrate in Wind River. Maybe we all get wasted at the Blacktop Tavern, sing bad karaoke, and I pretend my old life doesn't exist for a little while longer, but wouldn't that just be delaying the inevitable?

Both poles have a strong pull, and I'm being torn between them.

"We'll figure it out," I say. "We'll have to, won't we?"

He nods, reopens the book in his hands, and shows me the notes. "When did you do these?"

"How do you know I did them?" I ask.

He shrugs. "The handwriting and the doodles in your sketchbook. They are almost identical to the ones in here. Of course, the stuff in your sketchbook is a bit more refined now. More mature. Still, it wasn't hard to put two and two together."

"I was probably ten," I say and I tell him about Thanksgivings, the agreement me and Gramps made, and all the books I read by reading light on car rides home.

"You were an English major in the making," he jokes.

"I don't think I was doing any critical analysis. I just liked stories."

He stacks the book back on the pile, careful not to disrupt the balance of all the other titles nearby. "But you don't want to write your own like your mom?"

"Nope. Never," I say. "This is going to sound silly, but I always loved the big events in those books. The Jane Austen-esque parties, the big dance scene in *Little Women*, or Fezziwig's annual Christmas Ball. They set the stage for so many interesting interactions, different people coming together, making new connections. I think that's what I love about planning events. I make space for new stories to start and old stories to collect new meaning."

"That's beautiful." He flashes me a winsome smile.

"Thanks. But I'm so afraid of doing anything in a true, professional capacity because what if I fail? Failure seems to follow me everywhere these days. Success is the only marker of worth in my family. I've always been so afraid of what people and my parents would think if I put my mind to something and it fell apart." Prince-a-Palooza comes to mind too quickly.

"And now?" he asks.

"Now I'm still scared, but coming around to the idea of being a bit more fearless," I say. "Thanks for that, by the way." He shrugs it off. "What about you?"

"I think I want to follow in my mom's former path and do the academic circuit, while working on a novel or a collection of short stories. Maybe I'll do Spanish-to-English translations? I mean, that's the dream, but we'll see what happens, what grad schools will have me," he says, then stands suddenly. "My fear is that I'll always live in this uncertain in-between place. Forever a student. Forever on the margins. That I'll never be enough." I want to say that he's enough for me. That he always will be. But I don't want to interrupt.

"I don't know if I can do it. Any of it," he admits shakily. "I just don't know, dude."

"I think you might be the hardest-working person I've ever met," I say. Compliments have never come naturally to me, and yet with him, they flow freely without worry. "There's no *if*. You *can* do it. I know it."

"It's the dollars and cents of it all that scares me. How will I work off the loans? How will I make money? It's not a surefire pursuit, and what jobs are out there for us now anyway?" he asks. "Well, not *us* as in you and me. You don't really need a..." His voice trails off. "Can we stay away from the overarching-life-goals talk for tonight and just be together? These next few days are going to be hectic getting everything settled for the gala, and your grandparents are out..."

He doesn't need to ask me twice. I go to him, braid my arms around his back, and tug him close. He smells of laundry detergent and cranberry hand soap. I give each of his cheeks a kiss before planting one on his lips.

He gasps into me as if I'm a balloon he's trying to inflate. The longer we hold there, the more it's like I'm levitating over the ground, but still fully in my body. This isn't the anxiety-attack float I've become accustomed to. This is the out-of-body magical float that feels amazing.

With both hands firmly on his pecs, I press him down onto his back on top of the soft gray duvet lining my bed, a welcome change from the hard Great Hall floor. I straddle his hips and take off my shirt, careful not to crack my head on the bunk above, before helping him out of his pants.

I run my hands up his naked thighs. I'm in control of myself, yet he's controlling me. I'm controlling his pleasure, yet I'm obtaining pleasure from pleasuring him. It's nearly too natural—our now-naked bodies parallel and panting.

I take him in my mouth, the way I did his fingers. Soft, long strokes of my tongue and wisps of hot breath elicit strong verbal reactions that spur me on. My eagerness mounts in time with my speed. I try different tempos, allowing his shudders to dictate the pressure, the depth. The repetitive act is a calming reset.

His hands stitch through my hair, gripping at the roots. Guiding me toward what he likes. It feels amazing.

When it becomes too much for him, he switches it up, placing a gentle hand on my shoulder. "My turn," he purrs. He returns the favor with vigor.

Seeing him there—not just anyone, but *Hector Martinez*—between my thighs is enough to make me short-circuit. The edge—the oh-so-tempting edge—creeps closer, building and building beneath my red-hot skin. And right before I teeter too far, he slips a condom and lube out of a drawer in the entertainment console, as if last night had been foreshadowing this all along and he knew the prelude would pull us here. We both stop, uncertain. We're doing the who's-on-first bit with our eyes (as if the bit were about bottoming and not about baseball).

"I want you inside me," he whispers.

I couldn't be more game. It takes time and patience, gentle fingers and one of the smaller sex toys from his well-hidden collection. He's a beautiful mess of whimpering moans and satisfied smiles. When he can't take it any longer, the begging starts, and even though this role reversal is like a symphony to my ears, I don't make him wait…*too long*.

I suit up and slip inside him with some expected trial and error.

"There," he groans when I get it right. "*There.*"

A newfound bliss billows through my body once I settle into position. We hold *there* for a minute, two minutes, gasping, before beginning to rock in time with each other. Our communal breath becomes labored, and our bodies are ablaze.

"Are you okay? Does this feel okay?" I ask, noticing the profound emotion evident on his face.

"It feels more than okay," he chokes out. His hands find the back of my neck and he pulls me into a deep kiss.

We aren't just having sex; we're taking an oath to be tender and true. For now? For forever? Who's to say for sure? There are only this moment and the next few days.

And a while later, after we both come, I resign myself to the fact that's okay. Not everything can be as cut-and-dried as it is on the page or in my mind. There are infinite possibilities for what's ahead, and whichever possibility plays out, I'll make peace with it.

I curl into his pleasingly sweaty body right as he whispers, "We make a good team."

I quiver in agreement, thinking back on our baking challenge. Never has he sounded so sure, so settled on the idea of us as a pair.

Minutes go by before he shifts from our cuddle, stands, and offers me a hand. He grabs a set of towels from the rack near the door and we head into the bathroom together.

The water runs cold for a while before anything warm enough to step into spits out. Under the low shower head, rotating in and out of the steam, he takes the bar of soap from the dish and begins to lather it in his hands. With reverent strokes, he scrubs my chest, my back, my arms, my everything.

It's scarily intimate, yet invigorating. And when not a single toe hasn't been given its own attention, I return the favor. I allow my palms to become explorers on an expedition of uncharted crevices. They wander the hollows of his underarms and the dimple in his lower back, until he's softly moaning my name once more. I take this moment to snap as many mental pictures as I can.

"Round two?" I ask, wiping the water from my eyes, not wanting to ignore his growing fullness any longer.

A wicked grin gives away his enthusiastic answer.

CHAPTER 30

The night air nips at my puffy cheeks as we exit the Great Hall a little after 10:00 p.m. The paths are salted and clear for our guests. The parking lot is devoid of other cars, thanks to all the students being home for the holidays. It's just me, Hector, and the starry sky.

Everything is done now. Displays are set. Auction items are locked up. Guest lists are confirmed. The event is sold out. Grandma says it's the first time in four years that has happened. It doesn't feel like I can relax yet though. The execution is the most daunting part. Tomorrow night will be the true test of our work. Will it all come together? Or will it all come crashing down in one dramatic flourish? Only time will tell.

When we get to Hector's car, he stops and looks at his keys.

"Here," he says, handing them over.

"We are not playing this game again," I say.

"Come on. A few laps around the parking lot? You taught me how to waltz. I think it's time I teach you a lesson or two."

"I can think of a few other lessons I'd like you to teach me…"

He frowns at me, but there's a speck of intrigue there too. "Be serious for a second."

I hesitate. There's so much else to worry about that I don't need to add totaling Hector's car to the list, but he gets me with those damn dreamy eyes and I relent. I get into the driver's seat, shaking minimally.

He walks me through the PRNDL shift again. It's an automatic, so obviously I don't need to worry about changing gears. The only floodlights in the parking lot are around the perimeter, which is good because that means there are no glaring objects for me to crash into.

"Ease it nice and slow into drive and tap the gas," he says.

The car plunks into motion. I brake fast, scared suddenly.

"It's okay. Take your time. I'm here, and I've got my hand on the emergency brake." He makes a big show of grabbing the black plastic handle between us.

I glide the car through the parking spot and into the lane. He reminds me to keep my hands at ten and two like numbers on a clock face. We come to the end of a row, and I pause too long at the stop sign.

"Hand-over-hand turn, okay?" he says. I signal my blinker just to stall a second more and then I execute a crisp left turn.

"Maybe this *is* like riding a bike," I say.

"Okay, don't get cocky now."

We drive in circles for some time. It's peaceful and it helps me forget all about tomorrow night's jitters. Kelly Clarkson riffs through the speakers, giving me a diva boost into the stratosphere. Hector grows more comfortable, so he moves his hand from the brake to my thigh.

"Do not distract me right now. I'm in the *zone*," I say.

"Sorry!" he says. He asks if I'm up for a challenge. "A three-point turn, perhaps?"

"Again, Princes don't retreat when the gauntlet is thrown," I remind him.

"It's like you're drawing the letter K with the car," he says.

I take it in stride. My lines are jerky and my handling leaves a lot to be desired, but when I pull out straight, Hector smiles at me. Pride rockets in my abdomen.

"You're a natural," he says.

I cheer. "Think I can drive RideShare now?"

"I'm willing to put my own life at risk, but please don't play roulette with the citizens of Wind River." He grabs the handle above the door as I speed up a little, doing one final victory lap, banshee screaming the whole way, before putting it in park.

Looking out on the Havensmith main building, I can tell we're both playing back a montage of shared memories, all those sentimental moments that led us here tonight. Together. This isn't official and this may not last, but it is incredible right now.

Unless I decide to take Mom up on her offer…

"Do you think we're ready for tomorrow night?" I ask, sensing my own anxieties as rough stones in my stomach. I don't want to give myself over to them, but it's an ingrained habit at this point. What if I publicly screw everything up again? I can only take so many floggings before I become one giant bruise on the back of the universe.

He grabs my hand with assurance. The fears swiftly drain out of me.

"I know we are," he says.

And I choose to believe him.

CHAPTER 31

Hector and I stand flanking the double doors leading into the Great Hall. He wears a formfitting, maroon collared shirt and a skinny black tie. No jacket. But he doesn't need one to look debonair. Especially not with those wood-chopping arms straining the fabric of his sleeves.

His hair is down, but slicked back with pomade. He let me style him for the occasion, and I can't keep my eyes away as we greet everyone.

Townies young and old come up the front walk dressed to the nines for an evening of cocktails and conversation, music and merriment. I spy on Grandma, Gramps, and Mom as they find old photos of themselves in my Christmas Past mobile. The smiles they wear, complementing Grandma's shiny necklace and Gramps's shinier cuff links, energize me for the night ahead.

I feel good, prepared, the right amount of worried excitement. I've only asked myself *What could go wrong?* about twenty times as opposed to my usual two hundred. That's a major achievement for me.

I direct a young couple toward the leather-bound guest book just inside. Across the way, children in poofy, cupcake-like dresses and sharp, penguin-like tuxedos frolic in the Christmas Yet-to-Come exhibit, which, if I do say so myself, rivals even what the best Disney Imagineers could come up with.

People who I met when I was a boy, but whose names don't ring a bell, congratulate me on a job well done. I direct them to Hector, allowing the spotlight to soak us both. This isn't the basement bash they're used to. Sure, it's not the Met Gala, but to them, this is a night they won't soon forget.

As the last of the guests arrive, grabbing their table cards from the organized display, I head in to ensure everything is all right. We decided last-minute to do away with the tables right around the Christmas tree. In their place, we used leftover string lights to create a circular barrier between the dining area and the tree. This was both to give the Christmas Present section its own special moment and to create a ring where couples could dance.

Within it, Dean Graft holds his wife, a beautiful brunette woman in a shiny, deep-green dress. Wendy Samson is there too, looking ravishing in red. She dances with Kendra from the salon. All of them sway in time to Swingin' Six who are set up onstage, playing a jumpy rendition of "Rockin' Around the Christmas Tree." The air is abuzz, and the smell of the hors d'oeuvres wafts from roving trays. I stop one of Christina's girls, wearing spotless white gloves and rented tails, and grab a risotto ball.

Hector comes up beside me. "Look what we did."

"Couldn't have done it without you," I say.

"I told you hard work feeds the soul," he says. I roll my eyes, knowing he's right but not wanting to give him that satisfaction. "Can I have this dance?"

I take his hand. "Gladly."

He leads me out onto the dance floor, and I do a general sweep for Mom. I don't need her prying eye perceiving this perfect moment. Thankfully, she's dipping out the side door in the direction of the restrooms, phone in hand.

At ease locked in Hector's embrace (it's clear he's been practicing), I look at all the happy faces sampling food and sipping drinks. I'm hit with an overwhelming sense of pride and a second equally overwhelming wave of purpose. I spent so much time feeling like my friends and peers had their lives figured out for themselves. I felt such deep shame dropping out of NYU. Now, I see that this is my calling—this is what I'm meant to do.

I decide that when my accounts are unfrozen and when the world realigns itself again in the New Year, I'll go to Nan, Dad's mom, and ask for a loan to start my own business.

Yes, a loan. Not free money. I will pay her back. With interest. Like everyone else. Because while I may be from means, if these last few weeks have shown me anything, it's that if you don't earn it, it doesn't mean anything.

At the end of the song, Hector kisses me on the cheek. There it is—proof that Noelle's supposed holiday magic exists. It's in the way Hector's lips send a glitter elixir coursing through my body. I'm shining from the inside out.

"Am I a better dancer than Greta from the nursing home?" I ask.

"Tough call, but I think so." His laugh is soothing. "I should go check in with Christina and Siena to see if they need anything before dinner is served." He squeezes my bicep through my paisley blazer and disappears into the crowd.

I venture over toward the silent auction table. The SBA did an amazing job of reaching out to their members and getting the grade A bidding items I couldn't shake out of them myself. There's a full-service spa package complete with at-home robe and slippers. There's a basket full of expensive wines and all the makings for a classy charcuterie board. There are TVs, e-readers, and even season tickets to see the Patriots. All in all, our collection is valued at just over $20,000 and with the number of interested bidders, we're well on our way to making a sizable chunk of change for a good cause.

Grandma catches me peering over at her. She excuses herself from a conversation with Rosalie and makes a beeline toward me. She's wearing a flowing black skirt matched with a jade-colored blouse and a festive wrap.

"Dear, you do know how to throw a shindig for the ages," she says. She attacks with her usual cheek pinch.

"You're going to mess up my makeup!" I cry. I save all my best concealers and such for special occasions, so I decided to put on my full face for the evening. Even Hector, who I was afraid might go dude bro on me when he saw it, complimented me on my highlights.

"I'm floored with what you've done here," Grandma says. Tears appear at the edges of her eyes. I offer her my monogrammed handkerchief and a side hug.

"We did it for you. And the other businesses, obviously, but mostly for you. Hector told me the store is struggling, and I want to help. In any way I can."

"You've already helped so much," she says, gesturing to the crowd.

"Beyond this. I mean it." I wait a beat before I add, "I feel terrible for how I acted when I got here. I'm sorry. I know I've been distant these last few years. I think I got my priorities mixed up."

She shakes her head. "Dear, we don't hold it against you. You're growing up and figuring things out, deciding how family fits into the fabric of your life. It's a process. We went through it with your mother, so we know."

"I know she can be—"

"No," she says with certain authority. "Not tonight. She's here. She's present and she seems happy."

That's when I spot her rejoining the crowd. Not too far from the bar, she takes a seat next to Arthur, who cleans up quite nicely and looks handsome in his Christmas-tree bow tie. Their bodies are angled in toward each other, subtly giving away their history to the whole room.

"I'm happy too," I say.

Swingin' Six is closing out its first set. Hector pops up near the stage. It's almost time for my speech. I crack my knuckles, roll out my neck, and put on my cheeriest expression.

You'd think, as someone who spent most of his young life being paraded around on press tours and at red carpet events and galas just like this one, I wouldn't fall victim to stage fright. But, as I stand onstage before this town—one I'd previously seen as beneath me in many ways—I feel a lump in my throat. I can't tell if it's from nerves or intense feelings of gratitude. Hector gives me a big thumbs-up from the steps, and it's enough to buoy me for now.

"May I have your attention, please?" I say into the microphone. "My name is Matthew Prince Jr.—you may know me as Lorna and Doug Winston's grandson—and I am happy to be one of your co-organizers for this year's Holiday Charity Gala."

A rapturous applause erupts throughout the room. The sweat stops and the lump subsides. I ease back into my body and this exquisite moment.

For once, faces staring back at me are all in support, not looking to tear me down.

"This year's theme is Christmas Past, Present, and Future. Hector Martinez and I came to this idea through a mutual love of *A Christmas Carol* by Charles Dickens." There are numerous nods of recognition and adoration. "I hope you enjoyed the walk down memory lane. The tree, generously donated by the Bishop Family Farm, with its display of presents reminds us *the present* is the most important present of all. And the projection photo op was created in part with Let's Get LIT Productions in New York City.

"Before we move on to the food, brought to you by local hot spot A Very Fine Vine, I'd like to turn the microphone over to Patricia Myerson, president of the Small Business Association, to give you a bit of background about what they do for your—*our*—community and how your donations will help," I say.

Patricia takes the mic with a wide smile. Hector and I find our table with the other young people who preferred not to be seated with their parents. Noelle looks amazing in a romper and cardigan combo. She's wearing the dangly snowflake earrings she wore on the first day I met her. That feels like a little infinity ago. I'm so happy to know her now.

"For you," she whispers as she pulls out the chair next to her. Hector claims the seat on the other side of me. "This place looks stunning!"

"Thank you," I say.

"Hector better not hog you all night. Save me a dance later?" she asks.

"I think you might have your own dance partner," I say, nodding toward the double doors across the way. Siena stands there clearly trying not to make her demure glances so obvious. Noelle fights a smile, while squeezing my elbow.

We all tune back in to what Patricia is saying. Hector finds my hand under the table.

This night couldn't get any better.

CHAPTER 32

After the dessert plates are cleared, the children's choir does their annual performance, followed by the swing band again with a slower set to round out the evening. I meet Mom over by the bar where I ask for the signature cocktail, a Christmas Mule (the secret is a splash of cranberry juice and the cheapest vodka imaginable).

"It goes without saying that I'm proud of you, but I'll say it anyway. I'm proud of you," she coos uncharacteristically, ruffling my fluffy hair. The simple act is transportive. For a second, I'm the kid from the photo in the hallway again.

"It's nothing like what your publisher throws."

"No, you're right," she says. When my eyebrows go up, she adds, "*It's better.* It's better because it's personal. There's so much of you and your passions in this place. I–I wish I had seen this in you sooner. I'd have had you do all my book launches."

I cackle at that even though her bevy of compliments is more than welcome. After years of negative press, it's nice to hear encouragement straight from her plum-colored lips.

"No, seriously. You have an eye for design and detail." She fiddles with her sparkly clutch, overwhelmed but I can't tell by what specifically. "I was wrong for pushing you into NYU when you so clearly had a talent going unnoticed. I guess I always thought your parties were about likes and comments. It never occurred to me that they could mean something more."

Based on her questionable tone, I decide not to mention my mini revelation. I'll go to Nan in my own time and on my own terms. I take a sip of my drink out of the plastic, faux-copper mugs Christina happily helped us get.

"Though I was interested to find out that, according to a Pierce Brosnan–looking man in a white jacket, I'm delivering the commencement speech for Havensmith College next spring," she says.

"I meant to tell you about that..." I give her an innocent shrug as her nervous tic intensifies. Her fabric clutch is nothing but a ball in her hands.

"Did you get a chance to look through all the photos out in the entryway?" I ask, attempting to pull her out of her head. I've never seen her this flighty before. She prides herself on public composure. Part of the reason why even I, her son, never know what she's thinking.

I suppose returning to your hometown after so long will do that to a person—dig up old habits—so I grant her the grace of a distraction.

She nods sharply. "I did. It was a throwback I wasn't expecting."

I can't tell if this is a good thing or a bad thing. "It was a lot of work, but I think it paid off. People seemed to enjoy it. I think it reminded everyone how magical Wind River can be around the holidays."

I pause, giving Mom the space to agree and validate what I've come to know, but instead she briskly says, "Would you like to come home with me tonight? Oksana will do cinnamon buns tomorrow morning."

I don't answer right away. I knew this possibility was coming, but somewhere inside my head I'd convinced myself I'd fuck this up like I've fucked up countless times before. This gala was destined to be yet another misfortune brought upon the Prince family name. Yet somehow, someway, with a little help and a lot of heart, I aced the assignment.

Except this isn't the prize I once thought it to be.

"Your father and I want to do Christmas right this year." Mom's tone is persuasive. "You don't need to decide right this second. Maxim should be here in about an hour. Take your time." Though I'm not sure how much patience she's willing to spare. She hastily kisses my forehead and I notice her sight line land on Arthur across the way. He's standing alone, shuffling to the music. "Come find me when you know."

I can't help but allow my eyes to follow her over to him. The bag-squishing halts, and her supernova shine intensifies in his presence. I think about my own supernova shine, and the way it intensifies each time I'm beside Hector.

Hector. Hector. Hector.

His melodic name running through my mind lets me know that I need to tell him. This is a decision we should make together. Perhaps he'll be thrilled for me. He'll agree to come to my warehouse party. He said he's willing to be pleasantly surprised.

I hold on to that flimsy hope as I scan the room, but don't see him. Guests are trickling out, some with elaborate silent auction prizes in their hands. Jack, the now-recovered former organizer, has agreed to help with the teardown and is scuttling about the room at the ready.

Hector. Hector. Hector.

Where has he gone off to?

CHAPTER 33

As I make my way down the mostly empty corridor, all I hear are the sounds of the food crew cleaning up. Siena, in the catering uniform, comes hastening out of the swinging doors that lead into the kitchen.

"Everything was delicious," I say. It's hard to hide the hammering of my heart under the sound of my shaking voice. I desperately want to talk to Hector right now.

"This was such a beautiful event. Christina and I couldn't be prouder to have been a part of it," Siena says. She envelops me in one of those overly friendly hugs people love giving out around the holidays.

"Remind me, Hector has an old-fashioned paper check for you before you all head out," I say. "Oh, and the extra is to tip your waitstaff for such extraordinary service. Seriously, they were better than most of those out-of-work actors trying too hard to impress people with their pouring skills I've worked with in New York."

She shimmies around me with the bus-person trays to finish cleaning up. I call back once more. "By the way, I'm sure Noelle is still out there! Just in case you were wondering…"

"I've seen her." Her fierce blush lets me know what that really means. "She was actually looking for you. It seemed a bit urgent."

I rack my brain for a reason Noelle would need to talk to me, but can't find one. Maybe she wants to cash in on that promise of a dance. I'm on a hunt for Hector. She's on a hunt for me. I don't know where to go next. I thank Siena before turning around and coming face-to-face with a harried Noelle, clutching her phone like it's a stolen heirloom.

"I need to show you something," she says in a low voice. She pulls me into the nearby stairwell. It's freezing in here and our voices echo with a creepy, cave-like quality. "You don't have your phone with you, right?"

"No, I left it on silent in my bag in the kitchen. Didn't need the distractions. Why? What's up?" I ask.

"I wasn't sure if I should show you this, but I think you need to see it for yourself," she says. My nervous system switches into overdrive.

It's a Google alert for Mom's name followed by sensational headlines like:

Privileged Prince Jr. Buys Island Real Estate to Impress Mommy and Daddy

Bad Breakup Leads to Bad Investments: Yup, Matthew Prince Jr. Just Got Worse

It's like somebody turned the temperature up five hundred degrees. My skin feels as if it's about to burn up and slide off my skeleton. Culture writers *never* spare my feelings, which is rude considering I *always* give them something good to write about. They should be sending me Edible Arrangements, the fancy kind that include chocolate-covered strawberries, along with their thanks for being able to make their rent payments on time.

My eyes snag on another:

Poor Little Rich Boy Shipped Out of Manhattan after Prince-a-Palooza Plans Leak

Well, now I know word of my exile has hit the internet and that my failed music festival dreams, whipped up alongside my married ex-boyfriends, are open for anonymous ridicule. Even though the breakup was almost six months ago, seeing our joint brain-child chalked up to a laugh still stings.

I stand there, shaking but still, running but stuck in place. Somebody sold me out.

"I should've waited," she says.

"No," I force out. "No, I needed to see this."

Though what I really need is to block out the world with a soft bed, a weighted blanket, and blackout curtains. A dark, trigger-less box to calm myself down as every breath becomes shallower and the walls start to fall in.

Noelle's quiet for a long while. My heart feels dangerously close to escaping the lockbox inside my chest.

"Can I be alone for a minute?" I ask. Just her eyes on me are making this situation harder to handle. I give her back her phone.

"Are you sure? I can stay. I can get you out of here. What do you need?" she asks.

"I need to be *alone*," I say with more bark than I intend to.

Noelle just nods, pats my shoulder, and slips back into the hallway.

Krampus has usurped me this time, grabbed the reins and taken my mind on a sleigh ride straight to hell. I lose all sense of time and space, vision growing hazy at the edges. Fingers tingly.

I don't even notice I've grabbed my things and pushed back into the Great Hall.

I thought I had tamed my past, but now my brain is on the run again and so am I. My fast feet carry me away from here. The tinny sounds of "Matthew, what's going on?" ring out behind me, but I don't place the voice.

I'm convinced that everyone has seen this. Everyone is looking at their phones and laughing.

Hector. Hector. Hector.

My mind flips on repeat mode. If I find him, he'll know what to do. He has to. Even if he doesn't, he'll talk to me. He'll calm me down. He'll…he'll…

Searching for him among the chaos of the Great Hall is a losing game of Where's Waldo? Fuck, why didn't I think to dress him in a striped candy-cane suit when I had the chance?

Fuck. Fuck. Fuck.

I push out into the entryway. The Past exhibit, a former wonder, is now a snowstorm of overstimulation. The lights, the pictures, everything funnels together into a blurry mess until I'm barreling forward through the crowd without a sense of direction, no regard for who I'm shoving out of the way to clear a path.

I only stop when a manicured hand finds my shoulder. Mom is behind me, coat-check ticket in hand, worry creasing her forehead.

Without thinking, I collapse into her arms. A rush of relief comes, but doesn't stay. I tilt my head up at her, eyes seconds away from becoming waterfalls. I say like a little boy, "Take me home?"

She ushers me outside, sensing the urgency in my hiccupping voice. Probably embarrassed by my hysterics.

Counting. Breathing. Fake-event planning. All of it goes to shit as I stumble down the front steps. Coping is not in the cards. Surviving this moment is all there is left.

Wendy's Christmas lights are far too bright, so I shut my eyes—but the darkness waiting behind my eyelids scares me even more.

I'm not safe anywhere. That realization causes the truth to come out: "Island Gate leaked." I brace for the firm hand of disappointment to come crashing down on me.

"It did? I mean, it did." Mom's voice is distant, faraway, caught in her throat, but her expression is a neutral mask.

Fresh tears spring up to my eyes like a geyser. I'm trembling out here in the cold. Mentally and physically frostbitten. "Yeah. I don't know. I don't understand how it happened. I was careful. So *so* careful. I promise."

There's a millisecond where I fear she won't let me in the car. She'll get in, drive off, and leave me to sort through this myself. Instead, she nods for Maxim to open the door and allows me to slide in first. It's not the panic room I need, but its walls, leather seats, and tinted windows are enough to calm my senses.

"Give me a moment," she says, underscored by the door shutting. She's already got her phone out, looking at an email, lower lip becoming a chew toy.

"Is that Sarah? Does she know how it happened?" I'm frantic, needing every ounce of detail possible. Some nugget to help this all make sense.

She ignores me. "We'll handle it, Matthew."

"I didn't tell Bentley."

"We always handle it," she says.

"Baz and Spencer didn't know I was here."

"All right. Good. That's good."

I hug my coat tight to my chest to try to mute the relentless thumping. "How, then? I can't explain it!"

"Matthew!" she shouts, an unexpected burst of energy that fizzles out with a few deep breaths. "Sarah says a...young man contacted her stating that he had information regarding our family that they'd go to the press with if funds weren't paid promptly," Mom details slowly. "You must understand, we get threats like this all the time, and they're almost always toothless."

"But not this time?" I ask, sounding stupid but needing to hear it.

"No, not this time it seems."

"This is why you sent me here..."

"Well, it's complicated..."

"God, I'm such a selfish, stupid idiot." My hands rake furiously through my hair.

"Matthew, please. Pull it together."

"What was his name?" I ask. I'm coming unstuck enough to see my biggest mistake rising through the mayhem.

Mom blinks at me, her fake lashes cartoonish in the overhead light. "Whose name?"

"The young man?" I prompt her. Because if the name in my head matches the one on her lips, I don't know that I'll be able to handle it.

"His name?" she asks, dazed. Her eyes flick back to the screen. "This was a bit ago. I believe, well...I believe it started with an *H*."

I'm sucker punched.

Hector. Hector. Hector.

I don't dare speak his name aloud for fear that will make it true.

But it already is true. Isn't it? Mom has just confirmed what I couldn't see, I shared all the dirty details of Island Gate with him in confidence as I fell for him.

I was tricked. Hector played me for his own plane ticket home.

He didn't trust me, and I misplaced my trust in him.

"Hector." When his name finally comes out, it's nothing more than a raspy sob.

Mom nods. "Yes, now that I think of it. That's what it was...yes."

"I'm sorry," I croak, knowing those words will make me seem weak, won't be enough, but they're all I have left as the anxiety rocks me from the inside out.

Mom sighs, straightening her back and pushing her hair behind her ears. "It's not your fault, Matthew." Those are words I'd never thought I'd hear come out of her mouth. "Everyone wants what we have. Everyone wants *more* and some people will do dastardly things to get it or keep it."

Her words are a horse pill in my mouth, impossible to swallow.

As we pull away from the curb, Hector comes rushing out the front entrance. He paces in frustration, seemingly scanning the faces for mine.

I hate how utterly heart-stopping he still looks in the moonlight. I squish that thought like the pest it has become.

What I felt from the start was right. I don't belong here. Being here made me soft. It made me care. It opened me up, and it sent the bucket of paint on an impossible string slamming straight into my chest.

No more.

I face forward and find Mom's hand on the leather seat between us.

CHAPTER 34

Mom stays in the car while Maxim and I run inside to grab my things from the basement.

I'm grabbing items left and right, a Frankenstein's monster of mistakes causing destruction every which way.

In the bathroom, I catch sight of Hector's Breathe Right strips beside my SpectraLite mask. It makes me sick to my stomach how the sweetness could spoil so quickly.

Krampus roars right on cue. Autopilot prompts me to throw everything into the nearest bag without a care. Clothes, shoes, and toiletries are strewn into the suitcases, lotion bottles spilling all over expensive fabric. *Fuck it.* I don't have the energy to care.

I shudder, slinging one zipped bag toward the staircase. My moment of thought cost me necessary seconds because a text pops up from Mom.

Hector incoming, it reads. His car just pulled up.

My heart bounces up into my throat, and my vision narrows even more.

Bang, bang. There he is. He stands backlit by the patio light, looking like the Ghost of Christmas-Yet-To-Come finally here to claim me. I back away, needing a wider stretch between us. Otherwise, I might curl up into the fetal position and begin to cry.

I'm comforted momentarily, thinking the door is locked, but Hector has a key. I can't bear to look him in his stupidly handsome face. He's not even wearing a coat.

"Where are you going?" he asks. Maxim grabs the packed suitcase and lugs it up with his usual strength and speed. I don't want him to witness this, but I also don't want to be left alone with Hector.

Alone with Hector is what got me into this mess in the first place.

"Back to New York," I croak.

"What? You said you were staying. You said you *would stay.*" He's pleading, eyes puppy-dog dreary. A bungee cord, like the one we wrapped around the Christmas tree, constricts my heart, making me feel faint.

"That was before you…" I can't even complete that sentence. The betrayal burns through me at lightning speed.

"Before I what? Matthew, what are you talking about?" he asks like he doesn't have a clue. A spectacular act of duplicity. His face crumples up when I hold out my hand to keep him from coming any closer. If he punctures my personal space bubble, I might scream as loud as the piercing wails inside my head.

"This was the plan all along, right?" I ask, not looking at him or caring if he even hears.

"What plan? What are you talking about?" he asks.

"Make a profit off my big mistake," I mutter, ravaging the closet for anything left behind. "Think the worst of me like you have since day one." I'm laughing uncontrollably for no good reason. "Up there on your righteous high horse. Ha! You have everybody fooled."

"I have no idea what you're saying." He nearly gets hit with one of my wieldy, wayward kilts as I fling it off its hanger.

"Get out of the way," I command. He's standing between me and the last open bag.

"Not until you tell me what's going on."

The rage becomes too much. Krampus grabs hold of my voice box, lowering my pitch and pushing out frightening, protective words. "You're a liar and a bottom-feeder and a fake, and I'm the stupid asshole who believed you were different."

Shock covers up the confusion on his face. "You…you don't mean that."

"Don't tell me what I mean," I growl. I get to my suitcase and stuff and tug until I'm almost tearing the seams apart. "Have a merry little Christmas and a happy fucking new year at home."

God, *home*. Why won't that word stop assaulting me with its evasive meaning?

"Home? Please. Let's sit and talk."

I scoff. "I don't want to talk to you after what you did. My mom told me everything!" *I believe it started with an H.* She knew his name. She just didn't want to say. She needed me to make the conclusion for myself.

"Your mom? Matthew, please, stop for a second."

"No, *you* stop pretending you care!" I shout.

He's got his hackles up now. "Does it look like I'm pretending, dude? I chased you here to make sure you were okay, and now you're just up and abandoning me, this town, *us*."

"This town is a joke, and there is no *us*."

"Matthew." His tone dips to a calmer place, and his eyes are twin probes, attempting to placate me. I won't be a rag doll to his whims.

"Don't 'Matthew' me! There is no *us*," I hiss in a tailspin.

He puffs out his chest, stands his ground, and asks as evenly as possible, "What if we do that mental event-planning thing again?" His strong-willed composure has never been more infuriating, especially as he tries to help me using my own anxiety-coping mechanisms.

"Screw the event thing and screw you too!" I'm right up in his face now, heartbeat in my ears.

He closes his eyes. "A, uh, Christmas Cookie Exchange. Everyone gets a random recipe emailed to them and they have to—"

"Move!" I yell, but he refuses to free up the pathway to the stairs.

"—bake that cookie and bring one for everyone. Your grandparents judge them anonymously. We host it here, um, and you…you, uh…"

"Let…me…*leave*." I'm pleading now.

He blinks fast, holding back his own tears because he knows this is it. The end. "Is that really what you want?"

"Yes," I say on an exhale, seething. "Yes, yes, yes. That's *really* what I want."

After a beat, resigned, he says, "Okay." And steps aside. No more fight. No more fake event. Nothing. He turns away so he doesn't have to watch me go.

His cold stance only reiterates the fact that the only person I can trust is myself. My pompous rich boy act kept people on the other side of the moat, and that's the way it has to be. Otherwise, I end up impossibly broken, over and over.

I grab the side handle of my suitcase and run up as fast as my long legs will allow me. I know he's not chasing me, but I can't risk slowing down or my thoughts might catch up to me. I might realize that what I'm doing is stupid, what I said is a lie, and I won't allow those things to be true.

Encumbered by the physical bag in my hand, and the new emotional ones strapped to my back, I load up the trunk, slide into the back seat, and wave Maxim on. Grandma and Gramps's house disappears through the back window and I realize, again, I was right from the start. I never belonged here.

They say Manhattan chews you up and spits you out, but at least there you can Instagram filter your existence. The *real you* can live behind a pane of glass. You become a living window display to be gawked at, sometimes in admiration and sometimes in condemnation, but there's still that layer of protection.

Here? Everyone knows you. Everyone will bother you. Everyone wants or needs something from you. You must give everyone little bits of you or you don't belong.

I sit in the back seat, taking inventory of those little bits, making sure I packed up as many of them as I possibly could. At least enough to rebuild myself.

I need a bath, a stiff drink, and the old me back.

CHAPTER 35

Nothing beats waking up swaddled in Egyptian cotton sheets upon my memory-foam king bed done up in blues and golds. My soft, sheer canopy greets me, along with the extra hardwood square footage and large window with its remote-controlled blinds. I can sit up without fear of a concussion because there are no boards and no mattress above me, so why does my head still throb?

Oh, because there's no guy above me either.

The guy whose snores I memorized. The guy whose lips tasted like Burt's Bees and peppermint and happiness. The guy who taught me about hard work, and then sold me out so easily, sending me back here before I was ready.

I guess *ready* is another of those nebulous words. One can never be ready for emotional upheaval. Especially not around the holidays.

There's a rumbling dread in my chest when I remember what day it is. Christmas Eve. Since I've returned, I'm faced with another year of going through the tepid motions of togetherness. A half-ass parade of platitudes and last-minute presents and going our separate ways.

I think about lying in bed a while longer, letting everyone think I'm still asleep because an anxiety hangover is almost as hard to push through as an anxiety attack is, but then the scent of baking cinnamon buns comes in through my partly open door, and I remember what Mom said about doing

Christmas right. Resurrecting old traditions. If my nostrils aren't deceiving me, there's a freshly baked breakfast waiting for me in the kitchen, so instead of ruminating over the car crash wrapped around the telephone pole of my heart, I vault myself out of bed.

Avoidance is going to have to be okay for today. Even if my sluggish gait tells a different story.

I realize that I'm back to my real life and I must accept that. Hell, I should even celebrate that. I slide inside my walk-in closet. Stuffed like a secret behind a rack of old accessories, I find some tacky Yuletide pieces I couldn't part with for memory's sake. The Santa slippers from my youth won't even slide over my toes, and the elf hat is too snug for my head. However, there's an ironic red sweater that reads UGLY CHRISTMAS in white, blocked embroidery that calls to me. It was an irreverent gift from an old flame, and because I'm trying to extinguish a current one, I slip it on and snuggle into it, even if it smells stale.

I'm manifesting jolly with my gayest apparel, and nobody can stop me.

When I come into the kitchen, it's clear I wasn't the only one thinking this. Mom is wearing a matching Christmas pajama set from eons ago. I remember we all had our own pair for a Christmas-card photo shoot, back when those were still a thing, so mine don't fit any longer.

Dad is there too. No pajamas for him, but he is wearing a festive tie which I'm certain his assistant bought for him this morning because there are remnants of a tag still tacked on it. There's no briefcase to be seen, so that means he's off duty for the day.

For some reason, he always insists on icing Oksana's cinnamon buns, so he runs a knife across the now-cooled tops, making the gooey confections even more pleasing.

I pause before making my presence known. I'm wondering if I should tread lightly. Island Gate is the reason I was sent away, and now that it's out, it's only logical that I'll be lectured over the importance of staying mum when told to do so.

I'm surprised the wicked witch herself, Sarah Pearson, hasn't flown in on her broomstick yet, landing only to frantically sweep my indiscretion under the expensive rug.

Wow, what a waste of time. I served most of my punishment, and we still ended up in the place we least wanted to be. Or the place *they* least wanted to be.

But *they* don't seem all that peeved. *They* each notice me and sport a big, kind of unsettling smile.

"Good afternoon, Matthew," Mom says breezily. I didn't realize it was twelve already. In my defense, we didn't get home until well after 2:00 a.m. and even after settling back in, I don't think I fell asleep until at least four. My phone kept buzzing with texts from Hector. I deleted them all, unread, and then I blocked his number. Easier to sever the connection than keep the temptation where my itching thumbs can get to it.

"Matthew, bud, I'm happy you're home," Dad says, licking his fingers before coming to give me the hug equivalent of a handshake, fast and formal.

I'm happy to see one of my Pennsylvania-imported trees, trimmed with expert precision, presents wrapped and laid out beneath it. Dad's old Christmas CDs, the ones I'd assumed were chucked out ages ago, are playing from an old stereo dug up from who knows where. Springsteen croons and I cringe, thinking of Hector, the pharmacy, and the snore strips.

Hector. Just the thought of his name makes my muscles seize.

The hurtful things I said to him jumble together into a menacing word cloud in my head. I was tipped into such a dark, protective place, and the way I spoke to him frightened even me.

I try to focus on the present. I won't bring up the Berkshires, and I won't bring up the island. I can't tell what's happening here, but it's as if I've been flung through a time warp, some sort of hole in the universe, and I don't hate it. This is the cozy little Christmas complete with lit seasonal candles that I refused to let myself admit I'd been craving for so long. I'm not about to bring up a sore topic and ruin the vibes.

Instantly, my grinchiness minimizes. I let the kid inside me take over because that's what's convenient. That boy with the bowl cut comes out full-force as Dad produces a surprise from his back pocket. "Got your old favorite seats." He slides a triplet of tickets to the *Radio City Christmas Spectacular* across our marble island. I take a seat in the high chair and inspect them. Row JJ, center section. Not too close, not too far.

Overwhelming levity zings through me. This is a tried-and-true tradition reborn. That show was everything to me when I was a child. I'd count down the days all year until I was reunited with the Rockettes, a collection of high-kicking women that were the epitome of class and holiday cheer.

For the first time ever, I clock the price tag. Never once have I fretted over an amount, since we've always been able to cover any purchase, but being cut off like I was for those few weeks, it almost seems like our senseless splurging could be put to better use.

Dad's grin falters when I don't speak right away, so I thank him a million times over because he's making up for lost time with this—I think—and I appreciate that.

"I'll serve the cinnamon buns in the living room," Oksana says. She jingles as she goes, wearing a necklace of shiny bells. They remind me of something Noelle might wear. It hits me that I didn't even say goodbye to her.

I erase that oversight from my brain.

Mom, Dad, and I saunter over to the white Italian leather sofa. I sit between them like I used to, and even if time and experience have changed us, somehow nostalgia gets the better of me. Mom passes me the navy-blue Dior throw blanket to warm up under. The French press gets passed from Dad down the line until we're all graced with tiny, steaming cups of espresso, which we clink together.

The coffee is velvety, fragrant, and leaps and bounds better than anything Moon Beans could've crafted. Even if I do miss the homespun atmosphere and Noelle's entertaining gossip. I wonder if she ever perfected her foam art. If she ever *will*. I suppose I'll never know.

It's not like I can continue that line of communication when I've cast off that whole town for filth.

"How about a movie?" Mom asks, oozing cheeriness, before I can consider all I left behind in Wind River too long.

Dad and I agree. Mom starts up Mickey's version of *A Christmas Carol*, recalling it as my favorite from yesteryear, but then considers a second option: *The Muppets*. I nearly drop my remaining espresso in my lap before forcing the flash of pain away. This—family time around the Christmas tree—is all I've wanted for years. I need to stop thinking about a miniscule town and the selfish guy I left behind there.

Screw Hector. Screw Wind River. I'm back, baby.

"Could we do *Scrooged*?" I ask. "I could use a good laugh."

While it's true, it's also the fact that I need some distance from that story for a while. *Scrooged* is enough of a retelling that I can watch without having to feel the immense depths of my own despair. I know that sounds dramatic, but Krampus has a brutal way of reminding me of everything in my rearview mirrors.

"I prefer Bill Murray anyway," Dad says with a slight nudge.

"Whatever you want! It's Christmas!" Mom says.

I smile at them as the three of us snuggle in. Well, Mom and I snuggle in. Dad remains ramrod straight, feet planted on the floor, back with perfect posture. Relaxation looks different on him.

With the movie cued up and the Christmas tree looming over us, all is well for once in the Prince household.

Even if my shattered heart says otherwise.

When the film ends, I stand and announce that I'm going to run a bath. I brush the crumbs off my sweatshirt. "Is that okay?"

"Of course that's okay," Mom says. "Be ready by five. Maxim will pick us up for dinner."

Oksana, having anticipated my needs, swiftly gifts me a tiny plate of cucumber slices. She knows I need a quiet moment to myself.

"Is it that obvious?" I whisper to her with a light, self-deprecating laugh.

She shrugs knowingly and sends me on my way.

In my sprawling *private* bathroom, listening to the sloshing of the water as it fills the tub that could easily fit two, I stare at my naked body in the impeccably lit mirror. I chart the course of freckles across my nose and the mole on my right shoulder. My nipples look puffy and hairy, and my eyes look too sleep-deprived to function. Even the espresso couldn't counteract those less-than-designer dark bags.

Had it only been days ago that Hector touched me and I felt like the most desired person in the world? It couldn't have been that short a time since he ran that bar of soap across my skin in the miniscule shower we shared.

To distract myself, I pull my La Mer detoxifying and revitalizing face mask from a nearby cabinet, and I let out a sigh of relief as I step into the water. My body takes a while to adjust to the temperature shock in the tub. The water at Grandma and Gramps's was always slightly south of warm. I tip over a bottle of rose-scented bubbles, which is a mistake since it reminds me of Grandma's favorite tea. I light the candle near the window to counteract it.

I rest my head on a Mako cotton towel and use the luxury brush to paint on the mask. Each brushstroke tickles my sensitive skin, but I don't dare smile. Smiling feels wrong, and anyway, the mask will crack if I do.

Setting the cucumbers on my eyes, I wait for relaxation. When rising anxiety comes instead, I start planning a Forget About the Boy Bash. It would take place in a quaint piano bar. A fishbowl for tips would be set out along with a sheet-music binder full of show tunes. As the host with the most, I would perform a ravishing *Thoroughly Modern Millie* number.

Only hiccup is, as the fantasy goes on, I remember that that song's not in my range, and the idea of being gawked at and judged for anything more right now makes me super nauseated.

I grow even sicker when I realize how this spa moment is so much like the fake event I planned with Hector out on the porch at Grandma and Gramps's place. Churning starts when I remember how I shut down his attempt to help me last night. Would someone who threw me to the wolves do something like that? Maybe this was all an accident. Maybe I misunderstood.

Started with an H...

That's what it was...yes.

No. I'm firm in my knowledge that he did this. Mom may be spacey when it comes to parenting, but she wouldn't lie to me like that.

I wash my face, my hair, and unplug the drain. I grab a cucumber slice from the plate. Letting the citrusy notes dance over my tongue, I close my eyes and consider Hector for a second. Consider how weightless I was dancing with him at the gala. How supported I felt with him by my side on that stage.

It's incomprehensible that a guy with that much integrity could stoop so low. Just goes to show you, like he learned with Natalia, that people aren't always what they appear to be.

Once I'm dried, moisturized, and dressed in my cream sweater—the designer version of the sweater Hector had worn on that day in the bookstore (because I'm a sucker for self-punishment)—I slink into the kitchen for a predinner snack.

On the way, I spy Oksana in the living room. She sports bright-red lipstick and a short, tousled hairdo. In an oval mirror, she's attempting her eyeliner.

"Let me," I offer, holding out a hand. This is familiar for us. When I was young, I had a fixation on clothing and beauty. Naturally, this led to an obsession with watching Oksana put on her makeup. I'd beg to poke around in her makeup bag, back when she was still a live-in au pair.

Even after, I'd help doll her up for dates or parties or wherever her life took her beyond the walls of our apartment. Funny to think I never once asked where she was going, who she was meeting. For someone so firmly set in my life, I know so little about her.

"You always did do it better than me," Oksana says, giving me the pencil.

"After a lot of practice," I say. "Honestly, some of those attempts got pretty dicey. I'm surprised you still have both your eyes."

She laughs. "I trusted you, Matthew."

Hearing those words does something the bath couldn't. It fills me with bubbles instead of surrounding me with them.

I have her sit, and with a steady hand, I draw flawless lines beneath her down-sloping eyes. It's nice to channel my frenetic energy into something simple. There's a calming intimacy here that I've missed.

Makeup, I realize, is another way I costume myself to face the world. If I hide the blemishes, nobody can point them out or blow them up.

But on Oksana, even as I touch up her lips and powder her nose, it doesn't read like armor. This isn't the face she needs to take on the outside.

It's only meant to enhance the natural beauty she lets shine through every day.

"Are you happy to be home?" she asks.

That question is too much for my fragile heart. "Mm-hmm," I lie. Even if I'd like to pamper her some more, I drop the cone-shaped sponge and change the subject. "Party tonight?"

"Just a small dinner tonight," she says. "Big party at my place tomorrow. I know you have fancy plans, but you're always welcome to come by."

"Thanks," I say, already lost in my own head again.

Once she leaves, I fiddle with my phone, contemplating a call to Grandma and Gramps. I want to know if the gala was successful. If they made any more cookies. If they know what Hector did. They deserve some honesty from my end. But like with Noelle, I left without a goodbye. I can't expect everyone to forgive me just because it will clear my conscience.

I guess I'll have to learn to live with this.

$$\cdot * \cdot * \cdot *$$

Dinner ends up being a five-course feast. The steaks are bloody. The wine is bubbly. The conversation, if somewhat stilted, is still nice. It's been forever since the three of us talked, face-to-face. A meal like this one would've been a dream only weeks ago.

It doesn't even matter that we're sat smack-dab in the center of the dimly lit dining room when normally we'd request a corner table or a private room. Nor do I care when one of Mom's fans, older than her usual demographic, snaps a sneaky phone picture of us eating. I hope this one ends up on the internet and sneaks its way onto Hector's social media feeds. I want him to see me. I want him to know what he's done hasn't hurt me. Even if the whispers around us do get to me a bit.

Later, the Radio City Music Hall marquee shimmers in red, blue, and gold above us. Its dazzling Art Deco style makes me giddy as we emerge from the Town Car. Together. A trio out on the town like the old days. I'm ten and tapping my toes to the music that floats out from the lobby doors.

Dad hands out the tickets over the sound of "Is that Anna Winston-Prince?" and "Do you think she'd sign my forehead?" Usually Mom would ignore this kind of chatter from the attendees shivering in the admission line, but instead, she beelines right for them, stopping for selfies and kissing babies. Quoting her series to a riotous round of "Huzzah, hurrah! For glory and our kingdom!"

Maybe what she said in the tea room was real. *We're all due for some growth.* Perhaps this generous act is a small way to garner some good press in the wake of my scandal. Anna Winston-Prince making time for her fans while attending a sold-out show is the kind of thing that gets shouted about on all the forums and blogs.

I try not to read too much into it.

Inside the theater, the concentric golden arches welcome me home. It's been an eternity since I've been here. A kindly usher hands me a program and a pair of 3D glasses. The three of us shuffle down our aisle, sink into comfy velvet chairs, and prepare to be whisked into high-kicking and a thousand bell-ringing Santas.

The lights dim. The chatter stops. Despite everything, as the curtain rises, so do my spirits.

CHAPTER 36

There's no way to describe the Plaza Hotel on Christmas Day other than *dripping*. From the plush red carpets dripping out the front entryway and down its step to its ornate chandeliers dripping crystals, the gilded palace screams classic luxury.

Mom and I are primped to the nines for Christmas tea at the Palm Court, another bygone go-to from childhood. Back then, I hated being stuffed into my nice clothes and sheathed in a cloud of hairspray, but today, I sport my Givenchy metallic leather pants. The ones I begged a pranking Hector not to steal before I realized who he was and what was happening. The mohair jacket was the perfect touch to complete the ensemble.

I know it's wrong, but I expect to be photographed. Again, if a photo of me in this outfit happens to float past Hector's eyes while he's scrolling on his phone, so be it. Revenge is a dish best served in hot pants.

We check in at the underground dining hall's guarded passage with its gold railings, striking columns, and detailed floral carpets. Christmas trees alternate with palm trees on our right, making for a magical, if also confusing, indoor landscape. Ornate architectural motifs abound around us.

"Why is Dad meeting us here again?" I ask, nearly tripping up the steps I don't see in time.

"He forgot a gift with his assistant again. You know him," Mom says, blasé.

When we prepared to leave without him, I couldn't hide the confusion, but Mom brushed it off. Dad has always been an early riser, but Christmas Day was the exception. Not hearing him scuttling around the apartment, dictating last-minute emails was puzzling, but I decide not to harp on it.

All in all, we're back to basics (if breakfast at one of the most expensive spots in the city could be considered *basic*), and I don't want to risk that. I'm just happy to be included. Even though it seems a tad *too much*—as Hector might say.

I would've been happy with a second round of cinnamon buns. I might've even put my Wind River baking skills to good use beside Oksana.

But she has the day off, and I'm trying to scrub myself clean of that place. So I shelve the uncertainty.

Dad appears in the lobby. He holds an impeccably gift-wrapped box, corroborating Mom's story. He offers me another smile, another micro-hug.

The Palm Court is like tea in the Wind River Inn reading room on steroids. Faux orchids pop out of flower boxes behind high-backed booths. A stained-glass skylight stands as the centerpiece of a room sheathed in olive greens and bursts of vibrant pink.

We're set up beside a voluminous, titular palm in a bulbous pot. Its fronds hit me in the face as I sit.

Dad doesn't even let us see the menu. He orders the most expensive prix fixe—a decadent array of unlimited tea, coffee, and champagne. Promptly, a three-tiered circular display of clotted cream, finger sandwiches, and indulgent pastries gets placed in the center of us. My taste buds are eager for the festive treats. Especially the mini Bûche de Noëls.

"To another holiday here in New York. Good health and lots of happiness ahead," Dad says. We tip our glasses together, but nobody makes eye contact, breaking the cardinal rule of toasting. I'm unsure, but Dad's wedding band looks askew on his hand. Mom keeps dabbing her upper lip with the linen napkin, even though she hasn't eaten a bite yet.

I'm about to take my first taste when Dad says, "I bet you're wondering why we brought you here—"

"Matt," Mom scolds. She never uses his nickname, especially not in public. Her held-up hand is a blinking stop sign. "Present first."

Dad fishes for the gift he dropped beneath the table. I set down the sandwich I'd been planning to demolish in a single bite. My parents' eyes are expectantly cast in my direction. They haven't watched me open a gift with this much parental enthusiasm since, well, maybe ever.

Delicately, I pull the strand of silken ribbon and the box unfurls. In the center, wrapped in tissue paper, I find a Prada bifold wallet. My fingers brush over the pebbled leather and the metallic letters pressed into the corner. I know what I'll find when I open it. My cards, all new, all shiny, all set to be linked to Apple Pay. They're ready for me to resume my old life.

Shouldn't I be ecstatic? I feel anything but.

"The social media blackout remains in effect until after the New Year," Mom starts, taking the wallet and doing what my hands couldn't. She shows me that I'm right. Untouched cards are nestled in the fine black slips inside. "But we thought it only fair you should be given access to your funds once more."

"So you're aware, the island sold for a little more than what you paid for it. Honestly, even I was shocked. I guess having the family name attached to it hiked up the value a bit. I was lucky to fob that island off on an acquaintance. I spun a few tales like the ones you told me—all that *potential* nonsense. Glad he ate it up. You'll see that the profit has been deposited into your account," Dad informs me, very businesslike, producing a bill of sale from his pocket. "Be sure to put that in the lockbox I gave you for important documents."

This is all happening quickly. I thought they'd ease me back into the old way. It seems they are set on speedily moving past this. Which makes me wonder why those matching looks of upset linger on their faces. Mom takes a big gulp of her champagne.

"Th-thank you," I stammer, unsure if I'm grateful for the letup or fettered by the shackles of these sharp pieces of plastic again.

"You're welcome, Matthew," Mom says in an unrecognizable voice. What is she doing with that napkin?

Uneasy and unable to ignore it through this whole meal, I say, "If it was that easy, it's clearly not why you sent me to Wind River."

My statement sends a shock wave around the table, maybe through the whole place.

The "café," which is larger than most restaurants in New York City, grows louder. Families reunite. Tourists stream in with shopping bags and hugs to give. Overwhelming doesn't even begin to describe it.

"We need you to be smarter with your expenses from now on, okay? Your mom and I work hard for that money, and now…with, uh…" Dad pauses.

"With what?" I ask.

"We just expect you to be more careful and considerate of your spending," he finishes.

Mom speaks from the bottom of her first glass of champagne. "I think what your father is trying to get at is that, um, it's clear you felt a strain on our family, and rightly so because…"

I brace myself for news of a big move, an affair they've parsed through without my knowledge, a work snafu that needs to be hush-hush covered up. The classics all my classmates' families went through back in the day. That juicy gossip that got leaked to Deuxmoi.

"We're getting divorced," Mom concludes, voice low so no one overhears.

Right as she says it, an inexperienced server drops a portly white china pot nearby. The hot brown tea seeps into the lavish golden carpet. I watch as the stain spreads, begins to set, needing something to focus my eyes on that isn't my parents.

"You're what?" My ears are ringing too loudly for me to be certain I've heard correctly.

"Your father and I are getting a divorce," Mom says again. Her statement is blunt, declarative. It punctures me. "This arrangement is no longer suiting us, so we've decided to part ways. So you can see why we need you to be less spend-happy as we split our assets."

Quickly, I invent a fake Children of Divorce Dance. No parents allowed. Part support group, part drink-fueled rager. It's at a Midtown pub with mirrored walls and low lighting. The signature cocktail is a Daddy Issues Daiquiri and the food special is Mom's Not Coming Home Mashed Potatoes. (They even come with a tiny plastic mallet to do some heated mashing yourself.)

The details calm me enough to come around to it. It's painful, sure, but it's survivable. Right? It has to be.

"When you were young, you always said you wanted two Christmases," Mom offers. I guess a half-ass silver lining is better than no silver lining at all. I nod heavily.

"Matthew, I think it's fair to say your mother and I haven't been happy together for a long time, and…" I notice Mom kick him under the table, prompting him to speak up. Not beat around the bush. Summon some of his businessman steel. "I've met someone."

"He says he's in love," Mom tosses in for good measure.

"With who?"

Dad grows ruddy, won't meet my gaze. "Ellie Barton."

Dad's a polished man with nice hair and a lean figure, but he's leaps and bounds below former supermodel Ellie Barton's level. She's the kind of woman that breaks Instagram records for likes and follower counts. The kind of woman that leaves a trail of broken hearts in her wake.

Wow, I invited her to my New Year's Eve party last year. Baz and Spencer introduced her to me. I introduced her to Dad. How stupid had I been?

I'm tempted to ask if this strange arrangement dates back to the party. Was I the catalyst for this cataclysmic corruption of our lives?

But then again, what about me and my selfish actions? I haven't made it easy on them. I know that. Vying for their attention when they receive it in droves on such a grand scale became an obsession. I convinced myself I needed to work overtime to get them to see me.

Now, for the first time, maybe *I'm* seeing *them*.

"I want to explore what we have further," Dad says. Suddenly, it clicks why we met him here. He's been staying here. That's why he wasn't padding around the apartment this morning. Somewhere in his blazer pocket he's got a room key. Ellie Barton may be up in a suite waiting for this charade to end, the other shoe to drop.

"Understand that with me on tour or on set or writing and him working and traveling and taking meetings, our lives are like ships passing in the night," Mom says, calm enough to serve herself some chilled salmon, but shaky enough for it to be noticeable. "We'll do the formal announcement, the family interview in *Vanity Fair*. We want to give this the proper send-off it deserves. After the New Year, we plan to weave a tale of lost love and mutual parting and a family unit that will survive on respect and shared parenting. We expect you to adhere to that."

I exhale. "Okay," I say, resigned, like Hector was when I left the cabin. There's no fight wobbling inside me. I'm sure they were expecting an outburst, but I've matured since they last saw me. Wind River, even if it did betray me, taught me so much. If I can plan a stressful gala in two weeks, I can handle this.

"Oh." Mom's lips purse.

"Good," Dad says, straightening his tie.

I blink back at them for a minute. They're still holding their breath. "If it's all 'oh' and 'good,' why does it feel like there's more?"

It's Dad's turn to nudge Mom under the table. They think they're being so discreet. I can read it all over their faces. When did their refined facades begin to fade around me? Maybe I'm just more observant now.

"I have something else to tell you," Mom says, already pouring herself another flute full. Her hands can't seem to be idle even for a second. "I made a...*mistake*."

My stomach sinks. "What kind of mistake?"

"Less of a mistake. More like..." She's doing what Grandma does, searching for the right word around the room. Their similarities have never been this striking. "An error of judgment."

"Anna, tell him," Dad says.

She's balling her napkin like she balled her clutch the night of the gala. "It's about the island-story leak."

Hope instantly ignites in me. "You got the name wrong? It wasn't Hector?" I'm pitched forward, impatient.

"Something like that," Mom says. Dad chides her again. I'm growing agitated the longer she draws this out.

"So?" I ask.

"So, I lied," she says quickly, head bowed. "There was no young man. I made that up in the heat of the moment based on your assumptions. Hector reached out to Sarah about an unrelated matter earlier. He had informed her of your charitable work with the gala, thinking she could sprinkle out some good-will for you in the press, but he had nothing to do with the island story leak. I fabricated that as a cover." Her truth nearly topples me right out of my chair.

"Wh-what?" I'm dumbstruck. Stuttering. Confused beyond belief.

"An anonymous source came forward saying they had proof your father and I were divorcing and would run the story unless we gave them something more sensational. We sent you away and tried to snuff it out, but their insistence and the pressure kept mounting. Sarah said we had no other choice…We gave them the island story in exchange for our privacy. I'm sorry, Matthew," she says, apology profuse and unrehearsed. I haven't heard her say that in so long. It's strange that it's coming now and not for any of the other times she's put her needs before mine. "Things got out of hand and, well, you have to understand that these matters are delicate. Our careers hang in the balance of…the image we sell."

"Why did you wait so long to tell me? And why today? Why *here* of all places?" I ask-shout, an anxiety attack nearly as big as the one from the night of my almost-escape shimmying up my spinal cord.

Everything I said to Hector in the basement comes rushing back to me. None of it was true, and all of it was cruel. He'll never forgive me for not letting him speak. I can't believe I silenced him when I should've taken his help.

"Because…well, because we knew you would *get like this*." Mom's tone is tart.

Like this. It's practically code for anxious, a kind way to tiptoe around the fact that I have a GAD. Her fingers drumming on her forearm are send-ing a telepathic message to my father.

"Which I know you get from my side of the family, from…" Mom's flab-bergasted voice grows more frog-like. I have no idea what she's hinting at but, in a second, she's off like a speeding train in the other direction. "I–I–I panicked, okay? I panicked when you asked who did it. I was so impressed by the Matthew I met in Wind River and all you did for that town." She holds her heart right below her necklace. "*My* old town. I was riddled with guilt. The source wasn't supposed to run the island story until the New Year. We were going to contain it. The number of outlets that picked it up the other day blindsided us. Can't you see?"

I *can* see.

I can see how one person's heated, selfish, spur-of-the-moment action can cause a domino effect of destruction. Something I've done a time or twelve million in my twenty-one years. It's just a shame I'm sitting in the rubble of someone else's right now. That I hurt someone I care deeply about because of it.

"So, that's what all this was? The movies, the cinnamon buns, the show, this tea?" I push my plate away from me, stomach burrowing into the depths of the earth. "This was all some big show to assuage your guilt? One last hurrah before we break apart?" It's almost evil, downright diabolical. Show me what I had, let me revel in it, and then snatch it away again, all the same. I wish they'd just been straight with me. It would've saved me the second heartache.

Mom sits up taller. "No, Matthew. No. We wanted to make one last family holiday memory together. We thought that's what you wanted."

"You have no idea what I want," I mutter.

Dad chimes in. "Matthew, your mother's indiscretion aside, you must see that we're letting you off easy." His volume lowers, and his tone becomes piercing. "That island could've cost us a lot. We cleaned up your mess for you. Yet again, I might add. You're seeing a lucky payday off a massive misstep."

I squint at him, hoping if I distill him into something smaller he might make more sense to me. He's crunching everything into facts and figures, blacks and whites. If I was expecting emotional honesty, I don't think there's enough champagne in the world to make that happen. He's a walking, talking calculator. And missing the point entirely. I don't care about the money anymore.

I only care about Hector.

"How could you let me believe Hector did this?" Mom doesn't answer right away. "Just because you made me doesn't mean I'm a character in one of your books. You know that, right? You can't just rewrite something if it doesn't suit you."

"Of course I know that, Matthew. I just don't want to see you hurt."

"You don't want to see me hurt?" Incredulity is a furious dragon in my stomach, breathing fire into my lungs. "Where was that concern when Sarah made me stop seeing Lukas because it would ruin your TV show and his career? Where were you when I tried so hard to hack it at NYU but my mental health was spiraling and getting in the way of doing any work? Where were you when I was so heartbroken over Baz and Spencer that I bought a fucking island? Where were *either* of you?" I'm crying free-flowing tears now in front of this entire establishment, and they need to see it. Even if it is being captured on more than a dozen phones. "Did you know they did an opening monologue about me on *The Late Show*? Your son is a literal punch line."

"That was a silly throwaway joke," Dad counters.

"My life is a silly throwaway joke?" That hammers into my head. "Mom, you say you didn't want to see me hurt, but I've been hurting for a long time, and you've chosen not to see it. I finally find someone who saw that hurt and didn't make me feel bad or wrong or ashamed, and you let me piss away our relationship on your reputation."

"A *relationship*?" Mom asks, stunned.

"Please don't pretend like you didn't know."

She swallows audibly. "I swear to you, I did not."

I shake my head. "Even so." I shrug. "That's a poor excuse."

The desserts piled high between us, blocking my view of her whole face, only serve to remind me how sweet I found this life before when it was really nothing more than a never-ending, unhealthy sugar high. I should've known there'd be a crash this big.

I stand, hitching my dignity onto my back, wrapping myself in my coat. "I'm out of here. And don't you dare try to follow me."

"Matthew." Dad makes my name sound like a threat.

"I don't want any part of this any longer." I hold my head up high. "Merry Christmas."

Chest heaving, heart staccato, I turn on my heel and begin my march out of the Palm Court, leaving the rest of the room with a whole lot to talk about in my wake.

CHAPTER 37

Maxim pulls up to the curb of Bentley's Kent Avenue apartment complex.
My adrenaline is still surging.

From the back seat, I peer up at the luxury waterfront building that has the
geometric appearance of a child's lopsided Lego tower if the Legos were made
of glass. This will be the perfect hideaway while I regroup. I paw the spare key
in my coat pocket. Bentley's still in Aspen, so I'll have the place to myself.

"Is this not the right place, Mr. Prince?" Maxim asks when I've stalled
too long.

"No, this is it. Thank you, Maxim," I say, using his name for a change.
It's the least I can do for how I treated him previously. I wish I had money
to tip him, but the new wallet with its cards and cash was left behind on the
table at the Plaza. I know there's no going back for it now. "I want to say I'm
sorry for how rude I've been these last few years. I know this is a thankless
job even when your passengers are kind, and I've been…less than. So, yeah.
I know it doesn't mean much, but I'm sorry."

He nods, uncertain. The way Hector was when I apologized for, well,
anything and everything. "Apology accepted, Mr. Prince."

"Please, call me Matthew," I say, no longer wishing to be referred to by
the same moniker my father uses.

My father. Maybe names like that create distance. That's why Grandma,
Gramps, and the residents of Wind River did that with Mom. *Dad* is too
close to the heart. *My father* recognizes a bloodline, but separates us.

I say to Maxim, "Oh, and my parents told me to tell you to take the rest of the day off. You shouldn't be working on Christmas."

"Are you sure, Matthew?" he asks.

"Yeah," I say. "If they forget, tell them I insisted."

Maxim smiles at me, probably the first time he's done so for real. "Thank you, Matthew. Have a wonderful holiday."

"You too."

With a gentle honk, Maxim waves and pulls back into traffic. I'm left alone, shrinking underneath this architectural anomaly. A tiny reprieve waits for me inside.

The doorman checks my name on the approved-guests list. Despite Bentley not being home, I assure him she authorized my visit, fudging some remark about watering plants. A lie seems the least of my worries right now.

I take the speedy, aerodynamic elevator up to one of the top floors. The doors spit me out a few apartments down from Bentley's. A skunky weed smell permeates the place. A Mariah Carey song blasts through the floor above. This building has always been a party place. A hot spot where zillennials' mommies and daddies bankroll their modeling careers and dubious start-ups. Day drinking and drugs are only ever a knock away.

I pause before shoving the key into the lock, shooting off a text to Bentley.

We need to talk. My parents are THE WORST.
Staying at your place for a bit.

The whoosh of a sent message helps me relax, even though Bentley has been silent since Island Gate dropped. Not that I reached out in the past days either. Maybe I haven't given her a chance to prove herself. Maybe she's waiting for me to reach out to her for comfort. If she thought I needed space, that would be the kind thing to do.

A large majority of me doesn't buy that, but it's more comforting than the alternative: that I've always been a dormant torpedo poised to sink her shiny social submarine.

Regardless, she gave me the key with the express permission to come by and use her place whenever I needed to.

The need has never been stronger.

Her two-bedroom unit has a stunning view of the Brooklyn Bridge. The curtains are flung open, inviting in early afternoon light. There's not a Christmas decoration in sight. I'm happy to smell the familiar lemon floor cleaner over the scent of cinnamon candles or baking treats. My nose needs a break from Christmas.

I leave my bag at the door and drop the key in the bowl before shooting off one final text:

Let me know if you need anything done while I'm here. ♥

A phone chimes from the peacock-blue sofa. A sleepy Bentley shoots up and scares the shit out of me. When we lock eyes, we both scream.

"Jesus, Bee. What the fuck?" I clutch my chest, hoping my heart doesn't switch to overload. The cloud of her presence is overwhelming. It's been a while since we haven't had a phone screen between us.

Wiping sleep from her eyes, she shakes her head. "You're going to what-the-fuck me when you're the one who just broke into my apartment unannounced?"

"I texted," I say, holding up my phone while still holding my heart.

She checks. "So you did. Still. Knock much?"

"I thought you were supposed to still be in Aspen."

She groans, standing. She sports a cropped hoodie, a pair of designer sweats, and her signature thick eyeliner. "I was. Not that it's any of your business, but I got into a fight with my parents over the bajillion-carat, oval-cut, D-color diamond necklace from Tiffany I asked for and did not find under the tree last night," she says. "I took the private helicopter back to prove a point."

Ignoring her pettiness for a second, I strip off my coat and hang it by the door. She appears visibly peeved by the act, while she grabs a Voss from the fridge.

"I'm seriously so happy to see you," I begin. "Everything has blown up, and I can't stand to be alone right now. I need a place to stay." I step further into the kitchen, hopeful, while she drinks, never breaking eye contact. "Can I get one of those? I'm parched."

"No, you can't," she says, point-blank, unblinking.

"Why not?"

"Because you're not staying. In case you haven't heard, you're canceled, Matthew Douglas Prince. Hashtag PrinceaPaLOSER was trending for twenty-four hours. There's absolutely no way in hell I can risk having people see you coming and going from the building, let alone be seen with you right now." Her tone suggests this should've been obvious.

I huff out an incredulous breath. "Some kind of friend. What about our New Year's Eve party?"

"Oh." Bee makes a big show of thinking about it, even though I can tell her mind is already made up. "I made the executive decision to throw this one solo. I got all new invitations made. See?" From a pile on the counter, she hands me an envelope.

Once I pop the seal, the card bursts into a box, spewing confetti into the air with impressive velocity.

After it's done spitting out silver and gold glitter, I notice it has nothing but an address, a time, and a dress code. The other sides of the box are artsy photos taken by an up-and-coming photographer whom Bentley was intimate with for a few months last summer before breaking up with him in Thailand and going on a bender.

If you didn't know Bentley well enough, you'd have no idea it was her—a smooth, milky elbow on a lounge chair, black locks spilled along white, hot sand. There's no mention of me at all. I've been erased.

"It was a super-last-minute decision, Matty Baby. Don't be mad. It's what's best for the party," she says. "You know how it is. The rise and fall of the party people. You'll be back on the horse next year. I'm sure of it. But for now, you have to go."

"You can't be serious." She's nudging me toward the door.

"Unfortunately, I am." There's no irony in her voice. No mocking. She means this. To her, social perception is of the utmost importance. If she loses her crown, she loses everything.

I lost my crown somewhere between Wind River and here, and frankly, I couldn't give a flying fuck. I see that now, even if it burns.

"I thought we were friends," I say half-heartedly outside her door.

"We were... I mean, *are*." She does a bad job of covering her slipup. "We will be again once this all goes away. We'll do brunch. Bottomless mimosas and eggs Benedicts on me! I'll text you, okay?" she asks, but she doesn't wait for an answer. The door is already closing in my face.

I stand there, stupefied with the horror that the only friendship I've had for the last few years was never real. It was all built on falsities and posturing. I no longer serve Bentley so she leaves me with nowhere to go.

Well, not *nowhere* exactly. But not anywhere I want to go. Not anywhere I should go.

Yet what other choice do I have?

My fingers move to call Noelle. In Wind River, she wouldn't bat an eyelash at my outlandish predicament. She'd offer me a place to stay.

Hector's blocked contact taunts me. He'd know what to do too. If only I'd given him a chance to explain. Stupid me. Believing my parents and suffering the consequences. Once again. I'll never learn.

I can apologize all I want. It will never be enough for blowing them off, running away over a misunderstanding.

Coat flapping in the wind, I'm a dog with his tail between his legs, pounding the pavement in the direction of the only place I can think to go.

I'll show up, unannounced, and hope for the best.

✴ ✴ ✴

Hoping for the best was a stupid idea.

Bentley's brush-off was bad, but once I walk the gazillion blocks to get where I'm going, I'm greeted by the only doorman in New York City who absolutely hates my guts.

He's a short, built, bouncer-type with a dramatic buzz cut and a permanent scowl. He's despised me ever since I got too drunk on a night out and threw up in one of the lobby's ficuses. In my defense, it was the plant or his shoes, so at the time I felt I deserved a thank-you. Now I know better; I was in the wrong for overdoing it.

"Hello, Norman," I say with a congenial smile so he knows I'm here with good intentions.

"Mr. Prince, what a joy, a privilege, an honor." His deadpan response makes me wish I were dead.

"Sorry to bother you on a holiday." He grunts at that. "I'm just here to see Baz and Spencer."

His smile tells the whole story. "Sad to say they're gone for the holidays. They happily left for a getaway on some far-off island. You know all about those, don't you?"

"Suppose I deserve that," I say. I don't know what hurts worse, the jab or the fact that my exes are on a vacation, living it up without me. Not that I expected them to clue me in or be moping in my absence. If I weren't on a social media lockdown, I could've deduced this for myself, but nevertheless, I'm more upset than before. "Do you know when they'll be back?"

"I'm not allowed to disclose resident information," he says.

"You just told me they were away."

"No, I didn't."

"You—" I stop myself. He wants me to argue. I'm not going to give him the satisfaction. If Baz and Spencer can't provide me the holiday haven I need, then I know it's not meant to be. Scratch that. I've known for a while it wasn't meant to be, and coming here has only confirmed that their lives never needed me. I was ornamental. Fun for a time. But that time has passed. "Thank you for your help, Norman."

He aggressively tips his hat. "Merry Christmas, Matthew Prince."

Cue the somber Charlie Brown music as I rack my brain for a warm place to share a meal and spend the night. I never expected to long for Grandma and Gramps's cabin, yet here I am. Wishing for a place I wanted so desperately to escape.

I may have been forced to go there, but they never made it seem that way. They opened their home and hearts to me as if I'd been invited.

Invited. That thought reminds me of another invitation I received recently, so I recalibrate my GPS and prepare, against the abrasive cold, for one final pilgrimage.

CHAPTER 38

"I can't believe you came here last," Oksana scolds, piling my plate high with Christmas dinner. She spoons out samples of different vegan dishes. A woman holding a baby across the way encourages Oksana to give me more since I've never tried most of these delicacies except the kolach, a braided bread taunting me from the center of the hay-covered table.

"I left the candle in the window from last night and everything," Oksana adds.

"What does the candle have to do with anything?" I ask, peering at the tall white candle on a circular tray filled with pooled wax. Its flicker is calming, dancing with the breeze of each person walking by.

"It's a Ukrainian tradition. It's to let passersby know that all are welcome in the celebration of the birth of Christ," she says. It's a lovely custom, though I don't think more passersby could fit in this small apartment that's full up with party guests.

At my first bite of kutya—a cooked wheat treat with poppy seeds and raisins—I light up with pleasure. I missed Oksana's home-cooked meals so much. "Thanks for letting me crash here. I don't want to cause an issue between you and my parents."

"Oh, Matthew, I've worked for your family long enough. I can handle it," she assures me.

I've never known a world without Oksana. She was my caregiver when

Dad was at work and Mom was writing. She was my homework helper and my playmate before I had friends. She was my chaperone to some school functions.

When I was too old for an au pair, or in periods where Mom was less busy and Dad took days off, she became housekeeper and chef extraordinaire. The way she's adapted every step of the way, anticipating our family's needs, is a wonder to me. It's illustrated right now in the way she pours me a glass of water without asking.

I know it's not the time or the place, but Oksana is the only person close enough to even remotely relate. "I don't understand why they did it."

"No sense overthinking other people is what I always say. They do what they do, and they do it for them." Her wisdom has always been bountiful.

It's that wisdom that prompts me to ask: "Have you liked working for my family?"

She puzzles over this question, toying with a stray strand of straw in front of her. "I have. I didn't expect when I came to New York that I'd end up working for such a prominent family. It was stressful at first, but caring for you when you were young brought me so much joy. Caring for you now too." She smiles. "I have a younger brother, Amon, and I missed much of his childhood when I left. Seeing you grow up was a nice exchange. Now, I'm going to see him at his home in Italy for the first time in four years next month, thanks to your parents."

"Really?" I ask, wondering how I wasn't looped in on this.

"Yes, they offered me quite the lovely holiday bonus this year, so I used it to book two plane tickets. One for me and one for my fiancé," she says.

"Fiancé?" I ask. I've never seen her wear a ring. Though I guess if you're cooking and cleaning all day, there's too much of a risk that your rock might fall down a drain or end up baked into a loaf of bread.

"Maxim," she says. At the sound of his name, a tall man with a black beard turns toward the table. I'd know the back of that head anywhere. I have it memorized from the front of the Town Car.

"Matthew, what a surprise," he says, coming in for a handshake.

"Matthew will be staying with us for a bit. We'll need to fish out the linens for the pull-out sofa when everyone leaves," Oksana says.

They live together too? I want to ask how, when, and why I never knew this before, but the answer is so clear. I never bothered wondering about anyone but myself.I didn't even know Oksana had a brother. I feel like the biggest prick.

"I'm speechless," I say.

Oksana laughs. "Your mom introduced us. We've been together for four years, engaged for two," she says. Oksana is verging on forty. She was probably around the age I am now when she started with us. I was maybe four or five then. Awful that I never questioned her life outside of my apartment.

"I'm sorry I never asked about any of this before," I say, overcome with the urge to go back and do better, but I know that's not an option. Not in any avenue of my life. "Why haven't you gotten married yet?"

"We want to do it right and big with our whole families. Getting everyone in one place would be expensive. We're both old enough to know if we are going to do it at all, we're going to do it right," she says.

"If you could have your dream wedding, where would you want to get married?" I ask. My planning brain is turning on. Cogs are spinning. How could I make this happen for her? Especially since I realize she's spent approximately seventeen years of her life helping to raise me, treating me as if I were her family when her real one was living all over a completely different continent. What a selfless act. This is the best way to repay her for how I've acted and how much she's given me. I'm sure of it.

"I'd get married on the moon if it meant everyone I loved was in the same place," she says. Her sentimentality gets to me.

"Noted," I say.

Oksana tenderly pats my cheek. "Now, it's Christmas Day. Don't dwell on the darkness too much. Tomorrow, you can confront everything. Tonight, we sing carols."

She stands and calls the room to attention, moving into the living room where there's a keyboard in one corner. Oksana used to play the baby grand in the sitting room at the apartment for me when I was young. It always cooled my fervid temper.

Before I know it, I'm joining in the chorus, singing loud and proud for all to hear, unafraid to fly off-key or hit a wrong note. Nobody here is going to judge me. Nobody here cares. Everyone is just happy to be full-bellied and together.

Even if it started off shitty, this is the happiest, merriest Christmas I've had in a long while.

Once everyone leaves and I'm curled up on the fold-out, blanket pulled up to my chest, I take out my phone and make a call. The day's events have caught up to me since I'm finally alone with my thoughts.

"Matthew, dear? It's late. Are you all right? Merry Christmas," Grandma says, not an ounce of resentment over me leaving sitting between the notes of her singsong voice. That comforting sound makes the tears come on. "Dear, what's wrong? You sound upset," she says. The concern is palpable even through the phone. Even though I put this distance between us again.

"Everything is changing and I can't make it stop," I say as if the act of manipulating time and space were ever in my power. "How do I make it stop?" With the phone to my ear, I slide on my shoes and coat, lift open the window, and hop out onto the fire escape. Oksana and Maxim are sleeping, and I don't want to be a burden. More of a burden, I should say.

"Hold on." I fumble with the old latch. "I'm sorry. I'm sorry. I'm sorry. I'm sorry…" I keep saying it on repeat. All those years filtering it from my vocabulary and now I'm a broken record. It doesn't feel good, but it doesn't feel bad either.

"What are you apologizing for? Dear, did something happen?" she asks. But where to begin? God, I can't play her our greatest hits without croaking a full sob.

"I found out about the divorce," I tell her. "And how Mom leaked the story of my island to cover it up." The betrayal flashes fresh each time I call it out. "Everything is changing and not for the better."

Her sigh causes a crackle on my end. "I'm sorry you're going through that, Matthew."

"I keep asking myself *why*. Why did she do it? There's no real answer."

"Dear, it makes me sad, but I think your mother only shows you a small sliver of who she really is." Grandma sniffles. "Your mother has been struggling for a long time now, and she's gotten very good at hiding it, especially when you were a child and she stepped onto the world's stage." A tentative beat goes by. "I don't say this to excuse her behavior, which angers me more than you can imagine. I say this so you know there's more to her story than she puts on the page."

You get that from my side of the family. I slump against the cold railing, letting the biting frost seep through the pair of borrowed sweatpants I'm wearing. The cold is a shocking balm.

"Are you saying what I think you're saying?" I ask.

She clucks. "I've already divulged too much. I know you're probably not ready right now, but one day, when the time comes, ask her yourself. She may surprise you." Her tone isn't convincing even if it is hopeful. "None of this will be easy but Gramps and I will be here for you if you need us."

I think about what she said. Doors and windows into my life. "Even after I ran off like a scared little boy?" I ask. Shouldn't that have put a dead bolt in the way?

"Scared? Would the Matthew who showed up on my doorstep three weeks ago have voluntarily thrown a charity gala? Put his ego away to connect with a community he didn't know and wasn't a part of?"

"Probably not."

"Look, I'm not saying you were an oaf stomping around all the time before, but you always had your own interest at the front of the line. Something changed for you here. If you feel everyone around you is changing, it's because you're changing too. Enough to notice it," she says.

I wipe my eyes with the back of my sleeve. "I guess you're right."

"Oh, I'm a grandmother and grandmothers are always, always, always right. Never forget that," she says.

"I won't," I say, remembering the reason—the real reason, not the selfish one—I did all that work in the first place. "How did we do?"

"We raised a good chunk of change because of you."

Momentarily, I brighten. Only she doesn't say more, which makes me fearful.

I hedge, "Enough to save the store?"

"It was a record amount." It doesn't come out cheery. It's a simple fact, which lets me know that the event wasn't the smashing success it needed to be. "You did your part beautifully. Everyone is still talking about what a perfect evening it was. The money we needed was a long shot. Don't beat yourself up about it."

I resist the urge to argue. Instead, I simply thank her for the grace she's granting me in this moment—letting me know that I can't harbor hurt over something out of my control.

Maybe I need to apply that lesson to Mom's lies as well. The one thing I could control was how I responded to Hector as my mental health spun like a top off the table. All the other wreckage was an unavoidable by-product.

I sigh. There's a beat where I take in the sounds of the cabin. She's hearing sirens and the rattle of buses down below. We hover in an alternate reality where I didn't leave with Mom. One where I didn't go running at the first sign of impending doom.

Trying to be courageous, knowing there's a bigger apology meant to be made, I ask, "Is Hector in?"

There's a lengthy pause. Some whispering. "He's…not, dear. He stepped out for a bit. Or, um, sorry, he's sleeping." She's not accustomed to lies. Even tiny ones. "Would you like me to leave him a message?"

"No, no," I say, almost too quickly. The mean words I said to him flip inside my mind. I've been studying that scene repeatedly. If only I'd thrown out the script, forgotten my lines, been honest about my feelings and heard him out. Too late now.

"If you're sure," Grandma says. She's trying not to sound too dejected.

"I'm sure," I say. "Everything else okay?"

"Everything is peaches and cream, dear."

"Good…good. Merry Christmas," I say.

"Merry Christmas," she says. "I love you."

"I love you too."

Right as I hang up, a snow flurry trickles down from the ashen night sky. I stand there, letting it wash over me, not absolved per se but ready— *more than ready*—to turn over a new leaf. To care for myself the way I've been neglecting for far too long.

With my last iota of energy, I draft a text I should've sent ages ago:

Merry Christmas. Sorry to bother you so late but…
I'm ready to talk.

My final Christmas wish whisks out into the universe.

CHAPTER 39

"You've undergone a lot in a short period. It's valid for you to be feeling very strong feelings right now. It's a major step that you showed up here today to work through this, and I want you to know that the work will take time, but it will be worth it."

Work. Hard work. Hard work feeds the soul. Hector is everywhere. Omnipresent after everything. Still infiltrating my life in a positive way.

How do I pay that back in kind?

I guess that's what I'm here trying to figure out with my therapist, Josiah Barnes, in the Upper West Side office I used to consider a second bedroom. I know the fabric couch by heart. Its cushiest spots; its squishiest pillows. The way the air purifier hums and where to reach for a fidget spinner or a stress toy. The statue of a robin on the shelf across the way that I can fixate on when Josiah's eye contact becomes too intense, hits too close to the heart of the truth.

I've spent hours in here unpacking, tucking hurt into new drawers, reorganizing the closet of my childhood memories. Josiah Barnes has heard it all—from the fallout with Lukas Clifton to the NYU debacle, and now I'm ready to sort through the mess I left behind in Wind River and the new mess I've returned home to.

I'm ready to make this practice permanent again.

"I don't know how to not feel both hurt and remorseful," I confess.

"Those things aren't mutually exclusive," Josiah says, toying with a silver ball of beads. "We've talked previously about your aversion to apologies."

"I'm a vending machine full of 'I'm sorry' these days," I tell them. "But I don't think Hector wants to hear one. Not after I ran off and hurt him in a way I knew I could for something he didn't even do. And I'm not sure my culpable mom would offer another one. The one at the Plaza felt obligatory."

Josiah lets us sit with that for a moment, knee bouncing before a thoughtful breath. "What would you say to her if she did offer another one?"

Josiah has a way of smacking me with the heavy-hitting questions, even at 10:00 a.m. I may not be caffeinated enough for this, but I guess this is what I've always liked about therapy and why I've worked with Josiah for so long. Their eyes peel away the bullshit until I have no defensiveness left.

It strikes me that maybe that's what drew me to Hector. I'm pulled toward people that won't let my posturing stand in the way of what's real. I hold on to that revelation for a moment, and answer the question posed. "I'd say I wish she hadn't done it—either of those things, the leak and the lie—but that I can understand the scared place she had to have been in to have made such drastic decisions." I swallow hard, shaking my head.

Josiah's position shifts to something more upright. "Is that a place you've been before—that scared, rash place you just described?"

Flickers of the night I bought the island come to mind. The night I tried to escape Wind River. The night of the gala. I've cozied up in that dark place many times before, hissed at any sign of light seeping in.

I don't even hear myself say yes, but I must've because Josiah says, "Is it possible your mom might deal with some of what you deal with daily?"

It's wild that I'd never considered this before. Her buttoned-up public image bled into our home life so young. I was taught to hide my GAD because, maybe, she was hiding hers even better. It's how she thought she could protect me. It was wrong, but that doesn't mean it's without merit.

"Mental illness can run in families," Josiah adds.

My bobbing head only picks up speed. "You could be right."

"And let's imagine for a moment I am. Can we reconsider my previous question?" I'm so wrapped up that I don't even remember the previous question, so Josiah kindly calls it back. "What would you say to her if she apologized again?"

"I'd say I'm not ready to forgive her just yet, but that I want to." This might be the biggest realization I've come to in this office, which is saying something.

I don't want to hang on to this burden. It's only weighing me and my mind down.

They smile. "And what about Hector? Do you think you could find a way to offer a truthful apology to him?"

"Of course," I say without hesitation. One has been forming for days, though I know it will wither away with time in my notebook. He has no interest in hearing from me. "But him accepting it? That's another story entirely."

"Apologies aren't always about acceptance," Josiah offers. "Can you elaborate on this fear of rejection?"

"What I said was callous and kind of unforgivable."

Josiah exhales. "Would you say what your mom did was also quite callous and unforgivable?"

"Maybe," I say, confused by the string of logic.

"Okay, so by that token, if you could come around to the idea of forgiving her," Josiah says, about to rock my world with therapeutic reasoning, "don't you think Hector could do the same?"

I consider this from all its angles, and for the first time since leaving Wind River, the light spectacular spangled throughout my chest buzzes back on. "Do you really believe that's true?" I ask, allowing hope to visit me once more.

"There's only one way to know for sure."

$$*\ *\ *$$

Returning to my apartment the next day is a shock to the system.

Christmas has yet to be packed away; garland still gleams on the mantel, and ornaments are still hanging from the going-brittle tree. I let myself believe, if just for a second, that none of the bad stuff transpired.

Footfalls snap me back, and that's for the best. Fantasy doesn't hold water when Mom and Dad enter the family room with Sarah Pearson, my erstwhile nemesis, not far behind.

While I'm still not feeling the warm fuzzies when it comes to any of them, if I'm going to make amends the right way, I'm going to need their help. It's the least they can supply when they tipped my life into utter turmoil.

Granted, I did that to their lives first with my frivolity—I see that clearly now—so I've prepared a proper apology.

The assembled perch themselves across from me, all on a strict time crunch. Dad needs to return to the office—he rarely takes lunch breaks as it is, the workflow never letting up. Mom has an important meeting about her musical later today. The fact that they both took my request seriously and showed up—punctually even—is a wonder that I'm thankful for.

Sarah crosses her legs on the couch, tablet at the ready, eyes sharp like I've inconvenienced her. Like she hasn't been inconveniencing me my whole life.

I clear my throat and set my coffee down. Oksana has laid out a spread. Her presence in the kitchen radiates an aura of support. Whichever way this goes, I know someone will be there to comfort me unconditionally.

"Thank you all for coming. I won't take up too much of your time. However, I want to start by apologizing." I wait for Dad to interject about how apologies show weakness, and Princes are too strong for that. The way he remains silent lets me know he's here to listen. And he's only checked his watch once since sitting down, so score for me.

"I'm sorry for lashing out and buying the island. It was selfish. The music festival I wanted to throw there was about me creating something that set me apart from the two of you." Everyone shifts slightly at that. I had a feeling they would. We never discuss the massive shadow they cast over me and my life. "I've never not known this spotlight, and the truth is I've never quite known what to do with it. So I abused it, and abusing it for so long got me into a lot of trouble."

"I'll say," Sarah mutters. It's clear she thinks it's funny, and I'm more than satisfied when no one laughs.

Ignoring her crack, I say, "It was wrong of me in every conceivable way. I know you had to work hard to fix another of my big mistakes. All those actions came from a scared, defensive place of panic." I hope my word choice makes clear to Mom that we frequent the same shadowy corners of our minds. The chemicals a little funky and the decision-making centers a little out of sorts, but that's okay. That's our normal.

"That's very mature of you, Matthew," Mom says. Her tic is turned up all the way, fingers tugging on the edge of her blouse.

I can't go back and be kinder, gentler, and more understanding with her, but I can make a choice to do that going forward. "While my apology holds, it doesn't negate the fact that you all hurt me. Deeply. Even if I understand why you did it, my feelings are valid, and I need you to acknowledge that."

Dad bristles in his chair, clearly uncomfortable. I wish frank discussions didn't make him prickly—evidenced by his red neck and the sheen of sweat across his forehead. If we'd talk about my mental health more openly, or at all, really, we wouldn't be this on edge sharing our feelings.

"Acknowledged," Mom says.

"Ditto," Dad adds warily. A notification chimes in on his phone. He ignores it. That earns a smile. If he were anyone else, it wouldn't. But he's him, and I'm going to learn to accept that.

Just as I hope they can learn to accept me. Hidden parts too.

"Good, because…I have a generalized anxiety disorder. I know you all know this. Maybe in less certain, less clinical terms, but for some reason we don't talk about it," I say, allowing my pent-up frustration to roll through my sternum and pass. "I'm not ashamed of it—not anymore, anyway—and I don't want it to be some big secret hanging over me."

Naming it forces Krampus to lose some of his power; he shrinks in size and retracts his claws. The immeasurable weight of stigma falls off my shoulders.

I angle in toward Sarah, steeling myself for her icy-blue eyes beneath blunter-than-blunt bangs. I will not let her steamroll my life for salability any longer. "Since I can't shut off the spotlight, I want to talk about this publicly—help other people feel less alone. I want to get involved with organizations that uplift queer people who need mental health support and amplify less privileged voices. I'm done pretending having all this means I can just lean on it forever."

Sarah purses her lips. "We'll need to go over the approaches, run some tests, see how this might affect the brand." She spouts off more and more meaningless PR jargon until I can't stand it anymore. I'm about to speak up when Mom beats me to it.

"Sarah, that's enough." She folds her arms across her chest, taking the power stance I learned from her all those years ago. Never have I seen her use it on Sarah—the confidant, the keeper of the secrets, the one who's been here since the beginning. "You work for our *entire* family. Not just me and Matthew Sr. If this is what Matthew wants, then do your part to make it happen."

Sarah's clipped smile goes loose at the edges. "Anna, I understand you want to support your son. Believe me, mental illness is all the rage right now. We just need to make sure we're doing it in an *organic* way."

I audibly groan. "I'm not doing this because it's trendy, Sarah. And, honestly, that's a messed-up thing to say."

She stammers, tapping on her iPad as if it contains a reasonable excuse. "I'm sensitive to the issues."

"That *was* a messed-up thing to say," Mom says, coming to my defense, and after a bout of thought, she adds, "I think it's best if you go."

It takes all my self-restraint not to stand up and cheer. Like me, Mom has always bowed to Sarah's word, treating it like law. Now, Mom's standing up for herself. For me, really.

"Anna, come on. I misspoke."

Mom is having none of it. "This is a family meeting, Sarah. I'd like it if it were just the family from here on out."

Sarah huffs an incredulous huff, hesitating and then stuffing her tablet into her expensive red tote. Before she's out the door, Mom calls, "We can circle back on your place on our team in the new year."

Sarah doesn't deign a look back over her shoulder. The door clicks shut behind her.

Good riddance.

"Thank you," I say to Mom. Her speechlessness speaks volumes. "So, here's the deal," I begin before my nerves get fried or the residual anxiety of putting this off becomes unmanageable. "There are three things I need from you both."

My parents share a concerned look, but allow me to have the floor.

"First, I need access to one of the cars."

"Sure thing," Dad says, palming his phone. "We'll get Maxim—"

I stop him. "One of ours. For me to drive." It's clear they aren't understanding where I'm going with this. I don't care though. This isn't for them. "Second, Mom, I will need one of your signed *Game of Dark Dissension* first editions." It's a simple request, so she nods. "And lastly…"

Abruptly, Mom reaches out for Dad's hand, clearly scared that I'll write them off forever, and he lets her take it. He even squeezes it. The gesture makes my heart grow three sizes. Even if their marriage is ending, the love they built over the years won't die. It'll live on in me. Because of that, I make a silent vow to do right by it.

"I want you to cut up the cards again," I say.

Loaded silence gives way to rollicking laughter. I know my dramatic flair may have had them prepared for the worst, but come on, this is excessive. They're laughing as heartily as Grandma and Gramps do together. It's sweet, if a tad insulting.

Mom composes herself. "Oh, no, Matthew, we're not laughing at you." Instantly, the laughter turns to tears. Joyful tears, I think. "It's just when you asked to meet, we thought… Well, we assumed after what I did, you'd make good on what you said at the Plaza. You'd really want nothing to do with us. And for that to happen after my mistake, I would've been gutted."

I nod, trying to be as understanding as possible. "It's not forgiveness, all right? Not yet, anyway." I make sure I'm clear on this point. "I don't want the accounts back. I don't want my room here back either. I need my own space, away from all of this for a while. All I want is a new account made under my own name with the extra money you got from the sale of the island. Absolutely nothing more than the extra."

The extra is enough to support me for some time while I figure out the steps I need to take to live an independent life. What I didn't budget out for myself, I already have a solid plan for.

Dad speaks up. "That can be arranged, Matthew." His penchant for numbers relieves me for once.

"Thank you." I take a mighty deep breath, unburdened after all this time. "Is there anything you'd like to say to me before I go?"

Mom is slow to speak. "Just that I'm sorry again, Matthew. Not knowing you were in a relationship with Hector was not meant to be an excuse for my lies. I never want to stand in the way of you and love."

Love. Maybe it's the right word. Maybe I'll never know. Either way, it's obvious the apology extends to what happened all those years ago with Lukas as well. She's opening her eyes to the error of her ways. That's a solid first step toward—not repairing our relationship exactly, but building a new one perhaps?

"And that we love you, Matthew," Dad says in an uncharacteristic display of sentimentality. I knew there was a sappy inner life somewhere under those well-tailored designer suits. Maybe his new relationship has excavated a dormant part of him.

"We will never stop loving you," Mom adds.

"I love you too," I tell them, certain that this is what healthy progress looks like.

CHAPTER 40

The WELCOME TO WIND RIVER sign on the horizon looks different through the windshield. All snow-dusted and quaint, it sparks legitimate joy this time around. And when I pass it, my chest swells knowing I'm almost there with a Christmas redo in tow.

A bag full of better-late-than-never gifts rattles around in the otherwise empty trunk. Here I sit, strapped in to the driver's seat, sunglasses on my face, hands on the wheel. A road trip playlist of pump-up pop tracks blasts from the speakers.

"Are you sure you wouldn't like me to drive you, Matthew?" Maxim had asked when he dropped Dad's car off at my new rental apartment.

I told him I was sure, but that I could use some practice before the long drive. After renewing my license at the DMV—talk about a *humbling* experience—we trekked out to New Jersey to circle parking lots, merge onto highways, and not step on the brake erratically anytime a truck got too close.

As I cruise into the hillside sector, I applaud myself for not letting my anxiety talk me out of this. No matter what happens, this is an achievement all on its own.

When I pull up to the cabin, my motivation dulls a dash. There aren't any cars to be seen. No lights in the windows. I envisioned my return differently—everyone home, fireplace roaring. So much for that.

For a moment, I consider getting back into the car, but then I decide the walk will do me good. Stretch my legs out. I made sure to wear the appropriate shoes this time. I'm learning.

The heavy bag of presents slows me down quite a bit. Eventually, I'm marching toward Moon Beans. Noelle was supposed to be my last stop—a quick latte before heading back to New York—but I make an exception when I see her hard at work through the frosted front window.

I pause in the doorway, sheepish, when I notice she's serving Natalia at the counter. Their heads snap up simultaneously at the sound of the overhead bell.

Noelle pops her lips. "Look what the cat dragged in." She twirls her rag, almost tickled at how I've arrived on foot to grovel for forgiveness.

"Fair." I skip the greetings and get straight to the heart of why I'm here. "I'm sorry I ran off without a goodbye. You've been such a good friend to me and you didn't deserve that." I take a seat next to Natalia and rummage through my bag. "I come bearing gifts. I know that won't fix everything, but I hope it's a start."

Noelle eyes me with skepticism before ultimately taking the impeccably wrapped package. As she tugs off the paper, I turn to Natalia. "Sorry I didn't bring anything for you."

She laughs. "I think it would be a little weird if you had. You would've needed some serious psychic abilities to know we were going to run into each other today." Her ease with jokes and soothing voice help me understand what Hector saw in her when they were together. We're complete opposites, and yet Hector fell for us both. I can only pray he'll take a chance on me again.

Noelle's excited scream grabs our attention. "Are you freakin' kidding me?" Mom came through on supplying me a *Game of Dark Dissension* first-edition book signed by the entire cast of the TV series, and as a nice gesture, she threw in a promise of two tickets to the premiere of the musical in DC next fall. "Oh, wow. I take back every bad thing I said about you."

"What bad things did you say about me?" I ask with a playful squint, knowing full well there's been much worse said about me in much more public ways. But she's Noelle and this is Wind River and, fuck it, I'm happy to be back, so I let it go. I'm working on letting *all of it* go.

"Nothing, never mind," she says with a mischievous grin. "Please leave without saying goodbye anytime you want, especially if you're going to come through with such epic presents."

"Oh, I almost forgot." I hand her a smaller bag with a sparkly reindeer on the side, overstuffed with tissue paper. "Open this too."

Inside, she finds a Christmas-inspired latte art beginner's kit, stencils and all.

She licks her front teeth, fighting off a smile. "I hate you, Matthew Prince." But I know she means the opposite when she reaches across the counter and wraps me in a bear hug. "You are forgiven."

I release a sigh of relief. "If only it will be this easy with the others. Speaking of, they weren't at home."

"They're at Lorna's store," Natalia chimes in. "I was with Hector yesterday—not *like that*," she adds, anticipating a reaction out of me. "He needed a friend, and while we were together, he got a text from Lorna saying a huge anonymous donation was made to the SBA. They had just started prepping for a closing sale, but now they've gotta get everything back where they found it."

I smile to myself. Armed with that knowledge, I thank her, leave Noelle to her gifts, and forge onward.

When I arrive, Grandma's at the window of her shop taking down a barely used Going Out of Business sign. My heart flutters seeing her light up at the sight of me. "Matthew!" she calls excitedly from the other side of the glass.

The inside of the store is more barren. Books were beginning to be boxed up. Price guides had been pulled down. Maybe that was a good thing. Grandma could use some updates, and the money I wired is enough to foot the bill for plenty of them.

I won't tell her that though. She may assume. That's fine. I don't want anyone to feel indebted to me for something I wanted to do more than anything. Grandma and Gramps deserve millions of emotional dollars for putting up with me all these years. This year especially. A lump-sum donation is the least I could do.

Gramps grabs me and pulls me close, hugging me like he missed me. "What a surprise. Welcome back, Matthew." He eyes the bag. "What's all this?"

"Belated Christmas gifts," I say right as I lock eyes with a hesitant Hector coming out from behind the stacks.

He's wearing the red flannel and the corduroy jacket from the very first day. He's beautiful. Not like I'd forgotten, but being reminded causes tears to spring up into my eyes. I have to remind myself that this isn't forgiveness. This isn't happily ever after. Not yet.

"Oooh! Me first! Me first!" Grandma yelps, acting like a little kid.

I oblige. "It's a joint gift, actually." Inside an electric green envelope, Grandma and Gramps find two tickets to a taping of a popular baking competition series that films in New York City. "Since you loved the challenge Hector and I did, I thought it could be fun for us to go, get dinner, and then you can crash at my new place."

Grandma's eyebrows ruffle. "New place?"

"Yeah," I say. "I'm renting an apartment downtown now. It has a sizable guest room with its own bathroom. And an elevator! So Gramps won't need to worry about the stairs."

They beam at me, and I know they're proud.

"That's wonderful, dear. Sounds lovely. Can't wait." Grandma pinches my cheek in thanks before charting my gaze over to Hector. "Doug, let's go into the office for a second. I need help with, uh…well, just. Let's go."

Alone now, I take a tentative step in Hector's direction. "Hi."

"Hey." His posture is guarded, and I don't blame him. I'd be boarding up my heart too if he'd hurt me the way I hurt him.

"Before I give you your gifts, I wrote down everything I'd like to say to you so I don't forget anything." I produce a piece of paper from my back pocket, unfolding it with trembling hands. "Would it be all right if I read it to you?"

He nods, hesitant.

I breathe into my body and begin. "Hector, I'm sorry for the hurtful things I said the night I left town. Regardless of what I was told you did, you didn't deserve to be spoken to that way. My anxiety elevated to an eleven, and I dragged you into the darkness with me. That wasn't cool." I glance up a second to make sure he's with me. He hasn't moved a muscle. He hasn't even blinked. "If I had been thinking clearly, I'd have realized right away that a person like you—trustworthy, loyal, strong—wouldn't have betrayed me like that. I know in my heart who you are, and I wish I had listened to that instead of my sometimes unreliable brain."

"Matthew—"

"Would you mind if I finished first?" I ask, afraid if I stop I might lose my momentum. He nods again. "I think I needed to go home—well, not *home* exactly, but as close to it as I had before all this—to see everything that had changed and how my definition of *home* shifted in the short time I was here. You helped me see that *home* is not a place. It's people. It's the people you choose to invest in, believe in—the people you let hold your heart." I meet his eyes, so he knows I mean this bit more than anything. "I have never set my heart in more caring hands than yours." I'm crying now, swiping away stray tears. "So please accept these gifts as a small act of penance for, well, everything. Much love, the Grinch, a.k.a. Scrooge, a.k.a. Matthew, a.k.a...*me.*"

To free up my hands, I give him the note so he can see how many times I scratched out lines and rewrote sentences to get this to the level he deserved. Then I hand him a hefty box.

His expressive eyes flash from serious to overjoyed when he sees what's inside. "Is this a first complete edition of *Don Quixote*?"

I nod. "I had some help sourcing it. It wasn't easy to track down, but I'm told it's *bound in full calf.* Whatever that means. And that there's *gilt* lettering? Not sure I'm even saying that right."

"You are," he muses, awestruck.

"Anyway, there's also a not-rare-at-all paperback copy below that. I read and annotated that one since you seemed to enjoy that old copy of *A Christmas Carol* so much." I smile. "Apologies in advance for my wonky windmills. They're not easy to sketch."

As he opens the book, two rectangular pieces of paper flutter to the floor, landing beside his muddy boots. "Plane tickets?" he asks, picking them up.

"A promise is a promise," I tell him. "Or a deal is a deal, rather."

Inspecting them closer, he says, confused, "These are both to Dallas a day apart."

"I know. That's because I'd like to make a *grand gesture*. But I didn't want to just do it without giving you a choice or an out or whatever first, so..." I lower my voice so he can't hear how nervous it sounds. "If you take the earlier flight, I will be waiting in the JFK terminal for you to arrive. I have a ticket for that departure as well. Only if you want, I will tag along with you for New Year's so I can see where you grew up, get to know you better, and make up for those days we lost to my fears. If that doesn't appeal to you, you can arrive the following day—no notice necessary—and fly home solo to be with your family. I promise I won't be upset if you choose that option. And I won't read anything into it either. And...yeah."

He blinks at me, too stunned to speak.

I laugh uncomfortably to break the tension. "I know it's a lot, but, you know, *grand gesture* and all. So, um, I'm going to go now. I still have boxes to move into my new place and loose ends to tie up back in New York. I just wanted to deliver this personally, so you knew how sorry I was. Hector, I really, really am sorry."

There's more silence. He holds the two books, the tickets, my note. All of them probably heavier because of the emotions they carry.

I pick up my empty bag and zip my coat back up, escaping before nerves can get the better of me. "Grandma, Gramps!" I call into the back. "I'm heading out!"

"So soon?" Gramps asks, voice close. Almost as if they were eavesdropping by the door. "You just got here!"

"Yeah, can't you stay for supper at least?" Grandma asks.

I shake my head. "No, no. I need to get back, but thank you."

"You have a car waiting?" Gramps asks, peering out into the street. There's no idling Maxim to be found.

"No, I drove myself," I say. "Left the car up at the cabin."

"Well, let us at least drive you back to your car then," Gramps offers.

I shrug the offer off. "I'm fine. I can walk. I *want* to walk. I've been cramped in the car all morning." I hug them individually. "I love you both. I'll see you soon for the taping, okay?"

"Okay." Another sweet round of hugs warms me.

I wave goodbye to Hector, and after another stunned beat, he waves back. If this is the end of the road for us, at least I'll get to remember his half smile, the look in his eyes when he opened his gifts, and the crackling feeling still heating up my heart.

At the street corner, I pull one final apology from the pocket inside my coat—a stamped letter addressed to Baz and Spencer explaining myself and taking responsibility for my actions. I drop it with a flourish into the shiny blue postal box.

I tilt my head up toward the sun, finally embracing the light—*my* light; and that's the greatest gift I could've given myself this year.

CHAPTER 41

The long TSA security check is a cacophony of zings and rings behind me. Holiday travelers argue and roll their bags back and forth in impatient misery. I stand at the inlet with my Louis Vuitton carry-on in one hand and a plane ticket in the other.

I haven't seen him yet. Checking my Movado watch, I realize the minutes are ticking closer to departure. I didn't get any confirmation that he'd be here, but I promised myself I'd see this through. That's what Josiah would've told me to do. Even if my advance is rejected, I can begin the healing process. It's a personal win either way. Though one success would be much sweeter than the other.

Mom and Oksana return with a carrier full of sludgy peppermint mochas from the Dunkin kiosk. "He's not here yet?" Oksana asks. I shake my head, stuffed full of tissue paper.

"He'll show. He will," Mom assures me, but it does nothing to quiet my rumbling stomach.

I asked Oksana to come with me, and when Mom found out what I was up to, she invited herself. It's all part of her promise to be more present.

If they weren't here, I might've dipped by now, so I suppose it's a good thing. Their confidence, even if wavering, helps me stay strong.

I check my watch again. And again. Over and over for the full hour.

Five minutes late. There's probably traffic.

Ten minutes late. The parking here is a nightmare.

Twenty minutes late. My grand gesture failed.

He's chosen tomorrow's flight.

Acceptance is inevitable, but futile.

I sip my less-than-decent coffee, willing him one last time to appear, but he doesn't. For once, I do wish I was one of Mom's characters so she could write me a different ending...

"We should go," I tell Mom, sorrowful.

Oksana tugs me tight to her side. "You tried. That's what matters."

She's right. If it was meant to be, it would've been. Hector said it back at the lights spectacular, and now it's holding true.

That's okay. I'll ring in the New Year single, but I'll have plenty to look forward to. I've already begun contacting mental health nonprofits about volunteering. I put out feelers with Nan—Dad's mom—about a loan for my eventual event-planning business. I've even started decorating my new apartment, giving it all the Matthew Prince interior touches it needs to feel like *home*.

It's not such an evasive word any longer. I'm investing in me, believing in me, and holding my own damn heart in caring hands, forever and ever.

Home was inside me the whole time.

Just as I start heading toward the exit, a voice breaks above the ruckus.

"Hold the plane! Hold the plane! He's coming! He'll be here!" Gramps is jogging—not running—but jogging through the masses.

"You can't just hold planes. That's not how planes work," I say when he gets to us, winded beyond belief. I couldn't be more excited to see him.

"Well, *private* planes..." Mom offers. I give her a look. "What? I'm just saying."

"What are you doing here?" I ask Gramps. Then I see Grandma pulling up the rear in her snug coat and puff-ball hat. Noelle is beside her, giant replicas of the Times Square Ball hanging from her ears.

When they split off, a flushed Hector appears, rolling a suitcase behind him.

My heart catches, and my breath snags.

"I wasn't sure you'd come," I say.

"I wasn't sure I'd come either, dude," he admits. "It took a village just to get me here." He gestures to his posse.

"His car wouldn't start," Gramps says.

"And then Gramps lost his wallet," Grandma says.

"So they called me," Noelle says.

"And we had a terrible time finding parking," Hector says. *At least I got that part right.*

"Which is expensive as *hell*," Noelle cries. "I will be Venmo-ing you for reimbursement, thank you very much."

I laugh. "I got you. Don't worry about it."

But as I say it, my own worry rears its ugly head.

Focusing on my breath, I allow the atmosphere of this liminal space to settle in around us. We're far removed from the fantasy of Wind River and the reality of Manhattan. Somewhere in the middle of Queens, in its own zip code, Hector and I become uncertain reminders of a Christmas romance gone awry.

"Does this mean what I think it means?" I ask, needing to hear it to be certain that this isn't a holiday hallucination.

There is a long pause where I'm certain I've lost him to his own doubts, but then he smirks that delicious smirk and my body goes woozy. "When you first arrived in Wind River, I sincerely thought my whole holiday was shot to hell, dude. That my unfortunate situation had somehow gotten more unfortunate. Then we agreed to work together, and I thought, *Well, at least one good thing is coming out of this*. If I'm being honest, I never thought I'd get two good things. This." He holds up his plane ticket—the one for today. "And *you*."

Relief rushes through my body; his words mean everything to me.

"It crushed me that you wouldn't hear me out and that you left knowing that it would hurt me most of all, but I understand that the Matthew who believed the lie is not the Matthew I shared a room with, planned a gala with. Definitely not the Matthew that showed up with gifts and sincere apologies," he says.

"You're right." I'm suddenly scared. "That's right, but here's the thing: I can't promise that incoherent, spiraling Matthew won't come back. There's no cure or quick fix or reset button that will turn him off. All I can do is try and take care of myself."

He nods, understanding. "I know."

"Well, I guess…I guess I'm just saying I understand if that's too much for you."

His eyebrows knit together. "Matthew Prince—*too much*?" He laughs, oozing care. "No. Honestly, I don't think there will ever be enough. I was ready to say as much when you showed up at the bookstore, but why waste a perfectly good *grand gesture*, right?"

The lovely creases by his eyes let me know he's being genuine. It'll take some time to process all of this, but we have a whole plane ride together to hash it out.

"I forgive you, Matthew. And I know I said I don't believe good things last." Hector reaches out to touch me, and I lean in. "But I believe in our good thing, and I believe in *us*."

The wooziness multiplies. I stare back, at a loss for human words to describe the beautiful blasts booming inside me.

Right there in the middle of rushing commuters and frenzied guards, we kiss. It's the kind of kiss that reads like an ellipsis and hangs in the air over our heads, an uncertain piece of punctuation on a story we're still writing. It's a promise of something more to come. I surrender to his taste, his touch, his warmth, his life and then some.

The TSA security guard starts a slow clap for the absolute scene we're making. A horde of people join in. Gramps whistles. And for once I couldn't be happier about the sheer spectacle I've become.

New year, new me?

Nope.

New year. Same me. Better choices.

Starting right now with this one.

EPILOGUE

I'm in a relationship. So what?

It's not a perfect relationship. It's only been, like, six hours.

The guy is tall and solid and a little gruff, but underneath, he's intelligent and caring, and he sees my *potential*. I've always wanted to be with someone who believed in my *full potential*, so I asked him to be my boyfriend on the flight over, and he couldn't have said yes faster.

So here I sit in the back of a RideShare as our driver speeds up Route 121 North from the Dallas/Fort Worth International Airport to the very nearby suburb where my *boyfriend* is from.

Before we arrive, I check my social media. It shouldn't matter, but the way people are shouting about our airport reunion makes my heart beat faster. For once, the world gets to see the unfiltered me beside the person who makes me feel the most *me* I've ever been. Satisfied, I log out and delete the apps. I don't need a forced detox this time to trick me into living in the present.

To break up the silence, I ask, "Will I finally get to try some of this storied coquito?"

"Absolutely." Hector smiles. "Oh, and I forgot to ask. Do you like grapes?"

"What a highly specific getting-to-know-you question." We spent most of the flight over running down one of those internet lists—"200 Questions to Deepen Your Relationship" or something—to help pass the time.

"No, it's not that. I ask because my grandma *will* force you to eat twelve grapes at midnight to attract fortune and prosperity for the year ahead and if you don't participate you *will* be given the silent treatment by the entire family." He gives me worry-eyes.

"I will eat a million grapes if it will make your family like me. Promise."

Shortly after, we come to a stop at a vacant curb.

On a quiet tree-lined street sits a single-story house of brown and red brick. Expertly trimmed shrubbery lines the front exterior, adding softness to the sharp lines of the geometric home.

I hesitate before slipping out of the car, suddenly nervous. "You know what? I just remembered that I was cursed by a witch as a baby and now if grapes even come close to my lips I'll fall into a seven-year slumber."

"How do you explain all that wine you drink, then?" Hector rolls his eyes. "It'll be great. They'll love you." He offers me a hand as he hunches in the open car door, wearing a reassuring smile. "Come on."

I ride the wave of my emotions, letting the anxiety register and then roll away.

Hand in hand, we walk the worn path to the maroon front door. Hector knocks a unique rhythm, one the family must know by heart, and one my own heart saves away for later.

I take a breath—inhaling gratitude—and prepare myself for what lies beyond the threshold.

ONE YEAR LATER

I'm in the kitchen of the Cornelia Street apartment Hector and I are renting. Greenwich Village glows at night with a vibrant community and more sweet treats than my metabolism can take. I'm happy to be back in the city that raised me, in a new neighborhood that accepts me, living with someone who loves me.

I pour a glass of red wine to celebrate another successful event fully planned and on its way to completion—a holiday charity fundraiser for a mental health organization I'm affiliated with. I close my laptop. I'll start up again in January for Oksana and Maxim's wedding. Tonight, I'll bask in the pleasant uncertainty of an impending event blended with the cheerful certainty of helping others.

With Nan's backing, I finally opened Prince Charming Events, an upscale, boutique event-planning service catering to all walks of life and all budgets. I sometimes work pro bono, like I did for this evening's affair, but my usual rates have helped me manage my own bank account, independent of my parents' now equal-and-separate wealth.

Hector had been right: hard work feeds the soul.

Right on time, the key jangles in the lock. Hector slips inside. His hair is short now, tapered at the sides and trimmed at the top. He looks as handsome as ever as he slings his Herschel bag near the shoe rack and hangs up his coat. He's just come from his final class in his first semester as a graduate student in the department of English and Comparative Literature at Columbia University.

"Congratulations!" I call from my perch. I pour a second glass of wine and hand it to him as he greets me with a kiss on the crown of my head. "How does it feel to be free for at least a few weeks?"

"A student never stops learning," he says. He takes his first sip and *mmms* at the crisp, oaky notes. The bottle was an expensive gift from one of the celebrities whose vow-renewal ceremony I worked on a few months back.

"Well, you're going to have to keep your books in the bookshelf for this evening. I'm leaving in five and you should leave in, like, an hour just to be safe," I say.

"Oh, crap. That's tonight. Right." It's not like him to forget one of my events, but I shrug it off.

He sets his wineglass down near the toaster with a nod. "Guess I'd better get changed."

I follow leisurely behind him into our master bedroom where our king bed sits up against exposed brick and the large windows look down upon a relatively quiet sidewalk. I guess it was possible to find peace in this city of so many noises after all.

"It's business casual," I remind him. "You don't have to wear a blazer if you don't want to."

The way he relaxes makes me laugh. Dressing Hector up is a chore and a half. Mrs. Martinez told me he was the same way as a child when she broke out the scrapbooks nearly a year ago. It's one of the many quirks I love about him. If he wants to live in ripped jeans and beanies, that's his business. And besides, he looks so damn good in them.

I make myself comfortable on the edge of the bed, careful not to spill any red wine on our fresh, white duvet. I like watching Hector change. Taut, tan skin reveals itself like the gift that keeps on giving. He wiggles out of his jeans and into slacks.

As he lifts his shirt, I swiftly jump up and run a finger through his treasure trail toward his belly button. He giggles, which he only does, I've learned, when I surprise him. I wanted to see his smile.

"Keep it up like that and we'll never make it out of this apartment," he says, grabbing two handfuls of my ass with a low growl. The city looks good on him, I must admit.

Wind River Hector was tough and sure, but here, he's really transforming into a rare breed of self-assured man. I waited for this to scare me, but the fear never came. I thought somehow a catch with a face like his might meet another intellectual, stylish grad student and finally realize that while I might have been a Massachusetts seven, I was a New York City five.

Ugh. I throw that thought away like the trash it is. It's not productive. It's not *me* anymore. I'm working on it.

He fixes his button-down in the mirror. I come around behind him. The reflections staring back at us shoot happiness out in every direction. We're bright individually, but we're shinier together.

"Don't you have a staff to oversee?" he asks.

My eyes nearly leap out of my head when I check my Apple Watch. I fling on my coat and blow Hector a kiss from the already closing doorway.

I take the subway, which I've come to love in its own unreliable and grimy way, uptown to Queens. It's a bit of a hike but it will be worth it. The venue is everything I could've hoped for and more for this particular event. I settle on the plastic orange double seat and let the rattle and rock of the M train lull me as I do some meditative breathing.

Up on street level, I walk down the block and around the corner where the white, window-covered exterior of the modernist Museum of the Moving Image comes into view. Standing in front of the entrance, backed by neon-pink block letters, are a few of my highly skilled team members. They are all young, thriving, and willing to work for free this evening (though I secretly have holiday bonus envelopes stashed in my bag for each of them).

"Ready for some fun?" I ask.

Charlie, my assistant with iconic wire-rimmed glasses, pipes up first. "Everything in the café is in order. The centerpieces were a little more color-ful than we expected, but they give a nice pop against the stark white of the space." He opens the door for me to step inside.

No matter how many of these events I plan, I still get misty-eyed every time. I don't know if it's pride or disbelief or a combination of the two, but I'll never get over the feeling of something sprouting up inside my brain and then blossoming to life in a location like this. I take in the soft lighting, the view beyond the windowed walls, and the busy bartenders polishing glasses.

A tasteful banner draped across the ceiling reads: *Holiday Benefit for the LGBTQ Mental Health Alliance—Tis the Season to take care of your Mind, Body, and (Holiday) Spirit*. Not my subtlest tagline, but then again, nobody hires *me* for subtlety anyway.

Charlie hands me my iPad with my last-minute checklist already marked off. It's not like him to do my final sweep for me. "We all pitched in and figured you'd want some time to yourself before the event started. There are some early guests waiting for you in the exhibition."

"There are? I specifically said doors weren't open for another hour," I begin to argue, but rein it in. I remind myself that I can be a boss without being bossy. Charlie just shakes his head with a secretive smile. "What's going on? Who's here?"

"I think you'll want to see for yourself," he says, pushing his glasses farther up his nose. "I think you know where to find them too."

I start away, taking the stairs in twos. I bypass Tut's Fever Movie Palace with its ornamental marquee and the nearby prosthetics exhibit.

On the second floor, the zany orange and black of the Jim Henson Exhibition (*my happy place*) appears across the way. Mom stands there expectantly, dressed in complementary all-magenta. I can't help but pick up my pace.

"I thought you couldn't come," I say before giving her a kiss on the cheek.

"Matthew, we've been over this. I write *fiction*. I'm a good liar," she says. "More liars incoming behind you."

When I turn, Grandma and Gramps, in their Sunday best even though it's Friday, shout out to us, hands waving vivaciously. Hector, looking just as dapper as he did when I left him, leads the way. Hugs are exchanged. Cheeks are pinched. Nothing has changed. Well, everything has changed, but the good stuff has only gotten better.

"You boys look well," Gramps says, rubbing my shoulder. I think he feels like he played Cupid somehow. I'll let him have that one, since it makes him so giddy.

"Shall we head back down? Guests should be arriving soon," I say.

Hector shakes his head and pushes me toward the exhibition entrance.

When we turn the corner, with Hector's hand tucked safely in my own, we find three more smiling faces. Noelle is inspecting the creepy human hands of the Swedish Chef, and Siena, Noelle's now official girlfriend, is smiling upon one of Kermit's nearby banjos. Arthur, wearing the same outfit from the Wind River charity gala last year, towers over the cases.

"I can't believe you all came," I say, breathless with delight. Noelle nearly lifts me off the floor with the total force of her running hug.

Arthur goes in to greet Mom. Nothing official is happening there, but the ample times she's brought him up since deciding to get her own place in Wind River are more than enough evidence that something official could be in their future.

So many of my favorite people are gathered in a single room with so many of my favorite childhood comforts surrounding us. The stars are aligning for once.

We all branch off to take in the old set pieces and retired puppets, including my personal favorite—Miss Piggy in her wedding dress. Hector and I come here on date nights sometimes for special film screenings or just to reset after a long week. We've binged the entire Muppets back catalog together at this point.

It was his idea to host this event here tonight. I think my event management expertise has rubbed off on him. I wouldn't be surprised if he's started planning fake events in his head now too. Even though I'm doing it significantly less since my world has settled down. I'm learning to cope better.

"So, this was all your doing, I suppose?" I ask, knocking our shoulders together.

"Well, I figured since we'd be spending Christmas with my family this year, it seemed only right we get to all be together for at least a few nights," he says. "Oh, and Noelle and Siena are staying in our guest room."

"Ah, that must be why all those freshly washed and folded towels and sheets ended up in the linen closet," I say. "Oh my God. Did you just hear that? We have a *linen closet*. What's happened to me? Are we old? Am I *domestic*?"

"Do you want to be the ball or the chain?" he asks.

We laugh in the way only two people in love can, with a saccharine knowingness of their certain shared future.

Arthur comes over. "Let's enjoy the rest of the adorable sights later. We've got a movie to catch."

Mom passes out a series of donation-based tickets to the Redstone Theater, the architectural wonder that looks like the Epcot Ball had a baby with an intergalactic spaceship. I scamper back down to my team, who are already primed at the doors, allowing in a flood of luscious-looking people wearing smiles and festive pins in support of this evening's charity.

My family and friends take seats up near the top of the crowded auditorium right as the trippy, multicolored curtain gets drawn back. The projector blinks to life and the high-quality screen reads:

NOW PLAYING: SPECIAL SCREENING...
A MUPPET CHRISTMAS CAROL
TO BENEFIT LGBTQ MENTAL HEALTH ALLIANCE
IN PARTNERSHIP WITH PRINCE CHARMING EVENTS

I soak this feeling in.

Charlie runs me a microphone as the final guests arrive. Dad and Ellie shuffle into the front row with Oksana and Maxim close behind. With everyone I love present and accounted for, I begin.

"Welcome to the Museum of the Moving Image and thank you for supporting the LGBTQ Mental Health Alliance with your tickets to this evening's event. We begin with our showing of *A Muppet Christmas Carol* and will conclude with a dessert and drinks hour out in the café. The museum's exhibitions are all open for browsing at your leisure, and the Hot Circuits arcade games are free for unlimited use—unless somebody beats my high score at Donkey Kong, and then we're closing it down *immediately!*" Polite laughter rolls through the crowd.

"Please know that tonight's festivities are for a great cause. This time of year can be magical, wonderful, romantic." I steal a glance at Hector who may or may not be blushing. "But it can also be difficult for folks who struggle with their mental health, especially LGBTQ people who statistically experience anxiety and depression at a higher rate than their straight peers. The LGBTQ Mental Health Alliance works tirelessly to provide counseling and wellness resources to underserved populations. We hope that watching this film will remind you that the holidays are a season for giving. Sit back, relax, and enjoy the show."

Just as the lights dim, I take my spot, sandwiched between Hector and Noelle. I grab both of their available hands on the shared armrests, letting the center pieces and color schemes fade away into past-life nothingness.

A new, remarkable holiday tradition begins tonight.

NEW ADULT

by TIMOTHY JANOVSKY

Nolan Baker longs to be "thirty, flirty, and thriving" in this charmingly quirky LGBTQIA+ romcom that's *13 Going on 30* meets *One Last Stop*. Coming August 2023!

CHAPTER 1

Jokes, they say, are a lot like life and love: all in the timing.

Right now, I should be planning out the jokes for my next stand-up set, practicing the punchlines that are going to bring the house down during the upcoming open mic, but *no*. Instead, I'm doing *this*.

Come quick. It's an emergency, I type before throwing my phone on the bed like it's a bomb and assessing the unmitigated disaster that surrounds me.

Ever since my sister announced her surprise engagement and subsequent blowout wedding, my timing has been *way* off. Like life-in-utter-disarray off.

Case in point, I'm mid-crisis on a Saturday night, running majorly late to meet someone, and banking on my best friend to come through with a fix like he always does.

Footfalls bound down the hall to my right. The door flies open and a frenzied Drew—all six-foot-three of him (90% limbs, 10% other)—thrusts the fire extinguisher we keep stashed under the sink in the kitchen into my bedroom, nozzle first. "I told you not to light any more of those Doop candles if you're going to take a nap. You flail in your sleep. You're a flailer!"

He points and weaves, clearly trying to decipher where the fire is.

There is no fire. Not this time, anyway. Just socks. Lots and lots (and *lots*) of discarded socks, dumped from an overturned drawer and sprawled all over the floor. Tall socks. Short socks. No-show socks. Socks with zany patterns and TV-show quotes and corgi butts printed on them. But sadly, detrimentally, no dress socks.

There is, however, dress sock. Singular. And I am now dejectedly holding it up for Drew to see.

"It's not an I-accidentally-started-a-small-fire-by-flailing emergency. It's a do-you-have-a-clean-pair-of-dress-socks-I-can-borrow emergency." I look back down at my mess and correct myself. "Scratch that, even dirty dress socks would suffice at this point." I'd buy a new pair of my own if I were in any kind of financial position to do so. Perks of being a struggling stand-up comedian with a tip-based survival job.

Drew retracts the extinguisher, powering down from red-alert mode. "You couldn't have texted me that instead of making me think our entire building was going to burn down again?"

"Where's the fun in that? Where's the *drama* in that?" I waggle the sock in his face for emphasis, which he swats away, slight annoyance making his left eyebrow twitch. The one with the tiny scar above it from when he had to get stitches in high school after a bookshelf-building-attempt gone wrong. "Sorry, but in fairness you watched me throw out those candles after the incident. How was I to know the *Go to Sleep, Bitch* candle was going to put me to sleep in literal seconds? I don't fuck with witchcraft."

Drew snorts. "Of course, blame witchcraft and not your shifts that sometimes last until three a.m. or your off-again-on-again insomnia."

"I know you don't believe me, but there is totally something weird about where my sister works," I protest, launching into the same argument I give whenever somebody tries to upsell me on Doop, the trendy fad startup company my sister got in on the ground floor at. "Doop claims to be a lifestyle brand and yet they operate more like a cult. A very pretty, very wealthy, very health-conscious cult. It's creepy. And they definitely put something in that candle."

"I bet the Doop higher-ups possessed your body in your sleep and forced you to knock it over too." Drew's accusatory expression is completely unwelcome here.

"At least I acted quickly!"

"Yes. Your prompt yelling of 'Drew! Drew! Fire! Fire!' was both chival-rous and helpful."

I would dispel that absurd rumor of my inaction if it weren't completely true and I weren't talking to the world's leading Nolan-Baker-Bullshit-Detector. "At the very least, nobody was hurt and the damage was minimal."

"True," Drew concedes. "But we definitely lost our security deposit."

"Which is not a problem considering we're going to live here together forever and ever until we're gray and wrinkly and senile and then nobody will ever know about the unsightly singe marks until we're dead and buried." I shoot him with my most winning smile, musing a tad more, because *why not.* "Won't need that money when we're in side-by-side burial plots some-where shady and beautiful, perhaps with an oak tree and a bench."

Drew's expression warms. Red rising to the tops of his cheeks, matching the stark red of his hair that has always made him easy to pick out even in the largest of New York City crowds. Well, his hair and his previously mentioned height.

He's basically a giant. A gentle giant. A gangly gentle giant who is look-ing at me like I just solved the universe's oldest riddle. "You have it all figured out, huh?"

"Indeed." I give his cheek a light, friendly smack. "What I don't have figured out is what I'm going to do about this sock-cession..."

"Are you saying 'succession'?"

"No. Sock. Cession." I chop the air with each syllable. "A recession of socks."

Drew goes from thinking I hold the key to enlightenment to thinking I've swallowed said key and now we're going to have to wait days to weeks for me to poop it out. "Clue me in here."

"As in the value of my socks has greatly declined due to the fact that half of them have holes in them." I gesture to the pile on my left. "And the other half don't have a match." The sad, single socks sit on my right. An apt metaphor for my life.

Drew assesses the situation before dropping down to his knees and doing his damndest to find a perfect, put-together pair. How sweet and naïve he is to think I haven't scoured. Haven't hunted. Haven't prayed to Saint Anthony even though I'm as unreligious as they come. "How did such a deficit come to be?" He's evidently flummoxed by this, even if my general brand of disorder is commonplace by now. "Did you buy a million single socks or something?"

"Honestly?" I give him my best deadpan. "I blame the candle."

That gets a laugh out of him. "I'll be right back." He edges out of the room slowly. "Don't cause anymore chaos while I'm gone."

I cross my heart with my pointer finger and wait seconds for him to return. It's a sneeze-and-it-shakes small apartment.

"What are the dress socks for?" he asks upon arriving again, gracing me with a neatly folded pair of navy blues.

I flop way down onto my mattress, which doesn't have a bed frame (I like it like this, I swear) and slip them on, pausing over what to say. Drew and I have a no-lie policy as all the best best-friendships do, but in this case, I have to tread lightly. The last thing I want to do is let Drew, the bestower of blue socks, know that I'm slightly embarrassed and a little miffed over my evening plans. "I'm, uh, meeting someone."

If the sock-cession confused Drew, this news causes his brain to fry and his expression to sour. "You didn't put it on our Google calendar?"

It's funny how so much of my life is *ours* regarding Drew and me. This is *our* apartment. What he's referencing is *our* joint, online social calendar. These blue socks, for all intents and purposes, are now *ours*.

A lot of *ours* but there is no *we*.

"It was a last-minute thing," I say, not meeting his eyes while pretending to be amused by how big his socks are on me. You know what they say about guys with big feet…

"It takes two seconds to update our calendar." *Big* amounts of skepticism.

He's right on all counts. It would've been exceptionally easy to add a blue color block, the same shade as these socks, to the shared calendar that's meant to make our lives easier by blocking out work shifts (red), nap schedules (purple), nights we may want to bring another person home so the other should make themselves scarce (blue), etcetera, etcetera.

But the truth is, Nolan Baker using the blue is a rarity. Almost unheard of recently. "I have a...*date*." I nearly choke on the word.

There is an excruciatingly lengthy silence. "What happened to the whole *you're not going to date anyone until you've become a successful stand-up* thing?" he asks with a jagged edge to his voice.

The other truth is, Nolan Baker using the blue is a rarity (almost unheard of) because he's hopelessly, desperately in love with Drew Techler. But that's an admission only someone with a decent pair of matching dress socks is allowed to make. Love is not for those without a bed frame. Or so I'm told.

"That was all before my sister decided to be selfish and go and get herself engaged," I groan while crawling over to the open closet. I struggle to prepare myself for the onslaught of shoes. Being crushed by Mt. Ve-*shoe*-vius sounds better than having to face Drew about my feelings.

The feelings that are likely far too late and far too unreciprocated.

"Ah, yes. Love. The most selfish thing you can give another person." I don't even justify that with a proper response because I can't. I snort... or grunt...or something else stupid comes out of my mouth while I sort through the wreckage that is my belongings and try not to think about the inconvenient love lodged in my stupid heart.

When my sister announced her engagement to her co-worker to my whole family and told them Doop was footing the bill for an all-expenses-paid wedding as a marketing stunt, everyone else shrieked with excitement while I dutifully smiled, participated in the toast, and then sprinted to the bathroom to comb through my contacts for a suitable date. Even though the little audience in my brain was chanting: *Drew! Drew! Drew!*

Ted Grindr was a no-go because of his BO. Bill Tinder was a ghosting situation. Lamar Bumble was a chronic dick-pic sender. My phone was a long list of failed connections and missed opportunities, but I couldn't give up the search so easily.

Baker family functions, for me, go a little something like this:

Well-Meaning Family Member: "Are you still doing that comedy thing?"

Me: "Yes, Great Aunt (think of the oldest, crotchetiest name you can think of) I am."

Well-Meaning Family Member with an Old, Crotchety Name: "That's nice. Your Uncle (Insert Creepy, Generic Name Here) showed me one of your videos on *the* Facebook."

Me: "Oh, that was nice of him."

Well-Meaning Family Member with an Old, Crotchety Name: "Yeah...I didn't get it."

That's not even to touch upon the "Isn't New York City expensive? How do you afford it?" and the "Isn't New York City dangerous? Do you carry pepper spray?" and, by far my favorite, "Isn't New York City full of *the* gays? Shouldn't you have a boyfriend by now?"

All that passive-aggressive care is uncomfortable. I need a buffer by my side through it all. Especially for an occasion as lovey-dovey as my sister's wedding to her well-to-do, Connecticut-bred boyfriend. I'm going to stick out like the black sheep who can't stop *baaaaaaaaah*-ing loudly for attention.

"So, you're dating again because your sister is getting married?" Drew asks, obviously not grasping what I'm getting at.

As I carefully inspect the precarious shoe situation, I say, "I don't really think of it as dating. It's more like...*shopping*. Shopping for a wedding date. I'm basically going to the mall."

"As someone who lives and dies by romance novels, I don't love where you're going with that analogy." Drew has always been the one in our friendship with the mushy, hopeful heart, and honestly, that's part of the problem.

Not that he has a mushy, hopeful heart. I love that about him. Gah, *love*. Jesus.

It's more that he's a love-bug through and through, and if I make the wrong step while bumbling my way into adulthood, he could end up splattered on the sole of my shoe. A fate far worse than loving him from afar. At least from afar, I can't fuck it up.

That's what I'm telling myself, anyway. A smaller than small part of me knows I'm being governed by fear here.

Fear of awkwardness, rejection, having to find a new living arrangement because I've irrevocably fucked up the best friendship I've ever had by choosing an inopportune time to catch feelings.

Drew wants it all. The commitment. The cute Instagram photoshoots. The getaways and late-night phone calls. The whole works.

As for me, I want that stuff too. I want to give him that stuff. But I can't plant roots until I'm firmly progressing on my career path toward comedy stardom. With my family breathing down my neck, seemingly ready for me to fail, I need to prove that this move to New York City was for *something*.

For now, I'm fine, or pretending to be fine depending on the day, with casual, don't-bring-him-back-to-the-apartment flings. It all provides ample fodder for my stand-up material. Leave the strings for the puppets, I always say. (I don't really, but maybe I should start?).

Which is why when I turn around with two pairs of matching shoes, one in each hand, I'm hit with a niggling sense of mourning.

There's Drew. Handsome as ever, even in a pair of pale pink sweatpants and a matching crewneck. Someone who would make an excellent wedding date, and an even more excellent life partner. Someone who supports me and loans me socks and has kissed me on exactly two occasions and hasn't curled away in disgust, which has happened to me in the past, mind you! But in fairness, I had eaten a shit-load of garlic knots before said-kiss so I was basically vampire-repellant and this dude was wearing guyliner and a vintage My Chemical Romance T-shirt. You do the math.

God. I can't even keep a pair of damn socks together. How on earth could I keep a couple together when one half of that couple is *me*? Drew deserves more, better, *the world*. All I have to offer is this: half-heartedly begging for a pair of clean, matching socks on a Saturday night mere minutes before I need to leave for a date I don't even want to go on with a guy named Harry who's way out of my league. Honestly, Harry and I might even be playing two different sportball games, but he asked me out and I'm really in no position to decline a free meal at this juncture.

"Which pair?" I ask, forcing myself back to earth. Forcing myself to forget that I love Drew as anything more than a friend. (Note: this is impossible).

Resources

Mental health and mental illness are very important topics to me, as are recovery, safety, and healing. If you or someone you know is struggling, please reach out to a trusted loved one, a medical professional, or one of the support networks listed below.

You are not alone, and you are loved.

Hotlines & Crisis Resources

The Trevor Project
1-866-488-7386 or text START to 678-678

The Trevor Project is the world's largest crisis intervention organization for LGBTQ+ young people under the age of twenty-five. You can reach them by phone, text, or chat twenty-four hours a day, seven days a week.

Crisis Text Line
Text LGBTQ to 741-741

Texting the Crisis Text Line will connect you to a crisis counselor who can offer support. This resource is available twenty-four hours a day, seven days a week.

Trans Lifeline

1-877-565-8860

Trans Lifeline is a service devoted to offering care and support to transgender people. It provides peer support from a place of experience since the organization is staffed by trans individuals.

National Suicide Prevention Lifeline

1-800-273-8255

The National Suicide Prevention Lifeline is a free, anonymous resource for anyone who is dealing with suicidal thoughts or behaviors. By calling or visiting the site to access their online chat service, you can talk to a specially trained counselor who understands issues that LGBTQ+ people may be facing. Their website also offers a section devoted to lesbian, gay, bisexual, transgender, and queer issues along with information for friends and family looking to help.

LGBT National Hotline

1-888-843-4564

The LGBT National Hotline is for people of all ages and offers a confidential, anonymous place to talk about issues including coming out, identity, bullying, safe sex, anxiety, and other concerns.

Other Resources

Gay, Lesbian & Straight Education Network (GLSEN): Student Action

Gay, Lesbian & Straight Education Network (GLSEN) is an organization that offers information designed to help students take action and initiate changes in their schools and communities. Students who are interested in starting a Gender and Sexuality Alliance in their school can register to find resources and learn more about how student-led movements can help foster more inclusive schools for all students.

glsen.org

True Colors United

The True Colors United focuses on ending homelessness among LGBTQ+ youth. In addition to providing learning resources and advocacy, they also provide fundraising guides for those interested in raising money to support LGBTQ+ youth.

truecolorsunited.org

Pride Counseling

Pride Counseling offers online therapy to members of the LGBTQ+ communities. This service features counselors who not only specialize in helping people who are LGBTQ+, they also have experience with a range of issues including stress, depression, anxiety, sleep problems, trauma, relationships, self-esteem, and interpersonal conflicts.

pridecounseling.com

Q Chat Space

Q Chat Space allows LGBTQ+ teens to participate in online support groups that are professionally facilitated. All members are verified and the facilitators guide conversations and enforce group rules to ensure safety. The site also offers an option for Spanish-speaking LBGTQ+ youth.

qchatspace.org

Love Is Respect

1-866-331-9474

Love Is Respect offers resources for teens about healthy relationships and dating violence. The site has a section specifically for LGBTQ+ teens with information about dating abuse, personal safety, supporting others, and other topics. In addition to providing information about healthy relationships, they also have counselors available to provide support, advice, and education.

loveisrespect.org

The National Runaway Safeline
1-800-786-2929
The National Runaway Safeline works to provide resources and assistance to young people who have run away from home. They also work to help those who feel unsafe in their home or who are thinking of running away. They can provide assistance with transportation, shelter, counseling, and returning home.
1800runaway.org

Acknowledgments

This story first bloomed in my brain when I was a sophomore in high school supporting a deep obsession for ABC Family Christmas movies (yes, ABC Family—not Hallmark or Lifetime or insert other network here). I had binged to my heart's content but was still craving a holiday romance with leads who loved like I did, so on a trip to the Berkshires with my best friends, the idea of a disgraced rich boy and a struggling local college student falling in love popped into my head. I spent the weekend annoying everyone with my relentless barrage of ideas, details, and potential stars for a movie version (Dylan Sprouse, if you're reading this, you're still my #1.)

Since the inception of this book dates so far back, there are plenty of people to acknowledge for helping me (and humoring me) along the way.

Thank you to:

Tarah Hicks and Heather Hicks for many, many years of love and friendship that is more like family-ship, but also for taking me on the trip that inadvertently inspired this book.

The incredible editorial and marketing teams at Sourcebooks Casablanca, including: Mary Altman, Christa Soulé Désir, Diane Dannenfeldt, Deb Anderson, Stefani Sloma, Alyssa Garcia, Katie Stutz, and Jessica Smith, as well as our sensitivity readers and designers. I am forever grateful to you all for shaping up my little queer rom-coms and shepherding them into the hands of readers.

My agent, Kevin O'Connor, and the team at O'Connor Literary Agency.

My early mentors, Charlotte Sheedy and Ally Sheedy, whose feedback on this book was indispensable.

My first readers and close friends: Melanie Magri, Kelsey Scanlon, and Julie Matrale. Having good friends is a blessing, but having good friends who will read your messy first drafts is a downright miracle.

Robert Stinner, for your unwavering love, support, and unpaid editorial skills when I'm stuck or stressed or just "can't look at this damn thing anymore." My life (and work, let's be honest) would be significantly less full and swoony without you.

Alison Cochrun, I'm seriously unsure how I would survive—let alone thrive!—writing a book without you. Your feedback and encouragement made this story infinitely better, and your friendship is a cornerstone of commiseration and sanity in this wild career we've chosen.

Nate Rosario for your time and generosity in helping shape the characters.

The whole HoliGays22 team: Courtney Kae, Helena Greer, and Jake Maia Arlow. We made the Yuletide gayer this year, and for that I am most proud.

The authors whose support of *Never Been Kissed* and beyond has made this writing thing less lonely: Gina Loveless, Anita Kelly, Lisa Roe, Lynn Painter, Suzanne Park, Rachel Lynn Solomon, Ruby Barrett.

My parents, family, and friends for believing in me and my goals. Also for skipping the sex scenes like I asked you to!

My therapist for ushering me on my mental health journey and inspiring me to dig into Matthew's story—and in many ways, *my own*—in a more truthful and unfiltered way.

The online book community whose friendship and rallying have made this little author's dreams come true, especially: Kasee Bailey, Laynie Rose Rizer, Jacob Demlow, Simone Richter.

You (yes, you!) reading this book. Thank you for taking the time to engage with my words. It's a privilege and an honor. Catch you on the next one!

ABOUT THE AUTHOR

©Rebecca Phillips

Timothy Janovsky is a queer, multidisciplinary storyteller from New Jersey. He holds a bachelor's degree from Muhlenberg College and a self-appointed certificate in rom-com studies (accreditation pending). When he's not daydreaming about young Hugh Grant, he's telling jokes, playing characters, and writing books.

timothyjanovsky.com 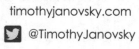 @TimothyJanovsky

@TimothyJanovsky @TimothyJanovsky